Holy Grail, Holy Grail: Quest East, Quest West

Holy Grail, Holy Grail: Quest East, Quest West

Gary Corseri

Copyright © 2001 by Gary Corseri.

Library of Congress Number: 00-192482
ISBN #:   Softcover   0-7388-4293-1

All rights reserved. No part of this book may be reproduced or transmitted in any form or by any means, electronic or mechanical, including photocopying, recording, or by any information storage and retrieval system, without permission in writing from the copyright owner.

This is a work of fiction. Names, characters, places and incidents either are the product of the author's imagination or are used fictitiously, and any resemblance to any actual persons, living or dead, events, or locales is entirely coincidental.

This book was printed in the United States of America.

To order additional copies of this book, contact:
Xlibris Corporation
1-888-7-XLIBRIS
www.Xlibris.com
Orders@Xlibris.com

Contents

PART ONE

1 Merlin's Dream 11
2 Lancelot du Lac 23
3 The True Story of the Holy Grail 42

PART TWO

4 Yamato 57
5 The Kami 75
6 The Peaceable Kingdom 96
7 The Peaceable Kingdom Revisited 117
8 Silk 145
9 Fire 173
10 The Battle of Dan-no-Ura 202

PART THREE

11 The Man in the Blue Seersucker Suit 241
12 The Petunia Petunia Show 268
13 The Disciple of Chi 292

14 The Quilt 311
15 Showdown 332

PART FOUR

16 The Ocean of Time 361

For those who reconcile along the Way.

PART ONE

Britain & the Grail

"We are such stuff
As dreams are made on, and our little life
Is rounded with a sleep."

—*William Shakespeare*

1 | Merlin's Dream

The mind of Merlin mickle brooded . . .

It rode the breakers up the Solway Firth, flitted with screech owls through the Forest of Celidon, swooped on the field mice cowering in tangled roots. It fell like mist over emerald lakes, rose with the morning sun, saw the first fires of the market blaze at York, mixed with the breath of farm boys and farm girls blowing on their hands for warmth. Over the York dales it moved down the spine of mountains, over the ancient land where Druid priests had led their wild-eyed worshippers to trees and stone and water.

Merlin slept, and knew he slept, knew that he dreamed in a spider's web of his own making—victim, and predator.

Then the girl came into his dream, the way she had that first day at Arthur's court. She'd thrown herself before Queen Guenevere with some petition over some imagined wrong, a minor princess from some minor fiefdom. She spoke the lilting speech of her country, and, though she was small, the abundance of her thick, red hair, proud emerald eyes and pouting chin assured she would not escape notice. Merlin glanced at her, then put her from his mind.

He had never loved a full-fledged human girl.

"But you are the wisest man in all the world," the redheaded girl had said.

What was the occasion? He could not remember. Only the lilting syllables and the way her freckled nose tilted towards his beard.

"What is your name, child?"

"Vivian, Great Sir," and she had curtsied.

"And how many summers have your heart-wings beat?"

Her sparkling eyes smiled. Merlin gazed into the pools of her eyes and beheld—more emerald green.

"Seventeen, Great Sir," she answered. "And if you count the summer of my birth, eighteen."

Merlin smiled gently. "You must not call me 'Great Sir.' My name is Merlin. It conjures well enough."

She curtsied again. "Yes, Great Sir."

And then it seemed that she was everywhere: tagging after, a *bonafide* nuisance wanting to know why grass was green, why eagles flew, what made the water boil, how fire worked, why men and women loved so differently, and how did great magicians love?

Not in so many words—the last—but intimated with nuances and glances. A nuisance! A coquette, whom the knights dubbed 'Merlin's pet,' 'Merlin's tagalong,' or—Sir Bors especially—'Merlin's pretty brat.'

One day she did not tag along and he inquired softly, was she ill? Had anybody seen her? Had she returned whence she had come? His mind wandered from his magic, he forgot a simple spell, misread a symbol, forgot a principle of Euclid's, wandered to the lake and knew that he was lost.

She found him there, slipped wordlessly beside him as he sat on the fallen, petrified tree, turned his face to hers and kissed him on the lips.

"Merlin, teach me all that you do know," she said.

And he knew that he would. Her green eyes fixed him, held him like a creature held in amber. A cool wind blew from the lake. He shuddered.

The spells of the witches he taught her, the sayings of the elves, the dances of warlocks, the words the worshippers of Marduk sang, the secret names of Re, of Maat—the Goddess of Truth—of Osiris, Horus, Isis.

And he had barely begun.

She answered boldly with her body. For every layer of the spirit he unveiled, she unveiled another self, gave still more of her body, molded her small form to his, sang to him, and soothed his brow; surrendered in a delicious festival of flesh, heat, coolness, light and shade.

She gave him mead to drink, and he drank. She told him the gossip of the court: which knights had broken vows, who slept with whom, and he listened. It was heady to be nothing but a human man in love with the flesh of a girl, to feel his heart beat with her voice.

Then Bors called him *her* tagalong. Lancelot winked at him. Gawain, the Courteous, shunned his company. Galahad, the Pure, looked away. Arthur—he had no time for Arthur now—Arthur seemed to understand.

"You have not taught me everything you know," she teased one day, playing with a stalk of grass, tickling his ear with it. "Still you hold back."

He leaned on his elbow and studied her. "What more would you know? You know how to fly with egret wings, how to be as still as a tree—and listen. How the wind blows this way and that—and why. How to look into the heart—"

"That last is my petition."

"How to look into the heart," he continued, "that alone takes time heaped on time."

She leaned on her elbow, tickled the gray hairs on the broad chest. "Two years I've been your plaything . . . Still you do not trust me." She lay her head on his chest. "Teach me your heart," she said. "I have not given all that I might give." She kissed his chest, kissed his lips, then scratched his face as with a tiger's claws, not altogether playfully.

He felt the wound. It burned his cheek. He undid the ribbon of her samite gown. He nuzzled his beard against her small, white breasts, and she moaned.

"Oh, Merlin, teach me all you know to make a love a prisoner." She drew him into her myrrh-scented breasts.

"You would undo me," he said softly, a strand of fear caught in his throat.

"Undo *me!*" she bid. She undid his starry mantle. Though his face was lined and gray-bearded, his body was that of a vigorous young man's. Her green eyes chided him and pleaded. Her velar moaning fired his blood.

Afterwards, she lay her head upon his matted chest. She stroked the gray-brown hairs. "You remember what you taught me once—about the Power? How it must not be misused, or Earth itself might fall? Do you think I have not learned? Trust me—show you trust me!"

"Why place that burden on such slender shoulders?"

"To take it off of yours! To share the world of him whom I adore—my liege, my lord, my Merlin! Make me co-equal in your power. No one can love you better." She twirled her tongue around his earlobe.

"I cannot see the future as it turns upon myself," he sighed.

"I know . . . You have said so."

"Of Arthur and his court I have strange glimmerings . . . Sometimes, clearly, I discern an image floating on a future sea. Usually, they come with music—these images . . . But for myself, only silence."

Then Merlin considered, and deceived himself. "If I taught you how to look into my heart, you could see my future, teach me how to better serve . . ."

She took his head in her hands and kissed him. "No better than you are I'd have you. But if another spirit means you harm—I'd see that. Before the curse fell from your enemy's lips, I'd catch it in a vial and seal it under the earth . . ."

"There are those who mean Arthur harm . . . They'd bring down Arthur by destroying me."

"Teach me to see, and let me be my Merlin's owl, with eyes revolving always in the night to look into the hearts of men and *screech* if one does mean my Merlin harm."

So he taught her what she wanted. And when he slept, after

their night of love—a wilder night than he had ever known—she walked around him three times three, clapped her hands, and said the ancient words. And when he woke he found himself immobile, under the branches of a hawthorn tree in the forest of Broceliande. But he thought himself in a tower, surrounded by his books and bibelots. And he thought that he could never go out of the tower. And this was true. For as he slept he heard her cursed words:

> Now in the tower that is no tower,
> amidst the hawthorn, in the forest quick,
> when owlet *"who's"* at the midnight hour,
> and future monarchs know themselves a trick,
> espaliered Merlin lies within his words' white runes,
> by a sly girl euchered of all he thought was good.
> So let him lie—until the five moons'
> night brings him balm from Holy Wood.

*

Now she came gliding through the air, her small body, bathed in belladonna, naked and gleaming in the moonlight. Every inch of her, save her flaming red hair, was dark blue with belladonna juice: from forehead to berry-blue lips, to her blue-black toes. She opened the highest window of the tower, far above the bed where Merlin slept, and entered on a feather of wind.

She had been with others of her kind, bathed in belladonna and monkshood. Drunk, with loins redolent with lust, they caught the currents of the air, skimmed above the sea, and floated into the Valley of the Rocks, where the Earth had been scooped to the shore as by a giant child playing at castle building. They dressed in the skins of she-wolves and called the Horned God, who rose from the center of their circle. Each of the twelve females had danced with him three times, wound their limbs around him, before he'd vanished.

Vivian was nineteen now, more lovely than when she'd first enchanted Merlin. She was taller, her face less angular, her breasts more full.

She floated down the moonlit chamber with its shelves that the magician stacked with hour glasses, bells, clay poppets, rings of garnets and opals, charts of the sky, gilded mirrors, flasks, weights, tallow hanging from looped cords, keys, hemlock, Henbane, the dials with numbers she did not understand, all manner of papyrus scrolls; and here and there, because he was forgetful, tucked between flasks of dreaming homunculi: a potent formula he'd not yet mastered. There were strange objects from his future-tripping: a shining, spoked wheel with the word "Chevrolet" emblazoned on it; a delicate black hat with a lacy net and an ostrich feather; an "I like Ike" button on a pin.

When her feet touched the floor she looked on Merlin's peaceful face. The soft, long beard rose on his mantle with each breath. She saw that his sleep was troubled, listened carefully for any word from him.

Since his confinement Merlin had begun to talk in his sleep. Nothing significant had passed his lips yet, but Vivian clung to the hope he'd utter a stray formula: something buried in his memory, revealed by the flooding of dreams and time.

"How did he sleep?" she asked Jasper, the gray-eyed cat.

Ever irreverent, the tomcat yawned, humped its black back and stretched its legs languidly. "As you see," he said, then leapt to its favorite spot on the first shelf.

Vivian covered herself with her samite gown. Her blueness would not shock Merlin, neither would ner nakedness. Nor would he be hurt by her communion with the Horned God. But out of respect she covered herself and sat on the oak chair and looked on Merlin's mantle.

There was the onk and David's star, the palm with the blinking eye, the Celtic cross and Jerusalem cross, a sliver of the moon, the full moon, the eclipsed sun's corona, and the sun with all its rays falling on gnarled trees and gnarly mountains. Around the perimeter, a moebius that seemed to undulate, and, moving as clouds move, within the purple mantle: faces of animals, humans, birds; godlike creatures, creatures of the lower air, dark creatures fading into light, all merging and emerging as one looked: grotesque and beautiful, changing colors, fading and becoming.

Merlin woke. He looked into the tower's high turret, gazed on Vivian and smiled.

"Did you dream well?" she asked.

"I dreamed of you—and what has been . . ."

She lowered her eyes. She held out her hands. "I brought you parsley from the forest, and endive from the hills."

"One to nourish, and one to keep me bound," he said.

Vivian sighed. "Merlin, will you ever forgive me?"

He smiled. "When Jesus gasped upon the cross, he asked his God to forgive all men. He did not say, `except for Judas.'"

She sighed again. "I am your Judas."

Merlin leaned on an elbow and gazed on her with kindness. Her blueness made her otherworldly, and fanned his passion.

"Will you bathe me?" she asked.

With a nod, Merlin conjured a marble bath and filled it with aromatic herbs and warm, clear water. He snapped his fingers and myriad, tiny, speckled fish swam against Vivian and tickled her clean. The fish then devoured the blueness and the water was clear again. The mage and his pupil relaxed in the warmth. She floated into his arms.

"Did you hear the future music?" she asked.

"No," he said sadly. "I have not heard it since the time . . ."

Then Vivian told what she had been thinking. "Merlin, you understand so much more than I . . . Is there a reason that I tricked you? Can some good come of this?"

"Morgana le Fay spun this web out of spite for her brother Arthur. You she used to quarry me. Now Arthur and his realm's imperiled—and I cannot help."

"Merlin, I was a child, and maybe I am still. Every day I

learn a deeper truth which contradicts the one I thought before. The Horned God I worship. Or let the Horned God worship me. When the sabat moon comes down, every female heart is one. For the sake of that lost knowledge, I enchained you here. Because, ten thousand years ago, God took my form, my female form. But the Gods of Greece and Rome drove my Goddess out. The God men pray to now—and the good wives of those men—is not my God. Somehow, we must not let our Goddess die. So we meet in the woods, and rub the flying ointment on our bodies, and make love with the Horned God who worships us—because he was there in the beginning . . .

"I thought you were my enemy, Merlin . . ." She paused. A tear of pity fell from her cheek to Merlin's. "Morgana le Fay deceived me there. Your knowledge I needed to better serve my Goddess; your strength to see me through a thousand years—or more—of darkness, which I know must come . . . Can no good come of this?"

Merlin caressed her white shoulder. "Before, I gathered toys from future walks. I saw gleaming cities of glass and stone—better than our best enchanted worlds. And in the midst of these, huge other cities of desolation: men and women without hope—and children killing children. I came back to my time and thought about these things. And so men called me wise. Somewhere, I picked a lock of knowledge and saw you, and knew you must betray me. I knew I must give you the means of my betrayal . . . But I know not why."

Then they kissed in the warm water, and made slow and gentle love while the speckled fish tickled them.

And a female being took root in Vivian's womb—a being who would gestate 1500 years.

Merlin ate the parsley and the endive and lay down on his stone couch. His charts and scrolls rose in jumbled order on the shelves above him, but he was too tired to think about them now, and he brooded on how to help Arthur, and how to release himself from his dream-life:

> Now in the tower that is no tower,
> amidst the hawthorn, in the forest quick . . .

But he could think of no way out. And though he loved the strange, wild girl and had contentment with her, he missed the landscapes of his mother's world: the Giants' Dance where the heroes lay, and the great locks of the north where the great serpents swam in the murky deep.

And though he might see and hear and feel and taste and smell in dreams—and he was learned in dreaming—yet the most poignant sense of present-*ness* constantly escaped him. The clarity and sharpness of life blurred and flamed out. He pined for summer flowers, spring rain, autumn colors, white winter's frosty breath; and the true voices of the men he loved; the dust and tumult of the jousts and tournaments; the damsels with their flirting eyes; and a view of the night sky from Land's End—endless, with a billion stars.

Instead: a tiny corner of Orion, framed by his tower window. Vivian watched the heavy lids close, knew that he pined, and grieved she had brought such sadness. Only after she had made him sad had pity been born in her. Only after she pitied him had she learned to love.

*

Now in his dream Merlin sat on the windy plain upon which stood the monoliths of the Giants' Dance—the place the Celts called Stonehenge. The night was moonless, but the stars were bright enough to watch the play of light and shadows on the stones. He breathed deeply, held his breath, let it out easily, and repeated. Even in his dreams, he was not bereft of power. He studied the Wheel of Time that the stones represented, but he could not decipher. He listened for the Future Music, but he could not hear. Something terrible would happen, but he could not say what. He sighed and a luminous tear curved down his cheek.

The falling star appeared in the corner of his dream. At first he barely noticed. He watched as it came towards him, shining brighter over the plain.

The long tail of the comet was the train of the angel's mantle. The shining angel paused above the stones. Merlin watched with fear and wonder.

"Merlin," said the angel. And the voice was like his mother's, and like his teacher Blaise's, but neither.

"Is the hour of my death at hand?" Merlin asked.

"You have barely been born," said the angel. "In that suspended animation which is now your state, the cycles of the ages barely ripple your appointed time . . . But, list well; I cannot linger . . ."

The angel hovered over the huge stones. The angel's mantle seemed to cloak it in a flame, and the stones reached up like tongues of fire. Yet there was no heat. The night was cool.

"All that you have learned, all you have been guided to—" the angel continued, "we need. All will be used. Nothing is wasted. The supernatural and the natural worlds that men divide, are one. You know, and you have taught it so. Others will come and also teach. But, lo . . . the darkness will descend, the dragons will descend: torture refined, exquisite, too terrible to tell, will come."

"Tell me what I must do," dreaming Merlin said aloud, so Vivian woke beside him, and saw his face lit with vision.

"I am Joseph of Arimathea," the angel said, "who guarded the Holy Grail from which Christ drank at the first Mass. And some call it the Sangreal, because—and it is true—they say it caught Christ's blood after the soldier's wound."

"The Grail that was at Glastonbury," Merlin marveled, "guarded by your children, and your children's children's children."

"Even so. For generations handed down until one culprit of my seed gazed upon a woman's inner thigh when she knelt down to worship."

"And then it vanished."

"Vanished, and but recently appeared when all the knights were seated at the Table. They had a vision and they swore to bring back the Sangreal. But, alas, they all must fail."

"They are the best men of the world," Merlin protested. "Is none worthy enough?"

Then the angel came towards him. The brightness dimmed, and he stood face to face with Merlin, like a living man. "They must fail," Joseph said, "because they seek the visionary thing, and not the real. Only the vision was at Glastonbury. Galahad will have the meaning of the vision, and become a vision of himself. But the real thing must be held! It is high time. That will release you from your Vivian's charm—and release humankind from their own delusions . . . One knight alone is qualified to make this quest . . . "

Merlin rose on his toes. "Galahad's our purest, and Gawain is courteous and brave. Sir Kay is noble, Sir Gareth prudent. Who is the one you mean, Resplendent One?"

"Only one," said Joseph softly, "and that is Lancelot."

Now Merlin wondered if it were a true vision he beheld or only a case of undigested endive.

"Lancelot of twenty years before," Merlin said. "The one who stole the hearts of everyone. The bravest, strongest, most handsome knight who ever crossed the Channel. But now? Lancelot as he is now?"

Again Joseph nodded. "He must go where knights have never ventured. Eastward, ever Eastward—to the edge of the sea; and then still further, beyond the sea—a chain of islands greet the rising sun—that land is Yamato."

"The land of the yellow men! I have no magic there," Merlin said sadly.

"Others do . . ."

"But," Merlin said, and he wanted to ask a thousand questions, but the angel's inner light shone again and Merlin covered his eyes as Joseph rose into the air, lighting the monoliths and the plain. The long trail of his mantle followed him into space.

Merlin stared at the vanishing light, and when it was no more, he shook his head, leaned against the nearest monolith, and said in a doubting voice, "Lancelot!"

And he woke with the name like a bitter taste on his tongue.

2 | Lancelot du Lac

Ansell the seneschal fidgeted and sighed.

Day after day, night after night, Ansell would go through the accounts: the reeves and bailiffs would bring taxes and rents and Ansell must pay for servants, livery, stables, mead, tournaments, imported pepper and ginger, hawks, hawk trainers, armor for the war horses, armor for the knights, bows, arrows, lances, entertainers—jugglers, dancers, singers—and on and on and on.

Lancelot's bounty was bottomless. On feast days, he'd select a random hundred villeins from his estate and dine them in his halls. Even the scullions who darted about the kitchen grabbing morsels that fell from the great pots ate better than the free men of other manors.

And now there was another call to court! Sir Galahad had had a vision and the other knights had caught his fever, so all of them were buzzing. Forever fasting, Pure Sir Galahad, no doubt craving a bit of wine, had seen the Grail the Good Lord had the sense to drink from, and the others, drunk as usual, had got religion, and made a vow to bring it back.

Lancelot and all the sensible knights—barons, really—now more concerned with revenue than saving helpless damsels, had been at home, tending their domains when Arthur's messengers arrived with the summons.

Lancelot knew what it meant: he'd have to journey to the Court, meet with the Grail-struck fools, wish them *bon voyage,* then devise with Arthur how to safeguard their abandoned lands. It was all too troublesome! There'd be the usual Court schemers, the hangers-on, and, of course, Guenevere: a little faded now, but still a handsome woman, light of foot. They'd get to recalling—just by looking—that affair of twenty years before. Lancelot would get maudlin, drink more mead than he should, and abuse his loyal seneschal—poor Ansell—and all else.

What could Ansell do? Squeeze the tenants for another farthing? He couldn't raise their rents. Poaching was increasing, grumbling spreading—he heard it from his spies. And Lancelot was, as ever, Lancelot—he wouldn't hear at all!

And now this damned expense! They'd have to bring the king a tribute. Lancelot would go in style. They'd have to go through London and the other towns, mingle with merchants, tradesmen, foreigners. Over the old Roman roads in carts and litters and on foot—for what? An adolescent's vision?

And what would it all cost?

*

If Wee Willie Wilkins hadn't wandered far from the commons, breaking his father's commandments again, he never would have beheld the most extraordinary sight of his eleven years. He'd been told to gather dry straw for daub for his sister's house, she being with child now and needing a place of her own. And his kind-hearted mother had told him to bring fresh rushes from the narrow river bank so they might put down a sweet-smelling floor for the newlyweds.

"Mind you return 'fore noon," his father had warned, cocking a stern eye towards his last son, the runt of the litter and the only survivor.

But Willie had wandered in the fog, charmed by the way it settled in the gorse and fennel, making earth and sky one. "If I had a sword like the knights, I'd cut the fog in two," he thought. "The larger part would fall back in the sky, but what was on the ground I'd gather up, and Mum would make a cloak for me and I'd put it on and walk around invisible." So thinking, he found a staff by the river's edge and swished at the air. Again and again he swung the staff and after a while it seemed the fog parted a little and a blurred white disk of sun spread warming beams.

Then he heard the sound of whistling a long way off. He ran up a knoll and searched the gray horizon. There were brightly colored pennants in the air, and floating beneath them, highborn men surrounded by shields with dragon crests and lion crests, moving without effort, floating over the plain. And he saw women such as he had never seen, with pink skin and shining eyes, wearing large, feathered hats. Not hard women like his mother and sister—big-boned and muscled from the fields, brown and yellow as hay—but delicate beings who seemed like wondrous butterflies, whose shoulders flowed with gossamer gold fabrics, and whose skin was white as sun-bleached bones.

He raced back over the hills, over the common fields, stumbling down the public way, into oxen and farmers who yelled at him, and he yelled back: "Fairy princess in a boat on the land—coming!" And the farmers shook their heads, for they understood Wee Willie well. They laughed and winked at each other, curled their forefingers round their temples, then went back to work.

But Willie's father was not amused. The big, beefy hand struck the boy's face hard. In spite of himself, Willie felt his hot tears flow. "How many times must I tell you not to fib?" his father yelled. He was about to hit the boy again when his wife stepped between them.

"Let the boy alone," she pleaded, her hand raised as a shield.

The other villagers were watching now. The big man let his hands fly at the faces of his wife and son. "Leave my Ma alone!" Wee Willie cried, as he tried to protect his mother. "Bill, Bill," their neighbors called, pulling the enraged man's arm. "It's true what he says. The baron and his court are coming even as we speak. Leave off the boy and woman. Look you to the collopes!"

Then father, son and mother, sister and her husband, flew

about their dingy house trying to hide the little food they had. They stuffed the salted meal into the straw in the roofs, the garlic and leeks inside the straw pallets they slept on, the dried fruit under a mound of earth in the crofts. Then they looked sadly at the razor-backed pigs they had not killed for collopes, and the scraggy hens that gave them eggs. There was no place to hide them now.

All the villagers listened in dread as the rumbling court of Lancelot approached, the highborn men pulled in high carts by palfreys, and the ivory and pink-necked ladies carried in horse litters, emerging out of the grayness like alien beings from another world. The doe-eyed villagers watched, and some of them scratched at their scrofulous skin, and some of them pulled at their patchy clothes and scabs. The highborn ladies turned from the reeking odors. The floutist made a merry whistling tune to entertain the court, but to the villagers it was the sound of doom.

*

The hooded goshawk preened its blue-black feathers with its bill and talons, cast a pellet of feather-ball and undigested insect from its throat, and defecated on the gloved hand of the man who held her. She did not see the man nonchalantly wipe his glove, but she felt the practiced hand stroke her with a long feather and she recognized Lancelot's soothing voice. She fluffed and shook her feathers in response.

It was two hours past dawn and the sun was still struggling to break the hold of intermittent clouds. The goshawk knew that the hunt would start. Its puny nostrils tried to scent the game, and, as usual, were overwhelmed with the smell of horses, men and dogs.

"She's straining at the jesses," the squire said.

Lancelot smoothed the orange breast feathers as his favorite hawking bird dug its powerful talons into his glove. He slipped the hood from the bristling head and, barely giving it time to blink, released the bird with an upward swoop into the air.

The hawk soared to a hundred feet above men, horses and dogs below. The tiny bells attached to its neck tinkled like a warning. Lancelot watched the five-foot wingspan, and the field of men began to beat the bushes with sticks, as the dogs yelped and the horses neighed and defecated in the confusion. A flock of cranes rose on a wave of white wings out of the underbrush.

In an instant, the goshawk's eyes detected the movement of the weakest crane. The blue-black wings formed themselves into an arrow and the bird swooped at two hundred miles per hour. Just before collision, it pulled its body back so its weight concentrated in its claws. The crane never knew what hit it. Its life was knocked out of it, but the goshawk binded with it until they hit the ground together. Spasmodically, the talons pierced the crane's soft whiteness, then pierced the lungs and heart. The dark blood spurted over the white breast.

"A good kill," said the squire, grinning, as the field rushed to the doomed crane before the goshawk could dismember it. Lancelot whistled and the bird returned to his glove. He fed it a morsel of meat and replaced the hood.

"We won't have to feast on peasants' pig tonight," Lancelot boasted, and his field laughed with him.

He'd taken the hawk as an eyas from the nest and carefully trained her himself. It was painstaking work with lures and patience and getting the hand to keep steady and the voice just right. It was five years ago. Right after he'd last been to Camelot. After he'd last seen Guenevere. Five years . . . Training the hawk had helped him to forget.

The squire carried the crane by its legs, held it up to Lancelot for inspection. Lancelot nodded, and the squire tied the crane to his palfrey, next to the one the hawk had killed an hour before. "One of the field says there's rabbit further up," the squire said.

"The day is young," Lancelot said. "Which way?"

They rode towards the warrens while Lancelot tried to keep his mind on the hunt.

Five years since he'd seen Guenevere and then he had saved her life! A villain, who schemed to kill Sir Gawain, had put a poisoned apple atop a silver tray of fruit. According to protocol, the unsuspecting queen would offer Gawain, the most dignified of the knights, first choice of the fruit. But between the apple's being placed and supper, the ambassador from Scotland had arrived. Now protocol demanded the Scot get first selection. Alas, his face had turned purple and he had choked to death on his own vomit.

A month later Sir Mador, brother of the poisoned Scot, demanded recompense: a life for a life. No one would stand for Guenevere. She was condemned to die.

Word had reached Lancelot in the forest. He had taken up the life of a hermit, forswearing women and drink, rich food and hunting. But he could not let her die.

He had his craftsmen burnish his old armor. Sir Mador fought him for six hours before they waned. Lancelot grabbed the beaver of Sir Mador's helmet and raised his broad sword above his neck. The knight could die or plead for mercy. He chose to live. Lancelot helped raise him to his feet and praised his strength.

Five years ago . . . And before that, ten years!

Now another face swam into his mind—sweet Catherine of Shallot. There was one who might have saved his soul! And one, above all else, whose life he should have saved! He should have looked beyond her sixteen years and taken her for wife! He saw her again: the barge upon the river with its cloth of gold, and the nobles gathered round. They parted when he came. They stilled their wagging tongues. He knelt beside her, saw how the river's breezes touched her flaxen hair, kissed the purple of her cold, hard lips. How white and cold she lay! All for the love of him! Because she'd seen his heart was still not his. Then he turned his back on all of them, and rode.

Fifteen years ago . . . He had been twenty seven. No entreaty could induce him back. Ten years he had lived as a hermit, asking the priests for guidance, practicing the penance of the New Religion. Then the news of Guenevere's imperilment had flushed him out.

Guenevere—he'd ruined his life for her! And she for him! For her he had abandoned Catherine. Now he had more gray hairs than blonde, and he could not wield the broadsword from noon to dusk, as once he could. What did he have to show for love? Now he was "Sir Lance the Wastrel," " Inebriate Sir Lance" and "Sir Laxity". He liked his mead and ale and hunting. And wenches—he could have his fill of wenches. His lands grew. Ansell tended to the rents and taxes and there was time for cock fights, jousts and tournaments. Guenevere's damned jealousy when he wore the Lady Shallot's colors faded from his mind. The pale face of the dead girl faded.

Some commotion up ahead upset his reverie. He heeled his palfrey forward.

"What's this?" cried the squire, holding a tattered peasant's cloak in his strong hand. Inside the cloak, four limbs and a small head squirmed to be free. The other men laughed. "It's a goblin," said one. "Let's skewer it through its navel."

"It's a serf's son—and he stinks!" said the squire, releasing the ragged captive into the bramble. The squire held his nose and the other men guffawed.

"Ouch! Ouch!" cried Wee Willie from the brambles as he tried to raise himself. But his bare feet were no match for the thorns.

Lancelot cast a bemused eye on the heap of patches. "What do you mean, boy? Do you spy on your betters?"

"Ouch! Your pardon, your Worship—ouch!—I'm Willie— ouch!—from Amargh—ouch!"

"Amargh-ouch, boy?"

"Ouch! No, Sir-ouch! Amargh—ouch!—Sir!"

"It's the village where we pitched our camp last night," the squire explained.

"Help the boy out of the brambles," Lancelot ordered.

So two men lifted Willie by the scruff of his neck and deposited him in front of Lancelot's steed. The steed snorted with contempt.

"How did you get so far from home?" Lancelot asked gently.

"Your pardon, your Worship . . . I followed the wagons when you left 'ere daylight."

"'E's run off," said one of the men.

"Is it true, boy?"

Willie lowered his shaggy head. "Yes, Sir," he said softly.

"Send the ragamuffin back," the squire suggested, and delivered a round kick to Willie's rump, which sent him sprawling by the horses' nervous hooves. The other men guffawed.

"Leave off!" Lancelot said angrily. He dismounted and helped the boy to his feet. "How did you follow us on the hunt?" Lancelot asked. "How could you follow the horses?"

"I ran, Your Worship," said the boy.

The field and squire tittered.

"Are your tiny legs so strong, boy?" Lancelot asked.

"I don't know, Sir. But in the village, no other boy or man could keep apace with me."

"What about your father?" Lancelot inquired. "He'll need you for the harvest."

The boy looked down at his hands. "'E's not my father, Sir . . . My father died. This other one—'e sleeps beside me mum, but 'e's a cruel one, not a good'un."

"Then, what about your mum?"

The boy saddened. "She's better off without me, since my father died . . . One less mouth to feed. And another baby comin' from me sis."

"Are things so hard?" Lancelot asked.

The boy seemed surprised. "I never thought of it as hard, Sir. Just how things are."

Lancelot studied his squire and the field of hunters. They were ill at ease. The boy disturbed him, too, but for different reasons. In the gray fog of the prior evening he could not discern the rags his serfs wore, nor the bony ribs behind the tattered clothes. He sighed. "Come with us now . . . We'll put you back on our return . . . Anyone with legs like yours may do some good."

The squire looked askance at his lord. Lancelot ignored him, and mounted. "Squire John," Lancelot commanded. "See that the boy is scrubbed till he hollers, and give him a good cloak to wear."

"Yes, Sir," said the squire. And added, under his breath, "Your Worship!"

*

Up to the earthen banks and walls of London there was little to indicate the humming activity within. Lancelot's procession bumped over the rough roads that had seen better days in Roman times. The gentle ladies and gentlemen were jostled in their carts and litters, requiring frequent adjustments to headgear and coiffure to preserve their sense of dignity. The knights and squires rode by quickly, indifferently spattering mud, boisterously calling rude challenges to each other, while the ladies averted their eyes.

Inside London's walls a vendor of bad meats sat in a pillory while meats were burnt under his nose. Children played ring-around-the-rosy in front of him. Lancelot's procession immediately created a stir and the townspeople gathered at the edges of the street to watch. Children were hoisted on shoulders and the simple folk tried to recall when they had seen so fine a sight.

"Is it the King?" a man asked.

"It is Sir Lancelot du Lac," another said, proud to recognize the heraldry, recalled from a tournament two decades before. The children and simple folk rolled the name over: "Lancelot of the Lilac."

"Is it a famous knight?" a woman asked. "He be a fine looking man!"

"Aye," replied a burgher, "but worn at the edges for jousting with his lance!" He gyrated his pelvis, and the obese housewives and fishwives held their bellies to laugh.

The procession, which had enjoyed the country air, was assaulted by the town's odors. The carcasses of animals lay in the streets where they had lain for days. Butchers were slaughtering lambs and pigs and the blood and offal drained into the channel in the middle of the street. Housewives threw night-soil and other garbage into the streets. From back alleys, the odors of tanning and skin-dressing wafted over the crowds as fishmongers and bricklayers, brewsters and bakers shouted the virtues of their commerce. The sea of drab brown and gray collected round the sumptuous colors of Lancelot's entourage. The squires and knights roughly pushed their way through. A crafty beggar put a cap on his trained dog and played a wooden flute and the dog rose on its hind legs and danced. The squires threw coins, which the townspeople rushed to steal from the beggar.

Pigs wandered and chickens cackled, roosters crowed, hounds and hawks strained at their tethers and jesses. Gamblers turned their attention from their cockfight, and a couple of drunkards stumbled out of a brewster's kitchen, relieved themselves against the wall, and stumbled back. "A gallon of ale for a penny!" sang the brewster from her door, and the squires licked their chaps and took note of the place for later.

Wee Willie gasped in awe. They passed houses with gardens, two-story houses with stables underneath solars reached by wooden stairs. Kitchens and dairies were separated from the main house, and there were courtyards for nothing except sitting. Clustered around the great-houses were the clapboard shacks of the poor, the immigrants from the country, the drunks and the failures. Babies wailed and children ran underfoot as housewives struggled to cook or clean, to make do, and to improve.

As they approached the street of inns, they saw a bear being baited. The chained creature's fur was ragged and torn by the dogs held in check by their masters. For a penny, a man was allowed to hold meat on a stick in front of the bear. When the starved creature lunged for it, other men would beat it back with clubs. When the bear wouldn't lunge, the dogs were set on it, and then it roared piteously and weakly. With its clouded vision, the bear, too, watched the procession, wondering what new torture came with the pennants and the banners.

*

After several days of traveling, they came to the edge of Camelot. They arrived at dusk, with just enough time to set up camp by the channel. From one end of the kingdom to the other they'd traveled, through towns, through London, over plains and forests. They had felt themselves watched by the wild people of the forests, the naked warriors with their rough-hewn oak-staff spears. The knights and squires held one hand on their swords as they passed through the land of the unseen. And the highborn women knew that brigands lurked behind boulders, and only the brave display of arms kept them at bay. Less potently armed caravans had been attacked, men slain, women's honors compromised, the most delicate white throats slashed even as they cried for mercy. And the brigands sucked the blood. Such were the tales and the times!

But now they paused by the inlet of the sea, bone-weary, but safe. They pitched their pavilions by the moonlit, lapping waters. In the far distance the spires and towers of Camelot rose, torchlight spilling dimly from turrets and windows, the full moon falling softly over its ramparts. The testiness of the knights and squires receded with the vision, and the highborn ladies—who seemed much less highborn after the ordeals of the road—had their female attendants lay out their best gowns and jewels, unguents and fragrances in preparation for the morning when they would scent their hair with myrrh and put on rouge and lipstick. At Arthur's castle all things were possible.

Now it was near the witching hour and most slept. A detail of knights and squires gambled around campfires, alert though at ease, their weapons and horses nearby. Others patrolled the foothills, for even so close to the seat of authority and the citadel of peace, vigilance was prudence.

Lancelot walked out beyond the campfires. His men saluted him silently. They had learned his ways, his nightly wandering.

He went down to the sea and watched the waves pour moonlit diamonds into the sand at his feet. He sighed deeply, then whispered her name to the salt-air breeze: *"Guenevere..."*

Half his life ago, he had held her in his arms and loved her more than his God or honor. He had betrayed his king, the noblest man in the world, who had risen above ancient justice and the rights of kings and husbands—to forgive, to pardon. Lancelot loved the bear-like man, yet he knew in his heart of hearts that if circumstances conspired thus, he would betray him again. "Guenevere," he said more loudly, then drew his sword for he thought he heard something strange.

It was Merlin that he heard, taking the form of a white greyhound, trotting along the strand. Merlin was still in his dream, of course, so his powers were limited. He could not make himself known to Lancelot, but he smelled his longing and fears. Like a good dog, he lowered his head to be petted and the man obliged, laughing at himself. "Are you a fairy dog coming from beyond the sea?" Lancelot asked, holding the dog's face in his hands.

Merlin looked back with large, curious, sad eyes, then trotted away. His magic was not strong enough to communicate from the dream state. The dream had called him back.

After a while, the weary knight rose and walked to the tree line. Summoning his strength, he struck at a large oak with his sword. Again and again, chipping away at the bark, tearing into the sallow wood, he vented his rage. The sword made a dull clanging while he grunted, and his sweat and fear flew in the moonlight.

*

Guenevere was glad the pesky fly that had been buzzing around her finely featured head gave her an excuse to swipe at her eyes. It certainly was odd how the fly so deftly evaded all chances of meeting its Maker! None of her attendants had been able to catch it or kill it either. But now she was glad because she could wipe her tears.

Lancelot, the cause of those tears, was making an ass of himself. They were hot into the tournament and Lance was sweating down to his gambesons. Decked out as he was in mail, helmet and shield, it was hard to know if he was enjoying the spectacle he made of himself. Surely he must have heard the jeers and laughter of the scaffolds as he tipsily rode into battle, and was pinned like a bug at the end of a couched lance. Helped to his feet by his squires, he made an elaborate bow to his howling fans.

Guenevere had observed him for two days: out-drinking, out-gambling, out-wenching, out-swearing, out-fighting men half his age. He had been stiffly formal with her. She had hoped that, now that their passions had cooled, they could at least be civil with each other, that they might learn to be friends. But his tone had been frosty and he had avoided her. So she was surprised when he'd asked to wear her colors in the tournament. They had just finished the first course of supper. The first set of candles had guttered out and the servants were replenishing them. Lance was wiping his hunting knife on the remnants of a half-eaten rabbit. (His manners had not improved in the twenty years she had known him; but, no one else's had, either!)

"Are you sure, Lance?" she'd asked.

"Nothing would give me greater pleasure." He winked at a pretty serving wench. "Well, almost nothing," he'd added.

Was he deliberately trying to humiliate her? Or proving to his men that he still "had it"? Arthur was busy leading a chorus of knights in an old war song from his Mt. Badon days, keeping time with his knife, slashing the air.

After gorging themselves on mutton, venison, geese and

peacocks, the wassails began in earnest. To great applause, Lancelot emptied a pewter pot of ale, then called for another. He emptied the second, then fell flat on his face into a tray of strawberries. He was carried from the hall by two of his squires, his face smeared berry-red.

"What ales, Sir Knight?" asked one rollicking punster.

"He's just berry, berry tired," said another.

"He looks like a poor pismire," said a third.

"He'll piss mickle if he'll piss at all," said the last.

And all guffawed.

Except, of course, Guenevere, who hurried from the hall. Was he trying to take everything from her, every tender memory? Would he never forgive her for the Lady of Shallot? What sort of fool was she to consent to let him wear her colors?

The fly buzzed noisily about her ear, and she swatted at it, then brushed away another tear.

As for Lancelot, there was no man more miserable. The five vows of chivalry—courtesy, loyalty, hardiness, largesse, and franchise—he broke each before noon. Well, not largesse, perhaps, though, truly, he was generous to a fault. If he could not play the lover well, he'd play the grand buffoon. He looked longingly at the scaffolds, saw Guenevere.

The aching love was still there, as intense as when they were young. There sat Arthur, the good, old, bear-like man. Arthur waved at him.

Now he focussed on the joust. His head still ached from the night before, and Sir Victor meant to make that sore head his trophy. Twice the knave had unseated him, the first time cleanly with the lance to the center of the shield, the second time glancing off the edge. Ansell had passed on the boast of Sir Victor's seneschal: his third lance would be aimed between the helmet and the mail. The stupid bastard meant to make his reputation by skewering one of the old heroes of the Table Round!

Now Arthur's team of twenty jousters gathered at their posts while Sir Victor and his teammates met at theirs. The steam rose from the horses and the men. The sun struggled through the clouds. Lancelot raised his visor, and took another glance at Guenevere.

At the signal, the horses rumbled forward, shaking the scaffolds. Lancelot couched his lance. Forty lances raced towards their marks, forty horses, forty riders, and death was in the air. He aimed at the center of Sir Victor's shield. He saw the enemy lance aimed high, aimed at his head. He heard the thundering hooves, armored men on armored horses, the grunts of his compatriots, and then the silence that always came in the last bursting moment. A cloud of dust enveloped the field, so the spectators saw a kind of dreamy flashing of metal, heard thundering hooves, lances splintering, a crash of armored horses, bones of men and horses cracking, and all going down into a screaming abyss.

No one could see the fly that had wandered into Sir Victor's visor, into the little crack where it was jointed. They could not see how it rankled Sir Victor and made him lose his mark, so that Lancelot's lance struck first at the very center of his shield and sent him tumbling back onto another of his team, and the two of them fell together in a heap.

Lancelot was more surprised than anyone to find himself the only knight still on his horse. He'd never heard such cheering from the scaffolds. He took his helmet off, dismounted, bowed. Guenevere awarded him the carcanet.

Twenty years of buffoonery and anguish faded in an instant. And Merlin the fly went back into his dream.

*

The night before they were to part, the knights retired early. All the best of Arthur's kingdom had pledged themselves to the Grail. They'd had their days of merrymaking, and nights of feasting, wenching and songs. Now the great task lay before them. In the morning, the high priest would bless their quest. Now, like good children, they slept.

And Merlin in his tower slept. He was getting better—moving in the dream. He'd re-learned what every amateur magician knows: no magic's perfect. Within the greatest web of magic, yet there was a strand such as a fly's eye might find, a hair's breadth weaker than the rest. His teacher Blaise had explained it once: "Leave the tiniest imperfection, so the spirit may get out." Vivian had enmeshed him; but through a hair's breadth rift in her magic, his spirit roamed, and changed its forms, and sought once more to be a man.

Arthur slept, too, the gray-flecked beard rising on his mighty torso. Uneasily he slept, with dreams of Mt. Badon when they had beaten the Angles and the Saxons back, and all his knights were young. Then he was the cheerful father of a brood of warriors, grand men all, and chief among them—Lancelot. With Excalibur before them, they'd cleared a path through Picts and Scots at Lake Lomond and established a reign of peace: an era for women to cultivate their arts, for children's laughter to ring out from the hills, for men to do great deeds. And then the vision of the Grail had come; and the real world that they'd sweated for, and all the years of peace, fell like a goddess's samite gown.

Of all the court, only Guenevere did not sleep. Barefooted, she wandered through the vast cellarium beneath the castle. Under the high vaulted arches her white skin caught the gold hues of scattered torches on spikes against the wall. The place was cold and she hugged her shoulders. A mouse startled her. The mouse was pounced on by a cat. She turned to go. Lancelot stood before her. She fell into his arms.

"I did not know if you would come," he said, after their first kiss.

"God forgive us both," she said, touching his lips.

"There's no forgiveness for such as we," he said sadly, resolutely. He held her tightly to him. "You are cold." He tried to warm her with his arms. The myrrh of her hair, the golden whiteness of her shoulders shouted in his blood.

"Lance, I'm frightened," she said, pulling away. "Some say

hell is a dungeon with no light. And some say iron melts there, and iron hearts cry out without an end."

"Aye," he said. And they kissed again. They lay down upon a sack of grain. She lifted her skirts, and the bleak years fell away.

*

Lancelot walked out into the cold night air. Her smell was still on him, lingered like a mist, and he hungered for her still.

A sentry saluted him, then cast a curious eye on his disheveled clothes. The man would probably squawk it about tomorrow, how he'd seen the great knight in his summer linens, forlorn and pining like a boy.

He didn't care now. He was past caring.

There was a site of stones down from the castle's hill, left by the ancient ones. Now he stood in the circle of stones. Farther still, a promontory rose above the churning waves. "Ancient Fathers, now have I sinned again," he said. He fell upon his knees.

Thunder seemed to answer him. It roiled out of the ocean. A flash lit all of Camelot.

He thought how he might run from the circle to the promontory and crash upon the breakers below. Their passion had claimed the Lady of Shallot; still it beckoned for more victims. Then he thought of Guenevere again. And he knew that they must die together. He could not leave her to face their shame alone. He imagined her body crumpled on the jagged boulders. Then the rain flushed out of the sky.

How could he break his trust with Arthur? How could he live on, away from Guenevere?

The cold rain pelted him, and he wept—for the shy girl Catherine of Shallot, for Guenevere, for Arthur, for himself. After a long while, he felt a hand on his shoulder, and looked into Merlin's face.

Lancelot jerked away. Like everyone else, he believed that

the magician had been killed by sorcery. No one had seen him for a dozens years.

"Be not a-feared, Lance, this is no ghost before you."

But he was not convinced. "The rain passes through you."

"I am speaking from my dream, Lance, and I cannot linger. To speak to you thus, takes every fiber of my will. For centuries I must lie still and dreamless to pay for these few minutes. That is my life now. I have no time to tell you more."

"Merlin, you are the wisest man who ever walked this earth. Can you see my guilty heart? What must I do?"

Merlin pointed with his staff. "There is a bog to which I'll lead you. Within the bog, a coffer. I'll show you how to pulley up the coffer. Within, three treasures: a mirror . . . a curved jewel called *magatama* . . . and a sword like no sword in this world. Guard these well."

"I shall. But . . ."

Merlin silenced him. "Listen . . . Three other gifts I give you. The gift to make yourself whatever form within that mirror. The gift to hear, through the curved jewel, the true thoughts of another. And the gift of the sword to separate the worlds . . . These are not my gifts, but the gifts of one greater than I. Even as your quest will be greater than all others."

"But, Guenevere . . . and Arthur?"

Merlin's voice was soothing and the rain abated now. "Don't tax me with details, Lance. Time's a-wasting. Up, to it! What will seem a thousand years for you, is but a night's long dream for Camelot. When you wake again, another hand must guide you. I have no magic in the land you go to. But, be assured, that way redemption lies."

"For love of that sweet word, I'd take on all the demons of the world . . . How will I know this other?"

"He will know you. In the land of the rising sun—Yamato. There, only there, is the true Grail."

"The Grail?"

"Aye . . ."

"How did it venture *there?*"

"Do I look like Father Time to you with time to play Twenty Questions?"

"Sorry, Sire, sorry . . . Just one more question, Sire. Shall I journey forth alone?"

Merlin pointed with a mischievous smile: "Go by that shrubbery, whose long shiny leaves resemble rabbits' ears. Pluck up an ear." Lancelot approached the shrub, and sure enough an ear stuck out—though it was pink, no ear of any rabbit! Lancelot plucked it and Wee Willie Wilkins rose and howled. "It's that nuisance of a devil of a boy!" Lancelot fumed. Still holding Wee Willie by the ear, Lancelot kicked the boy's behind.

"Be stern, but not too stern," Merlin advised. "Teach your page well."

"My page?" Lancelot let go. Wee Willie bowed repeatedly. "Sorry, Sir! Sorry!" Then Lancelot thought of Guenevere. "Have you spied on me this whole night, boy?"

"Be not embarrassed," Merlin told him. "The boy slept in the shrubbery."

"I am not used to such a fine house, Sir," Willie explained. "The other boys were talking of the girls, and what they'd do with them. I have no ear for such a talk."

Lancelot shook his head. "Merlin, perhaps, I'd better go alone."

"Prepare to see sights unimagined," Merlin answered. "The true Grail waits. How and when and with whom and why—I know not. Now, to the bog."

When Merlin swept his starry mantle around them, only the mortals' footsteps remained in the dirt in the circle of stones.

After a while, the light rain washed them into the pools of time.

3 | The True Story of the Holy Grail

Granny Esther squinted at her reflections in the little pools of wine left in the empty chalices.

She was in a sour mood. It wasn't simply her unsettled stomach—though that didn't help. Dried fish from Lake Tiberius, indeed! Who knew what mallet-softened hide she'd eaten! Last time she'd trust a sweet-talking caravan man! Last time for a long time!

And it wasn't just the chronic arthritis that stiffened her joints every time she got a paying job. What really got her dander up was having to work at all. A day short of fifty, she should be playing with her grandchildren—should be taken care of herself!—what with her dear husband dead these four long years and three no-good sons to support her!

She was gathering the dining utensils in the reed-woven baskets. Dishes, cups, spoons, chalices. A mess! Left-over bread, spilt wine. Apparently, there'd been some kind of ruckus! One chair was turned over on its side, as though someone had left in a hurry. Not that holy men were above ruckusing! Not that they were above the temptations of the flesh! Granny sniffed the air knowingly. Nope—no sign of a woman here! No dancing girls had jangled and spangled their way across the bare stone floor. This seemed to be an honest group of holy-rollers.

It was just that there were so many of them coming into the city now! All over Jerusalem—talk of the messiah! A new one popped up every week or two. Some claimed to heal the sick, some had wondrous visions. This Jesus of Nazareth—the party-giver—had come into town on a white donkey, with his followers strewing palm fronds before him. First there had been John who'd lost his head over some dancing girl—and now this follower of his was attracting even bigger crowds and making even more spectacular claims.

And had her life changed? Had any of the messiahs made it easier for the common Jews who worked and sweated under the yoke of the she-wolf's brats?

No wonder every fortnight brought a new messiah!

Granny paused at the chalice in front of the center chair. Joseph of Arimathea had promised her a tip if she brought him the chalice from which Jesus had drunk.

Now, this Joseph seemed a nice man! Granny bet he'd treat her right if she were his mom! Not like those boys of hers! How'd she ever raise such a crop? An Essene, a Pharisee, a Sadduccee! Weren't they all Jews? Didn't they believe in the One Without a Name? And in the Law of Moses? Fine points, fine points they argued—who should eat what, how the rabbi should be addressed, what to do and not to do on Shabbat, which law came first, what mattered most, how to pray, what to wear when praying—and then they stopped arguing and wouldn't speak to each other!

All Granny knew about her faith was what the great Rabbi Hillel had taught: he said a poor person could say it standing on one foot: Don't do to others what you don't want them to do to you!

Poor Granny couldn't remember her left hand from her right—and her children bickered over straws! And because they bickered, they couldn't look after her!

She'd put all the utensils away and she'd begun to swab the oaken table when Joseph of Arimathea entered the hall.

"Hello, good woman," Joseph hailed her.

Granny grinned half-toothlessly.

But Joseph was formal with her, not friendly as he'd been before. He approached the two baskets of utensils. "Which is the Lord's chalice?" he asked.

"The Lord's, Sir?"

"Jesus . . . Jesus the Lord's!"

Granny stared at the two baskets. She had carefully placed Jesus's chalice on the top of one of the baskets, but couldn't remember which one. She picked up the top chalices from both baskets. She hefted them, but they were the same weight. Joseph was frowning.

"Now I remember, Sir. I put it in the left basket!"

Joseph, who had watched her carefully, saw that she still held the chalice from the left basket in her left hand. He took it from her, dropped a few extra coins into her hands and walked out the door.

Granny stared at the coins. When she heard the door close, she woke from her reverie. "I meant the right one, Sir," she said to the door, holding up the other chalice.

*

The next night Jesus was arrested in the Garden of Gethsemane. No one remembered Esther the cleaning lady who had so carefully washed and polished the dining utensils. So she kept the utensils as a bonus, and from time to time sold a piece at the market in order to supplement the meager allowance provided by her sons. Two years after the crucifixion, the old lady expired, receiving the rites of baptism on her deathbed. All the utensils had been sold, save the last, the Grail. Esther never revealed the secret of the chalice, and it was passed on with many other items to her oldest son, the Sadduccee.

The Sadduccees were the richest of the Jews of Jerusalem, and, decidedly pro-Roman. In 66 A.D., the downtrodden masses threw off the yoke of their overlords. One of Esther's grandchildren, an Essene leader of the revolt, orchestrated the murder of another one of her grandchildren—a Sadduccee. The Essene grandchild distributed the bounty of his cousin's house, except for the chalice, which he kept as a memento of his irascible grandmother.

The Essenes and other firebrands were liquidated by the Romans.

The chalice, meantime, had been passed from one Jewish home to another. After the destruction of the temples in the south, the chalice was sold for a song to a trader from Antioch. This merchant shipped his odd assortment of goods from Gaza to Antioch, where the chalice remained for almost two hundred years.

*

To Antioch came the caravans from Persia, India and China: silk and jade, ivory, perfumes, myrrh and spices flowed Westward on the Silk Road; backward to the East: gold, silver, wool, jewelry, and dancing girls with alabaster skin. Through all the wars and revolutions, men and women sought the beautiful, the silken caress like breath on their skins; and the unspooled cocoons of the black-egged silkworm wrapped a delicate skein around the empires of the East and West.

Tasting the water from a spring near Antioch, Alexander the Great declared it sweeter than his mother's milk. Five miles south of Antioch lay the suburb of Daphne, named for the mortal who had shunned Apollo's lust. A laurel tree grew at the famous springs of Daphne, and it was said to be the very tree into which the fleeing girl had been transformed. A short walk beyond the tree, in a grove of cypress, the cool, clear waters of the springs of Daphne flowed from underground reservoirs into large, stone basins.

By these same springs, pilgrims had placed chalices so that others might refresh themselves. Some were finely-wrought, but most were simple household objects, carried on camel or mule back from distant lands, placed as tokens of gratitude for a safe journey. In the soft gold-purple of Daphne's evenings the chalices shone softly, catching the last glowing embers from Mt. Silpius. The chalice of Granny Esther shone among them.

*

Fat Brother Benjamin, the Deacon, flew about the old church like a stuffed goose fleeing a cleaver. Above his own hard breathing, his sharp ears strained to hear the chariot wheels rumbling across the five bridges linking the island to Antioch. "Hurry! Hurry!" he called to the altar boys.

Swooping over the altar, he scooped the Eucharistic vessels into his raised skirts. He summoned the most fleet-footed boy. "Take these to the house of Thomas," he ordered. He turned his skirts inside out so the goblets tumbled into the boy's sack.

The boy ran with the wind behind him. He had never seen a Persian before, and now Sapor himself was inside the city's gates. The boy ran over the rickety bridge to the oldest part of the city. On the bank of the river, Christians were loading their wares onto flatboats and barges. Officials in togas were also abandoning their posts, buying passage on overburdened riverboats. The boy saw a priest he knew, and ran to him, kissing the hem of his robe. "Please, Father," he stuttered, but the priest pushed him away.

The cries of victims of Persian swords and arrows grew louder, and, at the same time, the river scene took on a dreamlike quality. People of all ranks were mingling now. The few Roman soldiers who had remained in the city were discarding their uniforms and scrambling into boats with Jews and Christians. A dog barked wildly at a frightened girl. Out of the Old Church, near the shore, deacons, priests and altar boys hurried with sacred relics from the days of St. Paul.

The boy wanted to run to the house of Thomas, but his legs wouldn't work. He folded his hands in prayer and sank to the ground. A disdainful priest kicked him in the back of his head and the boy tumbled into the sand on the river bank.

He came to a couple of hours later. The entire city seemed to be in flames. All around him lay broken bodies, corpses with gaping gashes, spears through bellies, chests and backs. There were mutilated bodies, with men's bearded faces staring in death from atop the shoulders of bare-breasted women, and women's bodies with dog's heads on top of them; and there were still-breathing men with their genitals slashed off, and breast-less women clasping torn children to their flowing wounds.

But the boy was unharmed. His head ached terribly from the kick that had saved his life, but otherwise he was well.

He searched for the sack of Eucharistic vessels, and dimly perceived that it was gone. He could not know that it had been seized by a Persian charioteer, nor that among the vessels was Granny Esther's heirloom.

*

"Why do you bring such worthlessness?" demanded the captain of the charioteers, who had been rummaging through the spoils of his men. The charioteer stared forward, unblinking. "Are you a fool?" the captain taunted.

The charioteer spoke evenly, calmly, as befitted a horseman of the imperial guard of Sapor the Magnificent. "These are holy vessels from the ancient church," he explained.

The captain picked up a bronze chalice. "Can't you tell bronze from gold, you fool? Must we go to the ends of the earth for bronze?" He threw Granny Esther's chalice into the chariot, where it clattered against the Eucharistic vessels. The captain hurried to inspect the next man's collection.

But the charioteer was more clever than he seemed. He had secreted on his person, on his horse, and in every nook and cranny and compartment of his chariot, gold coins and jewelry raided from one of the villas of Antioch. A few months later, on another raid, he used an arrow from one of the enemy dead to wound himself in the thigh. His captain was happy to dismiss him from the guard. The charioteer had shown no aptitude for plunder. He had been spoiled by philosophy.

With his hoard of gold and precious stones, the charioteer helped outfit an expedition to Cathay. Silver, wool and colored glassware of trays, necklaces and small vases went West. Silk and jade came back. The charioteer made a handsome profit, and retired to an orchard to read his beloved scrolls, pay homage to Ormuzd, study the curious dualities of the world. As a remembrance of his good fortune, he kept an unpretentious bronze chalice in a special place on the family shrine.

*

Old Chang cursed himself, cursed his stomach, cursed his leach of a brother-in-law, cursed the yaks, and the cold, and his fate.

Again and again he had told that stupid Liu they were starting out too late, but the wine-drinking fool had been spoiled by the loose ways of the oasis. He no longer believed in propitiating the gods, in following the prescribed course. Always he lingered at the oases, tasting the pleasures of the fair-skinned dancing girls, joining the dance like a fool to entertain satraps and commoners.

Now he was dead, his corpse tied to one of the white yaks, his limbs dangling like a puppet's, and a curious grimace on his face, as though he mocked death, even as he was claimed by it.

They had climbed the Pamirs! The peaks were cut sharp as jade and disappeared into clouds. They'd skirted the desert of Takla Makan. Yaks were exchanged for camels, which were exchanged for mules, exchanged for camels, exchanged for yaks once again. They had traded their goods at the Pamirs, then started home again. They'd slept with the animals in heat and cold, alert, even in sleep, for the brigands. And, at last, because of the cold and their fatigue, they had slept too well and been raided.

Ten of the seventeen men had been killed and six of the yaks. The scrawny brigands, motivated by desperate hunger, made pathetic corpses. Old Chang wished them better fates in their future lives.

Now they were near the Jade Gate, but Chang wondered if he would live to see his old wife again. In spite of his grandson's poultices, the wound in his side had not healed. Riding on the yaks was too painful, but walking tired him easily.

He never should have taken Liu with him! He should have persisted against the pleas of his sister. Now there was only the corpse and Liu's bronze drinking cup—that worthless goblet some merchant had sold him for good luck.

If hunger had not driven them to the land of the barbarians, Old Chang would have died in the land of his fathers, honoring the household gods!

He leaned against the powerful shoulder of the yak and the animal grunted—almost, it seemed, in sympathy. The long, brown hair felt silky against Chang's roughened face. The animal weaved its head close to the ground.

Chang remembered how much he had enjoyed yak meat when he had first tasted it as a boy. He put his tongue out, and snow flakes quickly melted upon it. "How sweet!" thought Chang to himself. Soundlessly, he keeled over into the beautiful whiteness.

*

Suspended on the bamboo pole, on the gosling yellow cloth, glutinous silkworm eggs wavered in the April breeze like the dark froth of a miniature sea. The Chang family had prepared six trays of eggs, and all the men and women of the family—grandparents and mother and father, aunts and uncles, brothers, sisters and cousins, and Su-ling—had helped gather load after load of tender green mulberry leaves to serve the hatched grubs' appetites.

The jade chimes made a delicate clacking as the breeze from the Huanghe blew over the loess-rich fields and entered the Chang household like an honorable guest. Su-ling, the singing child, felt a strange stirring in her body as she arranged the yellow wildflowers in the foreign bronze chalice her family kept as an heirloom. Her mother watched and smiled.

Su-ling turned suddenly from the chalice on the sill. "Oh, Mother, isn't it wonderful how the spring days come after a hard winter? Soon all the flowers will be in bloom, and the crops growing, and the merchants haggling, and the boats will go on the river far into the setting sun. Isn't it wonderful, Mother?"

But Mother simply shook her head, a bemused smile peeking around her lips. She continued plucking the goose for the evening's meal.

Su-ling embraced her mother from the back, chair and all, her thin, white arms circling the broad, brown chest. It was not a proper gesture for a girl of thirteen, but Mrs. Chang indulged her daughter, just as everyone else did.

"Child, where do you get your ways?" Mrs. Chang wondered, patting Su-ling's clasped hands.

Su-ling squeezed her mother, then sang:

> "From the lark I learned a pretty trick
> when the flowers were in bud:
> I rose from earth on cloudy wings
> then fell back, sun-struck."

She tapped the willow-colored chimes. A rooster answered from the courtyard. "This year we have one more tray than last year," she observed for the second time that week. "We shall be even richer than the year before!"

"Su-ling!" Her mother"'s face reddened. "How dare you say such a thing again!" Mrs. Chang looked around quickly to be certain they were alone. Su-ling lowered her head. "Foolish child!" Mrs. Chang cried, then slapped her daughter hard.

The imprint of her mother's hand made a pinkish pattern on Su-ling's cheek. The girl stood silent, awaiting the second blow. Hot tears started in her eyes.

Mrs. Chang held the second blow. Carefully, in clean, white

paper, she wrapped a portion of the dried meat she had been saving for her oldest son's upcoming wedding. She put it in Su-ling's hand. "Go to Grandfather's grave, and ask forgiveness," Mrs. Chang instructed.

"Yes, Mother."

Then Mrs. Chang remembered her aunt's son. With slightly less care, she wrapped five purple plums. "And bring this to Li Ho."

Su-ling shuddered within at the sound of the name, but her face revealed nothing. "Yes, Mother."

"Wear your hat!"

"Yes, Mother."

Mrs. Chang watched from the window as her strange daughter left the courtyard. She hoped the gift to her father-in-law's spirit would appease the gods of harvests, silkworms, and wealth. Just to be on the safe side, she would have no thought of good fortune until after the harvesting—and after her son's wedding.

It was hard for her to discipline her child. But Mrs. Chang remembered another time, before Su-ling's birth. Grandfather and his brother had traveled to the Western lands to earn a few extra *ch'ien*. Both of them had died on the journey, but the goods the boy had brought back with him—and two fewer mouths to feed—had started the family on the road to wealth. That boy had become Mrs. Chang's husband.

Su-ling walked along the river and watched the farmers cultivating the pale-green terraced hills that would soon be rich with blondish wheat. Near the river's edge, the family of papermakers was cutting hemp, mixing hemp with water, treading hemp, and making potash from wood. The sharp fumes of ash and hemp paste rose from the brick, as the grandmother stoked the fire and fanned the smoke away. The strongest men of the family pulped the mixture while the women stirred it in a large vat of clear water; they dipped bamboo-stripped frames and set them leaning in the sun to dry.

"Hey, Su-ling!" one of the young men called. "Going to see your boyfriend?"

Su-ling blushed and hurried away as the family laughed good-naturedly at her.

She understood why her mother had struck her, and Su-ling harbored no ill will against her. She was incapable of harboring ill will. She watched the clouds gather over the dry, rumpled, brown mountains and imagined she saw a chariot with a great king holding the reins of the horses.

She left the dried meat at the shrine by her grandfather's grave. "Forgive me," she prayed silently. "I did not mean to tempt the gods of misfortune."

Five minutes later, she was skipping along the riverbanks. She took the steep hill up from the river. Near the entrance to one of the caves, she heard hammering. Her cousin stood on a stone ramp, chiseling the soft stone.

"Hello, cousin," Su-ling called brightly.

The young man turned to the girl's voice. His work had made his arms and shoulders sinewy and bronze, and his body glistened with sweat. Only a loincloth protected his modesty. Su-ling lowered her eyes, then cast a sidelong glance.

"What have you brought me, singing child?" her cousin teased, putting aside his tools and leaping from the ramp to land at Su-ling's feet.

"Oh!" she cried, then held the plums to him. "From my Mom."

Li Ho smiled. "You are too old to say `Mom,'" he advised, gratefully accepting the plums. "Anyway, thank her for me." He ate the purple sweetness.

Su-ling squinted at the carving that had consumed her cousin's passions. "Who is it?" she wondered.

Li Ho gazed reverently at his handiwork. His voice changed. "It is the Lord Buddha," he said.

"Why do you call him Lord?"

Li Ho took another bite of plum and chewed. "Because he taught us how to live. How to release ourselves from the chain of existence."

Now Su-ling squinted at her cousin. Of all her relatives she had always felt closest to him. They were not so far apart in age—just four years. He was the one who had carved her the willow-colored wind chimes, and he had carved her wooden dolls when she was a child. They were second cousins; that meant it was possible one day—it still happened—that they could . . . But she stopped the thought, lest the god of misfortune should hear it.

"Is he like Master Kung?" Su-ling wondered.

"No," Li Ho smiled. "Master Kung Fu-tzu was a great man. And the Master of the Tao was great . . . But Lord Buddha is not like them!"

But Su-ling had been disturbed for weeks, and now her heart was overflowing. "Cousin, the people say you are deluded, like your grandfather was. He lost his way from too much wine, and now, they say, you are god-deluded."

Li Ho smiled gently.

"Won't you come back to the village and make the jade wind chimes?" Su-ling blurted. "The people from the West like the chimes and will pay for them . . . Let the busybodies see that you are not a fool!"

Li Ho continued to smile. "But I am a fool," he said softly. Then he rose. "I must get back to work."

Su-ling was growing desperate. "But when you finish," she said, "won't you come back then, and help your father and your brothers in the field, and, some day, you will want to—some day—I mean, perhaps, you will want to take a *wife* . . ." She lowered her eyes, and repeated softly, "Some day . . ."

Li Ho searched her face. Because her mother always made her wear a hat in the sun, and long white sleeves—like the wealthy landowners' and officials' daughters—her face and shoulders and arms were white as ivory. The family had placed much hope in this daughter through whom they planned to ascend the social ladder. Even at thirteen she was a beauty . . .

He took up his mallet and chisel. "There are one hundred and ninety four caves here," he told Su-ling. "And at the entrance to each, I'll carve an image of Lord Buddha. And if I live a thousand years, I'll carve an image in every cave, and make caves within caves—and carve more."

Su-ling turned from him. She did not want to show her eyes.

"Go, pretty flower," Li Ho said in his heart. "Shed your petals in this world of pain."

She did not look back. She ran down the hill, and ran to the grave of her grandfather and wept. After a while, she looked between her legs and saw that she was bleeding for the first time. She watched her blood seep darkly into the earth.

PART TWO

Yamato & Heian-Kyo

"Bows and arrows heavy at his side,
Ice splitting his horses' hooves . . .
Since ancient times men loyal to duty—
All have learned to die."

—*A Ch'an Buddhist*

4 | Yamato

At the verges of consciousness, Lancelot perceived movement. He could not yet detect colors. He could not be certain how long he had been standing in his present position—and certainly not why. He understood that someone was standing beside him. He heard a great, roaring sound which he took for the bellowing of a dragon, but he found his limbs unable to respond. His whole body felt numb.

The scene before him seemed incredibly white. The whiteness stretched to the horizon in a fury of roaring sound. Cupping his hands over his eyes, he saw large, rounded, smooth boulders and a dozen creatures sure-footedly scurrying over them. The creatures were naked, or at least the males were—and they were poking long poles with netted baskets into the whiteness.

The whiteness was the sea and the men—if men they were—wore nothing but white loincloths, while the women, in long aprons and straw hats, stood a little further back, sorting the fish which the men emptied from their baskets. One of the men looked up at Lance and Wee Willie on the cliff. He grinned half-toothlessly, then sang out words lost to the waves.

In the distance, small, sturdy boats struggled into the dragon's breath. Nearer shore—for the film was lifting from his eyes now—Lance saw a large, craggy boulder, joined by a thick, straw rope to a smaller one. They had been wedded by some ceremony, even as the sea swirled around and between them.

Turning now, his eyes were flooded with colors. Blue-green

cyptomeria, wind-sculpted, stood behind him on the promontory, and behind the trees the stout red pillars of the *torii* held a double gate aloft—though who but a giant would enter there, he could not imagine. Beyond the *torii*, a blondish, wooden building cast simple, noble lines against gold and fiery maples.

"Ha!" cried the startled little man beside him. Lance looked, and saw that it was some sort of demon in the shape of a young boy with yellowish-brown skin and almond-shaped, black eyes. He reached for his sword. The boy-demon crumpled at his feet. "Don't kill me, Sir!" it pleaded.

The voice was familiar. But the words were strange, though understandable. "Why should I not kill you, demon?" Lance demanded.

The boy-demon hugged Lance's feet. "Oh, Sir, I be no demon verily, but only Willie of Amargh. I come hither I know not how, but for the sake of some magician's blackest arts. I mean no harm, Sir." The boy began to whimper.

"Willie?"

"Aye, Sir . . ."

"Are you Willie?"

"So I was when I knew myself."

Lance stared in wonder. "I'll not harm you, Willie."

The boy stopped whimpering and kissed the boots of his protector.

"Here, that's enough," Lance said gruffly, lifting the boy by his upper arms.

Willie stared into Lance's face. His expression of gratitude quickly changed to fear, then changed again as he tried to hide it. "Now, Sir, if I may take my leave," Willie said, backing away. The boy continued to step back more hastily, then turned to run.

Lance pursued, and the boy ran faster. After a few moments, Willie stumbled, Lance flew upon him, and the boy's eyes filled with tears again.

"Do you know me not, Willie?" Lance wondered. "What has happened to you?"

Willie continued to back away, pushing his body with the palms of his hands and the soles of his feet. "Oh, Sir—if Sir you be—I know your voice, but not your words, though your words I ken. But I never saw a face like yours."

"What is this babble, Willie? Who has transformed you? What craft has taken your power to know what others are and changed your features so? Know you not Lancelot, your Lord?"

"Aye, Sir. I know him when I see him. Him it is I seek to serve."

"Then seek no further; serve him here."

But Willie just stared at the man-demon's face. Then he remembered something from a long time back. Hoping to divert the man-demon's attention and run away again, he said, "Oh, Sir, if you be he—that great and noble Lord—you have a looking glass. I prithee, look within."

Lance, too, recalled, dimly, the mirror Merlin had given him. He found it in his satchel and looked. Then he dropped it as though his fingers burned. Warily, he crept to it, and gazed again.

A not unhandsome face gazed back. But it was no manner of man Lance had ever seen before: a man with long, straight, raven-black hair, high cheekbones, hawk-black eyes, a thin, black moustache that curled down beneath his chin. The skin was yellowish-brown. Lance stared and tried out different expressions—fierce, gentle, happy, sad. It was a good, manly, changeable face.

Willie, who had crawled twenty feet away, was about to rise and run again.

"Ho, Willie, you cannot serve your master if you flee!" Lance brought the looking glass to the frightened boy. "You bade me look. Now, look upon yourself."

The boy obeyed; looked away; looked again; shook his head; looked again; blinked; rubbed his eyes; made faces at himself that startled himself and, finally, looked, and stared.

"Great is your magic, Merlin!" Lance said. "And now it does come back to me: the storm, the precipice, the Holy Grail." He turned and saw the foaming sea, the breakers and the pole nets cast between them, the craggy wedded boulders, and the land that rose to dappled, mapled mountains. "Yamato . . ." he said softly. And Willie said, "Yamato . . ."

*

Their admiration of the strange beauty of the land was interrupted by the approaching sounds of drums, gongs, clappers and cymbals. Climbing a hill, they distanced themselves from the pounding surf, hearing more clearly the piercing sounds of the Chinese flute, and the reedy *sheng*. The musicians dressed in festive, autumnal colors; some wore conical hats, and others wore helmet-shaped hats of silk. Their robes and trousers were also silk. They wore white sock-like shoes and they tread upon a long, narrow fabric of woven straw. They went singly or two by two, beating drums, clanging cymbals, clappers and gongs, piping and chanting words of an ancient language Lance could not understand. Two priest-like men carried a large drum on a lacquered pole between them. One man beat the drum as the pair of them walked, and they were followed by other pairs of drummers, and after these, dancers with bronze animal faces.

Behind the dancers came men on horses: men of fierce, metallic faces with brush-like mustaches, wearing quilted clothing, helmets and slat armor, with long swords of iron at their sides, and long bows re-curved at the ends over their shoulders. They were men who decorated themselves with curved jeweled stones suspended from their necks. They rode with a trained, martial grace while small, black eyes darted disdainfully from behind their metal visors. Behind the horsemen came palanquins. Four bearers wearing black pantaloons carried the gilded carriages. A slender, white arm slipped out from behind black curtains, rode like a white wave in the dark of the frame. A hundred perfumes saturated the air from a hundred palanquins, and a hundred delicate, white arms slipped from behind black curtains, and Lance's blood stirred.

After the palanquins, a phalanx of the very fiercest horsemen surrounded a golden throne upon which sat a smooth-faced eighteen-year old boy. Arrayed in finery, the boy seemed bored. A white canopy protected the imperial head from sun glare, but even from a distance the alert observer could detect distraction in the eyes and a twitch that raised the lips in a sneer. From time to time the boy-Emperor—so Lance deemed him—would laugh in a high-pitched giggle.

The procession passed through the red *torii* gate. Lance and Willie edged closer. The boy-Emperor kneeled before the shrine. When he stood, the women in the palanquins emerged from their lacquered, black boxes. The whiteness of their skin contrasted sharply to the other yellowish-brown men and women Lance had seen. The boy-Emperor was also whitish; but pallid, not healthy looking. The women's shiny, raven-black hair cascaded to their ankles and their slender figures were cocooned in brocaded silk, tied at their waists with sashes. In their hands they held sprigs of the sakaki tree, as well as bamboo. To the accompaniment of the wooden flutes, they performed a sort of revolving dance around the blondish shrine, and then they stood in a semicircle facing the rest of the entourage. Lance had never seen more graceful creatures.

The palanquin-bearers lifted white canopies over their mistresses, as though more than a few moments' exposure to sunlight would wither their delicate blossoms. The high priest brought the boy-Emperor a tray of exotic fruits. The Emperor ascended the steps, presented the salver to the lintel of the central shrine, kneeled on the cloth-covered *tatami*, and touched his forehead to the wooden floor. Next he was served a bowl of white food, and then a chalice.

When the Emperor had completed this ritual, the high priest presented him with the very food and drink that had just been offered to the gods. The Emperor tasted each fruit and wiped his mouth daintily on a special kerchief. He tasted the rice and wiped his mouth again. He seemed much more eager to taste the contents of the chalice—which he drank to the lees.

Lance's eyes were riveted upon the chalice which the high priest bore aloft on a black cushion. "It cannot be the one," he said aloud.

"Sire?" Willie whispered with concern.

"It is!" Lance made a fist and hit the air. The high priest disappeared into the central shrine and the boy-Emperor ascended his gilded throne. Eight bearers easily lifted monarch and throne. The horsemen mounted their steeds, the women re-entered the palanquins, and the musicians and dancers commenced again.

But Lance was lost in thought. The Grail had been within sight. All he had to do was steal back at nightfall, penetrate whatever guard protected the shrine, seize the vessel and . . .

It suddenly occurred to him that he wasn't sure what was supposed to happen next. Merlin hadn't bothered to inform him. But somehow Merlin would get him back. He was sure of that. The sacred and the mundane came together in Merlin's realm.

"*Hata!*" someone called.

Lance looked up at the scowling man on the horse. He had been so lost in thought—or so focused—he had barely noticed the procession pass under the large red gate and back down the straw-woven carpet. The Captain of the Guard bridled his nervous steed. He gingerly dismounted and approached. Lance stood to meet him.

The next thing Lance knew he was on his rump and his cheek was burning. He watched the horseman through the fury of his tears. He was halfway to his feet when he felt the force of the man's kick shatter his cheekbone. Instinctively, Lance reached for his sword, but before he could draw it from its scabbard, his agile tormentor had him by his hair. Lance saw the sun balance upon the short sword which his enemy intended to use to slice his Adam's apple. He didn't even have time to say a prayer.

"Stop!" someone shouted, and the short sword stopped an inch from Lance's pulsing throat.

Commander Nakatomi ordered the Captain of the Guard back

on his horse. Through the haze of pain, rage and humiliation Lance barely heard a high-pitched, delicate tinkling sound—giggling—from the Emperor's direction.

"*Hata*," said the Commander, "are you so new to our shores you do not observe our cardinal rules? Should a learned man gaze on the Emperor of Ch'in? Would you gaze at the Sun? Did no one tell you of our customs, *Hata*?"

Though his head was pounding, Lance understood he'd been mistaken for a Chinese scribe. Merlin must have attired him accordingly. Now the curved *magatama* jewel gave him the power to understand and speak the strange language.

"Glorious Commander," Lance managed to reply, "I dare not gaze at the Sun, nor at the Emperor of Yamato . . . I was lost in thought, and gazed at nothing."

The Emperor wanted to know what all the commotion was about, and the Commander rode over to explain. After a brief exchange, the Commander dismounted, approached a trembling peasant, bid him stand, pulled his head back by the hair and neatly sliced through his throat with his short sword.

Blood spurted wildly from the head and severed neck. The torso seemed to balance precariously, then tipped over. The eyes in the head remained open—accusing, even as the life fluid drained from it. The Commander threw the head into a ditch. A barefooted peasant woman ran screaming to the corpse and threw herself upon it, then tried desperately to re-attach the head to the torso. The Emperor ordered his bearers to put his throne down, and the sock-clad, royal feet themselves stepped upon the white linen and the straw carpet. All lowered their eyes now.

The Emperor ordered two of his horsemen to raise the inconsolable woman. She was about thirty and in the later stages of pregnancy. She was drenched with her husband's blood. She stood trembling, but her eyes were madly defiant. The Emperor whispered something to the Captain of the Guard. The Captain approached the woman with his short sword drawn and, grinning, disemboweled her. She collapsed beside the headless corpse of her husband. Her hands tried to hold her warm fetus and viscera within, and then she died. A sickening, wrenching odor blotted out the light, the very color of the day. The Emperor threw his head back and giggled.

Lance retched. He did not feel the hands lifting him up, the rope that bound his hands together. The horse of the Captain of the Guard trotted forward and he was pulled behind it. The neck of his tormentor bobbed in and out of its cuirass, and when the long, black hair rose, the blue scales of a tattooed serpent's tail rattled on the nape.

*

Willie raced through the golden-yellow of the rice paddies. He was up to his knees in mud and a half dozen farmers were yelling at him and threatening his life with sticks. Out of range of the curved jewel's power, Willie couldn't understand a word. But he understood the stones they were throwing, and he splashed through the fields, making more damage, provoking more stones.

The curved jewel was with his master, who was a distant speck on the horizon now. It was dusk, the last half hour of daylight, and the purple mixed with the gold-yellow of the paddies, the dark greens of pine and flame colors of maples. If he could have stopped trembling, he might have liked the scenery.

He feared to get on the road. He feared to be seen. He feared for his master and he was determined to help him. Hunger pangs cramped his belly and he was most fearful of all of being alone at night in the country of Yamato.

Lancelot was also fearful. He had fought dragons and overcome them. To defend the honor of Queen Guenevere he had fought Mador from noon to midnight. In enchanted forests he had cut off the limbs of trees as they brandished swords at him. When Catherine had died he had conquered his grief. But now he was not himself. Merlin had transformed him into a Chinese scribe, and Lance did not know this man. How could a man conquer himself when he did not know who he was?

The Emperor's entourage stopped at one of his country palaces. Lance was taken to the stable, chained beside the horses, and left alone. An hour later one of the peasant attendants brought him a bowl of boiled millet, adzuke beans, a little dried fish, and a pot of hot, flavored water. Famished, Lance ate quickly.

The grimy peasant squatted in the dust and watched him eat. He seemed to find Lance's hunger amusing, and he laughed aloud several times, showing yellowish teeth. Lance found him very curious. His toenails and fingernails were as long as claws. Yet they were relatively clean. In spite of his obvious poverty, his hempen garments, unkempt hair, and scraggly beard, the man did not smell! Unlike Britain, where everyone smelled bad sometimes, and many people smelled bad all the time, no one in Yamato offended in that way. Except, of course, for Lance himself! Phew! What he wouldn't give for one of his monthly baths and a change of clothes!

The side of his head was throbbing with pain. He pushed the empty bowl towards his jailer's claw-like toenails. "Why am I being held here?" he asked the dark eyes.

The peasant patted his own hairless chest. "Tsukiwa," he said.

"Zoo-key-wah," Lance repeated.

The man laughed, then pincered Lance's cheeks in his hand and squeezed them to form a fishlike mouth.

"T'su, T'su," he said, running the "t" and "s" together.

"Tsu," Lance repeated, wincing, and Tsukiwa laughed and farted.

Lance turned his face away and held his breath. But Tsukiwa, who was not in the least embarrassed, began to tell him about his fat wife, his meddlesome mother-in-law, his three children and why he had run away to serve the Emperor. The Emperor was the Lord of Heaven on Earth, the child of the Sun-Mother Amaterasu, and he could do no wrong. If he, Tsukiwa, had not had skill in caring for horses, he never could have joined the Emperor's household. But he knew how to calm a nervous horse, what herbs to feed a sick animal. These arts he knew from studying the horse's shit, breath, eyes and teeth.

Lance listened while his cheekbone throbbed. After the man had finished, Lance said simply, "Why am I here?" and Tsukiwa stared blankly.

"You are here because you are not clean," a familiar voice said from behind a stall. Lance turned and saw Commander Nakatomi. He had not heard him enter. No animal had given a sign, nor had Tsukiwa, who was now hurriedly gathering the empty bowl and water pot. The Commander propped himself on a small stool he carried with him and ordered Tsukiwa to get out.

The thin-faced Commander picked his teeth with an ivory toothpick. "We cannot have anyone looking at the Emperor whenever he chooses, *Hata*," the sallow-skinned man explained. His voice was even, almost friendly. "Soon our peasants would lose their sense of place. Perhaps they would question the order of things: why they must plant rice for other men to reap, why this and why that. That would be unwise."

"How long must I stay like this?" Lance demanded, pulling at his chains.

"We will have work for you tomorrow. You can be of service to us." The Commander smiled at Lance's expression. His teeth were white as snow.

Lance stared at the man's penetrating eyes. He wondered if he had the strength to lunge at him, seize the throat between his hands and squeeze his life out. His hatred for this smug man filled him with a wave of nausea.

The Commander narrowed his eyes. "Save that hatred for a better occasion," he said.

But Lance would not be calmed. "Why were the peasants murdered? It was a savage act."

The Commander worked at a bit of food lodged between his molars. "Someone had to pay for your crime, *Hata*."

"Barbarians!" Lance blurted.

The Commander reflected. "Yes," he said coolly. "Perhaps we are. But we are a young nation, not venerable like the land of Ch'in. Perhaps in time we shall learn better manners." He leaned close to Lance, fought visibly against Lance's odor. He stared into the intense, black eyes. Again, Lance considered killing him. But he knew he could not escape. The chain would hold him to the wall of the stable, and he would die soon after the Commander's absence was noticed. He would die without redemption, his soul damned, and the Grail undiscovered in the heathen shrine.

The Commander smiled, as though he'd read his mind. Quickly, he reached into the sash around Lance's waist and withdrew the curved *magatama* jewel which Merlin had vouchsafed. He studied it carefully, reverently, then gave it back. "You see, we are not so terrible, *Hata*," he said.

And Lance loathed him. Loathed him because the Commander's intelligence could not be disguised, and yet he happily served a mad boy; loathed him because of his cynicism and complicity, and because of his savagery.

Where were the knights-errant of Yamato, the defenders of truth and goodness? Was the land so impoverished that it could bring forth no crop of heroes to restore it? The simple people did not seem evil, but the rulers were without a shred of chivalry.

Long after the Commander had left, Lance tried to make a pallet of straw, and sleep; but the cold of the night distracted him. He woke to stomach cramps from the unfamiliar food he had eaten. He retched violently, then tried to sleep again; but the fleas and tics aroused him, and he scratched until he bled. He cursed the long night and cursed the dawn, and, at last, the exhaustion claimed him for an hour until he woke upon wet straw, a horse urinating a steamy, golden stream three feet from his head.

*

The women were bringing him to someplace in the woods. They moved like nymphs, and he was their broken puppet. His head throbbed. Each pulse of blood sent white pain screeching through him.

There was the pretty girl who took pity on him, and the no-nonsense middle-aged woman who bore herself like a sovereign.

He was feverish. Sunlight shafted through the conifers, ricocheted off the *torii*, ran randomly in the white courtyard. The two men who carried the litter grunted and set it on the ground. Another woman in white robes stood by the entrance to a hexagonal building of skin-smooth wood. The middle-aged woman and the attendant exchanged some hurried words Lance could not interpret.

The two bearers helped him to his feet and half-carried him into the bright room. The attendant and the middle-aged woman stripped him and washed his body with warm water and sacred herbs. They led him into the well of warm, clear water. After a few minutes they disappeared.

A few moments later, the pretty girl appeared in a white, translucent gown with a wooden comb in her hair. She stepped lightly into the water and sat down quietly at the other end of the basin, some ten feet from Lance. It was serene for him to contemplate her exotic beauty. She sat motionless as a statue, without looking at him, caught in her own thoughts. The warmth of the water and the aromatic herbs soaked into his body and the pounding in his head dulled. He closed his eyes briefly.

The girl had moved without stirring the water. She was five feet nearer now, at the quarter circle. She still didn't make eye contact.

Lance wondered why the Commander had let him keep the curved jewel. The men of Yamato wore similar ornaments, but Lance doubted that they gave them instant understanding. He wondered, too, where Wee Willie was, and whether he had retrieved the satchel with the magical mirror. He hadn't seen his page since the peasants had been murdered, the boy curling himself into a ball and disappearing into the saw grass. Where was the troublesome boy, and where was Merlin's sacred sword? Surely the Commander had the sword now, but how was Lance to get it back? How was he to get the Holy Grail and get himself and Willie the hell out of Yamato?

He felt something silken brush his arm and opened his eyes from his half-dream. The girl was sitting beside him, her face as composed as a picture of a goddess. She looked at him and smiled, then lightly touched his shoulders and the back of his neck. She massaged him gently. She kneeled in front of him in the bath and massaged his shoulders. He saw her small, cone-shaped breasts caressed by air and water as she moved slowly around him, her dark nipples erect.

A few moments later the middle-aged woman and the attendant entered. Together with the pretty girl, they dried him with white towels and powdered his body with sedge pollen. They cut his hair, fingernails and toenails, and trimmed his moustache in the long, tapered style of Yamato. They presented him with a light cotton robe to wear close to the skin and a heavier one of wool to wear over it. They gave him comfortable leather sandals.

He was led into another small building where a table was prepared for him. As he sat upon a cushion, the pretty girl started to sing a touching folksong outside his window.

He ate the white rice slowly, savoring each morsel. How different it tasted from the rancid millet of the night before! The women had sprinkled flakes of dried seaweed on the rice. They gave him hot, flavored water that tasted of the forest and fields.

"This is sacred food," the middle-aged woman told him, offering a broth of herbs to drink. She showed him how to hold the bowl in both hands and rotate it three times, raise it slightly and then drink slowly, as with gratitude. It made him feel clear somehow.

They let him rest in the sun for an hour. He soaked up the heat like a lizard. After a while, the Commander rode up on his horse, leading Wee Willie on a palfrey. The boy dismounted, ran to Lance and embraced him. "We thought you might know this turnip," said the Commander.

"Sire," blurted Wee Willie, "I saw men walking on the green sea, and I walked, too. At night there were dragons around me. Morning I awoke and a kind goddess gave me food because she took pity on me. The houses were all off the ground, floating on the air, and the thatch of the roofs was heavy and sagging. Even the farmers' houses were clean and good-smelling. The woman pointed me down the road and I went. Then the Commander came and here I am happy to find you better than I left you— and when are we getting out of here?"

An hour later, they were riding towards the Imperial Palace. Outside the city was a line of trees, very long, straight and symmetrical, upon a mountain a hundred feet high. Gradually, Lance saw that the tree-line rose from behind a narrow moat into a mound of earth.

"Bow your head," the Commander ordered and Lance and Willie did so. For two hundred and fifty yards they rode along one edge of the mound. Around the slopes of the mound, in rows, were pottery cylinders with terra cotta figurines of men, girls, monkeys, warriors—each face with its own character.

At the center of the mound the Commander bade them to dismount. They passed over a bridge, onto a narrow island, passed a second moat, a somewhat larger island, then came to a great lake and within the lake a large island shaped like a keyhole. The Commader was silent. He looked around reverently, then signaled with his eyes that they must go.

After they had left the mound, the Commander spoke for the first time since the morning. "That was Emperor Nintoku's tomb," he said solemnly. "When he was born, an owl flew into his birthing room. It was an evil omen.

"But his father had a minister whose wife had given birth the same day. A wren had flown into that baby's chamber. It was a good omen.

"The older brother of Nintoku-tenno was destined to inherit

their father's throne. But he declined the honor. Nintoku-tenno would not go against his father, neither would he consent to have his brother's throne. After two years of impasse, the older brother killed himself.

"During the reign of Nintoku-tenno, farmers were exempt from taxes, canals and dikes were erected, storage houses overflowed with grain. The people lived long and happily, and Nintoku-tenno himself walked on the earth for nine and one hundred years. The Kami were respected . . ."

The Commander turned on his horse to face Lance. "Yesterday, you were polluted by death, blood, sickness and hatred. Had you not been purified, you never could have approached Nintoku-tenno's tomb."

Then they entered the Imperial City.

*

The *I-Ching* rendered the hexagram of "Teh-Khieu," with its double meaning of Great Accumulation and Major Restraint. Lance tried to decipher the oracle: "A mountain with heaven within it . . . The Gentleman stores in his mind the grains of history . . . Thus he knows rightness . . ."

Lance consulted the *Book of Judgments* and the *Appended Book of Judgments* to see what the scholars had said about it: "Firmness . . . correctness . . . Stay the course . . . Restraint together with accumulation . . ."

"What does not kill me makes me strong," Lance thought with some irony, then read on: "Virtue waxing . . If the Gentleman proceeds to gather his virtue, can impropriety serve him, can weakness? The Gentleman serves the public, the King smiles upon him, he undertakes enterprises of great height. He may cross the great water."

Now he put the books upon the straw mat, settled his buttocks on the cushion on the stone stoop, leaned back upon the bark of the pine. His eyes fell on the silver-gray surface of the man-made lake, followed the craggy stones that rose like islands, and the smaller slabs and discuses that came down to the shoreline like miniature mountains. A stone bridge connected his small island with a similar; then another stone bridge reached the shore. In the two weeks since he had stayed at the Emperor's Palace the maples had turned a fierce coal-red.

The Commander had assigned him the task of translating certain books from Ch'in. The Yamato people, he had learned, were unabashedly envious of the much older empire of Ch'in. They focused their envy by determining to learn everything they could about the wondrous people from across the sea.

From daylight to sunset, with Merlin's curved jewel resting in his sash, Lance translated from ancient Chinese to 5th Century Japanese. In the evening, after he had bathed and eaten, the words poured out to the Commander. Lance had not read so much in all his life, nor had he ever had a greater appetite for learning.

Especially he liked Sun Tzu's *The Art of War*. It was based on the theory of the opposites—the Tao—and trying to work with the harmony of nature to defeat one's enemies with guile—turning their own strengths against them. If it were possible to win by bluffing, was that not preferable to brute force? Force wasted one's own resources, as well as the enemy's. Brute force demeaned the warrior who used it. Better to defeat by guile, make the enemy one's ally, feed on his strength.

This was the strategy of the empty city: A general in an undefended city ordered the gates left open while a musician idly played a lute on the city's walls. The enemy general convinced himself that the city must have a huge army, allowing its citizens to act so casually in the face of peril. So he stole away.

Of course, it was all based on Kung Fu-tzu's idea of the Superior Man, the Gentleman. If the ruler behaved properly, if the general behaved with strength and dignity, then the common people and soldiers would follow suit. "Rectify the names," Lance said aloud, quoting Kung Fu-tzu. If the professed values of the society were the true values, harmony would reign.

The gold carp made a lazy streak through the watery shadows of the stone lanterns. Looking up, Lance saw the white-robed woman approaching—the one who brought him the fruits in the afternoon. It was Imbe-san, the no-nonsense, middle-aged woman who had bathed him with herbs, helping him to recover from his wounds and illness. Again he remarked the wonderful grace of the women of Yamato: women who spoke and acted as the equals of men, were accorded respect for their persons, and held positions of authority. As she stepped off the first stone bridge, a commotion broke out in the inner courtyard. Lance rose to his feet, gathered his books and joined Imbe-san. Together they left the garden and approached the sanctum of the inner courtyard.

All the busybodies were telling the story: In spite of the animal's uncustomary skittishness, the Emperor had insisted upon riding his favorite horse. Out of the city, the beast had placed its hoof in a gopher's hole and the royal bones had tumbled. Now the smooth-faced Emperor stood before the inns of rooms. His attendants mimicked his scowl. A pig was squealing in the distance. The noise got louder, until they saw that it was no pig at all, but a peasant being led by two guards who were twisting his ears. Lance recognized the grimy face, bushy eyebrows and talon-like nails of Tsukiwa, the jail-keeper from his first night of captivity. The guards pushed Tsukiwa to the ground in front of the Emperor. Tsukiwa groveled and cried.

The Emperor bid Tsukiwa to stand. His voice was mild, almost girl-like. The terrified peasant's legs kept buckling, and the guards pulled him up by his ears. Tsukiwa kept his eyes lowered as the Emperor looked him over. Though Lance was standing about fifty feet away, he thought he saw a quiver of a smile pass over the Emperor's lips. The potentate whispered to one of the guards, then told Tsukiwa that he need not be afraid. Again the voice was mild, the face expressionless. Tsukiwa stopped trembling. Suddenly, a third large and burly guard seized Tsukiwa from behind and carried him kicking and screaming to a post where he was tied up with leather straps. The guard to whom the

Emperor had whispered retrieved a pair of iron tongs from his belt and proceeded to pull the horse-trainer's thumbnails from their sockets.

Lance's heart hammered on an anvil within. He had never heard such cries, such pleading. He checked the faces of the witnesses. All except the Imperial Guard had their eyes turned. The Commander, who had arrived late, stood off to one side, watching coldly.

The Emperor approached his victim. Tsukiwa held the bloody stumps of his thumbs forward in supplication. The Emperor nodded and the powerful guard continued. The other guards surveyed the crowd, their hands cocked on the cords of their short bows.

After the fingernails were extracted, the torturer began on the talon-like toenails. Tsukiwa screamed and babbled and whimpered as the currents of pain broke through him. When the breeze blew in a lull of his screaming, the delicate wind-chimes under the eaves rustled against each other, and the sound of the Emperor's giggling was heard.

The Emperor bid his henchmen untie Tsukiwa. With spears prodding him, Tsukiwa limped out of the city. The Emperor and his entourage followed. The peasants returned to their chores.

Lance followed. He saw the Commander and wondered again how the man could hear the words of the *Five Ancient Classics* and Sun Tzu's words and yet serve a madman. Outside the gates, in the peasants' graveyard, Tsukiwa was forced to dig. The stumps of his fingers furrowed the earth as he cursed his fate and the first day he had ever looked at a horse. He begged that his bones be sent to his home village for proper cleaning during the *O-bon* festival.

The Emperor merely giggled. When the grave was deep enough, a guard swooped down with his sword and chopped off Tsukiwa's babbling head. The Emperor's dog was led forward on a leash. The animal turned, and with its hind legs kicked dirt over the gory head and torso.

5 | The Kami

The cry of the crane echoed through the late November sky. The red crested heads snaked forward and the gray sky gathered the white wings like a strange premonition. The flashing scissors paused in Imbe-san's hands and she said a silent prayer to the Kami.

Lance saw her worried face in the mirror, and thought he saw her lips move. "I guess that's enough for me," he said, rising from the chair, and brushing hair from his tunic. In the courtyard, monks of the religious clan walked hurriedly to their meeting with the Emperor. In the inner courtyard they would light joss sticks and say solemn prayers. The Emperor himself would offer new rice to the Kami of heaven and earth. Behind the white-robed monks, grimacing youths in nothing but loin cloths, strained against the weight of the *mikoshi*. The shrine bobbed like a gold lacquered wave upon their sinewy shoulders.

"Thank you, Imbe-san" Lance said to the woman he had come to regard as a friend. He turned to Wee Willie. "Up and to it, varlet!"

The boy rose sluggishly to his fate. As he settled into the barber's chair he turned a pitiful countenance to Imbe-san.

"Always there are festivals and ceremonies," Lance observed, as Imbe-san sprinkled water over Willie's unruly locks. The boy hunched himself and folded his arms. "Though I have read in the sacred books," Lance continued, "I find no reference to these ceremonies. Nor do I understand these Kami of which you speak."

Imbe-san showed a rare smile. "The Kami are before our writing," she explained.

Willie squirmed in his chair and cocked a wild eye at Lance. "Fussed over like milady's girl!" he muttered.

"I would like to understand these matters better," Lance continued, "but when I speak to the priests, they are close-mouthed."

"What is it you need to know?" Imbe-san asked.

"What we're doing here!" Willie answered.

"The names of your gods," Lance said, frowning at Willie.

"So," Imbe-san said. She reflected for a moment. "Are names of such importance in your father's land?"

"We have thousands of saints, and each saint has a name and a story. But the greatest name of all is Jesus"—here Lance crossed himself and kneeled—"in whose name all are saved."

"I have never heard of this Jesus," Imbe-san admitted. "Is this a new god of Ch'in?"

Now Willie looked with amusement at his sire. Lance cleared his throat. He had gotten carried away. "Only in certain regions," he told her.

"Yes, the western one," said Willie, and Lance scowled at him again.

"For us the names are not so important," Imbe-san explained. "But perhaps you can learn them, if you are ready."

"What must I do?" Lance asked. "I will do what you bid to learn the names."

"Aren't we done yet?" Willie asked.

"Can you 'scape whipping, varl?" Lance fumed.

"Sit still, boy!" Imbe-san commanded, and Willie slumped in the chair and stopped squirming.

"Tell me what I must do to learn the names," Lance repeated.

Imbe-san set scissors and comb on the dressing table. She looked around to see that no one else was listening. "Let the boy go now," she said.

"Stay within earshot," Lance told his page, and Willie skulked off, glad to have saved most of his hairs, but also scared of a tanning.

"Next month, not here, not far from here, there is a place I cannot tell you of . . . If you are ready, three days before touch no food nor water; hear no music; touch no unclean thing. Eschew the sick and the unclean. Also, there are words you must not utter. I will teach you these and give you new ones. But only if you are judged—prepared."

"But who will judge me?"

Imbe-san put the scissors and combs into her small, lacquered box, then fastened it under her *obi*. "You are already judged and are being judged," she said softly. "Now, I must attend to other duties." She bowed, and turned to go.

"What shall I do till then?" Lance wondered.

"As you have done," she said. "One cannot empty the storehouse of knowledge if one enters like a mouse seeking morsels." She smiled, nodded, and departed.

Lance realized he had just been gently reprimanded. His task, as far as *they* were concerned, was to translate the Chinese classics. Nothing else. To that end they put him up in the scholar's rooms, fed and dressed him well, taught him the pleasures of bathing each evening. The task was hardly disagreeable. Each day deepened his appreciation of the old culture of Ch'in. His gratitude to the ancient sages knew no bounds. And yet, he had come no closer to the Grail! Since he had seen it weeks ago at the Ise Shrine, he had devised no plan to rescue it from its bondage, to return it to Britain.

Without an ally he did not know how to manage. He had turned the problem over many times. The shrine was guarded by a hundred men. What sort of ruse would get him through? He did not know enough to devise a ruse. Without knowledge, all was hopeless. He carefully wrapped the sacred mirror in the velvet cloth and put it in the satchel.

There was the other problem, too. His sword had never been returned. Other scholars in the Imperial Service had swords so he hoped to have his returned. But when he had asked the Commander, the devil had squinted his eyes at him and laughed like a weasel.

"Willie!" Lance called, and the boy skulked forward out of the shadow of the eaves.

"How may I serve my Sire?" the boy asked.

"By holding your tongue, knave!" Lance said, then kicked the boy in his rump and sent him sprawling into the dirt.

A trio of young women were passing just then and they covered their mouths and giggled. Willie's face turned beet-red.

Lance went to the red-faced boy and helped him up. "Don't argue with the general in the midst of battle, knave."

"Aye, Sir."

Lance saw that the boy was near tears. "I won't have dissension in the ranks, boy!"

"No, Sir."

"Right, then."

Still covering their mouths, the trio of girls hurried away from the strange foreigners. "Get on with it then," Lance said sternly.

"Aye, Sir," Willie said, wondering what he was supposed to get on with. He dusted himself off and wished to God he had never seen Yamato, or the knight called Lancelot. Wished he had stayed in the poor village with his blessed mum. He missed her now, and worried about her, and wondered if he could take the Grail himself and get home somehow.

Satisfied he had taught the boy well, Lance returned to his books. But he had an uneasy feeling that there were probably better ways to teach the young.

*

Lance hunched against the cold, a scarf tied over his ears and around his neck, a fur hat on his head. Over a woolen tunic and trousers, he wore a coat of straw and a straw basket-like hat. He might have wondered how Imbe-san managed to sit with such straight-backed dignity beside him. She wore clothes less suitable than his. Nor did anyone else seem to mind the snow upon straw-sandal-clad feet. An updraft from the river dusted snow from the tree limbs onto Lance's neck. He shuddered in rhythm to the drums as the priest in the fox's mask and the animal robes danced and chanted to the gongs and flutes.

Some fifty people had gathered in the woods near a fork in a river. In the middle of a roped-off rectangular area, a large pine tree towered over the worshippers. Pebbles covered the sacred ground, and larger stones marked off the area, and the rope linked four red corner-pillars. Banners and streamers clapped to summon the attention of the Kami. Thanks to the sacred jewel, Lance understood the fox-priest's chanting:

> "Amaterasu, Goddess of the Sun,
> shamed by the misdeeds of Susanawo,—
> her brother the Thunder-God:
> to all good men a scourge—
> enclosed herself in a grotto
> and plunged the world to blackest night.
>
> "The Kami of the forest wept,
> the stones and trees and rivers—
> all things that love the light—
> set to bring the Goddess to her throne.
>
> "Ama no Uzume kicked her heels,
> showed her breasts, dropped her skirts;
> the assembled gods could not contain their laughter—
> though they grieved.
>
> "Amaterasu stole from her abode
> to see what all the laughter was about.
> (Dance and laughter brought the light around.)
> Her light clung to a mirror hung before the cave.

"Who had put it there—no one knew.
Perhaps the Kami who understand all things.
Entranced by her own light, she floated forth.
The buds of the field drank deep again.
And peace reigned in Yamato."

Lance had not eaten for three days. He had isolated himself in his rooms to avoid contact with any unclean thing or person.

Now a hundred voices rose in thanksgiving. Cooked rice and salt were brought to the makeshift shrine and offered to the Kami. Husked rice and unhusked rice, rice wine and saltwater fish, rice cakes, wild fowl, sea plants, waterfowl, greens and sweets came forth from the participants. The aromas brought water to Lance's mouth and his belly grumbled from three days of neglect. After the food offerings came *Ema*—wooden plaques covered with painted horses and prayers. From beneath their robes, the devotees produced statuettes of men and animals, and these, too, they brought to the shrine. Finally, heavy white paper, inscribed with prayers, were tied around the branches of a sapling.

Lance strained to see the Kami, but saw nothing, though everyone else seemed transformed by their presence. The moon cast shadows from tree to stone to face to hands. The fox-attired priest began to stamp his feet and chant from deep in his belly. His voice was that of a man's and also that of an animal's, punctuated by barks and howls:

"From under the bellows of mountains I come
with grief . . . with sadness . . ."

"Why do you come from afar with such a burden?" asked Imbe-san. And the drums beat louder as a misty snow began to fall.

"Now I shall tell all . . . Who listens here?"

"I do."

"I."

"We do."
"All are listening."
After the chorus of affirmation, the fox-dancer continued:

> "An eight-headed serpent ravaged the land,
> and Susanawo, the Thunder-God, chopped off the heads;
> opening the body, found the grass-cutting sword."

"That was a sword of swords," sang a drummer.
"Even the wind could not withstand its blade," sang another.
The fox-dancer continued:

> "Susanawo, the God,
> gave the grass-cutting sword to Earth,
> to make peace with Earth,
> to divide the reign of Heaven
> and the reign of Man.

"What could separate truth from falsehood, the good from bad without the sword?" sang the drummer.
"No dark, no light, no clarity, no purpose," sang Imbe-san in a voice that was sweet and young.
Then the old drummer chanted:

> "Fifty five states in east Japan,
> sixty six states in the West—
> great is the glory of Yamato!"

Twirling madly, leaping in frenzied arcs, the fox-dancer sang through his pain:

> "Nintoku brought peace with the grass-cutting sword;
> For eighty six years the Sun Goddess
> smiled on the prosperous realm.
> For eighty six years Nintoku

built the canals and the bridges,
the granaries overflowed,
the peasants danced in the paddies.

"Five generations later,
Buretsu piles ruins on ruins.
Because of this foul boy-Emperor
the sacred mirror
shows us no shape of the land.

Because of his foulness, the curved jewel
dazzles no eyes of the realm.
The grass-cutting sword is vanished."

"Men must have *wa*," the older drummer incanted.
"Without *wa*, the gods of heaven lose their bearings."
"Without *wa*," answered the other drummer,
"death and madness are the lot of men."

"How shall we restore this harmony?" sang Imbe-san.

And the fox-dancer seemed possessed. With his right arm stretched out straight, he began to turn in place. He made a whirring noise like a windmill in a storm, a great beating, a humming. He became a blur of light.

Lance blinked. When he opened his eyes, he saw the fox mask and the fox robes in a heap on the ground. Everyone gasped. The drummers stopped drumming. The devotees nervously searched the shadows.

Then Commander Nakatomi stepped from behind the sacred tree. He wore his armor, and in his arm, raised over his head, was Lancelot's sword—Merlin's sword—the grass-cutting sword of Yamato! The Commander looked into the eyes of each of the spell-bound devotees. "With this," he said at last. "This restores *wa* to the land."

The devotees rose with a shout. And Lance saw that they

were not simply worshippers, but warriors. From beneath their straw coats, short swords appeared, which they raised above their heads. "Nakatomi!" they shouted, "Nakatomi!"

And Commander Nakatomi answered with his eyes. Every man and woman there—and a third of them were women—looked into the dark eyes. He held the grass-cutting sword aloft, and the plangent cry of a raven echoed over the fast-running currents of the river, through the dark woods. The scudding clouds passed over the moon. Everyone held their breath. Then the full moon broke through the clouds again, the soft snow fell onto the torches, onto the shoulders of the river, dusting the world with exultation.

Commander Nakatomi put on white ceremonial robes and transformed himself again. Now he presided as the same offerings which had been brought to the altar were distributed to the people. Those who could bring more had brought more, but now everyone shared equally in the banquet. The torches lit pyres, and rice was stuffed into green bamboo and heated. *Sake* wine was poured into stone vessels and heated. Imbe-san brought Lance a serving of sacred food. He feasted on sweet duck and spicy greens, and when the hot rice wine came he drank deeply and the cold and discomfort passed.

"Now you are one of us," Imbe-san said, with one of her rare smiles.

"Apparently," Lance answered. "But who exactly are you?"

"We are the *uji* of the rites," she said.

"The family . . . the keepers . . . the clan . . ." she continued. Her eyes shone with pride; at the same time, the contours of her face lost some of their military edge. "Long ago, the gods gave the grass-cutting sword to Yamato Ihare, the first Emperor."

"But, the sword . . . how . . . ?"

Imbe-san raised a finger, and then continued. "In ancient times, two kingdoms flourished in the land—Izumo and Yamato. One people, two kingdoms; and all men worshipped the Kami. First among the worshippers, was the *tenno* of Yamato—the Emperor Most High. Then the Emperor said to the priests of Izumo:

`Come and join our brotherly kingdom. Let us subdue the wild, hairy Ainu white men of the north and make this land our own. Let us subdue the people across the sea, for they are divided. Over all public functions, over all ceremonies of Emperor and his court, let the priests of Yamato preside. Over all private functions, over all that the people hold sacred in their hearts—let the priests of Izumo hold sway.' So the priests of Izumo joined with the Emperor of Yamato."

Now the Commander, who had been listening behind them, spoke up. "This arrangement worked well for a long time," he said. "The *uji* of Yamato performed the public ceremonies. The *uji* of Izumo maintained the people's shrines, taught the people to honor their ancestors—for this gives pleasure to the Kami." He looked up at the moon, swept by the pine branches. "Well," he said with a sigh, "nothing lasts forever. The great Nintoku reigned for eighty-six years. After, dissension and intrigue ravaged the land. It must have been then that the three treasures vanished. We think the functionary priests of Yamato have known it all this time—for the treasures were entrusted to their safe-keeping years ago when the two kingdoms joined. We cannot say. The Kami hate unclean thoughts or deeds. Most abominable of all—our current tenno, this mad boy-Emperor who kills for pleasure."

Lance tried to digest it all. His mind burned with questions. Where did he fit in—if at all? How had the three treasures of Yamato come into Merlin's possession? Why did they allow him to keep the curved jewel and the sacred mirror? Why had the mirror seemed to lose its power to show the true face of things? "The peasants," he blurted. "Why did you kill the peasants?"

The Commander nodded. "Had you lingered at that gory scene, you would have seen two reptiles crawling from the smoke upon the grass. To win the mad boy's trust, I shuffle forms then scatter them."

"And Tsukiwa, the horse-trainer?"

"I trust he travels in a better world than this. That one I

could not help. The lines of his fate were knotted long ago. Much I see, much I cannot see. Yet I walk the path that chooses me."

"But—"

"We should be getting back," Imbe-san remarked. She studied the sky, as for portents. "The gate-keepers are our men, but still . . ."

The Commander nodded. Imbe-san rose and kicked dirt into the fire.

The Commander and Lance rose. Nakatomi peered into Lance's eyes. "We must restore *wa*," he said. "Without *wa*, there is no proper relationship between men, between men and nature, men and women, men and the Kami. If we thought you were merely a scribe, you never would have come this far. I read your heart in your eyes and I know you are with us. Steel your heart for giant purposes and let no one else discern your cause . . . For now, *Hata-san,* for now, *Lancelot*, fare thee well."

*

In the training grounds outside of the Imperial Gate, Wee Willie had been watching the swordsmen for hours. With one slanting blow they cut the thick bamboo stalks in half or slashed the straw-stuffed mannequins. They pounded each other on helmet and armor.

They had long ago gotten used to the strange Chinese boy and often let him tag along on unimportant missions. His quiet and his wide-open, eager-to-learn eyes, set in a cute monkey face, endeared him to the warriors, and they adopted him as their mascot. They called him *"Saru-chan"*—little monkey. And Willie, who understood quite a few words of their language now, relished the nickname. In his own country his looks had never appealed to anyone, and he felt it better to be thought cute as a monkey than ugly as a boy.

Lance watched Willie from the second story reading and writing room. He was not watching Willie so much as he was trying to work out a meaning in a text. He had been pondering the character *"junzi"* in the analects of Kung Fu-tzu. Considered a certain way, it meant "superior individual," as in a member of the ruling class. But rendered into Japanese, *"kunshi"* meant "ideal person," and, as such, a model for all to follow. Had the great sage merely written a guide for the rulers of the country; or were all people capable of striving so highly—the meanest peasant bound by principle and goal no less than a king?

Lance watched as Wee Willie raced towards the apartments...

In a sacred spot in the forest, marked by stones and rope, Commander Nakatomi cast the foretelling bones. Imbe-san watched with rapt attention as, once again, the sallow finger-bones pointed to the inescapable conclusion. "Lancelot!" the Commander said.

"But he is not of the *uji*," Imbe-san protested again.

"The bones have said it—twice."

"I will tell him," Imbe-san said, resigned. "He trusts me."

"It is much to ask of him," the Commander reflected.

"He is the one," Imbe-san replied. "The bones have spoken..."

In the reading/writing room, the boy flung himself at Lance's feet. "Great Sire," he said, "never have I asked a favor, or had a prayer, but one—to be of service to you, my Lord... But, but now—oh, one more favor, Great Sire, I beseech you."

"Stand up, Willie," Lance commanded. "Speak like a man!"

Willie stood, and he did seem to have grown a half head taller since he had first pestered Lance in Britain.

"Well?" Lance prodded.

"The... the... the *magatama*, Sire," Willie said, having learned the word for the curved jewel Merlin had bequeathed to Lance. "If I might borrow it for the shortest time."

"Have you, too, become a translator, Willie?"

"Oh no, Sire!" He looked at Lance's stack of books and scrolls in half dread. "I want nothing of books, as books want nothing of me."

Any other time Lance would surely have said no. Perhaps he would have cuffed the boy for his insolence. But the boy's eyes had not been so earnest since he had first begged to be allowed to serve. And there was something else, too.

Lance withdrew the *magatama* from his buckle. "Do you understand the nature of this weapon, boy?"

"Is it a weapon, Sire?"

"Aye, boy, for it cuts to men's hearts and bleeds their words to common understanding." Nestled in his two palms, Lance held it forth to Willie. "You have your mission, too, lad. Now, list well. Keep this in your buckle fastened tight. Nor move nor touch it aught. Understood? Guard it as you would the milk in your mother's breasts."

Overwhelmed, Willie kissed Lance's hand, carefully placed the *magatama* inside his own buckle, placed his hand over it, and practically danced out the door.

Lance watched the boy stride forth into the sunlit courtyard, and he made up his mind that instant that the great sage Kung Fu-tzu had indeed intended that all people should strive for the ideal. The humblest peasant might comport himself as a king. And the revelation shook him. He had to reach out for a beam for balance.

On the training grounds, Willie's back-clapping swordsman had fashioned his mascot a sheaf of split bamboo, bound together by leather thongs. "Are you ready now, little monkey?"

Willie approached with fear and excitement. "Yes, Great Sir."

The warrior held out the bamboo sword. Willie closed his hand on it. The warrior's face tautened. "First is the yelling," he said. "It must go through the body, through every reed of the body. If the spirit is great, the enemy will run before he ever sees the sword. He will tremble when he hears the yell . . . Now I will address you as a man. Understand?"

Willie could only nod.

"If you have great spirit, you will defeat your enemy even

before he lifts his sword. You must yell sharply as you fight, and watch your enemy as from a distance, as a hawk watches, so even the slightest movement is detected. Your physical power is directly related to the power of your voice. The sword moves first in your voice. The voice shows your spirit, and the sword understands this spirit and responds accordingly. Your body will move smoothly and the sword will move like lightning in your hands if you yell loud and true so all the Kami of the mountains—both good and bad—can hear you." The warrior took Wee Willie's measure. "Have you understood?"

"*Hai!*" the novice shouted.

"Every word?"

And louder, he shouted, "*Hai!*"

"What was that?"

And with exuberance, he shouted, "*HAI!*"

*

In the Valley of the Bountiful Joining of Forest and River, the owl whose daily sleep had been disturbed by an earthquake ruffled its white feathers and searched the winter landscape for food. A little beyond the sacred enclosure where Lance had witnessed the fox-dance, the Commander sat in white ceremonial robes and a conical hat, pouring the contents of various packets onto a flat, lacquered dish. He carefully mashed the herbs and roots with a wooden mallet, then emptied the mixture into a pot of steaming water and stirred. After a few moments, he lifted the pot onto the wooden table and let the brew cool.

On a small shrine, there was a flame-shaped terra cotta vase. Four terra cotta tongues of flame curled around the rim of the vase which narrowed into a fist-sized base. It looked like a torch and it was carefully supported in a wooden frame that had been specially built for it. A curious design of rope patterns of whorls and double vortices covered the vase. The Commander did not know that the vase was over 2,000 years old, nor that it had been made by the first inhabitants of the islands. He only knew that his teacher had given it to him, who had received it from his teacher—and on and on.

He ladled a cup of the still steaming brew and offered it to the Kami of the vase. He ladled a second cup and drank it. After a few minutes, he settled back upon the wooden pillow and shut his eyes. He felt the effect of the potent herbs, and he uttered a moan as he settled onto the wooden platform pillow.

He was walking beside a carriage, dressed in uncomfortable clothes with a rope of cloth tied around his neck. Something was over his eyes, too. When he lifted the small green windows, the world became much brighter, the sunlight almost unbearable. He put the windows back in place.

Throngs of white people were cheering and waving red, white and blue kerchiefs on various-sized sticks. Some of them held black boxes at their eyes, and the boxes had eyes of their own which reflected the sun.

Soon he realized that the focus of attention was the man and the woman in the carriage. There were other carriages behind and in front of them, but the Emperor and the lady in the carriage he walked beside were the star attractions.

The Commander had never seen such a handsome, vital young man, nor had he seen a more beautiful woman. The lady wore a tightly fitting pink tunic and skirt and the Emperor wore a tight black jacket and trousers. The Emperor's white shirt was also fastened with a rope of fabric.

A stiff bit of leather in the shape of a fist bobbed over the Commander's heart. Something hard, cold and somehow menacing rode in the palm of the leather. The Commander was about to explore this thing when thunder shots rang out and the Emperor's head exploded. The Commander saw the blood and brains flecked on his own white shirt. The lady tried to get out of the carriage. Puffs of smoke rose from a grassy knoll and some people were pointing in that direction. Men on rumbling white horses sped forward, and a man rushed to the black carriage and pushed the lady back, and the carriage sped away.

The Commander woke in a sweat. He sat up and dried himself. He slid open the door of the hut and let the fresh, cool air wash over him.

Each time he went on a journey he had a different experience, and he could never predict what it might be, not even who he might be. He only knew that these were moments from another time, though how the puzzle pieces fit together was beyond him.

He watched as Imbe-san approached the hut, her surefooted steps lightly imprinting the snow. She entered wordlessly and sat down at the wooden table, waiting for him.

After a few moments the Commander spoke. "A great Emperor was murdered."

"Ours?"

"Nay . . . Another time, another people . . ."

"We will not see further then," she answered. "Only the great sea battle—"

"Dan-no-ura—"

"And the time beyond that. Victory at the beginning will bring destruction at the end . . ."

"So I saw. So I understood . . ."

"Unless Lancelot helps."

"By changing the outcome."

Imbe-san removed her woolen shawl and placed it on a peg on the wall. The steam rose from the wool. She sat beside the Commander.

"Have you told him?" he asked her.

"As much as I know . . . He is ready . . ."

"Does he understand what this involves?"

Imbe-san put her hand on the Commander's hand. "He is a good and wise and brave man. And he has a wound in his soul. To heal that wound he will go into the possible worlds. He will do as we ask."

"Why have the Kami chosen a foreigner?" the Commander wondered aloud. Imbe-san put her finger to his lips to hush him.

He removed her outer garments. In the glow of the fire her skin was yellow and lustrous. "Before he does battle, we must nourish his soul; he must be ripened by our books and arts. The boy, too, must mature."

"There is a time we both have seen," she answered. "That elegant Heian court . . . Send them there. Let them store grain against the winter's siege."

The Commander smiled. "You are as wise as you are beautiful." He pressed his lips to a spot between her throat and shoulders. She shuddered. Under her cool skin, he felt the warm pulse of her blood.

*

Lance shifted the satchel from one shoulder to the other. The water boy poured him a cup of coolness and he drank gratefully. In spite of the lingering dusting of snow, the sun was high, and the long walk had made him hot. He watched the gently swaying haunches of horses and envied the Imperial Guard. He hadn't been on a horse in . . . what was it? Only three-four months? It seemed much longer.

In front of him the Captain of the Guard let the dark gleam of snake twine over the top of his body like the thick vine of a tree. The oddness of seeing a man with a pet snake had not worn off after three days on the road.

Now one of the foot soldiers laughed and pointed to a crossbeam up ahead. There were stones placed upon the beams, and more stones lying in a heap nearby. One of the Emperor's hounds ran over to investigate, got a nose-full and hurried back. The soldiers laughed and the Emperor threw a bone at the dog.

When they were closer Lance saw that the stones were the heads of variously aged males, some with their eyes open, some with eyes closed, some with calm, dreamy expressions, others with expressions of rage, shock or sorrow. The flies and the crows had gotten to them; only the cold had preserved some semblance of life.

"So much for the rebels!" one foot soldier muttered to his companions.

"But did they get them all?" another soldier answered.

And an air of uneasiness settled over the men, who stiffened their backs and watched the horizons.

Willie followed the foot soldiers. Every now and then he would remove the old sword from its scabbard and the sun would flash on it. He would practice one of the maneuvers he had learned. He had graduated from bamboo swords to a rusty, iron cast-away. When one of the swordsmen rode by he would scowl at Willie and the boy would quickly sheathe the corroded blade.

They walked the same road they had walked a season ago, and yet everything had changed. They forded a fast-flowing river, and Lance noticed how the water swirled around the horses and the men, streamed through the carriage wheels and made double whorls behind the boulders.

The snake curled its way around the Captain's torso and Lance thought about the image in the *Book of Changes* and how everything seemed to turn into something else—even its opposite!

"You understand what we are saying?" Imbe-san had asked him just yesterday. And he had replied what every chosen one since the beginning of Time has replied, "Why me?"

Imbe-san smiled ironically. "That we cannot answer. You were sent here for one purpose, now we have grafted another onto you. How these paths converge, we know not."

He had agreed to help them. In return, they promised him the Holy Grail. All he had to do was to stand like a boulder in the way of the flowing river of history. He merely had to alter the course of Time!

Now the procession halted at the promontory. The wintry sea lathered the rocks where the fishermen had stood a season before. The Commander rode forward from the back of the procession.

He rode to the Emperor's sedan chair. Lance walked to the carriage, too. The guards let him pass. He was just a harmless scribe. Willie followed.

The Emperor sat twitching in his throne as the silk canopy floated over his head. For an hour they watched as the little boat struggled against the waves and the loin-clothed men removed the rope that "married" the two huge boulders. Finally, the sailors brought the rope to the priests for inspection. The priests studied the fibrous threads, every tatter, every rip and discoloration. Then they declared that the rope had worn well and the next year would be fruitful. The Emperor blessed the old rope, then blessed the new one. Once again the small boat struggled against the surf and the sailors "married" the boulders.

Everyone was bored and tired. Willie sat on the ground, holding the unsheathed sword in his hand, breaking a cardinal rule. No one seemed to notice. The Emperor was brought rice wine, and he blessed it and drank and had wine sacs passed to his soldiers.

"What entertainment have you prepared for me, Commander?" the Emperor asked. "I am tired of singing birds and jugglers. Puppeteers try my patience. But perhaps we can find a fat peasant to roast. I have been wondering about the taste of human flesh."

The Commander and the soldiers laughed. "We might have trouble finding a *fat* peasant, Your Excellence. Perhaps we could raise peasants instead of sheep . . . ?"

"Yes," the Emperor mused, "I'm sure the babies would be most tender." Then his eyes fell on Lancelot. "How now, dour Scribe, have you tired of your reading? Your eyes are furtive as a virgin girl's. Have you no wit from your books? Look in my eyes, *Hata!*"

The Emperor stood face to face with Lance. Lance felt the boy's hot breath, smelled the sickly-sweet decay of his teeth.

"I have learned one thing from my reading, Your Excellence."

The Emperor shared a sneer with the Commander who was

watching him closely. "Amuse me, or die!" the Emperor said, and the nearby snickered.

As Lance reached into his satchel, the nearby guards grasped their swords. The Emperor stayed their hands. "I have learned one thing from my reading, Lord of the Sky, Descendant of the Sun. And it is this: If we cannot see ourselves clearly, we cannot see the world." Then Lance held Merlin's mirror in front of the Imperial face.

The boy looked and beheld. The knoblike bells of the mirror jangled softly as Lance's hand shook slightly. In the mirror, the smooth contours of the boy's face blurred, the lips curled back in a piglike sneer. The boy giggled nervously. "A fine trick, *Hata*. For this amusement I'll spare your miserable life."

Still Lance held the mirror. "Look again, Most High. You have just begun to see."

The Emperor sighed and looked again, drawn to the mirror by some unknown power. Again his features blurred, but now the sneer was like a corpse's, the cheeks drawn and cankerous. Unable to look away, the Emperor saw worms and maggots crawl out of the rictus of his mouth and nostrils; then they ate his eyes and bored into his cheeks. He giggled insanely. The Commander raised his arm. "Kill him!" the Emperor shouted to his guard. "Kill the Chinese bastard!" But before the Emperor had spoken the last word, the Commander had lowered his arm and his insurgents had struck with their short swords, and half the Emperor's men fell like a pack of cards. Then the Emperor's loyal troops rode forward on their horses. In the paddy fields, scarecrows turned into men with bows and they shot at the Emperor's troops and slew them.

The Emperor ran from Lance and the mirror. He stumbled back from the onslaught. One of his dead soldiers fell off his horse and fell upon him. Freeing himself from the dead man's limbs, the terrified boy-Emperor stumbled forward onto Willie's corroded sword.

Astonished, Willie stared into the dying face, the eyes turning glassy before him. The Emperor wondered who this boy was, how he had gotten in the way. But he did not wonder long. Something was eating his guts out. He looked and saw the blood spurting from his abdomen. He giggled delicately and crumpled at Willie's feet.

Reinforcements had already been alerted. At the nearby shrines they tolled the great bells. Lance appeared on a horse and swooped up Willie behind him. Arrows whizzed past Willie's ears and one of them clipped an earlobe.

The Commander rode up beside them. The Emperor's men appeared over the hill. "That way!" the Commander pointed down the road with his bow. The Emperor's men were coming up that same road. Lance hesitated, hoping he had misunderstood. "Ride!" the Commander shouted. "Ride like the whirlwind!"

And Lance rode into the storm of men. He rode better than he had ever done before, Willie clinging to him as a vine to a tree. A couple of spent arrows bounced off Willie's back and neck.

Lance saw the archer on the hill aim at his horse. He watched the arrow move towards the horse's muscular throat. At the same time, a cold, portentous shadow passed over the road and the hill and the warriors. A howling, fierce wind blew; but there was no wind, only the howling of wind. Lance watched the arrow enter the horse's throat and the horse galloped for a moment before it realized it was dead. The horse's forelegs crumpled like paper and the three of them—horse, Lance and Willie—fell tumbling over each other. The circle of the sky closed slowly above them and they fell for a long time into an abysm of darkness.

6 | The Peaceable Kingdom

Old Nurse could not keep her teeth from chattering. Her bones seemed to be made of icicles. Though she sat close to the brazier at the bow of the boat and Sagami had lent her her outer robe and even rubbed her hands and feet—the dear, silly girl!—the mere sight of the rippling dark waters brought the chill again.

It was the last possible night to go cormorant fishing, and the girl had had a dream about it some weeks before—a dream of banqueting in the Emperor's palace, a lucky omen—and so, of course, they must go, waiting, of course, for the most favorable date—the last and coldest night possible. Of course!

Old Nurse sighed deeply—loudly!—and raised her eyes to Sagami who smiled back in that childlike, endearing way of hers. The effect of brazier light on the girl's smooth, tawny yellow skin momentarily warmed Old Nurse's heart—until Sagami parted her lips slightly and her straight, white, shiny teeth gleamed like a she-demon's.

What was to be done with her? She was well past the age when she should have blackened her teeth to attract a good man. How often Old Nurse had tried to explain that men feared women with shining teeth like she-demons'! Men feared such women would bite off their tongues, or noses—or worse! Old Nurse shuddered, thinking of the worst, and looked about quickly to see that no evil spirit had overheard her thinking.

The flaming pine logs of the braziers attracted the silver-finned *ayu* fish, which peeped from underwater to see what made the strange, little gold suns slice like silk through their darkness. In the boat the master fisherman and his assistant checked once more the lines tied around the cormorants' necks. Too tight, and the birds would slowly suffocate; too loose, and the birds would swallow the big fish as well as the small.

Then over they went—one, two, three—fifty birds flung from the black pine boats to the tourists' cheers. Sagami's straight, white teeth gleamed, and her dark eyes shone.

"Poor child!" thought Old Nurse. What a karma she must have, great granddaughter of Sugawara no Michizani—Buddha bless his soul! And yet she was a lovely child, and when she played the biwa and sang, none of the court ladies could match her, no not one. But she was cursed with her great grandfather's fate. And cursed again with that no-good husband of hers—the drunken, gambling fool who had got his foot into the 5th Rank of Nobles by marrying the girl. And had the old fool given her a child after three long years of marriage? What had he done except use up her income, gambling and drinking?

Well, what was to be done? It was all determined long before the poor child's birth when the Fujiwaras had exiled her great grandfather and his ghost had come back to haunt them. There were earthquakes and floods and fires in the capital and the soothsayers decreed that only a shrine in honor of the scholar-official could calm his troubled spirit. So the Kitano Shrine was built north of the capital, and the family was restored. And then, and only then, Michizane's spirit rested.

Sagami moved to the front of the boat to get the best look. Already the boatman had pulled back some birds and forced them to disgorge their fish. The silver fins quivered in the gold flames of the braziers and the tourists were passing cups of *sake* to celebrate. Sagami's movements were graceful, catlike, but not feminine like the other women in the boats who huddled against their husbands and lovers. She did not powder her face white as they did, nor did she pluck and shave her eyebrows only to pencil new, more dainty ones a half inch above where the natural ones had been. The only bow she made to feminine-cultivated charms was the color she wore on her sensuous full lips and the scents she enjoyed mixing. A year ago, a retainer of an important lord from one of the provinces had visited the capital and she had taken him as her lover and known for the first time the feeling of high tide of woman's bliss. But her self-assertive ways had soon put him off and he happily returned to his province, convinced he had been bewitched.

Beyond the circles of the braziers, the more adventurous of the large, black birds were attempting to swallow two very large fish. Well, perhaps they were not fish, but floating islands. But they were not islands, either, for they moved freely, dreamily, to fend off the cormorants' beaks. An arm waved. Another. They clung to a bit of driftwood and a leather saddle, and their strange clothes ballooned to give them buoyancy.

The master fisherman felt the cormorants' movements through the cords in his fingers, and he pulled them back. Sagami, who had the eyes of a cat, as well as the grace of one, saw the man-islands even before the master fisherman. Her heart leapt to her throat, and she cried out, "Men!" and pointed. "Two men!"

Had any of the others spotted the islands first they would no doubt have shouted "Goblins!" or "Demons!" and forced the captain to hasten away. But Sagami now urged the captain forward, and the other tourists, cowed by her air of command, were still.

They were indeed islands of men: blue men, blue from the cold. With great grunts the fishermen heaved the frozen bodies into the boat. Had they been at the scene a few minutes earlier, they would have heard the men plop out of the water and fall back into it.

They had been falling for a long time, falling down a bottomless pit while the circle of light closed above them, closed on the world of the Commander and the mad boy-Emperor. They fell through the darkness and the terror with their screams echoing after, and when they were too exhausted to scream, they continued falling until the air grew wet and damp, then cold and watery and black. The inky blackness filled their lungs and exploded in their brains and they would have died but for the dull gold lights of the braziers above, off the horizon, and they swam kicking towards the gold lights.

"They are demons," Old Nurse said. And she prayed to the Kami to protect her. "Throw them over!" one of the female tourists cried.

Sagami moved her face towards the dark, blue shapes. The blue men's eyes opened wearily. They could barely stand to keep their lids apart. In the soft gold light, the tawny yellow face of a goddess smiled a blessing over them. "They are men," Sagami said softly. Then she ordered the fishermen to let the cormorants settle on their quivering bodies. The birds shook the water from their wings then settled their warmth on the blue men who slept and dreamed.

*

As the crow flies, the distance between Mt. Hiei in the northeast corner of the capital and the three hundred acres of the Nine Fold Enclosure in the north center of the city was a mere test flight of wings, a glide of a few minutes. But the journey by ox-drawn carriage, at the bumpy and uncomfortable speed of two miles per hour, would take an afternoon, especially if traffic was bad—and it always was. Now Lance watched the crows descend from the roofs of the temples of Mt. Hiei towards the Nine Fold Enclosure of the Son of Heaven and he ached to sprout wings and fly with them. His confinement weighed on him. In spite of the kindness of the priests and nuns, in spite of all he wanted to learn of this new sect they called Buddhism, he yearned to join the traffic of the city, add his voice to the hubbub of street and market place—and find a woman! He really needed to find a woman!

For the magic that had transported him some four and a half centuries into the future—from the primitive tomb-builders of Yamato to the refinement of the Heian court—had also managed to clip some twenty years from his age. He was still that exotic looking Chinese scholar-gentleman, but he was now in his vigorous early twenties. Even the nuns were starting to look good to him!

And the very air reeked sensuality. Soon after his recovery he had discovered that the temples of Mt. Hiei, being closest to the city, were favorite trysting grounds for lovers. The monks seemed to turn a blind eye. The faithful visited the shrines and temples, made offerings, and made arrangements to meet in the nearby inns. As long as the offerings were made, the monks went about their business reciting the Lotus Sutra, glad to have freed themselves from the fleshly struggles of the floating world.

"Do you find these women attractive?" Will had asked him the day after their arrival at the temple.

Lance plucked a persimmon from the bowl upon the table. "Do you find this fruit tasty, Will?"

Will showed his impatience with the superior tone. "I can leap in front of your speech," he said. "For my faculties are sharpened. And the answer is that I eat for nourishment. What nourishes me tells my tongue it's tasty. But as for these women—with their mincing walks and their pasty faces, with their hideous, blackened teeth and those false eyelashes—raised in continuous exclamation; as for that rose bud of a mouth and all their swaddling clothes—pah! get hence if you're enamored of'em. As for the pasty, silky men who circle round these doves—they make me laugh if men they call themselves."

Lance stared in wonder. Indeed, Willie's faculties were sharpened, and their relationship had changed. The time-hole that had clipped some twenty years off Lance, had added half a dozen to Willie. They were more like brothers now than knight and page. "Where have you got your wisdom, Will?" Lance inquired. "Did you suck from the tit of knowledge as we tumbled down the pit? Did you drink knowledge from the air?"

"I'm amazed at myself," Will said, "and if I knew the answer, I'd as soon you had it as I." He looked about to be certain no monk was lurking in the shadows. He moved a bit closer, lowered his voice. "The real question is, what do we do now?"

And with that Lance was stumped.

Now he watched the crows descend, and he was still stumped. In search of the Holy Grail he'd gone to Yamato. The Grail had been within his grasp, but the Commander had withheld it, enlisting Lance to his own design. "Sometimes the shortest distance between two points is a detour," the Commander had homilized. "Turn the screws of the instrument lightly and the strings will play a fuller measure."

Now, behind him, the novices walked down the narrow road, led by a priest swinging an incense burner. A crow glided close to Lance's head and Lance looked up into the shadow. The crow cawed and dropped a small leather pouch at Lance's feet. Lance picked it up, loosened the strings at its top and peered at the roots, herbs, earth, feathers and assorted elements within. His senses reeled. The pouch smelled of Britain. Somehow Merlin had managed to remind him.

The monks passed him now, murmuring softly, as rain on eaves:

> "I spoke to my children of the evils of the world,
> in order to save my children,
> but they would not heed me . . ."

Lance tucked the pouch into his robe, under the curved magatama suspended from a lanyard around his neck. He watched the clouds gather in the sky, the wind ruffling the monks' delicate robes. And he thought of Britain, and of long ago.

*

The crow caught an updraft of air and veered in the direction of the city. A hundred thousand citizens gathered in the confines of the city's walls: six feet high, with nine foot ditches on both sides and eighteen gates; nine square miles criss-crossed by straight streets and avenues. The crow flew over the Nine Fold Enclosure of the Greater Imperial Palace where the boy-Emperor, having escaped early from the afternoon counsel with his Fujiwara regent, hurried to the apartments of his aunt—his newest concubine. The crow flew over the Palace of Administration with its lacquered red pillars and roofs of glazed green tiles. It flew over Red Bird Avenue, the great street that ran from the Imperial Palace to RashoMon, the elaborate gate where the lowlifes of the countryside gathered to beg from the "good people."

The "good people" looked out from their carriages along Red Bird Avenue and saw the crow flying and wondered if it was a good or a bad omen. They urged their drivers to make haste before the drizzle turned to torrents, and the drivers coaxed and prodded the oxen all along the three-hundred foot wide avenue. The good people thought of their assignations of the night before, or the ones to come, and how they must respond to the latest poems from their lovers, and whether their kimonos were of-the-current style, and the next night of moon-viewing, the approaching ceremonies, perfume contests, music contests, and how sad and tender and beautiful life could be.

Towards the Fourth Ward where the nobility lived the black crow flew like a bad and good omen. It landed in Sagami's garden, on the branches of the plum tree and it lingered as she played the biwa and sang of the red leaves of autumn, already fading amidst the cries of distant deer. The crow heard her sigh in her chambers as she put the biwa aside and heard Old Nurse shuffling to close the lattices to the rain. Old Nurse beckoned the servants to stir the coal in the braziers. Oil lamps were lit and Old Nurse and Sagami sat together in the semi-dark, waiting for a message, a letter, a poem to relieve the monotony.

The black crow shook the rain from its feathers, but it was useless, for the downpour had started. The bird tried to fly, but its drenched wings would not lift it from the branch. It struggled, but its talons seemed stuck in the branch. One black eye looked with love and terror at the rain-soaked greying world, then it folded its wings and grew smaller, and smaller, crying out once in a shrill voice.

Merlin woke with the crow's screech ringing in his ears. Vivian kneeled over him. "Did you dream again, beloved?"

Merlin wiped the sweat from his brow. "Aye . . . Aye . . . I am great with dream."

She gave him fresh towels and a clean, white robe. Gratefully, he dried his wet body and put on the robe. Vivian returned to the arcane books. She knew he would want to be alone to sort out the images.

He had heard the Future Music when he first lay down, and he conjured a form, the form that was latent in the music. He had seen what needed to be seen.

But where had he been? And why?

He had felt Lance's presence, though he had not seen him anywhere. From that presence he had followed a line of destiny over a magical city. He had lingered in the destiny, trying to absorb it, to know it utterly.

But he could not know it. Vivian's spell continued to confound him in webs of mortality: beginnings, endings, songs of endings.

*

Oiwa rubbed his nose on the bare floor in front of the straw mat. The Fujiwara prince watched the display with growing contempt. Though he had lived in the capital for decades, Oiwa had never managed to slough his country habits. No doubt his marriage to the cat-like Sagami had only coarsened him. Only a bumpkin could have so badly miscalculated his marriage politics. While "good persons" married women to gain advantage, Oiwa had simply deepened the contempt the world felt for him. The prince shook his fan out to show his irritation.

"You say you have important news, but you tell me what I already know. Really, Oiwa-*kun*, what shall I do with you?"

At the word "*kun*"—junior—Oiwa could not suppress the slightest trembling in his shoulders. He managed his voice prudently. "I had no other thought than to warn your Lordship of possible dangers. The old books say, 'Even the hawk must sleep.' And, 'The more ears, the better.'"

The prince yawned at the man's tedium. The fact that he misquoted the texts only compounded his disagreeable ways. "For goodness sake, raise your head, Man! These are not ancient times!"

Oiwa craned his neck back.

"Did you think I would wait all these days to get a report on these interlopers?" Prince Fujiwara continued. "Are you the only one with ears at the temple? Fom the first, these 'blue men' have been under my surveillance. It is no secret, as you tell me, that the Taira and Minamoto clans are restive in the provinces. Yet the Minamotos have proved useful in the past, and may again. Not for nothing do we call them our 'teeth and claws.' As for the Taira, since their last routing, they are thoroughly demobilized."

"But—your Lordship's wisdom live ten thousand years!—"

"Yes, yes—"

"What about this other news? Another blue man discovered by a fisherman, nursed to health by that same good man, and then beheaded for his troubles?"

"No doubt a domestic quarrel getting out of hand. The fisherman caught by his wife with his *hook* in another fishpond! Country people do not understand these things. They say the Yellow Emperor had twelve hundred mistresses. I'm sure I need not elaborate to you. Country people are prone to violence by their nature. A fisherman is slain. So what? The Peaceable Kingdom has stood two hundred years and more. We've reason to believe these 'blue men' come from Ch'in, that their boat capsized. Naturally they act confused after their dipping. Perhaps they're scholars or missionaries with another slant on Buddha's

Law. Perhaps they're diehard Confucianists who want to overturn the Law. The smartest thing Sugawara no Michizane ever did was to stop our official contact with that land!" Here the Prince and Oiwa both looked around to be certain Michizane's ghost was not lurking in the corridors. Assured, they both breathed a sigh of relief.

"You do not serve me well with this," the Prince continued. Then added wearily, for who knew when the man *might* be useful: "Yet I thank you for your trouble." The Prince rose, withdrew a small purse from his robe and let it drop near Oiwa's bowed head. He proceeded to the lattice windows, slid them open, letting the light in, and admired the tubbed trees and the white gravel, carefully raked into small hills and valleys. Or were they whirlpools such as those at Naruto?

He dismissed Oiwa and didn't give another thought to the "blue men." Everything was under Heaven. The Fujiwara family controlled the Emperor, and the Emperor performed the ceremonies and served the ancient Kami. The Buddhist sects were too contentious towards each other to pose any real threat. "Divide and conquer," Sun Tzu had advised a thousand years before, and, of course, he'd been right.

There was talk of a great strongman coming to the capital. Now the Prince dreamed of a splendid festival. The strongman would take on challengers, and then they would have a perfume contest, a poetry contest—some sort of contest to bring the ladies out of their dark apartments. Now that was worth thinking about! How up-to-date it would be! How grand!

*

On the sixth morning after their arrival at the temple, the sun broke through sashes of pink and purple sky. The mist rose from the trees and temples on moulded hills like the backs of an army of war horses.

Will was glad to feel the sun at last, to escape from the stuffy apartments of the temples. Warmed by a breakfast of vegetables and *miso* broth, he explored Mt. Hiei. Hundreds of Buddhist temples and Shinto shrines rose in a city of gods. In and out of the city, Shinto priests in purple silk robes, crowning themselves with black hats, weaved between Buddhist monks in gold robes covered with black cloaks and bald heads.

Will gawked. In the village he had come from, the village of his childhood, a rustic cross upon a bare stone wall was all men had to symbolize devotion to an idea greater than themselves. The priest had said Latin words, made little speeches in high-falutin' words, then doled out bread and wine. Will had always liked the wine part best.

But Mt. Hiei was a different world. Perhaps, Will thought, they had entered Heaven itself. Perhaps Jesus himself was waiting for them to find him. Beyond the temples of the other gods, Jesus and Mary lived in glory, waiting for their worshippers.

"That's possible, Will," Lance had said, in that annoying way of his. "But I think we would have heard of it by now."

Will had persisted. "But maybe they live beyond here, in another part of the city." Will appraised his master's critical eye. "You haven't lost your faith in the one true God?"

Lance crossed himself. "My faith is of adamantine rock. I love the Mother of God and her Son. He speaks blasphemy who speaks otherwise."

Out of a knowledge he did not know he had, Will answered: "Place adamantine rock in a river and the currents wash it smooth. Perhaps your faith is growing smooth—washed by a current of ideas."

Lance had to sit down for that one. It was a problem he had wrestled with himself. The more he learned, the more he questioned. Yet his faith alone kept him even-keeled. He could not relinquish his faith. "From what waters have you drunk to make you wise?" he said at last. He rose from the table and opened the chest of drawers in the corner of the room. He withdrew a statuette covered with brocaded cloth. When he removed the cloth he set the wooden figure on the table. "The high priest brought me this yesterday," he said. "I looked at it all morning . . . In the afternoon, I let it look at me . . . What is here? What do you see?"

Warily, Will moved his head closer to the statuette. The details were so precise, he wondered if it might be alive. He moved his index finger to it, touched it gently. Lance laughed.

"It is a starving man," Will said at last. "Yet he sits upright."

"Yes," Lance said. "A starving man who sits upright. Now, look again. Look at the eyes."

Will shuddered. "They are the eyes of death. I won't look anymore."

"You should look more," Lance advised. "They are not the eyes of death, but eyes that have looked on death, one's own death. And yet, they are at peace, they are calm. Hunger has scooped out the valley of the eyes, and yet the eyes gaze with peace from the hollows. This is their god. This is their new god whom they call Buddha." Lance took the figure in his hands. "It is merely one of many representations." He locked eyes with the figure's. "I have been trying to understand . . . I have been trying to understand what it is that consumes the body but makes the spirit burn like a thousand tapers . . ." He looked at Will and saw that he, too, was trying to understand, and the gulf between them—master and page—dissolved a little more.

"When I was a lad in Arthur's court," Lance continued, "about the age that you are now, I went to the chapel in the woods and there on the cross upon the wall some artist had carved the image of our Lord. Gaunt he was. Wasted, and twisted with the world's treachery and sin . . . And yet, the eyes were like these. That is what I have been trying to understand, Will . . Perhaps they understand here. In Britain, the gods of the rocks and the trees are hounded underground, hunted out in the forests, driven deeper into the hills. But here they flourish. The old gods become the guardians of the new, and their priests walk together, and one may hear the chanting of one group overlay the chanting of another—a warp and weft of music, offered without discrimination, without judgment . . . And this is what I have been trying to understand . . ."

Now the sun rose a little higher, and the sky was twelve sashes of blending colors, each complementing each, revealing each, like the twelve kimonos of a lady-in-waiting, overlaying one another, the top one an inch shorter at the sleeve than the one underneath, all perfectly revealed at the sleeve. Will gazed down the avenue of stone lanterns and he saw the warrior-monks returning from a week of toughening in the woods. Three dozen, four dozen—three columns of sixty men on powerful horses. Who were these men with their long, double-curved bows and quivers of arrows? Never had Will seen such men! He rushed to the edge of the tree-lined avenue to watch the militant monks return. The more placid monks walked in the streets as before, holding their little books before them, chanting the words of the Lotus Sutra over and over, indifferent to the men on horses. A head monk beat time on a wooden block. And the men on horses rode by with eyes straight ahead, with their horses snorting, with the reins of their horses light in their hands.

*

A few days before the descent of the frost, in the hour of the dragon, Sagami's sister Sachiko arrived at her gate in the Fourth Ward. Sachiko's palm carriage was a far sight better than Sagami's stretched-straw carriage. Shrewder, if less wise, than her sister, Sachiko had married the old minister and moved a rank above Sagami. Now, as soon as she saw her sister approaching, followed closely by Old Nurse, Sachiko began to complain.

"Greetings, Elder Sister and Old Nurse. Is it not a bitter cold morning?"

"Greetings, Younger Sister. We shall warm soon once the sun rises."

"Even the sun wants to sleep long on these cold days," Sachiko continued.

"And yet the world goes on," Sagami rejoined.

Sachiko didn't know why she bothered. Somehow her sister always got the better of her, and yet she could never resist her. Perhaps it was because they had no brother to look after them. She only knew that since childhood she had looked to her sister for guidance. Sagami was strong and unique, and Sachiko was a little, chubby woman with a cute face and generous breasts. For those breasts her aged husband had overlooked her inferior rank and taken her as his concubine, and even installed her in a wing of his own house. For those breasts, the Old Counselor rejected the bed of his principal wife and snuggled beside his concubine. Alas, the Old Counselor's jade stem had seen better days, and even the glories of Sachiko's "white snow" could not awaken the dead.

"I do not see why we must go to Mt. Hiei to worship," Sachiko complained as they moved into the bustle of the morning traffic, with the commoners rushing about with their cargoes of wood and wares.

"We don't see enough of one another," Sagami said calmly. She smiled, and her sister quieted down again.

Sagami wasn't really sure what was driving her to the mountains. She regretted having to bother Sachiko and Old Nurse, but she really couldn't go by herself.

"Couldn't we have worshipped just as well at the Kitano Shrine?" Sachiko complained one hour further down the road. "It has always been good enough before. And, after all, it's the shrine erected to honor our dear, departed ancestor."

"Yes, Sister, but I told you, now they say that the God Hachiman has more power than all the ancient gods. Only at Mt. Hiei can we find his shrine."

"That god is loved by the warriors," Old Nurse muttered.

"Indeed, what use have we for the God of War?" Sachiko wondered.

Sagami shrugged. "Well, one never knows . . ."

Another hour out of the city, and they were being tossed here and there in the carriage and Sagami had to lean out the window and scold the outriders—a most unladylike thing to do. Old Nurse was scandalized to hear Sagami's mannish language. Sachiko had to laugh.

No, she would never be as bold as her sister who flouted the conventions, who would not even shave her eyebrows or blacken her teeth. They had been born under very different stars. But sometimes she wished she could be more like her, if only for a while.

And sometimes Sagami wished she could be more like Sachiko, whose life seemed so uncomplicated, who spent her days hearing the fashionable romances recited, and supervised the sewing and dyeing of her most thoroughly up-to-date kimonos. How pretty she looked with her white, round face and rosebud mouth, framed by her long, black hair.

They arrived a little before the strongman's carriage arrived. They had barely given the innkeeper their instructions when an enormous oxen pulling a tiny cart arrived with a mountain of a man. Will let go an arrow at the target and the warrior monk who was coaching him nodded, impressed with the young foreigner's natural ability. Lance closed the book he was reading upon his forefinger, the words of Ono-no-Komachi still ringing in his ears:

> "The flowers' beauty faded
> while I lost myself in idle thought,
> entranced by the long rain."

And the mountainous wrestler stepped out of his cart, nearly toppling it. His spry, little handler jumped out after him. The mountain roared with laughter. "I am Hajikami," he proclaimed, "strongest man in all Japan." Even the indiffrent monks stopped their chanting and broke ranks to have a look. The warrior monks stopped their swordplay and ran to see him.

Sagami's eyes found Lance's, the "blue man" she had come

to see. He did not recognize her. But he found his eyes pulled from the giant to her lithe, graceful form, and her face—so different from the other female tourists he'd seen.

Sachiko looked beyond the giant, too. She caught her breath. She raised her fan to her face then looked out over it to the tall, young foreigner with the bow and the quiver of arrows. He wore a small vest and his arms were bare and muscular. It was out of the question for a gentleman to display so much of himself in such a setting in broad daylight! Even the wrestler was covered in robes! Yet, over the rim of her fan, her eyes darted back to the bowman.

"When do we eat?" roared Hajikami. And everybody laughed.

*

Prince Fujiwara had organized the festival, so he took the seat of honor next to the empty Imperial throne. The Emperor himself was suffering from a minor upset stomach, and, according to the ancient Way of the Kami, isolated himself. In one of the many residences of his wife's family, the Emperor was irrigated by Chinese Taoist herbalists, pierced by acupuncturists and burned by moxabutionists—all in the name of ritual purification. And all under the watchful eyes of the Fujiwaras—the Emperor's inlaws. As the physician lit the powdered leaf cone on the Emperor's bare stomach and the heat traveled quickly to the sensitive skin, the Emperor cried out, and asked himself, again, if being Emperor was all that it was cracked up to be.

The good people were delighted to find themselves celebrating another festival, so close on the heels of the First Day of the Boar Festival, and shortly before the Festival of the First Fruits. But life was good! The income from the rice plantations filled the coffers steadily, the Emperor performed the rites to please the ancient Kami, the monks prayed for salvation in the next life, and the Fujiwara wisely managed the conflicting claims of the various clans and kept all in harmony under heaven.

And it was a bright, crisp autumn heaven that they gathered

under. Will and Lance were filled with high spirits. They had finally been allowed to venture forth from Mt. Hiei. They sat with the militant monk-archer who had befriended Will, and with one of the masters of the Tendai sect, a monk with whom Lance had enjoyed days and nights of long conversations. It was this Tendai leader who had reported directly to Prince Fujiwara and persuaded him that the so-called "blue men" were not the spies of an invading army.

Will shook his head. "Why are you grinning like a hyena?" Lance asked him.

"Never have I known two autumns, Lance. I'd almost take another spill down the pit if I could be sure of choosing my seasons. Not to mention my years."

The Tendai master and the militant monk looked on. Though Will and Lance no longer conversed in English, they spoke a very peculiar Japanese. They often used words and constructions from centuries before, and they spoke with a strange, wild—though not unappealing—poetic imagery that baffled and intrigued their overhearers.

A few weeks after their arrival at Mt Hiei, Lance had instructed Will to call him by his given name. Will had protested, but Lance had insisted. "I'm in greater need of a friend than a page," he'd explained. Overcome with emotion, Will had fled from the room, lest he show his tears.

They were in the Imperial Gardens, the Divine Spring Garden, south of the Nine Fold Enclosure. These thirty acres were the best in the city of Heian-kyo, and were graced with a pavilion, a spring, a hill and a carp-filled lake. Nothing in London, nothing in Camelot, nothing in the Western world, could compare with the landscapes of Heian-kyo. As they had traveled down from the mountain, the two men had gaped constantly at glazed, green tiles, lacquered red pillars, willow-lined avenues as wide as Will's village had been, and chock full of oxen-drawn carriages with smartly dressed outriders and stately women within. These women would artfully allow a sleeve to dangle from their carriage windows. Their character and beauty might be surmised by the blending of the colors at the sleeve.

Now the giant Hajikami approached the specially constructed arena. A murmur went round, then a cheer went up. Never had the good people of Heian-kyo seen such a formidable champion. Neither had Lance nor Will seen such a man in Britain.

"Jesus and Mary!" said Will. "The man is naked!"

In fact, the mountain had a thick coil of rope around his middle, and a white hawser shielded his ponderous jade stem and massive ballocks from the delicate eyes of the ladies. A Shinto priest entered the arena to bless the ceremony. First, water was sprinkled on the sand. The priest in his high-peaked hat daintily wiped his hands on a towel offered by an attendant. Now the priest flung salt into the air to purify the sacred circle.

Sagami estimated the arena about twelve feet in diameter. She and Sachiko had spread their straw mat on the hill earlier, and now they had a commanding view. She leaned forward as Hajikami entered. The size of the man's buttocks amazed her. Sachiko turned her eyes. Why she had allowed Sagami to talk her into this affair she could never fathom! She turned her eyes and saw Will half risen on his knees, a hundred feet from her.

"Isn't it wonderful!" Sagami explained. "So up-to-date!"

"Oh yes," Sachiko muttered, still staring at Will. "So up-to-date!"

Hajikami bowed to the Four Directions, honoring the ancient Kami of the place. His little attendant gingerly stepped in after him, though what exactly he was doing there nobody could tell. In a high, squeaky voice the spritely attendant begged for attention. The *sake* cups paused in mid-air, the fans stopped their fluttering. "Good citizens of Heian-kyo, most glorious capital of the sixty-two provinces and the two islands, we humbly thank you for your patronage."

The good citizens showed their appreciation by remaining quiet through the sprite's lengthy explanation.

No man in the provinces had ever managed to bring the giant

down. To even things up, Hajikami would wrestle his first opponent with his hands tied behind his back!

Now the *sake* cups were passed again, and the fans were fluttering. How could a man wrestle without his arms? All admired the giant's sense of sportsmanship.

The crowd's champion entered the sacred circle. He, too, bowed to the Four Directions. He was a member of the Taira clan; a roughneck raised in the provinces, now serving with the Imperial Police. He was powerful and tall, but the giant towered a foot above him and was double his weight.

"Surely a member of the Taira clan will acquit himself well," Sachiko told Sagami. And everyone agreed. After all, he could use his arms!

The Shinto priest lowered his fan and the Taira clansman moved in quickly to place a well-aimed kick at Hajikami's privates. But the giant saw it coming, crouched forward and took the full force of the kick in his stomach. A crunching sound echoed to the back of the audience. The clansman howled and Hajikami grunted. The giant had broken the man's foot. The match was over.

Now the sprite begged for attention again. The next proposal was this: the giant would battle two men at once.

Two members of the Minamoto clan now rose to uphold the honor of the capital. They were also powerful men, and they had fought the hairy Ainus of the north and their prowess in battle was celebrated in poems and songs.

"Two men controlled Hannibal's beast," Lance told Will. "Methinks the giant has met his match."

"Perhaps the beasts allowed themselves to be controlled," Will answered, as the priest in the circle lowered the fan again.

The Minamoto men immediately dove for the giant's legs, one at each trunk. Hajikami let them struggle until they exhausted themselves. Then he calmly grabbed each of them around the midsection, lifted them upside down, then let them drop with a thud. The stunned warriors took a full minute to recover.

Hajikami's attendant handed him something, and soon the giant was calmly picking his teeth with a toothpick at the opposite end of the arena. The giant's oversized gestures and total nonchalance delighted the audience. When his two opponents stood again, Hajikami turned his back on them, leaned over and let loose a noisy blast of foul wind. This humiliation infuriated the warriors. The more volatile one immediately jumped on Hajikami's back, riding him like a horse while he punched at the bullneck. Hajikami whirled and the other warrior rammed his head into the mountainous midsection. Hajikami fell down upon the warrior on his back. Those closest to the action were sure they heard the cracking of the pelvis. Hajikami stood up, lifted the other warrior above his head and flung him among the front row spectators.

"This is too terrible," Sachiko said, as the man with the crushed pelvis was carried from the ring. Even Sagami had seen enough. She wished the Prince would halt the tournament. But inside the pavilion the Prince had moved his seat forward and was leaning forward to get a better view. The men of Heian-kyo were fascinated in spite of themselves. In a single afternoon—and only *for* a single afternoon—they had forgotten the refinements of two hundred years of court life.

Now the sprite made his last announcement. He hoped the preceding performances had convinced one and all that the giant could not be defeated. So he challenged the last brave opponent merely to touch the coiled rope around the giant's midsection.

"That's a gauntlet I'd as soon not run," Lance told Will.

Will smiled in return, then rose to his feet. "I accept the challenge," he called above the murmuring crowd. And he started to move forward.

Lance grabbed his wrist. "There's nothing at stake here, Will."

Sachiko sighed audibly and Sagami looked at her, looked at Will, looked again at Sachiko.

Will shook himself loose of Lance's hand. "The old order has changed, Lance. Nothing's at stake. That's why I go."

The warrior-priest nodded affirmation, and Lance gave it up.

He watched the headstrong youth approach the arena. The Tendai monk tapped Lance's arm with his fan. "All things under heaven . . ." he said.

"He is like my son," Lance said.

The Tendai monk and the warrior-priest raised their eyebrows. "You mean, he is like your brother," the monk corrected.

Will entered the ring. He bowed to the Four Directions. When he took off his shirt, Sachiko sighed again. "I cannot watch," she said. But as Will smeared sacramental oil over his body, her eyes fluttered above her fan.

7 | The Peaceable Kingdom Revisited

When the referee lowered his fan for the third time the giant squatted on his trunk legs and Will squatted on his muscular legs, and they seemed like a great oak and a sapling. The giant extended his thick, branch-like arms, and Will extended his wiry arms—and they waited. The giant's turtle-like head settled into his massive shoulders, and Will's head seemed to stretch upward, alert like a cat's—and they waited. The audience held their breath—and still the contestants waited. Hajikami's attendant looked about nervously, and then the giant moved.

He surely would have squashed Will if Will had been where he was. But he wasn't. The giant searched, but Will was behind him at the opposite side of the ring. Will could have touched the *shimenawa* rope girdling the giant's waist and ended the match in an instant. Instead, he landed a quick kick to the massive buttocks. The crowd gasped, then laughed, then applauded, then laughed again. Hajikami turned in fury. His face reddened. Like a bull elephant, he meant to stamp out the life of his tiny tormentor.

The tormentor had other ideas. He ran straight into the branch-like, outstretched arms. But when the arms closed around him, Will wasn't there. Hajikami grasped air. Will had squirmed out of the giant's arms, his well-oiled body leaving Hajikami nothing to clasp. As Hajikami hugged himself, Will landed two swift blows to the giant's face. The first one broke the broad, flat nose; the second one shattered two incisors. Hajikami's howl curdled the blood of the spectators and made the little hairs stand up on necks and arms.

"Jesus and Mary protect him!" Lance prayed.

"Buddha protect him!" Sachiko prayed.

Will should have left well enough alone, and a more experienced warrior would have. But the cheers of the crowd drunkened him. As Hajikami advanced—slow and deadly, Will leapt into the air, and brought his two arms hammering down on the region behind the clavicle. The pain shuddered Hajikami's form like a jolt of electricity; his arms bolted out, and he grabbed Will by the throat. The vise-like hands began to squeeze. Will's face turned red. Try as he might, he could not struggle loose.

Lance rose to his feet. "Stop the match!" he shouted. "Stop the match!"

Will put his forearms together as though praying. He tried to wedge his arms between the giant's. He tried kicking, but he couldn't get his legs off the ground.

Sagami rose to her feet. "Stop the match," she shouted. Sachiko fainted. All of the women fainted, or turned away, or wept, and some of the more sensitive men wept to see so brave a hero so badly used. The Shinto priest watched Prince Fujiwara for a signal, but none came. The Prince could not determine if it was more beautiful to have the brave warrior die a tragic death or to rescue that warrior at the last possible moment. Lance rushed towards the ring. He was restrained by the Imperial Police.

Will felt like he was swimming underwater. Above his head was the sun, and someone was trying to push him back into the water. He heard the watery cries of the townspeople and heard his mother's voice crying, "Oh Willie, Willie, Willie!" If only he could kick himself free of the water! If only he could kick, he'd break through.

Hajikami's pain and rage were unchecked. The little creature in his hands had hurt him more than anyone ever had. Not only hurt him, but humiliated him. He meant to squeeze the life from him. He'd squeeze until the blood burst from the ears. He lifted his victim into the air and watched the face turn purple.

Will heard his mother's voice again. "Come back, son! Come back to me!" He kicked towards the surface of the water. Weakly at first, and then with the last strength of his body and life.

The last kick struck the pendulous testicles of Hajikami. The giant doubled over and Will crumpled at his feet. Hajikami fell back on his buttocks, holding his bruised testicles like little robins in his hands. Will stretched his hand out of the surface of the water. He lifted his head above the water. He gasped for air. He lifted his upper body up by his forearms and he began to swim towards the white mountain. The townspeople were cheering again. The white mountain looked down on Will. Will lifted his arm towards the *shimenawa* rope. He grasped the rope and wouldn't let go. Then he rose on his knees and hugged the mountain for dear life. And out of pity and honor and mutual pain, the white mountain cradled him like a baby and brought him back to life.

The "good people" had never seen anything like it. They hailed Will's courage, they hailed Hajikami's strength and honor.

"This is most splendid, most splendid," Prince Fujiwara proclaimed for all.

Sachiko and the other fainted women were revived. The crowd rose to their feet.

"Where did he learn such prowess?" Oiwa said to the shadowy figure beside him. Oiwa and his companion had been lurking in the shade of the pavilion stands watching the proceedings. "No warrior in our present day can fight like that," Oiwa remarked.

"That is what I've been telling you," the third blue man said.

Oiwa shook his head. He still did not believe the blue man's story. People did not simply drop through the earth in the age of Yamato and emerge five centuries later in the Heian age! Not even the Kami of old could accomplish such feats. But that the three blue men were sorcerers Oiwa entertained no doubt. He watched now as Lance helped Will from the ring.

Should he go to the Prince again? No, even now the Prince was waiting for the heroes, waiting to bestow honors. Those Fujiwaras were far too smug, far too "up-to-date" to put any stock in sorcery. An occasional ghost, of course, but sorcerers? Unlikely! They'd go through the motions at the ceremonies, perform the rituals, then turn around and put on the cloaks of the New Religion. Expedience they worshipped above all. Oiwa would show them. He, too, could be expedient.

"You scared me out of my skull," Lance told Will.

Will grinned. He had his arm around Lance's shoulder. "Now have I met my Sir Turquine," Will said.

Lance laughed, nodded his head to acknowledge the tribute. "That was a fight to the death, Will. I pray you never need fight like that."

The Prince presented Will with a magatama of green jade, a *kenukigata* sword, an inkstone and writing brushes, penknives with jeweled sheathes, a decorated fan, and a lapis lazuli-inlaid belt that had traversed the Silk Road from Afghanistan. To Hajikami he presented warrants for a year's supply of rice from the Imperial graneries. "We do not want our giant to go hungry," the Prince jested.

Hajikami looked at his spritely attendant. "After my friend has eaten his fill," he said, "I fear I may yet go hungry."

When the awards ceremony was over, Will handed the inkstone, brushes and decorated fan to Lance. "You're more the scholar type than I," he explained.

Lance opened the fan. It showed a perfect cone of a mountain, reddening in the setting sun, framed by white-pink cherry blossoms. Without a thought, he handed it to the woman he had seen at the temple, the woman who stood behind him now.

"Perhaps the lady can make better use of this," he said.

Sagami blushed. She looked around quickly before accepting

the gift, which she secreted in the folds of her kimono. She smiled faintly, showing her straight, white teeth.

"Have you lost your senses?" Sachiko decried after Lance and Will had been coaxed to join Hajikami and his entourage. "How could you accept a gift from a stranger in broad daylight? Even for you, this is too bold."

Perhaps it was. Never had a gentleman been so forward with her. She was quite flustered. Yet the stranger's eyes were kind. If he had been indiscreet, it was from ignorance of their ways, not malice. The eyes were good and wise, even as she had seen them in the boat during the night of the cormorants. Even as she had confirmed them to be at the temple on Mt. Hiei. It was an innocent gift, given with generosity. Looking around first, discreetly she withdrew it from her kimono and admired it while Sachiko frowned. Sagami folded it carefully and placed it back above her heart, above the hardening peak of her white snow.

*

The "good people" gathered again that evening by the Kamo River. Since the moon was full and the clear weather held, Prince Fujiwara had announced a moon-viewing festival. The "good people" had gone and changed their apparel. Will and Lance had been feted by monks of the Tendai and the Shingon sects, by the Imperial Police and Prince Fujiwara's bodyguards. Musicians played on zithers and flutes and chanted songs from the *Manyoshu* while ladies sang sweet songs about life's touching shortness.

Old Nurse had thrown up her hands. "What? Are you going out again? Twice in one day? What's the world coming to? And who are these strangers everyone is talking of? Shall I not come along? Who will take care of the nightingales? Oh, of course, I will feed them, but who will sing to them in your stead? Oh, I don't think this is a good idea. Is it an auspicious night? Surely, it is not auspicious!"

"Old Nurse, be quiet!" Sachiko had commanded. She did not want to hear any talk of inauspicious occasions. She turned to Sagami, "Have you prepared the scents, Older Sister?"

"For some time now."

Sachiko took her sister's arm and they walked like conspirators to the carriage. She didn't know why she felt so giddy. Perhaps it was true what they said about the moon.

They arrived just before the scent contest was to begin. The "good people" had allowed a select number of vendors onto the roped-off riverbank. Under the flares of torches, the vendors moved back and forth selling grilled eels and hot, sweet *sake*.

Prince Fujiwara himself was the judge of the scents, and all agreed this was right for his sensibilities were the most refined.

Sagami was in a giddy mood, too. She had won the scent contests twice before, and she fancied herself an expert. "Let the ceremony begin," a nobleman of the Second Rank declared. One after another, the highborn men and women presented their blends of scents to the delicate nostrils of the Prince. Meantime, lovers stretched on their straw mats under the autumn leaves and a lantern-lit pleasure boat drifted on the rippling Kamo.

Blends of cinnamon, sandalwood, musk and sweet pine competed with ground conch shell, white gum and Indian resin. Aloes, musk and cloves delighted the Prince's finest sense. Sagami was the last to present her mixture. And it was so delicate and subtle, yet sophisticated, it brought tears to the Prince's eyes. "This is a scent of quiet longing," the Prince declared. "The ingredients play on one another like the instruments of a celestial orchestra. The scent fills one with nostalgia for lost love—first love—and blends it with childhood days when we were easy with all the colors of creation." Indeed, everyone near the contestants was filled with thoughts of the past, and these mixed with hidden yearnings for days and nights to come. "It is the sad, sweet essence of things," the Prince declared, and he was about to announce Sagami the winner when Lance stepped forward. "Might I be so bold?" he asked.

Prince Fujiwara nodded. Sagami covered her precious blend.

"I've only a little," Lance declared as he poured the contents from the pouch onto the laquer tray. It was the same pouch that Merlin the crow had dropped from the sky one lovely morning at Mt. Hiei.

The Prince seemed to dream as he inhaled. He smelled the fennel of the Yorkshire Dales, the heather of the moors, the cold winds racing down the Black Cullins on the Isle of Skye, the limestone caves of the Cheddar Gorge. More: sheep *bahing* in the Penine hills, farmboys gathering autumn hay; in the prosperous kitchens: fresh bread baking. And still more: Boadicia, the Iceni Queen, raising her white arm, the crude sword in her hands, the smell of courage like a heady wind bearing down on the Roman legionnaires. And Merlin's world, too: Original forest; sparrows' eggs in mossy oaks; the dark, ponderous smell of granite bathed by dragon whirlpools—whirlpools eddied by stirring dragon wings—and the hot breath of dragons.

The Prince stepped back, unable to absorb it all. But he must taste another draft:

The waves against the cliffs at Dover, the whiteness of the cliffs, the spine of the Penines, the Celtic soil, the iron forges, hyacinths and apples—every manner of scent overwhelming and refreshing and making one forget and making one remember what one did not know one knew.

All those in the vicinity of the contest were likewise overwhelmed, filled with nostalgia for what they'd never known.

"What is this?" Prince Fujiwara asked breathlessly.

"I call it Britain," Lance said.

And the Prince pronounced him winner.

*

As the gift presentation ceremony concluded, the moon reached its zenith, and a small, flat boat carrying musicians drifted by on the river. The boat was little more than a platform with a dragon masthead, four women in heavy blue kimonos poling at the corners while male musicians played a *taiko* drum, a zither and a flute. The cry of a deer came from the hills beyond the river.

"Oh," said Sagami

Lance turned to her. Now, in the moonlight, with the torches' gold reflected from the Kamo, and the watery silver of the moon a liquid ore bathing the grass, the *toriis* and the people, her unique beauty struck him full force. "Is anything the matter?" he asked.

Her black eyes shone. "Just that it's all so splendid . . . The Prince, and the moon, and the musicians, and the scents, and lovers on the grass, and the deer's cry . . . and . . . and . . . and all of it so sad, too. So tender. Fleeting as a dream . . ."

Lance looked around. Truly, he had never been in a more enchanted place. Jeweled nets were suspended from the branches of exotic trees, under which jewel-bedecked boats carried moon-viewing lovers on the river. Peacocks fanned their iridescent tails, strutted freely, cried in girl-like voices, while the Prince watched benevolently from a pavilioned stage of gold and silver floating on crystal elephant foundations. Under a distant willow, Sachiko and Will sat down together to share a decanter of *sake*.

"Fleeting, indeed," Lance agreed, "yet I assure you, I am no dream."

"No, Sir, verily, no dream. And yet our lives are brief as fireflies' light, and joy floats like a lotus on a world of pain."

Lance looked at her again. Never had he heard a woman speak as she did. Nor man, either. "They tell me this is a symbol of long life," he said, handing her the jade turtle he had been awarded for the contest of scents. "Take it, and live long. And put away these thoughts. Let the memory of this evening live long in your heart . . . You have changed me, Madam."

"Oh, Sir, please, you have already gifted me with kindness. I am one who dwells on the fringes of life. Draw me forth no more."

Sagami urged the turtle back. Lance closed her hand gently upon it. "If truly you dwell on the fringes of life, then fringes are new continents. I am captained to a will greater than my own. That will bids me to explore. Tell me soft your name."

"Sagami . . ."

"Sagami . . ."

"And you, Sir?"

"It is a secret name. Yet I am unspied. My name is Lance."

"Rance."

"No, *Lance*."

"*R*ance."

He couldn't help but smile. He exaggerated the "L" sound and said his name again. With thumbs and forefingers, he stretched his cheeks into a smile to get the sound right. Sagami imitated his gestures, but it still came out "*R*ance." They both laughed. "I will call you `Britain,'" she said. "Is it a good name?"

"Yes," he said. "It is a very good name."

Wordlessly, they strolled towards the riverbank. A vendor asked them if they'd like grilled eel. The vendor brushed a sweet sauce on it, and they sat down beside a willow upon one of the straw mats that had been spread before. Parties large and small formed circles where they passed *sake* and dried fish and fruits, while singing songs and composing and reciting poems for the moon.

"The other women blacken their teeth," Lance said. "But not you . . . They shave their eyebrows and paint on new ones an inch above. Why are you so different?"

"Do you find them pretty, these gilded lilies?"

"I found them interesting . . . until I saw your face."

"And your face, Sir, I find it . . . more than interesting."

Lance smiled. "Perhaps you would not find it so, if you saw my *true* face."

Sagami was half alarmed. "Are you a demon, Sir, who puts on faces as he puts on clothes?"

"Neither demon nor sorcerer."

"Then, pray, what would you be?"

"I would be . . . lover . . ."

Sagami looked towards the musicians' boat. She did not want to show her eyes. The stranger's spirit matched her own for boldness. Apprehensive and enticed, she struggled with herself. They said nothing for a long time.

"I'm sorry," he said.

"You are too bold, Sir."

"I am ignorant of your customs."

"Are the men of Ch'in so bold?"

"The men of Ch'in?"

"You play with me, Sir. I must go." She tensed to go.

"Oh, Lady, Lady, forgive me, please," he entreated. "I am new to Heian-kyo, and you have made me young again. I am foolish and drunk with the taste of these light years. Youth has made me impetuous again. Please stay. I shall unlearn me of my youth."

Sagami half-relaxed. "How odd you are! How have I made you young again? The dew still sparkles on your cheeks! Oh, I do fear a sorcerer has bewitched me. Let me go, Sir. Or I shall never find my way again."

"Nay, Lady, stay."

And then the moonlight faded, the silver circle edged by black. *"Look! Look!"* the "good people" cried. And they knew it was an omen, though whether for good or bad none could say. Prince Fujiwara summoned his counselors. "There will be trouble in the land," the first counselor said. "Nothing to worry about," said the second. Prince Fujiwara, who had settled in for the night with his favorite concubine, decided to believe the latter. And most of the good persons followed his example. Those who put caution first gathered their belongings and left. Those who remained sang lustier songs, danced more sensuously, and wrote more vigorously as the eclipse gradually drew its dark curtain across the moon.

"The dragon is swallowing the moon," Sagami said. "This is the strangest day of my life, Britain . . . Now I know you are indeed a sorcerer."

"Then I've caught myself in my own snares, Sagami. Like the spider who wove a splendid web, then lost his way amidst the dazzling strands . . . Won't you let your long hair down?"

Sagami placed the ivory comb upon the mat. She removed the ivory pins that held her hair in place. Then the lustrous blackness flowed over her shoulders. It caught the remaining silver light and flowed like black silk over her kimonos. It spilled onto the straw mat and onto the lawn. Sagami stood up and her hair reached her feet and curled in black eddies beyond her feet.

Lance gathered the ends of it. As the dragon swallowed the moon, and the torches burned themselves out, he brushed the dark river of silk against his lips. He drank in the fragrance as she looked down on his uplifted face. The black silk of her hair shimmered with the fading light as it cascaded over Britain, her Britain.

She covered him with her hair.

*

Prince Fujiwara installed Lance in a scholar's home in the Third Ward. With access to the Imperial library, Lance happily whittled the daylight hours poring over one of the 1500 Chinese classics, or learning the new *kana* script of Japan.

After his morning studies, he'd spend a couple of afternoon hours wandering the streets of Heian-kyo. The sounds, scents, costumes, busyness and efficiency stirred his pulse. And always: the unanticipated beauty of willow-lined avenues at dusk, a noble's courtyard glimpsed through a bamboo gate, a maple's red reflection in a back street canal; and the forested, circling hills and valleys, sluiced with streams and cataracts, and mirror-like lakes with their god-birthing mists.

Sometimes he'd wander into a less-traveled alley, past the commercial districts of the Seventh Ward where stall merchants hawked chicken, fish, wood, clothes and household goods. In the Western half of the city, earthquake and fire-damaged estates had lain in disrepair for decades and huddled cottages crowded out the tended lands of the well-to-do. Once, lost in daydreams, he'd wandered to RashoMon, the vast southern gate, and when he looked up he saw the hardened eyes of the dispossessed, the outstretched hands of beggars and ruffians. The days had grown shorter and darker, and men and women gathered around open fires, and the men looked at his fine warm clothes with envy. Luckily, the Imperial Police were in the vicinity, escorting a court noble through the gate. Lance turned on his high platform shoes and walked hurriedly in their train.

He had good reasons to forget himself.

It was a wonder he could think at all, study at all. At night, after dining alone and studying again, he'd walk through the quiet streets the short distance to Sagami's estate. He'd knock three times on the bamboo gate, and Old Nurse would let him in, grumbling under her breath, but with eyes twinkling with mischief. Old Nurse would lead him through the dark, drafty halls, past the sliding doors, to the inner apartments. In the dim light of the inner sanctum, behind the portable screen, he'd glimpse Sagami's hand resting on her lap, pillowed by kimonos. Old Nurse would leave, and their greeting ritual would commence.

"What lost soul troubles me at this unruly hour?" Sagami challenged.

"One parched for a kind word, milady. One whose eyes have looked too long on crows' feet on old scrolls."

"What does this lost soul seek of me?" she'd answer.

"As one who has travelled long at sea seeks a green shelter from the harsh sun; as a schoolboy runs from his books to help with summer harvesting; as a nestling seeks the warm updraft of air to cradle its first flight: so the lost soul seeks shelter in your arms, to gather, with you, the joys of summer harvest, and the ecstasy of flight."

Then she would suppress her girlish laughter, her hand would reach out under the screen, and he'd kneel and kiss her hand.

"Britain," she'd say when he came behind the screen. "The day is too long, the night too short."

He'd kiss her parted lips, their tongues playfully jousting in each other's mouths. They were joined at the mouths while he undressed her, one layer of silk kimono falling to the floor, and then another and another—even Salome had not so many veils—while she led him to bed, the frou-frou of falling silk mingling with sighs and murmured endearments. When she stood naked in his arms, she hurried to undress him, too. They breathed the air from each other's lungs, and fell breathless and swooning onto the kimonos.

No one had ever kissed as she—not even Guenevere. Or was it the intoxication of his own recaptured youth, the years sloughed, the wounds of battles sloughed, until he lay pristine in his lover's eyes? Her restless hands caressed his body while he sucked female essence from her breasts. Her tongue bathed him, and in her mouth he forgot the court of Arthur, the Holy Grail, the pledges of Yamato, the books, the battles, the guilt and the glory.

She taught him new words. "Say this," she said, leading his hands over her mound of Venus, "Sedge hill."

"Sedge hill."

Then he parted the "wheat buds" with his fingers and "sipped the vast spring" until she surrendered her "high tide." The musk of her "cinnabar cave" mingled with the perfumes she rubbed on her body—nuances of different scents on thighs, feet, belly, buttocks, back, breasts and throat—so she drunkened him as he kissed her.

When his yang weapon was "angry," when he could no longer hold back, she led him to the jade door. "Does the ambassador wish to visit the celestial palace?" she'd say.

"Yes. He wishes to pay his respects."

With Guenevere there had been the passion of guilt, the passion of forbidden fruit. With Catherine, try as she would, the guilt of original sin clung to her body, and when she was barren, more guilt turned her inward, filled her with herself until there was no room for him. But Sagami was guiltless. She luxuriated in his body, poured balms and oils over her breasts and buttocks and slid against him like a fish, deliciously wanton.

"To make yourself strong, you must eat this ginseng," she advised him, giving him the weird looking root. "Slice a few pieces each day and chew well and swallow." After a month, he found himself more eager than ever to take hold of her. From a large *makie* box of inlaid wood, she withdrew an *emaki* of the *Secret Prescriptions for the Bedroom*. In the dull light of the moon and brazier of charcoal, Lance wondered at the illustrations and the advice. If a man held his seed, the Taoist author claimed, he could give joy to a woman several times a day, cure himself of ailments, and live to a ripe old age. "I am afraid now I will not be enough for you," Sagami teased.

The wonder was that he kept up with *her!* She never tired of trying one of the new toys which Old Nurse happily obtained for her. Underneath him, on top of him, side by side, she lived now only for her lover's mouth, skin, touch and thrust. The dreary winter days trudged by. The Boar Festival passed, and the Festival of First Fruits. The General Confession came when *Kannon* blesses the sinners, and the priests came from Mt. Hiei and from Nara with their painting of the demons of hell.

What did she care of demons who ate the heads of children, who breathed fire at unrepentant sinners? She could not believe in the mercy of Kannon and the demons of hell at the same time. She could not believe that the God who made her lover's body would cast her into hell for worshipping that body. All the priests had their own slant on things and none of them agreed on anything, so how was she to know? She only knew the longing of her heart through the cold, dreary hours of the day. With Old Nurse she'd prayed for rebirth in the Pure Land of the Western Paradise, then she stopped praying when she learned that women could not enter the Pure Land except they be reborn as men. Reborn as a man and lose Britain's love? She'd rather risk damnation!

*

"Aren't you making a fool of yourself?" Sachiko complained. "Who is this stranger, anyway? Where does he come from? Who are his parents, and his parents' parents?"

Sagami had gently reminded her sister that questions of lineage had not over-concerned her when she mated with the wrestler the night of the eclipse.

Sachiko dismissed the charge. "That, of course, was madness. One night's excess—and not a few others parted the leaves that night! What you are doing is altogether different. Altogether. And, besides, it's risky. People are talking."

Sachiko had conveniently neglected to tell her sister about the morning-after letter she had addressed to the handsome foreigner.

"What do you make of this?" Will had asked the warrior-priest of Mt. Hiei. The priest knew what it was even before he read it. Sachiko had attached red maple leaves to the package and used the finest colored papers, a collage of gold and white and blue, decorated with maple-leaf brushwork and gold flakes. It was scented with dried wisteria blossoms. In her finest hand, she'd written her morning-after poem:

> "Will the hands that conquered the mountain
> return the wren to its nest?"

"Very touching," said the priest. "Most irregular, but very touching."

"I don't get it," Will said.

So the priest explained the tradition. "Of course, it is usually the man who sends the first poem. I suppose she has made allowances for your being a foreigner."

Will scratched his head and laughed. "She's going to have to wait till hell freezes over if she wants a reply."

The priest laughed, too. "Don't you like her?"

Will shrugged. "She made me feel good last night, that's for sure. And now that I know what it's all about—this thing between men and women—I suppose there are others who can do the trick when I want it. I've seen some pretty ladies serving drinks at the inn. I think they can do it just as well—and don't need poetry after . . . Now, weren't you going to show me how to shoot while riding a horse?"

It had taken weeks for Sachiko to recover from her humiliation. Now she wished both foreigners ill. Let the demons of hell devour them!

Sagami had also written a morning-after poem following the night of the eclipse. When Lance read it, his heart cantered with boyish joy:

> "As the pearl of moonlight overwhelmed the dragon,
> the scent of your limbs lingers in the morning air
> drunkening all senses."

It had taken him hours to frame a response:

> "Though the dragon disgorged the moon,
> greater wonder by far—
> your face in its silver light."

Lance had been shy about sending it. He was certain it was awful.

But Sagami had joyed to receive it. Rebel though she was, a part of her loved the traditions. Thus she would make Britain wait while she arranged herself behind her screen of state. Against her better judgment, part of her yearned for acceptance from the group whose values she flaunted. Perhaps it was the spirit of her great grandfather, still pining in his banishment, craving acceptance. In the autumn, she would put a basket of persimmon in front of his shrine, and each winter morning, a bowl of hot rice gruel to pacify his spirit.

Now she had taken a step which would earn her everlasting contempt, and even the spirit of Sugawara no Michizane would not be able to rescue her. How hard her ancestor had labored for redemption! In the dreary hours of daylight she prayed before the household shrine. "Forgive me, Great Grandfather. You alone understand. Compelled by your heart's reasons, you took the unpopular course. Even your friend, the Emperor, deserted you. Yet you spoke your counsel. Oh, forgive me, that I cannot still my heart, wildly beating for the foreigner!"

She had better reasons to be concerned. On the fifteenth day of the first month of the new year, the Imperial Water Office presented the Emperor with a special gruel of herbs guaranteed to promote health and longevity. That same day Sachiko arrived with her friends from the provinces.

"Hasn't Sagami's complexion changed!" Sachiko remarked to her friends.

"All grow white in winter," Sagami reminded her. "Except for simple folk."

"Indeed," Sachiko teased, "yet I do recall how you always hated the `pasty' look. And, to speak frankly, I have never seen my sister white as snow!" She held a clump of snow up to Sagami's cheek. Everyone agreed they were the same color.

"Her cheek is white, but her eyes are black and lustrous," said Sachiko's friend. "And I've never seen her in a better mood."

"What's the secret?" Sachiko teased. "Has the foreigner taught you new tricks?"

"Don't wag your tongue like a broken rudder on a run-down ship," Sagami cautioned. "Keep the keel even, or the ship will falter!"

"That's right," Sachiko said, withdrawing the peeled elder wood sticks from where they were concealed within her robes. She handed each of the women sticks while Sagami backed away. "Younger Sister! What are you doing?"

Sachiko and her friends descended on Sagami with the sticks, striking her loins through her robe. "Stop, stop!" Sagami cried, half laughing, half in tears.

The others were also laughing. "Have men children!" they shouted. "Men children only!" *Strike!*

"A woman's lot is a poor one!" *Strike!*

"She sits and waits all day for her lover." *Strike!*

"And when he comes, his head is full of the affairs of state!" *Strike!*

"Or he's dreaming of his latest conquest." *Strike!*

"Or composing a poem in his noggin!" *Strike!*

"For some other lady!" *Strike!*

"Enough, enough!" Sagami cried, fleeing into the courtyard. She scooped the snow into her hands and clumped it into snow balls which she aimed at her playful tormentors. Outnumbered three to one, she was nevertheless the most agile and she scattered them.

"Peace!" cried Sachiko. "We were only joking!"

But when the Festival of the Spring Prayer came in the Second Month, and the blood did not flow from the jade gate, Sagami knew it was no joking matter.

*

Imbe-san wiped the beaded sweat from her lover's forehead. Commander Nakatomi breathed deeply, then spoke, eager to get the words out before the memory faded. "In the belly of a great bird I sat, harnessed like a horse, and I looked through the great bird's eyes. To my left and right there were other great birds and I could see men behind the eyes, and the men's faces showed fierce determination. Each of the bellies of the birds was spotted with a red sun. And the great birds roared towards the distant horizon, above the clouds.

"I was filled with fear, and yet a strange, wild hope. The great birds' wings dipped in formation and we dove lower and I saw the glittering sea. At the edge of the sea were several islands, and I knew that my destiny lay there; and that my destiny was death. The face of a child and a young woman appeared before my mind, and I fought back tears.

"Now there was black smoke exploding around the great birds, but below us, out of harm's way. I pushed on a wheel in the great bird's throat and the bird dipped forward into the exploding sky. On the large islands below there were other birds—many—in formation, and there were smaller islands from which the black smoke came.

"We kept getting nearer the water. A great bird on my left burst into flame, and then my own bird was hurt in the wing, but not badly. `As a cherry blossom falls from the sky,' I thought, and I saw the great birds to my left and right and the islands before me, and the high sun above, and I thought: how beautiful and how mysterious. I lowered the wheel of the great bird and the beak dipped into a turret on a flaming island."

Imbe-san handed him a hot broth, then sat down on her heels beside him. "I have remembered," she said. "Let us call this, the *Great Bird Dream*."

The Commander sipped the broth and felt the lineaments of the dream fade. He felt the pulse of his blood, the fatigue of his muscles, the throbbing in his forehead. He finished the broth and waited for his body to calm down. He practiced his breathing exercises, and, at length, felt like himself again. "It takes longer to return," he said.

Imbe-san took his hand. "Train me, Husband. Let me take this burden from you."

He patted her hand. "Soon . . . Soon . . ."

"Will Lancelot prevent what you have seen?" she asked.

He shook his head. "Not this one. Prevent it, and the next one will be worse. Of that I'm certain. This is not for him to alter, but, rather, something to be realized—or the next one will spell doom.

"There is only one small chance, one tonal change in the chorus of time, one quivering moment—an event so small—and yet it moves through time like a ripple and it gathers strength as it moves until it rises like a tsunami and alters the course of the world." He sighed heavily, exhausted from his vision-questing: "If I have seen correctly," he added humbly. "If I have not misunderstood."

Imbe-san was about to reassure him when they heard the sounds of horses galloping through the woods. Had their shelter been discovered? Would the camouflage of foliage protect them? Or had the Emperor's guards come to wreak revenge for the shedding of Imperial blood?

"Commander!" the familiar voice rang out.

"It's Gonsai," the Commander sighed. He peered through the window of the hut, parted the foliage with his hands. Gonsai rode with the rebel party. The Commander pushed the door and the foliage gaped open.

Gonsai dismounted. "I bring good news," he proclaimed. "Buretsu's men are routed. Keitai will make peace with us and claim the throne. He declares a general amnesty, fair treatment for the peasants, taxes levied for the common good. The Kami are restored! Yamato is saved!"

The men cheered. The Commander held up his hands. "The Captain of the Guard who disappeared over the hill when the foreigners vanished, was his body discovered?"

Gonsai looked at the other horsemen. "In the general confusion—"

The Commander turned to Imbe-san. "As I feared . . . He must have tumbled down the pit I made for them . . . There's one who can thwart our plans—the element of chaos, the poison root in the elixir. We have won peace for our time, but the world remains imperiled."

"You can help the foreigners—"

"I don't know. Up to a point, no farther."

"The Kami will—"

"Which Kami? Those who suffer when we bleed, or those who salt our wounds?"

Unsettled, he stepped forward to greet the troops. *"Banzai!"* they shouted, lifting their crude bronze swords. *"Banzai!* Live a hundred years! Live a thousand years! *Banzai!"*

*

"May you live a thousand years!" Lance said, raising his cup to Will.

"And you, *Sensei*, at least as long!" The two men downed their tiny cups of *sake*. Sachiko covered her mouth with her fan, laughing delicately.

"Am I *Sensei* now?" Lance wondered.

"First and foremost," Will declared, unaccustomed to drinking, and already a little tipsy. "And brother and friend."

"We have traveled far from the village of your birth," Lance said.

"Aye," Will agreed, and a tinge of sadness was in his eyes.

It was the Festival of the Snake during the Third Month. The first crocuses had pushed against the sod, eager to taste air and light. In the south, cherry trees were already adorning themselves with evanescent blossoms. In Sagami's womb, new life also stirred.

The wine cups came around again. All about the streams of the Imperial Garden devotees offered toasts and gave thanks for girl children.

All morning Sagami had decorated tiers of shelves in her shrine room with *Hina* dolls and tiny household articles. Each shelf was covered with a bright, red cloth, and the *Hina* Emperor and Empress sat regally, attended by their ministers, ladies-in-waiting, and musicians. In every household of the good people, the tiers of shelves were decorated and the female children were honored. In their tailored, bright brocades, even the Minister of the Left and the Minister of the Right were at peace for once, and in the miniature world of the dolls self-serving stopped for a day.

Sachiko had brought her little girl to let her see her aunt's display. "What good taste," the child remarked. "Excellent good taste!" Then, after devouring a dish of sweet rice cakes, she asked, "Won't Auntie have a little girl so I can have a playmate?" she'd asked. Sagami had looked at Sachiko searchingly, but Sachiko only laughed and gently chided the child.

Now Sagami's hand rested momentarily on her amply covered abdomen. Impossible to detect anything through the multilayered kimonos, of course. But what on earth was she going to do? She had heard of noblewomen having children in secret, going off to monasteries in distant regions, and giving their children to be raised by the priests and nuns. But how could she give up her child, Britain's child?

Sometimes a husband recognized the children of his wife's lover, raising them as his own. If Oiwa-san saw any political advantage in it he wouldn't hesitate. But why would he? Perhaps he would like to be thought capable of siring a child? Only at the beginning of their four-year marriage had they attempted to mate and the outcome had humiliated Oiwa and frustrated Sagami. The old factotum had been childless with his former wife, too! No, he was much more likely to denounce his unusual wife, hold her up to public censure!

What then? She and Britain could travel to one of the eastern provinces. Britain would offer his services as a scholar. But who would take him? Outside the capital, scholars were thought slightly ridiculous. There would be few books, few pleasures outside Heian-kyo. And what if Britain rejected her?

He smiled at her now, lifting another cup of *sake*. His eyes were full of tenderness and dreamy longing. Praise Buddha, she was certain of his love! No matter what happened they must be together. They had been born to complete one another.

Will stretched back on the mat. "All I'm saying is . . . your Confucianists don't have the last word," Will declared, the heat of the *sake* in his voice. "Nor your Taoists, nor Buddhists, either."

"And I suppose Sun Tzu does?" Lance parried.

Will nodded. "When it comes to warfare, yes! Look . . ." Will sat up to make his point, "All warfare is based on deception. That's basic Sun Tzu. Do you think your "Superior Man," your "Gentleman" is going to deceive his enemy? No! He's going to perform his rituals and his ceremonies and lead his spotless life and hope for the best. Then the enemy comes at night and cuts his throat!"

Sachiko laughed. "There are no enemies in Heian-kyo," she offered.

"If men would follow Master Kung," Lance countered, "there would be no war."

"Aye," Will said, "and there's the crux. If pigs had wings they'd fly from the butcher." He winked at Lance. "If every maiden's chastity were sure, there'd be no need of chastity belts . . ." He leaned back on his elbows. "Sachiko, hand me that bowl of fruit, will you?"

"Am I your handmaiden, Lord?" Sachiko chided.

"It's not your hand that most entices me, fair lady. But that will do in a pinch."

She slapped his hand. "I fear you make light of me, Sir!"

"And I fear you have read Sun Tzu, also. For you pretend inferiority and encourage my arrogance. While I'm cockadoodling, you're sharpening the knives."

Sagami laughed and helped herself to a wine cup. Poor Sachiko didn't know what to make of her sometime lover. The greater his indifference, the more she sought avowals. "It's our turn to recite a poem," Sachiko declared, and the bordering wine parties waited on their words.

"Oh, this constant poeticizing," Will complained. "All right, I have one:

> 'Wine, women and song
> Make a man healthy, wealthy and long
> in the ding-dong.'

Will made an appropriately haggard facial expression. The bordering groups of party-goers looked about embarrassedly and Sachiko blushed deeply. Even Sagami's complexion flushed; though, after a moment, she laughed a deep throaty laugh like a man.

"Is that a poem?" Sachiko wondered.

"It sounds like a poem," Will declared.

"It has no hidden meaning," Sachiko expounded, obviously piqued by Will's ribaldry. "It has neither delicacy nor poignancy. Who would care to remember such nonsense? Suppose yourself ill, would such words bring comfort?"

"For me they would," said Will.

Sachiko sighed. Now she was irritated. "I'm afraid you are incorrigible, Sir."

"You may encourage me any time, Madam," Will assured her.

"What is your poem, Sister?" Sagami asked.

Flustered, Sachiko cleared her throat and read:

> Though the wine cups are empty,
> no true words have passed between us.
> The days grow warmer, but not our hearts.'

On the bordering mats they nodded their approval, and even Sagami was impressed with her sister's production. Perhaps there was hope for her, after all.

"I still think mine was a poem," Will said. Sachiko pushed him over, and he fell onto his back laughing.

"All right, Britain," Will said on his back. "Scatter your pearls!"

"I never claimed to be a bard," Lance demurred.

"Sun Tzu again," Will declared. "Pretend inferiority and provoke your enemy's arrogance. On with it! Thrust, Knight!"

Will took note of those on the bordering mats. "These scanty-bearded popinjays await your gleaming insights."

The scanty-bearded popinjays didn't know what the young foreigner was talking about, but they laughed in fellowship.

"All right, then," Lance said. He took a quick peak at Sagami:

> 'I may drink my fill of wine,
> but my thirst for you is unquenchable,
> as that of a man who has travelled
> centuries in desert realms.
>
> Though we part for a thousand years
> I'll return to your waiting arms.'

"Now you're talking," said Will.

"It's very lovely," Sachiko sighed. She looked askance at Will. "Very *sincere*."

Lance and Sagami said nothing. Their eyes spoke for them.

The surrounding popinjays nodded their approval and raised their wine cups to the foreigner.

"You're last," Sachiko told Sagami.

"Last, but not least," said Will, sitting up.

Sagami cleared her throat. The charmingly contradictory aspects of her character, her boldness and shyness, made gentle war in her; she blushed, as her eyes grew lustrous:

> 'I have drunk wine and bitterness and passion,
> but only love has made me blossom.
>
> The warm days follow the frosty heels of winter.
> Sweet is your face in bright sunlight,
> yet the long nights of winter were sweet for embracing.
>
> Let the wine cups passing on the stream of life
> gather reflections of our myriad selves.
> In a thousand wine cups I am looking at you,
> and hold forth my selves for your savoring.'

Will took a long look at Sagami, whose eyes were locked with Lancelot's. For the first time he envied Lance, and yet was happy for him. Sachiko wiped a tear from her eye.

On the bordering mats they were silent. Some of the more sensitive wept and everyone agreed it was a splendid festival and life was sad and beautiful. It was, of course, somewhat irregular for a woman to be so bold with her lover. But it was thoroughly up-to-date, they agreed. Most thoroughly up-to-date.

*

On the Kamo River rowboats of pine were stuffed with the *Hina* dolls from last year's ceremony. In the lead boat two powerful oarsmen pulled six boats linked with chains. The tiny emperors and empresses and all their attendants were heaped together in their colorful disarray. In a little while the boats would be set afire so the souls of the dolls might reincarnate in the Pure Land of the Western Paradise.

Lance didn't know if he would reincarnate there. The concept was strange to him. Yet he had traveled through time, and that was a kind of reincarnation. He wasn't sure what he believed anymore. He only knew he had a mission and in the completion of it lay his personal salvation. And he knew, too, that he could not leave Sagami. No redemption made sense without her. No heavenly paradise could rival what he'd found in her arms.

He played the biwa as she had shown him, serenading her with folksongs.

An hour earlier, when Will and Sachiko and Old Nurse had wandered off to watch the boats being stacked with dolls, Sagami had offered him rice cakes filled with sweet beans.

"Are you trying to make me fat?" he asked. "Like the wrestler, Hajikami?"

Sagami laughed. "'Spinning the silkworms' would prove difficult then."

Lance smiled at her allusion to the man-on-top position. "'Cranes crossing necks' would still be fun."

Now she blushed. The woman-on-top position gave her the greatest pleasure.

"Perhaps 'spinning the silkworm' will prove difficult sooner, rather than later," Lance suggested.

She looked askance. Lance wished he could touch her. But it was out of the question. Merely sitting together they were breaking all the conventions. "How well you've mastered the poet's art," Sagami declared, "the art of indirection."

"I saw you looking at the dolls," Lance admitted. "And there was a secret in your eyes, a joy tinged with sadness. Your face has never been as lovely, nor your hair so lustrous. In the dark, in the moonlight, I've learned your body's contours. In the daylight hours, apart from you, my hands release their memories. My hands have found a fullness that wasn't there before . . . That fullness is our child."

Sagami drew her breath in sharply. Then slowly let it out, relieved. Britain's face was calm, accepting. Even better, he was proud! "I didn't know how to tell you . . ."

"There was no need to hesitate."

"Please forgive me. I never meant to upset your life."

"You have put me back together. I was broken; now I am whole."

There was a tear in Sagami's eye. He had never seen her show her tears before. "What? What's wrong?"

"Nothing but the dew on the rose's blush of happiness," she said. "But what will become of us? And of our child? How difficult it will be!"

A shout went up downriver. The first boat of dolls was being set aflame. The man with the torch touched it to the dry strawbed of the tiny court and the colorful costumes lit with the purifying fire. The tiny emperor and his tiny ministers sat stolidly in the flames, as though they were already reborn in the Pure Land.

Sagami could not suppress her tears. "It's so beautiful,"

she said. "So sad and so beautiful. *Mono no aware*, we say. Death in life. The pathos of things . . . I'll never forget this day, Britain. Because you gave me your strength, I can meet whatever challenge comes."

They joined Will, Sachiko and Old Nurse at the riverbank. The torchman was about to light the last boat of dolls. The oarsmen were already pulling the other boats. Only the chain to the last boat lay slack. The torch went down and the straw lit. The oarsmen pulled and all six boats were flames on the water. The first boat had already disintegrated. But its steel keel held the links to the lead boat and the others.

The torchman held the torch above his head in an awkward gesture. Lance turned to look at him, and thought he recognized him. The man smiled wryly. Reflexively, Lance smiled back, then, in an instant, recognized the "blue man," the Captain of the Guards of Yamato. That face was the last one he saw before the world exploded into fire. Lance didn't see Will grab the Captain's arms, he didn't see them struggle in the light from the boats on the river. Dimly he heard Sagami scream. He couldn't take his hands away from his eyes.

Someone led him into the water. There was shouting behind him, shouting on all sides. "Oh, Lance!" Will cried. "My God, Lance!"

"Where are you taking him?" Sagami cried.

The water soaked his robes. Many hands were pulling him down, and he still could not take his hands from his eyes.

Then the pain burst like lightning in every nerve of his body.

8 | Silk

Will swam underwater, pulling his blinded confederate who thrashed at the pain. He pulled with his left arm, since his favored arm had been badly cut by the Captain of the Guards. Tendons had been severed in the bicep and now the arm hung like a useless fin at his side. After a minute or two—but what seemed like an infinitely longer time—he pushed his head tortoise-like above the dark waters. Lance gasped for air, then heeded his old instincts and remained still.

Will looked about, quietly towing Lance after him. All the fires were gone, the festival goers were gone; it was earlier than it had been—late dusk now. Someone with a hoarse voice gave orders which were invariably followed by a pause and a dull *thwack*.

Will grabbed Lance by the scruff of the neck and pulled him with his wounded right arm. He paddled with his left towards the opposite bank of the river, but he had to struggle to keep his head above water. Lance began to moan softly.

"What's that?" one of the men on shore wondered.

The Lieutenant put his hand on his sword hilt, then looked around warily. "Hah-ha!" he laughed. "Are you afraid of ghosts?"

"Nay, not ghosts. But Minamoto arrows—yes!"

The Lieutenant huffed, "Should we fear children when they play at war?" The Lieutenant laughed again. "Truly it has been said, 'Who is not a Taira is not a man.' As Lord Kiyomori dredged the Inland Sea, so now he dredges the nation's pond, and rids us of this Minamoto scum."

The soldier, whose hearing was sharper than his lieutenant's, knew better than to argue. He strained his eyes over the river. In the shadows, he thought he saw something bobbing, but perhaps he was wrong.

Will strained his eyes, too. Towards the Lieutenant, the soldier, and their kneeling prisoner. In the darkness he could not see how the shore which had been festive moments before was now stained with blood, how the torsos of the prisoners lay in unkempt rows with their severed heads scattered about them.

The Lieutenant lifted the chin of his last prisoner, a teenage boy with delicate features. The face kept trying to make a mask of itself, and it kept failing.

"Don't waste your tears, laddy boy," said the Lieutenant. "Soon you'll join your insolent dad. What sweet delicacies the Lord of Hell has waiting for you! It makes my mouth water to think of it!" The Lieutenant and his minion laughed.

But the eldest son of Yoshitomo Minamoto did not laugh. Finally, he set his face into a rock-like scowl. "Having raised his banners against the tyrant Kiyomori, my father's spirit now resides with his illustrious ancestors. I eagerly join him, and leave this world of lies to foul-smelling vermin like you."

The Lieutenant's gloved left hand flew forward, encircled the boy's swanish throat, squeezed without mercy. When the pink tongue emerged, the Lieutenant grabbed it with his right hand, pulled it out as far as possible, then kneed the boy's jaw shut on it. The teeth cut the tongue raggedly, and the Lieutenant ripped out what was left. The boy flapped like a fish out of water, then choked to death on the remnants of his tongue. After the writhing stopped, the Lieutenant nodded and his minion lowered the sword. *Thwack!*

Will gasped. Lance, who had passed out, now revived, and moaned loudly.

The Lieutenant and his minion rushed to the water's edge.

The Lieutenant carefully aimed his arrow as Will pulled himself and his sire under again. The razor sharp tip of the arrow grazed Will's ear underwater. He had dove without inhaling and now he quickly surfaced again. He waited for the arrows to end his life.

But it was quiet. He saw the oil lamps lit in the shacks that now lined the Kamo. Towards the capital, wives and concubines of wealthier merchants lit the fires of *ofuros* for the fifth-day baths. On the half hour, bowstrings were plucked to frighten evil spirits, while young women settled into long games of *go* and gambling men argued over *sugoroku*. Some two centuries had passed since Will and Lance had run into the river to escape the third "blue man," Yamato's Captain of the Guards. And twenty more years had passed since Yoshitomo Minamoto's eldest son had choked to death on his tongue. From the second story of his palace at Rokuhara, Taira Kiyomori coolly surveyed his domain.

Lord Kiyomori, who had placed his two-year old grandson on the Emperor's throne, whose authority superseded the abdicated Emperor Go-Shirakawa's, strode uneasily atop the ramparts, while the dark waters of the Kamo churned and the Kami wove erratic threads of fate and Will and Lance fell exhausted onto the riverbank.

And somewhere, far away, the God of History and the Goddess of Myth danced together on the moonlit plains.

*

On the morning of Buddha's birthday three holy women gathered before their small forest temple, clapped their hands three times, and bowed their heads in solemn prayer. Gio, the eldest, poured the sweet tea over the tiny statue of Buddha Sakyamuni. The fragrance of chrysanthemum, from which the tea was brewed, filled the mountain air, as Gio handed the wooden ladle to her sister Ginyo. Ginyo repeated the ritual, then handed the ladle to Kaoru. When they had completed the ablutions, they bowed again and prayed again, then sighed for the passing of another year.

"How quickly the years pass," Kaoru said, expressing each one's thoughts.

Ginyo nodded towards the mulberry trees crowded along the river. "Already the green buds peep into the world. Soon we'll wash the bamboo trays and unwind the white cocoons."

Gio laughed. "Hold your horses, Little Sister. There's much to do before then. Money won't jump into our hands. If these hard times last . . ."

She need not complete the thought, for the other two could read her mind now. They had lived together for a dozen years in the little cottage the people in the village had built for them. There had been four of them, but Gio and Ginyo's natural mother had died four years before. Now they waited to live out their days and join the other in Paradise.

The "hard times" might indeed hasten their progress. Since Taira Kiyomori had moved the capital the year before, overruling the geomancers and other diviners, nothing had gone right. The court officials, nobles, ladies-in-waiting, tradesmen, artisans and soldiers had traded their comfortable apartments in the 400-year old capital for the bracing winds, salt air, dust, smoke and the constant clatter of a city a-building. The warrior monks of Mt. Hiei had protested the removal of their patrons. They sent out feelers to the Minamoto clans and Go-Shirakawa, the cloistered Emperor: little notes of greeting and well-wishing in which disaffection was expressed by an offhanded reference to an ancient Chinese poem, or a comment that the crocus had been slow to bloom.

"Wasn't it foolish of the Priest-Premiere to proceed with his plans to transfer the capital?" Kaoru said. "In spite of the ill-omened wind!"

"He has always been stubborn," Gio agreed.

"They say sixty houses were destroyed, including mansions. Children were lifted into the air, and their brains dashed on the stones of RashoMon."

"Buddha preserve them!" Gio said.

"And now he is back with all his troops," Kaoru said, "and they say he mourns his son from light to dark."

"They say the capital will be moved again—back to Heian-kyo," said Ginyo.

"Wasn't it foolish to move it in the first place?" Kaoru insisted. "And now poor Shigemori's dead . . . He was the best of the Tairas. Nothing has gone right all these years."

"The brewer's son told me that the Great Fire took the lives of hundreds of nobles," said Ginyo. "Even sixteen 'good persons' were caught napping in their robes, and their fine brocades burst into flames."

The three sisters bowed their heads. "The southern gate of the palace, the Home Office, the University buildings—all are ashes now. And after the fire, came the whirlwind—four city wards flattened . . Last year there were the floods, and so many poor people took to the roads. So many people without rice, with their hands out, and their eyes bulging as though they have seen more than they can bare." Ginyo paused to catch her breath.

"We must pray for better days," Gio urged. But inwardly they knew they were in the Last Days of the Buddha's Law, and everything would get worse. "We must pray for the souls of the dead," Gio advised, and they bowed their heads again and prayed.

They were lost in prayer when Will approached them. He led Lance by the hand now. Lance seemed shrunken and much older. Will's right arm was torn and suppurating.

"Oh!" Ginyo cried, the first to open her eyes.

"*Namu Amida Butsu!*" cried Gio and Kaoru together. "Praise Buddha's Name!"

"Kind sisters," Will said in a husky voice. "A little rice, for pity's sake . . . "

The two of them could barely stand. Lance's face had been disfigured by the fire. The three sisters were horrified. They had all been women of the nobility before taking the tonsure. Now they fluttered about, helplessly inspecting the wounds, frightened of the men, and compelled by their faith to render aid.

Finally, Gio took charge. "Get the priest, Kaoru-san. He'll know what to do."

So Kaoru ran down the mountain to summon the Shinto priest while Gio and Ginyo helped the men to the cottage. Mountain roses grew in profusion in front of the lattice windows and along the walkway. Inside, the straw mats were fresh, and the wooden floor scrubbed clean. Will crumpled onto a straw mat and slept.

Slept for a week, lingered in a limbo between life and death, came to with one of the sisters mopping his brow, then heard his father's or his mother's voice beckoning him to some chore—to gather the harvest from the croft, slaughter the pigs or chickens, plant the seed. He dreamed of his father's meaty palm descending on his face and woke with his cheeks burning and the Shinto priest shaking a bundle of anise leaves over his face, while the sisters hovered in the background.

"Lance?" he worried.

And they led the blind and shrunken knight forward. The flesh was healing, but the eyeballs had melted. Lance put out his hand. Will grasped it and sank into fever again.

"Where is the Holy Grail?" he cried, and he saw the face of Jesus on the crude wooden cross of his village church. The face became his grandfather's, lying dead in the hayfields, the ragged kindly face turning ashen as the small boy shook and cried.

He was running, then, across the paddies, pursued by the soldiers of Yamato, trying to flush the image of falling guts from his mind, trying to find Lancelot—the only sanity he knew. But when he found him again, his face was gone. Then he cried in his dream, and the three sisters wept in sympathy, and Lance would have wept but his tear ducts were destroyed by fire.

Then everyone was cheering for him. He was fighting the giant Hajikami . . . He had got the better of the giant and a crowd of strangers was cheering. There were beautiful women, too. He had become a man, and his form was pleasing to women and three of them were looking after him, mopping his brow and feeding him soup and talking to him gently, reassuringly. The giant was squeezing him, and the giant's face was the face of Buddha, and the giant squeezed harder and harder until he burst awake with a shout.

"Will, Will, forgive me," Lance said, taking his hand.

"Nay, Lance. Don't beggar me with asking what I've naught to give. Having earned naught of my displeasure, you cannot earn forgiveneness now."

Then Lance squeezed the hand tightly. For the first time in a week he knew his friend would be well. And now he sank into his own darkness. A door opened in a dark room, and beyond the door was darkness, and beyond that, ten thousand other doors opening on darkness.

*

The poultice of clay and herbs which the Shinto priest had applied each day to the torn ligaments of Will's arm had a most remarkable effect. As it healed, the arm grew considerably thicker and stronger than it had been before. By the end of the second week of his recovery, Will regarded the arm with a kind of veneration. Though he didn't know it yet, it was a bowman's arm.

Now he accompanied Ginyo to inspect the mulberry trees. They passed the hemp fields, just recently planted, and the dry, furrowed paddies which would soon be irrigated and planted. On the road Will turned his face from travelers or slanted the conical straw hat rakishly towards his shoulders. He was still wary of Taira Kiyomori's spies; nor yet recovered enough to take on the "blue man." He had little sense of where he was anymore, nor what had happened to the elegant court of the Fujiwaras.

The road scenes should have convinced him the current crop of leaders had more to worry about than the whereabouts of two wayfarers from a previous century. There were many on the road now, from barefooted basket sellers with poles on their shoulders to itinerant priests with altars on their backs. Shaggy-haired orphans pulled on his robe and put their palms to their mouths in gestures of eating. To the most pitifully thin ones Ginyo gave rice cakes and strips of dried fruit. People with the remnants of fine clothes on their backs also wandered the road—cast-out concubines, no longer supportable, and scholars weighed down by their cherished books, bewildered by how the world had changed.

Will heard talk of skirmishes beyond the hills, where the Minamoto clans gathered like locusts, and the Taira warriors, decked in splendid armor, met to hold the line. But who were these contending families? What did they want?

Secretly, Will searched all the faces for the torchman who had blinded Lance. Where was he now? Was he still in that other world, the elegant capital with its courtiers, that life of pomp and leisure?

"Just a little further," Ginyo advised, as she led him off the road and down the trail into the valley. Then it was up the valley walls, and Will wondered how the sisters had managed to half-carry him and Lance to their cottage. What extraordinary women these nuns were!—so unlike the helpless damsels of the capital. They had nursed them back to health, given them their cottage while they converted the tiny temple's storeroom into a bedchamber for themselves. "It is quite adequate," Gio had said. "There is little enough to store now, except ourselves."

The squat mulberry trees had leaves the size of Ginyo's little hands. "Very fine," Ginyo said happily, and, almost immediately, a cloud passed over her features.

"What is it?" Will asked. He watched a tear form in her eye. Ginyo sank to her knees. "There will never be time to harvest these. The fat cocoons will wither on the vines. Gio says we must leave."

"Leave? But where will you go?" He felt an urge to put his hand on her shoulder, to comfort her, but he held back.

"For eleven years we have lived in these hills, always struggling, but, always, somehow, with the grace of Buddha, managing. Our dear mother died, and is buried in this region. Always the village people made provisions for us—just enough—and we prayed for them and taught their children. They built the little temple for us when they saw our sincerity to follow Buddha's Law. Now they haven't a scrap of rice to spare."

"Can Prince Fujiwara do nothing?" Will wondered.

"Who?"

"Prince Fujiwara . . . the Emperor's regent."

Ginyo looked at him oddly. "How strangely you talk, Sir. The Fujiwaras have been mere chatterboxes for over thirty years. The Tairas are the scythes that rule Japan. Men fall like weeds when they turn. Lord Kiyomori's the head reaper. Lord Kiyomori!" She spoke the name with venom. Her face colored with hatred.

Will was startled. Had an era passed when he dunked his head under the Kamo? Now that the gilded age was gone, he regretted its loss as a child who had been eager to leave home is filled with nostalgia on hearing it is gone.

Ginyo's eyes were still filled with anger. It spilled over, in spite of her vows.

"What did he do to you?" Will asked.

Ginyo sighed, hesitated. "We should return," she said abruptly, gathering her skirts to rise. Will touched her hand. "Nay . . . Tell me—" Discreetly, she withdrew her hand. "We are friends, are we not?" Will asked.

"I saw you teeter at the Gates of Hell. I called you back . . ."

"More than friends then. So . . . you trust me?"

"I saw your weakness, the strength within that weakness. A boy's tender soul in the body of a man. A boy strutting like a man."

"You saw more than you know . . . Won't you tell me what disturbs you now?"

"Sir . . ."

"Will . . ."

"Will?"

He nodded.

"It's just . . . I have never known someone like you, Sir . . .

Will . . . Sir . . . Will . . . I have never been with a man so long alone. Oh, one of the farmers, perhaps, one of the old, garrulous ones, and with the young ones—the very young ones. Oh, what am I saying? I am afraid Gio will be angry with me when she learns I took you here."

"She asked you to oversee my exercise. I heard her myself."

"To walk on the road, Sir . . . Will . . ."

He watched the range of emotions play over her face. As she struggled with things she did not understand, with feelings she had never known before, the sure compass of her features altered, the set of her shoulders slouched. Though she was over twenty-five, he saw the girlishness that lingered, that had never been known or valued by others.

And he recalled that the face that had hovered over his bed most often during his illness had been hers.

He repeated the question. "What did he do? This Taira Kiyomori?"

Ginyo gazed fixedly on the scattered years. "How long ago," she said. "How long ago . . . when I was a child, or barely beyond my childhood . . . Then Taira Kiyomori was the first man in Japan. My sister Gio and I danced the white-suit dance. And when he saw her, he gave her his heart. Well, our mother and me he set up in a fine house. Each month rice and coppers came. Oh, so much! I am ashamed to think of it now. It was so long ago. Just after he entered the priesthood, and that was but a year after he became premiere . . .

"Gio held his heart, as they say. We'd visit her in the great palace at Rokuhara. For three years then we lived rich lives."

"Were you a dancer?" Will wondered.

"Yes. That was our trade. I was just a girl. Thirteen, but . . ."

Will wanted to press her more about her "trade," but he bade her continue.

"It was long ago," she said, as though reading his mind. "It is not like now with the dancers . . ."

"Please go on . . ."

"Well, for three years all was splendid. We really had wonderful lives, respected and favored. We rode in the ox-drawn carriages. And wore the latest fashions . . ." Her eyes flickered a moment as her gaze rested on her simple homespun. She smiled an ironic smile. "I know now, it was just a floating dream."

"And then?"

She sighed. "Then Lady Buddha came."

"Lady Buddha?"

"So she called herself. She had made a name for herself in the provinces, performing the white-suit dance . . . Well . . ."

"She performed for Kiyomori?"

"Yes . . ."

Ginyo shrugged. "They say women's hearts are fickle. You know the expression: `A woman's heart and the autumn weather.' But I think no heart changes so quickly as a man's when a woman has aroused him . . . Gio was ordered from the palace. She had less than a day to leave." Remembering now, Ginyo began to weep bitter tears.

"Please . . Please don't cry . . ."

She calmed herself. "Forgive me . . Even now the cruel injustice that befell my sister makes the waters rush over the dams of my eyes."

"I suppose this Lady Buddha had a similar fate," Will mused.

"Yes," Ginyo answered, wiping her tears on her sleeve. "But not as you may think." She sighed heavily. "Poor Gio could not accept her destiny. How could one plunge so quickly? She had been the most favored woman in the realm. And she always had a tender heart. How strange it all is! It was she who urged Lord Kiyomori to give Lady Buddha his audience. And you see what happened! Well, she resigned to drown herself."

"It is sin to kill oneself."

"Sin?"

"Yes," Will said firmly . . . "It is wrong . . ."

"That's what my mother said. She pressed her old, gray head

beneath my sister's nose, and pleaded with her not to leave her helpless in the world. At last, Gio relented. Though some would say the path she chose was just as bitter as the path of death . . . She took the tonsure . . . No one ever had more lovely hair . . . And if she had a single vanity, it was her hair. When I saw those black locks gathered on the floor, like a black fire, shiny and alive, I decided: in such a world that treated women so, I did not wish to live as a woman . . ."

Will lowered his head. Anger at injustice warred with another new, indefinable emotion.

"It was long ago," Ginyo added, as if to soften his discomfort.

His chin trembled. "It was a damnable thing for him to do, this high and mighty Kiyomori!"

Ginyo smiled. But it was not so much a smile as a gesture, and the gesture meant: Such is life; what can we do?

"And Lady Buddha?" Will remembered. "Did the gods take retribution?"

"Not the gods," Ginyo smiled again. "You must not misjudge her. She was just a sixteen-year old girl when she caught Lord Kiyomori's eye. Headstrong and proud, to be sure, but not unkind, not insensible . . ."

Yellow moths flitted between the cryptomeria as cirrocumulus clouds rippled the sky. A red bird alighted on a bell-shaped white flower. Will flicked a speckled insect from his forearm. Ginyo wiped a thread of moisture from her upper lip and Will settled back on the granite stone. He plucked a stalk of grass and played it between his teeth.

"Three years after we had taken the tonsure our mother and we sisters had made our peace with the world. Life had settled into a routine. There never seemed to be enough, and yet we always managed. Then, one night, there was a knocking at the door . . ."

"A knocking?"

"Yes . . . It was . . . Lady Buddha . . . It was autumn then, and she swept in with a cold breeze. As soon as she saw us she wept.

She begged forgiveness. Then she took off the cowl that covered her head. She had taken the tonsure, too."

Will understood. "It was . . . Kaoru?"

Ginyo nodded. "She had begged Lord Kiyomori not to dismiss my sister. But he turned a deaf ear. Lord Kiyomori was powerfully built, and handsome, and proud. Women were eager to serve such a man. But Lady Buddha—Kaoru—grew cold under his touch. Yet Lord Kiyomori was enchanted with her beauty. He kept her as one might keep a nightingale, merely to look at, and to hear the song. It was a sad song . . . It is a sad story, is it not?" She smiled her Japanese smile.

Some woodcutters were hauling large, long poles of bamboo down the hillslope. Their splayed feet seemed to cling to the muddy path. Will looked at Ginyo and tried to define what he was feeling. It was compassion—something he had never felt before.

"The Hour of the Sheep comes on," Ginyo said, gazing at the sky.

"I'm sorry," Will said softly.

"Yes. It is a sad story what happened to those two."

"I'm sorry for what happened to *you*," Will said.

"Me? Oh, my life . . ." She made a gentle sweeping motion as though she were brushing away a falling leaf. Her life was of so little consequence.

A bamboo cutter at the top of a hill called to the men below. The cutter spoke quickly, excitedly. Will couldn't catch the words.

"Come!" Ginyo said. "We must hurry!"

They scrambled up the hill, behind the bamboo cutters, Ginyo lithe and supple as a dancer. At the top they looked towards the road where a troop of Taira forces were riding by on horseback. The captain of the force was a young man with delicate features. Upon a roan horse, he wore a cobalt robe brocaded with golden lilies, and on top of this, a suit of teal blue armor. The lamellae of armor flapped easily on his shins and shoulders, and the sun caught the gold horns of his silver helmet. The men who followed were almost equally well-appointed.

"They look too pretty to fight," Will said.

But the bamboo cutters said they were going to fight and fight soon. Who were they going to fight? Will asked. Where had they heard it?

The bamboo trees had told them! The bamboo had been agitated for days. The head cutter could not remember when they had been so agitated.

Did the bamboo know who would win?

Yes, they knew, the cutters assured them. But they weren't telling.

*

Lord Kiyomori listened as the hundred dextrous fingers plucked the strains of "Evening Breeze." He especially liked the flute solo in the second movement, with its triplets and semiquavers, and the sure though delicate ripples of the zithers. How fine it was to lose oneself in music!

His retainers raised their cups of *sake* to him and the Priest-Premiere acknowledged their flattery. He was in one of his sentimental moods. They had dined sumptuously, and the entertainment for the evening had only just begun. Kiyomori wondered how many more times they would share a table between them.

It had been a busy month for him, his favorite month, actually, when the curtains were changed to let more light and air in and summer attire was donned. For the first time since his son's untimely death nine months before, he felt that his life had meaning. Soon after the Kamo Festival, with the fragrance of hollyhock still pungent in the air, his daughter's child, Antoku, had been coronated the 81st Emperor of Japan.

Now he had passed his 60th year, and like the ancient goddess, he held all the threads in his hands. Go-Shirakawa, the Cloistered Emperor, he had confined to the North Palace of Toba. He had enjoyed the wily fox over the years; the game of *go* they played so well together; the intrigue, simulated losses, feints and parries. The Cloistered Emperor knew how to keep his hand in the game, lending the dignity of state, the aura of divine descent. But soon there would be little need of him. He had overplayed his hand when he had confiscated the estates of his dear, departed Shigemori. Now he would cause trouble no more!

Yet, with it all, Kiyomori slept uneasily, his nights filled with dreams—old battles, old enemies. The central graneries were diminishing as the stupid peasants balked over every little tax increase, thwarting him in his grand designs. He felt himself ringed in by hypocrites, liars and slanderers waiting to make use of the ignorant masses, to turn them against him. The sleepless nights and the years and his beloved son's death had taken their toll, and he wandered through the fog of daylight struggling for sharpness. Prince Mochihito bore watching, he'd think, then wonder what he must do, his old acuity failing. The monks on Mt. Hiei are up to their usual mischief, he'd tell his aide, and then forget to take appropriate precautions. Mostly he feared some threat from the north, the hick Minamotos with their affected country ways and their disdain for the solemnities of court. Somehow, before he left, he must rid the empire of the Minamoto scourge. For their rashness, for their lack of vision and appreciation, he would wipe them out like so many weeds in the garden. Then Japan would be a garden for his grandson. Antoku would finish his projects. And peace would reign for a thousand years.

Antoku, now but a babe of three, would establish an imperial line to rival the Fujiwaras. Indeed, Kiyomori had mastered the game of the Fujiwaras and bested them. Only twenty years before, he had supported Go-Shirakawa against the Fujiwaras. Working together, they'd sent that effete tribe packing!

Now, as the white-suit dance began, the patriarch let his mind drift back. The performer was about the same age that Lady Buddha had been when first she danced for him. After a decade, he could still feel the weight of her small breasts in his hands—like two wrens. How youthful she had been—a white rosebud. For the love of her he had dismissed Lady Gio. Lady Gio! Of all his many women, only she had truly loved him!

Sometismes it seemed to him that women had been the cause of all his troubles. Perhaps the Buddhist fanatics were right in calling them demons. The face of Tokiwa floated above his mind: Tokiwa the peasant girl, whom he had loved best of all. With tears she had entreated him to spare the lives of her children. He had wavered. Then his stepmother had joined the chorus. "What have you to fear from children? Haven't you beheaded Lord Minamoto's eldest son? Let these Minamoto babes be raised as priests, under our watchful eyes. To show mercy at this time will be a sign of strength. The `good people' have had enough of killing. All the Minamotos are not our enemies. Some will join our banners if we temper firmness with mercy. There has been enough killing. Let us build our dynasty."

All else she had said had come true. Only in this judgment had she proven wrong.

That was a woman who could dream! She'd take him to the seashore as a boy and he'd watch the boats on the Inland Sea: boats from distant provinces, from the southern islands and beyond. "Isn't Japan surrounded by the sea, Mother?"

"Yes, of course. Izanagi and Izanami plunged their jeweled spear into the roiling waves. They were the first real gods, you know. They stirred it up until it thickened like a soup. When they withdrew the spear, drops of brine fell from it. These were the Japanese islands."

"Then we are the people of the sea!" Kiyomori said, jumping up with his childhood revelation. "We are the sea people!" he shouted. "Unlike all the other people, who are the land people." He did a cartwheel. And his mother clapped and laughed.

He had never forgotten the insight. Born of the sea, their future was the sea and the great trading ships that brought the world to market. For this purpose, as a provincial governor, he had dredged coastal areas of the Inland Sea—and vastly enriched the coffers of the Tairas. He had vanquished the pirates, and won the favor of the Emperor. He had founded Kobe and re-established trade with China and Korea. Let the Minamotos have their destitute northern provinces where barefooted farmers scratched out a rodent's sustenance on a few grains of rice a day! Land was limited, but the sea was infinite. For that purpose, that destiny, he had moved the ancient capital to the sea, so that the people might be mariners, men of vision, shipbuilders and traders, invigorated by the salt sea air!

But here he had failed. Something had gone wrong. He had displaced the Fujiwaras and lived to see his own soldiers' eyes mirror the affectations of their predecessors. The people had not kept up with him. The Taira aped the Fujiwara manners, and their gestures grew effete. They plastered their hair with pomades and powdered their plumpish pusses. They had lost their balance.

Meantime, those damned Minamoto boys had escaped the watchful eyes of their guardians! Damn Tokiwa and her wiles! Damn women and the sweet venom of their lips!

The noose was tightening, even as the music played the last strains of the evening. One of his retainers stretched inebriated fingers towards the *sake* bottle, and it went spinning across the table. Deflected by dishes, it stopped at the edge, and poured its warm contents into Taira Kiyomori's lap. The retainer didn't seem to notice. His eyes were fixed on the fifteen-year old white-suit dancer. He wet his lips with his tongue, while Lord Kiyomori sat and stared at the slowly spreading stain on his brocaded robe.

*

The itinerant Shinto priest examined the wound on the stranger's arm. He turned the arm in his thick fingers, as though it were a fish he was haggling to buy. "Pain?" he asked.

"No pain," Will assured him.

Will regarded the man's appearance. He had a white cloth covering his scalp and forehead and he wore a very large sleeved white half robe that fell to his upper knees. His calves were also wrapped with white cloth and on his thick-toed feet he wore rope sandals. A straw box of herbs and—as near as Will could tell—

magical sticks was suspended from a lanyard around his neck. The man carried a long, thin bamboo pole taller than he was.

"Good as new," the priest declared. "I never saw such a fast recovery. The gods of earth be praised!"

"It's better than new," Will said. "I can throw a stone twice as far as before." As if to prove the point, he cast a stone beyond the rice paddies on the far side of the river. It hit a scarecrow between its straw temples and knocked it over. "It got thicker and a little shorter," Will declared.

The priest laughed. "You will have to run faster to catch the young women," he joked.

"But my aim will be better," Will said.

The three nuns blushed. They turned their attention back to Lance who had isolated himself in a corner of their vegetable garden. The priest had been blunt with him: He would never see again.

Gio paid the priest with rice and fresh vegetables. He returned all but a small portion, blessed the house and its occupants, and bade them never to forget the ancient Kami. Moving down the hill trail, he seemed a large white moth caught in spring breezes.

Lady Gio asked if there was anything she could do for Lance. "Aye, Lady. Give me a moment's use of your eyes. I'd like to see what keeps me in this world of phantoms."

"I wish I could lend you my eyes," Lady Gio said. "For I am tired of what they teach me."

Lance sighed. "Had I but known it was a dream, would I have awakened?"

Lady Gio stopped in her tracks. "'Because I slept while my heart was yearning . . .'" she said softly.

"What was that?"

"You quoted a poem, Sir. By Ono-no-Komachi:

> 'Did you appear in my dream
> Because I slept while my heart was yearning?
> Had I but known it was a dream,
> Would I have awakened?'"

Lance sighed again. His gloom cast a pall over all of them, especially Will, who sank his head into his hands. Will had no words of comfort.

"Well, my friend," Ginyo said to Will, "shall we set that scarecrow fellow upright? Or have you other targets you need to knock down first?"

Will apologized and Ginyo's eyes sparkled. He was easy to tease, and teasing him brought out her mischief.

"I will inspect the mulberry trees," Kaoru volunteered. Gio would remain to look after Lance.

Beside the river which traversed the village—more a stream than a river—women and children in their cotton kimonos knelt over the flowing water, gabbing while they washed the trays for the silkworms. Some of the silkworm eggs of the peasants' families were already tinged green. Other families' eggs were still black. Those who gabbed the most had the most green in their eggs, and less to worry about.

"Ho, Sister Ginyo, have you got your handsome young man in tow again?" called the fishmonger's wife. And the other women laughed, and the children snickered.

"Yes. I thought I'd better keep him safe from you old fishwives," Ginyo joked back, pausing with Will on the little wooden bridge.

"After you've done with him, pass him along," joked another middle-aged woman. And she guffawed at her own boldness.

"Auntie, dear," Ginyo called, "the days when you caught slippery fish in your hands are gone with youthful sighs. And they say men are harder to catch than fish!"

"They are harder to catch," said a third woman, "but better to hold."

"And they kiss better, too," said the first, and all the women chortled.

Will and Ginyo set the scarecrow right. "They are funny old girls," he said, watching the women at the river. Out of earshot, the women had returned to their tasks. Will and Ginyo watched as the brewer's son ran up to tell them some news. The women crowded around the boy, nodding their heads and cackling like chickens.

Ginyo sighed.

"What is it?"

She gazed off. "I just remembered, when I was a girl, the washing in the river. My father made silk kimonos for the ladies of the court. In winter, we would don our high boots, trudge to the snow-covered banks and set long bamboo poles in the icy water. The silk fabric was fastened at one end, and it would flow out on the clear, cold water. We had already painted our flower designs on the fabric." She sighed again. "It was touching, somehow—to see the delicate flowered fabric gently stretched on the ice-cold water."

"You seem to have had a happy childhood," Will observed.

Ginyo shrugged. "Our childhood days . . . are wrapped in a gauze of wonder. So light it is, we never feel it, we never know it's there. But everything that touches us, touches us through that gauze. When the gauze comes off, we feel how cold the world can be." She studied Will's expression. "Wasn't your childhood happy?"

Will flashed on his father's broad-splayed hand burning against his cheek, the closed-in poverty of his village, the darkness of the clustered hovels. "I wasn't smart enough to know better," he said. "I guess you can't be sad, if you don't know you're sad."

"It's a strange idea," Ginyo said. Then she looked at him straight on. "Each soul has its own path to salvation. Within each of us, a seed of Buddha grows. When we nurture it, we bloom with happiness."

"It is a hard thing . . . to nurture a little seed."

"It is a little seed—but strong and hearty, too. It only requires a dash of sunlight—call it `right attention.'"

"And a few drops of water," Will added. "One might call that . . . `love.'"

Ginyo smiled her sweet-sad smile. "Yes. We can never forget love."

When they crossed the wooden bridge again the village women summoned them. The brewer's son had passed on the latest news. Prince Mochihito, Go-Shirakawa's son, had been discovered in a plot with one of the Minamoto lords. A sensitive youth, the Prince had watched his better years slip away as Taira Kiyomori had thrown up roadblocks to his ascension. Desperate, the Prince had cast his lot with his allies in the Minamoto clans and disaffected leaders among the warrior-monks. But the plot was betrayed and aborted.

"The Prince left the capital disguised as a lady-in-waiting," said the brewer's son, grinning.

"It is nothing to laugh about," Ginyo rebuked him. Then her face softened. "Has anything else been heard?"

Chastened, the boy shook his head stiffly. The village women lifted the heavy bamboo trays from the river and set them to dry.

A few days later they learned that the Prince had been surprised by Taira forces at the Uji bridge. A Minamoto lord had sacrificed his life so the Prince could escape.

After the silkworms' eggs turned green, they were stuck to strips of cloth which the women of the village held like babes against their breasts. Day and night, the women incubated the tiny eggs. Even Ginyo and Gio and Kaoru, who had never suckled an infant, held the eggs against their breasts. The village was quiet; men and children walked about on tiptoe so as not to disturb favorable spirits. When news came of Prince Mochihito's death in battle, the grubs began to wriggle out of the eggs, blood-red peonies flared on the hillsides, and the mulberry leaves were harvested for the grubs' voracious appetites.

*

Ginyo's premonitions of disaster had proved half right. They had watched the black worms grow fat on mulberry leaves, they had kept the fires burning while the cocoons were spun on the racks. The silkworms squirted their fluid and spun. In the capital, the

Taira prepared for war. In the provinces, the Minamotos rallied their forces. The price for silk plunged. Wily merchants arrived from the capital and offered ten percent of the silk's value. "How can we pay our taxes?" the men complained to the silk buyer.

"Surely that is no concern of mine," the buyer said. He was eager to part company with the malodorous rustics.

"How do you expect us to live?" Ginyo asked. She appealed to his mercy. "Won't you tell them in the capital how hard it is for us?"

The silk buyer shrugged. "It is hard for everyone. Life is no bed of roses, you know." Then he ordered his attendants to take the bales of raw silk. He cast hard eyes on Ginyo. "We have heard stories of two strangers living in this area."

Ginyo answered in measured tones. "There were two wayfarers who stayed awhile: a biwa singer and his nephew."

"We must not forget our good fortune, must we?" the man sneered. Ginyo was being warned to keep quiet. If the buyer had suspected that the wayfarers were important people, he would not have mentioned them at all. He would have passed the news to one of his friends in the Imperial Police, and earned himself some credit. He simply wanted the little nun off his back. He hated to be preached to.

"Well, see you next year," the buyer saluted them, then turned his back.

"Was the price that dismal?" Lance asked as Ginyo approached the farmhouse.

"How did you know?" Ginyo sat beside him in the garden.

"I heard it in your footfalls."

Ginyo sighed. She had broken her vows. She had lied to the buyer. Now she felt very weary. "I do not care for myself," she said, "but the poor people worked so hard." She wanted to cry. "Soon the taxes will be due again, and they have nothing."

"What if they refused to pay?" Will wondered over dinner.

The three women looked with astonishment. Poor people refuse to pay taxes? Who had ever heard of such a thing?

That night Will watched the sky. A comet flared on the

horizon. The Milky Way was strewn with stars as far as the eye could see.

Who had placed them there, and to what end?

Shame burned inside of him. He had known for weeks that he must leave. He was no farmer. Though he worked hard in the fields, he could not make things grow. Yet his appetite was as keen as his recovery. He ate more than he earned. The women, these kind, amazing women, encouraged him, took joy in his strength and health. Yet he burdened them, in spite of himself. They would never admit it, but it was so.

Then there was Lance. He ate like a bird now. He had shrunk, literally. He had aged. Whatever great purpose had once propelled him so that he had cast his fate like bread upon the waters had burned away like his eyebrows. He walked about like a sleepwalker who had misplaced a valuable object but could not remember what it was. The great knight whom he loved first as a father—as a god!—then as a brother—he pitied now. He hated himself for it, and yet, what other emotion filled his heart when he watched him stumble, when he saw the bottomless dejection which ravaged his soul?

Yet, with it all, it was not for Lance that he remained. In truth, Will knew Lance was better off alone with the three sisters. Together, the two men would be easy marks. If the Captain of the Guards still pursued them . .

Will could scavenge for them both, but he'd always be looking over his shoulder, always concerned about Lance. His concern would endanger Lance. That was the irony. Lance was better off with the nuns. They would surround him like camouflage.

Inside the farmhouse Lance plucked the strings of the biwa Gio had given him. Did he think of Sagami, whose tunes he sometimes played on the instrument? He never spoke of her.

Will watched the fireflies glow in the garden. In the adjacent temple, the oil lamps were lit in the nuns' apartment. "What a silly ass you are, Will," he said to himself. Not that he lied about his love for Lance, and his concern for him, but that he had struggled so mightily with the truth, and even now could scarcely say it.

After a while the oil lamps dimmed. The biwa strings stopped quavering. Only the stars and the fireflies lit the hills.

He wondered how she must have been before she took the tonsure.

She must have been a formidable beauty! Even now the years sat easy on her, in spite of her uneasy lot. Formidable—that was the word! She was too stubborn to let hardships wear her down. Will smiled to himself, remembering how she'd jut her chin to overcome some obstacle. What a world she was! Stubbornness and gentleness made friends in her. For the love and honor of her sister, she had sacrificed her life. The other two had known men, had known the world and turned their backs on it. She had turned her back on her youth as simply as a child gives up a doll she has outgrown. Her goodness and purity made him tremble, filled him with a longing to do something, something to be worthy of walking the same earth with her. As long as she lived in the world his life would have a lodestar to which he'd turn as surely as a compass needle. "Ginyo," he whispered . . .

The Milky Way turned on its fulminant axis. Over and over, the fireflies swept a wave of cool flames over the trees.

*

The three sisters watched the brewer's son rush up the hilltrail. His bare feet leapt over the rocky path and his tattered cloak sailed out behind him.

"Why do you rush so, boy?" Kaoru laughed.

"Holy Sister, Holy Sister, Holy Sister," he gasped, "and Sir and Sir . . ." He bowed to each in turn. "I came to say goodbye."

"Shall we have no more beer in the village?" Will wondered.

"Oh no, Sir. My father stays here, as his father stayed before him... and his father before him. To brew the best beer one hundred leagues around."

"Then where are you off to, little beansprout?" Ginyo teased.

"To the wars, Holy Sister."

Will laughed. The boy narrowed his eyes. He perched in the dignity of his eleven years. "Sir, it is not proper to address me so."

"Did I address you?"

The boy ignored him. "Well, I wanted to say good-bye. Miss... and Miss... and Miss... You've all been very kind to my kin and me." The boy did not look at Will.

"I do believe he's serious," Lady Gio said.

Kaoru knelt in front of the boy. His face was fixed in his decision.

"Surely the Taira army can spare a little boy?" Kaoru asked.

"I don't go to fight with the Taira, Sister... And I'm not so little."

"Son," Will said, kneeling beside Kaoru. "What do you mean to do?"

The little face lit up with pride. "If I can carry water for the Minamotos, Sir, that will be enough. If I can bring a warrior his armor, or cook his food—that will be enough."

"Can you carry armor?" Will asked. "A sparrow cannot build his nest with logs." Again, the boy ignored him.

Now Ginyo knelt in front of the boy. "But your family?" she said. "Surely they need you here."

"Here? Dad says two thirds of everything we own is grist for Heian-kyo. We cannot feed ourselves. I have heard him say: the Taira strut like peacocks and break the Emperor's laws. The Cloistered Emperor they placed under arrest, and now his son is killed. Minamoto Yoritomo will avenge these wrongs."

"The sparrow's wiser than his years," Will said admiringly.

The boy's eyes shone with pride. "Good-bye," he said, then turned his back on them, and on his childhood.

"How do you like that?" Ginyo said when the boy had gone. "Our little beansprout!"

"Can the Minamotos be so close?" Will wondered.

"The women say that there are bands that come and go in the night," Kaoru volunteered. "Lord Yoritomo Minamoto is raising armies to avenge the Prince's death."

"Many will need our help," Gio said.

Will looked out across the hills, searching for signs of the elusive Minamotos.

"But how can they take on the Tairas?" Kaoru wondered. "All the other clans together do not control as many provinces."

"And the Taira are well organized," Gio observed.

Will dropped the trowel he had been using to weed the garden. It clattered on a stone. The sisters turned to see his face flushed with self-accusation. He tried to say something, then ran up the hill.

"At last," Lance said softly.

"Now what do you suppose is wrong with him?" Kaoru asked.

Gio and Ginyo exchanged glances. Gio nodded. Ginyo excused herself and went into the temple to pray.

Some thirty minutes later she found Will on the high hill overlooking the village. He was so engrossed in his thoughts he didn't see or hear her approach. She stood and looked at him for a moment. Her heart was still beating hard from the climb, and sweat glazed her face. But it wasn't only the climb that quickened her heart. Wordlessly, she sat beside him on the lightning-cloven tree. Five minutes passed . . . Ten minutes . . . Fifteen minutes . . . At last he turned to look at her.

"I am a fool," he said. She shook her head. Her eyes were kind and patient.

"I lost my way," he said.

"Buddha put you on the path to our door," she said.

"That may be . . . but now, he puts me on another path."

She withdrew the small, lacquered *makie* box that she had tucked into the bodice of her summer kimono. A pattern of black and white wheels was half submerged in a river. They seemed to be bobbing along in the current. She handed it to Will. He looked at her quizzically. "Open it," she said softly.

Inside there was a sash of white silk. "I do not want to touch it with my dirty hands," Will said. Ginyo smiled.

"It is all that I have left from the floating world," she said softly with the slightest tinge of regret. "When I performed the white-suit dance, I wore this sash." She thought back to the court, the 'good people,' the courtiers, the pageants. "It was long ago," she said, jutting her chin. She smiled her ironic smile. "Now it is yours."

Will got down on his knees. "Milady, you have honored me more than you can know." He kissed the hem of her garment. Her hand trembled lightly through the air above his bowed head, then she withdrew it. They stared at one another. His eyes entreated her to let him rise to embrace her—once, just once. Quietly, firmly, without reproach, without judgment, her eyes said no.

"When will you leave?" she asked him.

"Tomorrow morning..."

She stared at the little silver band that was the stream that bound the village's life. Above the river, on the road from the capital, the destitute and the ambitious rubbed shoulders, crisscrossed each other's paths.

"Do you think, if we had met...?"

She shrugged. "Who can say? I was such a silly creature... I doubt you would have loved me then..."

Now he could say it. She had allowed him to say it. "I would have loved you then, even as I love you now. I have crossed an ocean of time to find you. Only to lose you again... Your Buddha is unkind."

She smiled indulgently. "When the seasons alter, when the leaves fall from the trees, should the limbs say to the roots, 'Buddha is unkind?' When the rains come, soaking the parched land, and the water runs in rivulets, and the rivulets run together into a mighty river that floods the low-lying fields, taking the lives of men and women and children, should those who mourn the victims say, 'Buddha is unkind?'" She sighed heavily, trying to collect her thoughts. "There is the Law and there is Buddha's response to the Law."

"Didn't Buddha make the Law?" Will asked. "It stinks!"

She put her forefinger to her lips to hush him. "Nay, friend, dear friend, it is neither good nor bad. It only is. Only our response to it can matter."

Will wanted to protest the Law. He would tear up whatever stood between them. Yet, he also knew, it was her devotion to the Law, her serene acceptance, that inspired him. Yet he grieved.

"Shall we meet again, dear sister?"

She smiled, not ironically. "As surely as the stars will glitter in the sky ten thousand years from now, so, surely, we will meet again."

They sat together in the glow of the afternoon heat. They watched the sun spread a rosy veil as it glided towards the horizon. Silently, alone in their togetherness, they walked back under a silken tent of sky.

9 | Fire

They were just two more forlorn creatures in the street: a holy sister in her mid-twenties leading a crouched blind man. From time to time the holy sister would seem to speak encouraging words to her companion, who was led, for the most part, impassively. The man seemed unaccustomed to blindness; now and again he would raise his head and seem to strain against the darkness. "I know this street!" he would declare. Or, feeling against the stone wall, he'd halt a moment, trace the splintered wood of a gate, and announce, "Yes, I know this gate. This is the mansion of the Minister of Archives." Then Ginyo would look at him and wonder. Long ago it might have been the said dignitary's mansion, but it had changed hands several times in the intervening centuries.

They were searching for the house of Ginyo's aunt. Kaoru and Lady Gio had remained in the countryside, hoping to eke out a living. All four of them could not survive there, especially if, as was feared, the Taira raised taxes again. After the Tenth Month, after harvest time, Kaoru and Lady Gio hoped to have enough provisions to reunite with Lance and Ginyo. In the meantime, Lance would use his fine voice to try to attach himself to one of the noble families. Even in the worst of times, the arts had been supported. A blind biwa singer could at least earn his meager keep, and Ginyo would serve as a nurse in one of the temples. With the grace of Buddha they would weather the afflicted times.

Within an hour of entering the capital Ginyo realized how

naive they had been. Heian-kyo had been transformed. The stone walls that had surrounded the great estates were overgrown with weeds and pockmarked where children had hurled stones. The artificial lakes had been left unattended, the carp and gaily-colored imported fish left to die and putrefy in the scummy water. The shells of houses destroyed by the great fires or quakes of recent years had been left to stand, overrun by rodents and rodent-like cats.

The streets themselves were appalling. The famine that had begun three years before had its epicenter in the capital. Those who clung to former dreams of glory starved on the diets of blasted hopes, false pride, misdirected loyalties. Even as the world had once seemed immovable, unchanging in its rounds of perfume contests, poetry recitals, cherry-blossom and moon-viewing, so now the fixed center of things had shifted, and events of state and economy moved with dazzling and poorly comprehended speed, stranding the blurry-eyed inhabitants on an island that was too harsh, too bitter—yet all they knew, all they could imagine.

"I know this smell," Lance said. It was the smell of death on the battlefield, the odor of decay. It sent him back to Mt. Badon and the great battles with Arthur. It was an odor he had hoped to forget. For Ginyo, who had no experience to call upon, the sights and smells were daunting. She leaned against a chinked stone wall and retched.

Lance rubbed her back. "Dear Sister, leave this place. Leave me here—one more misfit to make his way among the ruins. This is my fate, not yours. In my youth I swaggered, I did wrong to one who loved me as his son. What wrong did you do? Your soul is clean. Go and be kind where your kindness may do good."

Ginyo jutted her chin. "Good Sir, your path and mine—and your good friend's and mine—are bound together like a sheaf of straw in a farmer's hand. If my aunt is living in this city of corpses, I must find her, help her. If I can do some kindness, let me do it here."

So they proceeded along Red Bird Avenue. Under the willows,

emaciated mothers roped themselves against tree trunks to suckle their emaciated babes. Some mothers and some infants had died in the posture, so the dead suckled the living, or the living suckled the dead. Corpses strew the streets of the three-hundred-yard wide avenue, kicked to the gutters by barefooted soldiers who cleared the way for the ox-drawn carriages of those who had scurried above the rat heaps. Children and brigands ransacked the dead and dying. Wooden images of the Buddha of Mercy were stolen from temples, used for firewood. The favors of girls were hawked by their fathers—boys, too. And those who rode in the palanquins pulled the curtains tighter against the light, or sang old songs to drown out the cries of the hungry. Those who had not been touched by the disasters considered themselves blessed by the virtue of their former lives, and shrewder than those who had fallen. They doubled their offerings at the family shrines, and doubled again the time they recited the sutras. And they hardened their hearts.

But Lance's heart was filled with pity. He had seen the great city in yesterday's dream, and he remembered it as clearly as the face of new-found love. As Ginyo described the scenes, a dam burst inside him. Now it seemed to him that the great capital was enveloped by flames of hatred and indifference. Words he had heard in a small church long ago now spilled out of his heart, and he sang the hermit-monk's words:

> 'And the Lord said unto Cain, Where is Abel thy brother?
> And he said, I know not. Am I my brother's keeper?
> And He said, What hast thou done? The voice
> of thy brother's blood crieth unto me from the ground.'

Those who stood near Ginyo and Lance stood still, and wondered who this strange pair were, what twists and turns had caused their fall. The clear voice of the singer still rang in their ears when they heard the gruff orders to disband.

The orders were given by a vanguard of military men.

Suddenly Red Bird Avenue was a hive of efficiency. The stragglers who had crowded the street were hurried along, pushed by halberd-wielding foot soldiers. Large screens were set up all along the avenue so that a stray glance would not disturb the imperial entourage. The cavalry now whipped the oxen which had been bearing the carriages of the 'good people' at their steady 2 and 1/2 miles per hour. The tormented animals lumbered along the potholed streets, shaking up passengers who were lost in nostalgia. A cloud of dust rose as the procession from Rokuhara entered Red Bird. Six-hundred cavalry protected the carriage of Kiyomori's son, wife and grandson. Munemori, Lady Nii, and, most precious cargo of all, 3-year old Antoku, the 81st Emperor, rode by in sublime oblivion.

Save for the clatter of hooves on the road, save for the wheels of the carriages turning, and the footfalls of his Highness's entourage, a strange quiet settled over Red Bird Avenue. The beggars who moments before had wept openly over their fate, the merchants who had been hawking their wares, the pimps and the prostitutes hushed themselves and waited. Only the cranky voice of the 3-year-old Emperor of Japan was heard from behind the silk curtains. Only that illustrious, revered voice of the Sun-Goddess's offspring; and then, softly, unmistakably, the strings of the biwa were plucked, and another voice rose from behind the screened streets:

> "'In Thee, O Lord, do I put my trust:
> let me never be put to confusion.
> Deliver me in Thy righteousness . . .
> Be Thou my strong habitation . . .
> Deliver me, O my God, out of the hand of the wicked,
> out of the hand of the unrighteous.'"

Ginyo's mouth dropped open. After a shocked moment, the Captain of the Cavalry ordered the screens that hid the voice torn down.

"Hurry, we must run!" Ginyo pleaded, pulling Lance's arm.

But, possessed, he kept singing the strange words. His voice was pure and strong. The words were Japanese, but no one had heard such combinations before.

And an odd thing happened. Behind the white curtains, in the carriage where Kiyomori's wife, son and grandson sat, the cranky three-year-old Emperor clapped his divine hands together, smiled, and said, "Good!"

A brutish foot soldier kicked down the screens and was about to sever the head that had dared disturb the royal procession. The foot soldier looked to his Captain, Ginyo stepped in front of Lance, shielding his body with her own. Only her intervention delayed the order. The foot soldier would have been pleased to behead them both on the spot.

The Captain raised his arm. The foot soldier raised his sword. From within the carriage, Lord Munemori, Kiyomori's son, called out "Stop!"

Lord Munemori stepped out of the carriage. Like a pack of cards falling, hundreds of foot soldiers dropped to one knee. The cavaliers quieted their horses. Dressed comfortably in his carmine hunting suit, Munemori moved with easy grace, like a sunset cloud amidst his guard. He approached Ginyo and Lance. Ginyo was trembling like the last leaf in the autumn wind. And Lance sang again:

> "'Let my mouth be filled with Thy praise
> and Thy honor all the day.
> Cast me not off in the time of old age;
> forsake me not when my strength faileth . . .
> Now also when I am old and gray-headed,
> O God, forsake me not;
> until I have showed Thy strength unto this generation.
> Thou, which has showed me great and sore troubles,
> shalt quicken me again,
> and shalt bring me up again
> from the depths of the earth.'"

Behind Munemori in the curtained carriage, the sweet voice of Antoku laughed and sang out, "Good."

"Who is this?" asked Lord Munemori.

Ginyo, coming to her senses, dropped to her knees and burrowed her forehead into the ground. "Oh, Mighty Lord, please forgive this babbling old man. He means no harm. Too much sadness has unhorsed his mind. His voice runs wild without a saddle."

"Hush!" Munemori said, and Ginyo hushed, trembling. Munemori studied the blind man's face. He walked around Lance, looking him over. "It is an interesting face," he told the Captain of the Cavalry. "Ugly, and distorted . . . but interesting."

The Captain warily nodded.

"I do not know what nonsense the man sings," Lord Munemori said to his troops. "But he has a pleasing voice. The Emperor has been restless all day. Frankly, his divine whining was driving me nuts."

Lance laughed. "That's well-said, Sir,"

Ginyo shook more violently. The foot soldier's hand opened and closed on the hilt of his sword. The Captain watched for a signal from Munemori. After a moment, Munemori smiled. "You are too saucy for your own good, Singer! For now, however, you please me. His Highness is amused by you. I bid you join our entourage." Munemori examined Ginyo. "This female is your daughter?" he asked Lance.

"As near to me as my sun," Lance said.

"You speak in riddles, old man. We'll take your riddles for our baby's rattle. The woman, too. She may unriddle you when you have perplexed me."

"She may indeed, Sir."

Munemori bid Ginyo stand. He studied her face now. Something about it seemed familiar. "Have we met before, Madam?"

Ginyo hesitated. "You might say we met in another lifetime, Sir."

Munemori smiled. "Another riddler! Well enough. Two birds

with one stone!" He looked beyond the screen at the haggard bodies of men and women who were bowing and trembling in front of him. "Restore the screens!" he ordered.

*

Commander Nakatomi's assistant stoked the coals in the forge with a rake. The flames sizzled around the double fist-sized block of iron. Dressed in white trousers and white shirts, with white bandanas around their scalps, the Commander and his assistant worked in the semi-darkness of the hut, their eyes trained on the glowing iron. The Commander worked the bellows with his left hand while turning the iron with his right. The bellows, which the Commander had invented, allowed him to control the temperature by adjusting the flow of air. The bellows, and trial by fire, had enabled the Commander to manufacture the best swords in the world.

It had taken him ten years to perfect his techniques. Ten years after Buretsu's assassination, Yamato enjoyed prosperity under the reign of Keitai. But when he looked into the flames of the forge, the Commander saw other times when there was no peace and the blood-lusting Kami flourished. So he pumped the bellows and turned the block of iron.

Wordlessly, he removed the iron, brushed off fiery debris with a sheaf of strawstalk that smoked on contact. He lay the glowing iron on the anvil. The hammer rose above his assistant's head, then clanked on the coal-red metal. Over and over. Over and over. Muscles bulged. Sweat flew and sizzled against iron and charcoal. Another assistant took over the hammering. Heating, hammering, turning, heating, hammering, turning. And when the metal sang in a certain way, when the glow was the color of sunset in a particular mountain village on a cold, bright day in early winter, the folding began. A little water was poured onto the molten block and the sword was folded back on itself, thrust into the forge again, hammered again. Twenty times the metal would be folded and thrust and hammered until it had more than a million layers. Each hammer blow put the strength of the hammer, the resistance of the anvil, the cunning of the man into the iron. Each layering would give flexibility, resilience and strength. They would use twenty-five bags of charcoal—and only the charcoal of pine trees would do. And after six weeks they'd produce a sword that would not rust, though it lay for centuries at the bottom of the sea. A sword as alive as the earth from which it came, as subtle as the man who wielded it in his hands.

Commander Nakatomi thrust the sword-in-the-making into the forge. The flames shot up.

*

The flames hissed as one of the Minamoto foot soldiers poured water over the makeshift stove. "You've left a piece of rabbit to burn," said his companion.

"Leave it for the farmers," said the first.

"We'd better be joining the others," said the companion, looking around anxiously.

"They'll never miss us," said the first.

"They will if there's trouble," his companion warned. "Yoritomo Minamoto does not abide loose discipline. I heard of a soldier in another unit who broke ranks to go and forage for himself. He wandered in five minutes late for some such drill. He has no ears to break the cold wind now."

The first foot soldier had heard similar tales. "We'd better hurry," he said, anxious now. He kicked dirt over the stove. The two men seized their sickle-bladed halberds and ran off into the woods.

After a decent interval, two hands parted the bushes. Furtive, feral eyes looked out. A hollow, sunless face peeped out. Then the woodsman came forward into the clearing.

Will sniffed the air for foot soldiers. Waves of nausea swept over his body. He fell upon his knees and retched. Breathing hard, sweating, he brushed the dirt off the rabbit meat and stuffed it into his mouth. It hurt to chew. He had already lost a tooth to malnourishment. All of his teeth were loose.

His eyes filled with bitter tears, remembering his humiliation. The Minamoto warrior had shone in his lamellaed armor, his helmet with its golden horns. He looked down at Will from the mount of his horse, also armored and glittering in the sun. Will had bowed like a suppliant. That's what he was.

"This beggar wants to join our forces," said the foot soldier Will had first approached.

The horseman looked Will over shrewdly. "Where do you come from, *soldier*?" The horseman used the word derisively. The onlookers tightened their cheeks to keep from laughing.

"From the north, Sir."

"From the north? You mean like the wind?" The foot soldiers tittered.

"I can shoot an arrow, Sir!" Will blurted.

The horseman steadied his restive mount. "You can shoot an arrow, yet you have none. Nor armor neither, save for your thick skin. Get back to your rice-planting, country boy! We need men with horses, men with weapons and armor. Not scarecrows who have lost their stuffing!"

Will ate the dust of the retreating hooves. His face burned red with shame.

Yet he had followed them. Always trailing behind, and scavenging on their leftovers. He had watched the farmers level their little plots of ground, firm the earthen banks around them. The little dikes were raised and the water flowed into the plots, covering them. They sowed the seeds, and then stood knee-deep in the water—men and women, old and young, children and grandchildren—bending their backs in the hot sun, transplanting the delicate, grasslike shoots—one by one, bending, pressing in the earth, bending again in backbreaking toil. Sometimes they sang to relieve the monotony. Sometimes they'd stand up straight in the fields to watch him pass—a tall, gaunt, scarecrow figure who piqued their curiosity and relieved their tedium for a moment. The days grew longer, hotter, moister and the farmers and their families guarded the vulnerable plants against the ravages of insects, storms and thieving neighbors.

Will slept in the rain under a dripping lean-to shelter of leaves. He wondered what had possessed him to leave Ginyo and Lance. He wondered if they fared better in the capital. He prayed for their safety. To the Gods of Britain he prayed; to the God of Rome; to the Gods of Yamato at Heian-kyo; to any God who would listen.

He longed to return to them, to share their fate. But he could not. He must not.

Under the blanket of the summer night, he watched the shooting stars, listened to his stomach growl, and knew that whatever had lifted him from the marshes of Britain to transplant him to the rice paddies of Yamato had not done with him yet. Carefully, he unwound the cloth binding around Ginyo's *makie* box and opened the lid. The silken sash shimmered under the shooting stars.

He'd get back to them, somehow, back to those he loved. But first he'd finish what he'd started. He would not return a failure, to burden their hard lives. He'd come back with prosperity and position—the spoils of war, won by courage and endurance.

Upon the loom of the stars the comets shot silk threads of light this way and that. And Will slept and dreamed as the hammers fell repeatedly and the charcoal blazed and the blade was layered in the distant forge.

*

On the fifteenth day of the Eighth Month, Kiyomori himself opened the cages of all the household larks. Lord Yukitaka, his principal confidant, demurred over so unusual a gesture. But Kiyomori, in high spirits, assured his ally it was a fitting tribute to Hachiman, the God of War. The song birds rose into the air, floated on air currents, sang their poignant melodies, then plunged back to their cages. The servants had to shoo the confused birds away.

Kiyomori laughed. "It is even so with men," he declared. "They think they want freedom, they sing lovingly of it, and then they don't know what to do with it."

Lord Kiyomori had not been in such high spirits earlier that morning. He had awakened from a perplexing dream. An army of farmers was transplanting seedlings on a vast plain. A headless man walked down the country road. The man was attired in ceremonial robes. When the farmers beheld this headless man, they stopped their work, dropped to their knees and bowed, burying their faces in the water of the paddies. The headless man toppled over an embankment and blood began to pour out of the severed trunk. A great stream of blood gushed into the fields, darkening them, reddening them. Never lifting their heads, the farmers drowned in the maroon waters. Then the rice stalks began to grow—as a man and higher. They transformed into sickle-bladed halberds.

Immediately on waking Kiyomori summoned officials from the Bureau of Divination. The Yin-Yang Masters were frightened by the dream, but reluctant to speak of it. They hemmed and hawed about the ambiguities, how symbols might mean one thing one day and quite another the next. "Idiots!" Kiyomori stormed. "What are you paid for?" He was about to dismiss them all when the youngest stepped forward. The others watched with a dreadful curiosity. They knew the upstart was taking his life in his hands. The young man knew it as well. It was his bid for power and influence. Besides, he was certain of his skills.

"The army of farmers is simply . . . an army of farmers," said the young man, and the others breathed a sigh of relief. "They are doing what they always do: attending to their simple chores and acting stupidly." Here the listeners smiled and nodded in agreement. "Go on!" Kiyomori ordered.

"The headless corpse is, of course, the late Prince Mochihito. The traitor's head was never found, but there can be no doubts about the body that was found."

"Yes, that was my thought, too," said Kiyomori.

"Well, it is relatively easy from here," said the young diviner. "The Prince's blood spills into the fields, as if to nourish the seedlings. That would be the usual interpretation." Here the diviner looked haughtily at his colleagues. "But the stupid farmers are drowned in the blood," he continued. "Those farmers are the army Yoritomo Minamoto hopes to field."

Kiyomori clapped his hands. "Yes! I knew it!"

"And the rice stalks that turned into halberds?" the careful Lord Yukitaka asked.

"They are Lord Kiyomori's weapons," the diviner announced, turning to the Priest-Premiere. "Just as in your dream of many years ago when the Goddess of Itsukushima Shrine handed you the halberd and you awoke to find it by your side. As the halberds rise over the bodies of the farmers, so the invincible Taira will rise over the Minamoto locusts."

Kiyomori clapped Lord Yukitaka on the back. "Didn't I tell you? Even as I thought."

The other diviners raised their eyebrows to one another. They were not so certain.

But the young Yin-Yang Master was awarded with a promotion in rank.

Two days later Yoritomo Minamoto led a ragged band of followers in an attack against the Vice Governor of Izu Province. Surprising the Taira officer in his sleep, they slew him, then fled into the hills. It was Yoritomo's first act of armed insurrection. It also marked the last time the young diviner would ever practice his art.

Upon the crossbeams with the common criminals, the young diviner's head seemed out of place, as it tilted back into the shawl it had once worn so proudly. The marbled eyes gazed meaninglessly at the yin and yang of the world, and the mouth sneered tellingly at those who had gambled and lost. His little sister stood before the head and waved the joss sticks of incense back and forth, back and forth to sweeten the journey of her brother's soul.

*

Had Kiyomori been less impetuous, the Yin-Yang Master might have lived a few months longer. After he had slain the Vice Governor, Yoritomo and three-hundred mounted soldiers barricaded themselves at Ishibashi-yama, some three-hundred miles north of the capital. A Taira force of a thousand decimated the Minamotos' ragtag outfit. Yoritomo would certainly have been killed were it not for the intervention of an unarmed farmer.

When it was clear that the Minamotos were lost, this scarecrow-creature crept out of the woods and raced to the body of one of the fallen archers. The man seemed to run between the whizzing arrows—fleet as a fox and twice as agile. In seconds he let fly a dozen arrows, ten of which found their marks, delivered with such force as to pierce the armor of his assailants. The Minamotos cheered the newcomer with the short, thick forearm, and the Taira, who had been preparing for an easy rout, paused to regroup.

That pause gave Yoritomo a chance to escape. He fled into the mountains while the thick-armed stranger covered his back. The remaining Minamotos fought with renewed courage and the Taira fell back. The lull in the battle lasted long enough for the stranger to undo the armor from one of the slain warriors. When the Taira pressed forward again, they saw the thick-armed stranger rise like a phoenix over the corpses. His light blue armor with lacings of green silk seemed to shimmer like the calm sea in the midst of the grayness of battle. Their best archers aimed at this blue-green sea, but the sea melted into the earth.

When reports of the battle reached Kiyomori he thought he had put an end to the crisis. Of course, the reports neglected to mention the curious, thick-armed archer. Neither could they measure the ferocity with which the northern yokels had fought.

Armed with bow and arrow, Will hunted for himself now. His sinewy body filled out on a diet of rabbits, herons and deer. He learned to smell men, and to hear them at great distances—their breathing, whispers, spitting, shitting, farting, pissing. The half-hearted attempt the Tairas made to pursue the Minamotos was easily eluded. In the forests that surrounded the perfect cone of Mt. Fuji, Will learned the ways of the hunter. He bathed in the cold mountain lakes and caught silvery fish with his bare hands. The weather grew cooler, the days shorter and some instinct told him it was time to leave his mountain fastness. He followed the Tokaido Road along the coast. At the extreme Western end Yoritomo had established his military headquarters.

At the Eastern end, in Heian-kyo, the Taira nobles tried to forget the recent unpleasantries. In the Ninth Moon they drank wine steeped with chrysanthemums. In the Tenth Month, they ate special cakes to protect against illness and misfortunes.

Will concealed himself in the underbrush, behind the mugwort and the rushes. Out on patrol, the Taira soldiers chatted like old women. He'd catch a word here, a phrase there, sometimes a whole sentence. He felt the sea breezes blow off Suruga Bay and the gulls called to him, "Don't wait! Don't tarry!" So he thanked the gulls and went on his way.

*

In the Tenth Month the farmers harvested millet, rice, hemp and beans. They made offerings to their household gods, and joined together in ceremonies at the village shrines. Lord Kiyomori and his son Lord Munemori traveled from Rokuhara Palace to present their sacrifices at Itsukushima Shrine.

"It is a floating temple!" Ginyo remarked wonderingly. "When the tide comes in the whole temple rests on pylons in the water, and it seems like a great bird taking its leisure."

"And the *torii*?" Lance asked.

"The apple-red *torii* is submerged up to the first crossbeams. It is like a Chinese box kite floating on the water. When the tide goes out, the fishermen and women gather around the *torii* searching for clams in the mud. The tallest amongst them cannot come one third up to the crossbeams."

The principal Shinto priest who tended the shrine at Itsukushima, removed the 32 sutra scrolls dedicated to the House of Taira. Kiyomori and his sons had personally copied the sutras onto the gold leaf paper. Gilt and crystal knobs turned the scrolls, which were hand-painted with scenes from nature, literature and the court. "Surely the Kami will smile on us," the Taira thought, justly proud of their shrine.

But the Kami had plans of their own.

Seventy-thousand Taira drove into the Eastern provinces. The Minamoto forces retreated like ebbing water. When they were pressed, they offered no resistance, and yet they seemed to be everywhere surrounding the invading army. Taira Major General Koremori was twenty-three years old. He needed better recommendation for office than simply being one of Kiyomori's grandsons!

To learn the number of Minamoto that confronted them, Major General Koremori relied on the testimony of a captured messenger who could not count above a thousand. "Tell us the number of the Minamoto forces!" Koremori demanded.

"For a week or more," said the messenger, "on plains, rivers, mountains and seas, the soldiers swarm like migratory bids."

"How many?" pressed Koremori.

The prisoner scratched his chin. "I have heard it said that the Minamotos move like a great wave over the land. They take what they need and then move on. They don't take more than they need. They are not frightened when their bellies growl. Thus they gain allies. The other clans are flocking to them. All those with some grievance against the Priest-Premiere offer aid to the Minamotos, add their banners to their pennons."

Koremori's adjutant slapped the messenger. "How many?" he barked. Koremori stayed the adjutant's hand before he struck again.

"I have heard two-hundred-thousand," said the messenger.

Koremori blanched. "It cannot be," said the adjutant. "This dog lies. Behead him for his lies!"

But Koremori had a noble heart. "Let him be treated as any other prisoner of war." Then he looked pointedly at the adjutant. "Let this news go no further."

"Let this news go no further," the adjutant said later that day when he repeated the number to his trusted confidant.

"Let this news go no further," said the trusted confidant to his lieutenant. And by nightfall the phrase had been repeated hundreds of times, so that every officer knew. In each of their hearts the longing for wife and child or mother and father grew hourly.

In the mornings the men saw their breath about their faces, they shook out the dampness from the mats they had lain on the ground. Day by day the two massive armies advanced, while the great cone of the slumbering volcano cast giant shadows, caught sunrise and sunset and moonrise, and seemed to mock them all. Like Sumo wrestlers the armies advanced, pounding the earth and posturing, and waiting, waiting to wear out patience, waiting for the attack.

On the morning of the twenty second, the adjutant escorted Sanemori to the Major General. Koremori studied the rough-hewn, pock-marked face.

"We are told your village borders the Eastern provinces," Koremori said. "As you are our finest archer, tell us, truly: the men of the eight Eastern provinces—are there many who can match your prowess with the bow?"

Sanemori raised his brows. "Am I your finest archer?" He smiled ironically. "Thirteen handbreadths I can draw an arrow. In the East, they do that for hunting hares. I have heard of an archer who draws fifteen handbreadths on his worst days. It takes five ordinary footsoldiers to bend his powerful bow. His arrows can pierce three armored suits in a row . . . You have heard, I suppose, at Ishibashi-yama a warrior came out of the woods and loosed his quiver of arrows in the blink of an eye. Bamboo cutters have thick right arms from hacking all day long. Their eyes are keen as hawks. Now they are bowmen!

"The Lord of a small manor can support half a thousand men. Because the Lord has shared their hardships, because he knows their names and families, they fight for him and will die for him. The horsemen of the East fly with their horses over the worst terrains. Hearing that their parents or their children have been killed, they do not pause, but rush headlong into battle.

"In the West, it is another story. Hearing that their parents have succumbed, the warriors retire from the field and recite the Buddhist sutras to comfort their parents' souls. Should their children be killed, they cannot fight at all; so filled with grief, they care not for victory or defeat. Those men grouse at winter cold, summer heat, rain, flies, the moldy rations. The Eastern soldiers take such things in stride."

The adjutant objected. "Our officers are skilled in the civilizing arts. Each one of them is a gentleman. Each one of them can think for himself. These qualities more than match the country skills of our enemies!"

Sanemori crooked his eye at the adjutant's smooth face. "That so? Well, that may be . . . But somewhere I heard it said in *The Art of War*: a general must know the landscape well. These are Minamoto woods, not Taira. Strategy counts far more than numbers. Guard your backs! I for one expect to see my wife and babes no more."

"What a preposterous little man!" the adjutant said, after Sanemori returned to the ranks. But he watched his back more carefully. So did all the others.

Over the peninsula of Izu, all along Suruga Bay, the farmers and fishermen said: "Today we must leave." "Surely the battle will come today." But there was no place to go, and their instincts bade them stay. Will thought, too, "The battle must come today," but he remained aloof, still concealing himself, easy in the woods in the shadow of Fuji's cone.

On the twenty-third day of the Tenth Month the two armies faced each other from opposite sides of the Wisteria River. Now they could avoid the battle no longer. The farmers grabbed their wives and children and headed for the plains, the mountains, the forests. The fishermen and their babbling families took to boats on the river, on the sea.

"Beansprout," the brewer's son, who had just managed to catch up to the dust of the armies, but could for now advance no further, blissfully innocent, kindled a small fire to keep himself warm. Seeing that one fire from a distance, a farmer thought it well to kindle one of his own. When all the farmers and fishermen had kindled their fires for their evening meals, the hearts of the Taira soldiers plunged. "See the fires of the Minamoto soldiers!" they cried. "They cover the plains, the mountains and the sea. They are more numerous than the stars. The messenger spoke the truth!"

Will heard their lamenting, and he slipped into the woods. In his fur shoes he walked to the marshes where he had made his home. Thousands of ducks lay with their heads curled back, resting on their folded wings, one eye open, while the other eye slept.

Will knelt down and whispered to a beetle: "Thousands of men are coming, even as I speak. They will set fire to the plains and the forest. For the mercy of Buddha, I tell you. Save yourself, but tell no one else."

Then the beetle said to the grasshopper who was about to devour it: "Spare me, and I will tell you something to save your life."

And the grasshopper told the sparrow who would devour it. And the sparrow told the mallard who was its friend. And the mallard told its cousins who slept with one eye open. The drakes raised the alarm. With a storm-like whirring of wings, thousands of mallards rose into the air, casting ghostly shadows. Then the ospreys rose, dropping the fish from their beaks. The egrets and the cormorants cried out. And the herons beat white wings like the sound of a thousand bows releasing.

"The Minamoto are coming!" cried the Taira sentries. The officers feared they would be attacked from the rear. The twenty-three-year-old Major General ordered a retreat.

Fearing encirclement, some of the warriors left their bows behind, some left quivers full of arrows. Some jumped upon horses that were still tethered, and whipped the poor animals, who bucked and neighed. Some rode around in circles. Some officers ran from tents in their undergarments, frightened prostitutes clinging to their arms.

At dawn, the Minamoto warriors lined the banks of the Wisteria River. Three times their battle cry was lifted to heaven.

In the Taira camp, a lone, whimpering prostitute lay in the rubble of the night's confusion.

*

The bamboo rustled like the plumes of giant pens. The upper section of the latticed window was open to the autumn weather. In the weaving room Lance and Ginyo stretched the *obi* on the wooden frame. She led Lance to the bin of dyed silk threads, of various colors, curled and ribboned like the finest human hair. His hands played over the threads. He lay out a dozen upon the linen cloth on the straw mat. His fingertips caressed them, and his fingertips remembered Sagami's hair. "This one," he said. "This . . . this . . . and this . . ."

Ginyo studied his selection. "Yes, it will work," she said. "Not what I would have chosen, of course." Then her mind went to work, striving against the limitations. Her mind worked harder than it would have, and gave her better results. Lance, of course, chose only by texture and intuition.

In the courtyard, the official time keepers plucked their bowstrings and warned evil spirits to behave themselves for the next half hour. A gong beat out the hour of the day.

Ginyo sat back upon her white *tabi* socks, and rubbed two silk threads together in her hands. What would the daughter of Munemori like for her first adult kimono? She thought of the girl's character, how long she held a gaze, the tilt of her head. It was hard to think of pretty designs when the world was at war, but Ginyo shooed the other thoughts away. She decided on wildflowers under an autumn sky.

"Ginyo-san, I have been wondering about something," Lance said softly.

"Yes, Uncle?"

"Are there no songs from the tenth century in which a woman expresses longing for a stranger from another land?"

Ginyo pondered. "Let me think . . ." She ran the first stitch through the cloth, then plunged the needle back, half a fingernail away. "From another province?" she asked.

"Nay. From another land, from the ancient land of Ch'in?"

"No, Uncle, I don't believe there is such a song."

Lance sighed. Had Sagami never written about their love? It seemed inconceivable she would not have expressed her loss in song. Then what had become of her?

Ginyo heard the sigh and tried to deflect Lance's sad mood. "They say the capital will move back to Heian-kyo."

"Perhaps we will get word of Will," Lance said hopefully.

Ginyo pricked her finger at the name. Quickly, carefully, she moved her forefinger away from the sash. She pressed it with her thumb. A tiny droplet of blood appeared. She sucked on it.

In the capital, the 81st Emperor of Japan sucked his forefinger. He followed his grandfather's example and poked a small, wet hole in the paper *shoji* door. His grandfather dandled him and cooed. "Such a clever boy!" Taira Kiyomori summoned his attendants. "Save this screen," he ordered. "Mark this hole with the Emperor's characters. This one, with his loving grandfather's. Record the date here."

A chill wind blew from a drafty corridor and Kiyomori shuddered. He hunched his shoulders, and rocked the three-year-old Emperor in his arms. He coughed and bid Lord Yukitaka take the infant, and barked out orders for someone to find the confounded draft.

Two months later Kiyomori still did not feel like himself. It was one month after the capital had been moved back to Heian-kyo.

According to his spies, the Minamoto resistance was encountering internal dissension. Meanwhile, the Taira had fortified their positions. Kiyomori had had auspicious dreams. Yet he did not feel right. Perhaps it was because of his malaise that he decided to settle an old score. Three days before the New Year, he ordered the burning of the Nara temples.

He had been wary of the priests since their support of Prince Mochihito seven months before. Since then the militant monks had insulted his emissaries and rebuffed his attempts for reconciliation.

The images that had been chiseled from single cypress trees burned like torches. Bronze images melted into their alloys and spilled molten death through the halls where the children recited sutras. Perhaps Buddha opened his eyes wide with horror. Women ran through the halls and succumbed to the choking black smoke.

They had pulled up the ladders to escape from the soldiers. Now the flames spread rapidly from roof to roof in the fierce wind of the Twelfth Month. The tiles caved in on top of the worshippers. The scrolls of the founders perished in the flames.

Horses in the stables kicked against their stalls. The Buddha that was sixteen *jo* in height, polished by Emperor Shomu's hand four-hundred years before, melted and transformed itself into grotesque shapes. The bronze lotuses crackled and sizzled. The lame and the old were caught napping. Some priests dove into the flames. They could not bear to live in the world anymore.

Kiyomori's sons shook their heads when told. They remembered the ancient Emperor's saying: "So long as my temple prospers, so will the country; as my temple declines, so will the country."

Ginyo wept all day when she heard. "To kill the warrior monks!" she cried. "They, at least, were men with weapons! But why torch the buildings? Thirty-five-hundred men, women and children dead! Do the Taira think they can destroy our history?"

Perhaps if the Priest-Premiere had been in better health he

would not have made so stupid a blunder. The volatile warrior monks had been agrieved over ancient slights. A little sweet talk would have won them to Kiyomori's side—or at least induced their neutrality. Now the faithful throughout the Empire conspired against the Taira.

At the Hachiman Shrine in Kamakura, Yoritomo Minamoto made oblations for the New Year. As he ascended the wide, steep stairs, one green roof rose above the other like two birds settling to land. The columns that supported the first of the roofs were simple, elegant—as befitted the shrine to the God of War.

Yoritomo hated the ostentations of the Taira shrine at Itsukushima, the obsequious posturings of the court. He promised himself he would never go back there. He would not make the mistake of the Tairas who had allowed themselves to be seduced by refinements.

He had chosen his headquarters well. The fishing village of Kamakura was flanked on three sides by wooded mountains. An unlikely attack from the sea would allow the defendants to pull back, and harry the invaders from the mountains. Attack from the rear was even more unlikely and untenable.

During the lull in the fighting his men trained vigorously, shooting arrows from galloping horses. Among many champions, the one with the short, thick right arm often distinguished himself. With such men, and with the War God's help, Yoritomo was sure he could not lose.

Each day he was in contact with the clan leaders of the Eastern provinces. He learned how to ask for favors, how to summon aid, how to offer protection and appeal to common interests. The most capable soldiers were those in his own family. Blood will tell, Yoritomo thought with a note of self-warning. Their capacities required the utmost vigilance!

*

Ginyo adjusted the last screen against the lattice. Even with the screens up, the room was cold and drafty. She and Lance were dressed in thick, winter kimonos. The charcoal braziers sputtered and gave off insufficient heat. Outside, the wind howled across the Kanto plain, drove the frothing waves of the Inland Sea, carried ice and malice in its beak and talons, mountains of snow on its wings. The bamboo bent like bows and scratched the lattices like the long fingernails of the dead.

The time-keepers beat the gongs. Even the fierce weather could not still the gongs.

"I shall never finish!" Ginyo said with a frown. "And now we're to leave again! In this weather! At this time of year!"

Lance tried to keep her talking about the gods. That was their way. Their conversations kept them sane, helped get them through the dreary months. Each evening Lance's fingertips inspected the embroidery. "Tell me the colors," he'd say. "And she would answer: damask rose, emerald, teal blue, carnelian. "Yes, I see it!" he'd say. "It is good."

"It is slow," she'd complain.

It had always been tedious work, but she seemed to feel it more now. Each day she'd wait for the gossip from the capital. She'd get a morsel here, a tidbit there. "Had the rebels been vanquished? What of their internal rivalries? Were there prisoners?" In Lord Munemori's palace, rumors crested like the waves of the sea and the frail vessel of the human heart was tossed and battered.

In the First Month, the Priest-Premiere sent his eighteen-year-old granddaughter to the Cloistered Emperor. The result of a tryst with an Itsukushima shrine maiden, the lovely girl, accoutered like an Empress, arrived with a panoply of nobles, courtiers and ladies-in-waiting. Now fifty three, Go-Shirakawa received his trophy happily.

"The Priest-Premiere hopes to make amends," the rumor-mongers whispered. "It is too late," said the others.

"Perhaps there will be a general amnesty for the rebels," said the loose tongues.

Then Ginyo worked well at the embroidery, her fingers moving surely, swiftly. The next day someone would have had a dream, or a two-headed baby would have been born in the provinces. Then it seemed that a long war was inevitable, that Hachiman himself was drawing the bow of Japan. Then Ginyo's fingers erred and she'd have to start over.

Sometimes, staring at the unfinished wildflowers, a tear would moisten her cheek. She'd dispel the thought, and try to dispel the face that swam in her memory. But at night, in her dark apartments, the tears would run into the whorls of her ears, and she would try to remember every detail, every syllable she and Will had spoken.

Sometimes it seemed Lance heard the tears she wept in silence, reproaching herself for weeping, and reproaching the reproaches. Then Lance would ask her questions only scholars could know. She would compose her mind and try to be helpful.

"You were telling me about the gods," Lance reminded her now.

"Yes, the gods," Ginyo said, laying her needle aside. "In the old days it was very simple. The people worshipped the Kami—the good and bad spirits of the land. Sometimes the Kami were ancestors. An emperor might return as a Kami. Or a demon might be a Kami. Do you see what I mean?" Ginyo blushed. She tried to avoid the word "see" when she spoke to him.

"Please continue . . ." he said in a comforting voice.

"Well, it was all very simple, but complex, too. I mean, the idea was simple. But each village had its own Kami. If the people thought a particular place was beautiful, if they felt a spiritual peace there, they would enclose that place with sacred ropes and they would worship there, and the Kami would come."

"Yes, I remember," he said.

She looked at him curiously. "It is still like that in the countryside."

"Yes . . . I have seen it . . ."

"Well, everything changed in the 6th Century, of course. A Korean ruler sent images of Buddha. The Emperor was so moved by the beauty of one image, he trembled, and he said he felt as though he were looking on the face of God. For a long time there was an uneasy truce between the religion of Ch'in and Korea and the religion of our forefathers.

"In the 8th Century, the Emperor planned to build a massive statue to Buddha. Gyogi, a powerful monk of the time, was disturbed about the propriety. He journeyed to Ise, and asked Amaterasu, the Sun-Goddess, if the plan met with her approval. For seven days he fasted and prayed at Amaterasu's shrine. At last she answered him in Chinese verse . . ." She tried to think of a simile. "It is like the threads that I wind together in my hands. The needle drives them into the fabric, and they become one. So these religions are threads of the same truth."

"And Hachiman, the War God?" Lance interjected.

"Ah, yes . . . you don't understand . . ."

"You told me he, too, was Buddha."

"Yes," Ginyo said, "one of the aspects of Buddha. A Bodhisattva."

"The God-realized one?"

"Yes . . ."

"But the God of War—Yet Buddha is the spirit of peace!"

"Yes . . . How can I explain? Dear friend, you are so full of questions."

"I tire you . . ."

"No. But I haven't all the answers. I wish I did . . . Buddha . . . Hachiman . . ." She remembered what the prists had taught her years ago. "Hachiman is a Shinto god. He has been around from the beginning. Today we know that all the Shinto gods were Bodhisattvas. Amaterasu herself is the Buddha of Mercy. These are all incarnations of realities we have always known."

Lance heard the strain in her voice, and did not press her. There was much he did not understand, much that amazed him about her faith. How could Buddha embrace both the Goddess of Mercy and the God of War? The old faith had made peace with the new and both had grown stronger.

What curious people they were—welcoming, adapting, willing to change, but always holding to a core of beliefs! Stubborn and flexible. Hard and bending—like their marvelous swords!

Late in the Second Month, Ginyo and Lance followed Lord Munemori to the capital. Kiyomori's spies had delivered their assessments. The Minamoto clans had settled their differences. Worse, clans that had supported the Taira for centuries were rallying to the rebels. On the twenty third, Munemori rose in the War Council and declared his intention to lead the Taira to victory. "The honking of ducks will not cause me to turn tail," he said. The ministers applauded his bravado, and wished in their hearts that his far-more-capable brother, Shigemori, was still alive to lead them.

Four days later, on the day of his departure, Munemori was delayed by his weeping wife and children. "When shall we see you again, Papa?" the young girls cried, grasping his stirrups, heaving great sighs. Munemori's own eyes were wet with tears when his Lieutenant General galloped into the courtyard. The Priest-Premiere was gravely ill.

By the thirtieth of the Third Month, Kiyomori writhed in agony. None of the doctors could relieve his misery. "This is not a normal illness," the doctors whispered among themselves. "Even at six paces from his bed, I could feel the heat!"

"A demon has taken possession of the Priest-Premiere," the ladies-in-waiting whispered.

"Even the water he tries to drink bubbles in his mouth," Lord Yukitaka told his wife.

For once, the rumor-mongers did not exaggerate. The Priest-Premiere's face turned red as a ripe tomato. "Hot! Hot!" he cried, and no amount of fanning helped. The attendants drew water from a spring on Mt. Hiei. A stone tub was filled. Guards with heavy towels protecting their arms lowered the frail body into the cold water. Soon the water sizzled, then it boiled. "Get me out!" Kiyomori cried. "Get me out!"

They replaced his bed with a smooth pine board. A pipe was

fitted to run cool water over the board. All day and night the Priest-Premiere rolled himself back and forth, his raw flesh seared like cooking eggs.

"My enemies have done this to me," he wept, and he spit out their names with a volley of curses that made the hair of his listeners stand on end.

Lady Nii, Kiyomori's principal wife, offered gold, silver and jewels to the ancient Kami, to the new gods, to all the gods.

"Another cart is leaving for the temple," Ginyo told Lance when he asked what the clattering was.

"Stand aside!" the guard commanded, but the voice was weary of its own authority.

"There are bows and arrows, helmets and swords," Ginyo told her companion, hastening him to the side of the street. "Ceremonial swords with rubies and emeralds, and battle swords that glitter in the sun . . . A gold-studded saddle . . ."

Something fell off the cart, splattering the hems of their garments with mud. It leaned against Lance's foot. He stooped to pick it up. His fingers slid over the narrow neck, the round base, over the flare and into the dark mouth. He knew the shape! He could not be mistaken in that shape! He had seen it in Yamato at the Ise Shrine!

The horse-whip sizzled across his cheeks. The guard's boot caught his jaw and sent him sprawling into the mud.

"Can't you see he's blind!" Ginyo pleaded, shielding Lance's body. The guard dismounted, pried the Grail loose from Lance's hands. "That's no excuse," the guard huffed. "Let him mind his fingers."

Later, when Ginyo applied ointment to the wound, Lance asked for his biwa. He sang in melancholy tones:

> And it came to pass, when Rehoboam had established
>   the kingdom,
> and had strengthened himself, he forsook the law of the
>   Lord,
> and all Israel with him.

They were in a small apartment, down a long corridor, far from where the Priest-Premiere lay burning with fever. Countless sliding doors, countless chambers and corridors separated them from the Priest-Premiere. But a cold wind carried the melody into Kiyomori's chamber. He felt the wind suck the heat from his body, and he sat up sputtering, "Rehoboam . . . the law of the Lord!"

Munemori stared at his father who stared back, surprised to find himself naked on a damp pine board with a pipe dripping water on his limbs.

"What's the meaning of this?" the patriarch demanded.

Cautiously, Munemori approached his father's body. He touched his fingertips to the forehead. The fever had abated.

"Truly no one has karma like the Priest-Premiere's," the ladies-in-waiting quacked to one another. Everyone marveled at his recovery.

But Kiyomori was not deceived. He gathered his nineteen sons and daughters around him, then called for his eleven grandchildren. "I have come back from the fires of hell for a reason," he said. His offspring moved closer, huddled around his bed. "Now I am in transit from this world . . ."

"No!" his children protested.

He raised his hands. "When I am set forth on this road again, I won't come back. Take my bones to Harima, where I was happy once. There is a monastery in a quiet wood. You know the place." He nodded to Munemori. "When the *O-bon* ceremony comes, when you polish my bones, say simple prayers, nothing elegant, nothing refined. Let no prayers be uttered in this capital of fools!"

Now the younger grandchildren wept. Kiyomori touched their heads in benediction. He fell back on the bed. "For thirty years I was the Emperor's sword. Against his enemies I showed no mercy. For this, the Gods and the Emperor rewarded me. Born humble, I rose to be Premiere. I gathered wealth—for my family, for our clan. Through my daughter, our blood sits on the Imperial throne! I have accomplished all that I set out to do . . ." He paused.

He seemed to be listening to something. The shadows lengthened on his face.

"When I am gone," he continued in a weaker voice, "do not tarry; leave this place." His breathing was stertorous. "Be soldiers, not courtiers. Learn to hate the gilded pomp."

"Father, do not go!" cried Munemori.

Now the old man propped himself up. His doctors fixed satin-covered *zabutons* against his back. He raised his forefinger. His eyes sank into the caverns of his skull. "One thing more," he said, and his voice was already from beyond and yet was strong. "Yoritomo Minamoto—hunt him down! Never cease! When you have slain him, skin him. Let his bones lie bleaching on the ground. Never bury the bones! Let no funerary rites be said!

"Build me no temple, build me no pagoda. Only the head of Yoritomo Minamoto! Bring that to my tomb! Hang it on wires before my tomb! Let the flies and the weather and the maggots rot it! Let it swing by a wire through its ears before my tomb!

"Do you understand?" he asked softly.

His children and his grandchildren wept. By nightfall, the fever had returned. They moved him onto the pine plank again. "Hot! Hot!" he cried, writhing like a snake. Then his body shook for an hour. When it stopped, it stretched creakingly into the cold.

10 | The Battle of Dan-no-Ura

Meanwhile, back in the 6th Century, Susanawo was up to his usual tricks. As his sister Amaterasu ruled over the Heavenly Plain, so Susanawo ruled over the Sea Plain. His sister oversaw the rise and fall of the sun, the planting of crops, the harvesting. All things orderly, predictable, beneficent flowed from her milk-rich breasts. Susanawo never could overcome sibling rivalry. He brooded in dark caverns under the sea, hammered his fists against his watery domain—and tidal waves rose above him, crashing on frail vessels, killing terrified sailors. Sometimes he floated on his back, brooding over his fate, his weird appearance—huge nostrils, a horselike mouth, and a barrel chest like an ape's. Amaterasu was worshipped, he was feared. So he'd make the most of it! He'd get the wind churning in his chest, pumping his lungs like bellows. It would come rushing out of his lungs and swirl in his horsemouth, bulging his cheeks and flaming his nostrils. Then he'd take aim and blow against a seaside village for hours until the shutters of every house were ripped off and the huddled occupants perished in his blasts. Or, if he were feeling particularly spiteful, he'd eat some noxious food—rotting octopuses, last year's seaweed, the bark of dead trees—he'd take himself to a swamp, strip, bend over and let loose a gas so foul the haricot beans exploded, the millet grass frothed like rabid dogs, and humans in the vicinity choked themselves to death rather than inhale.

Now he concentrated his ire on the little forge where

Commander Nakatomi worked. All in white, the two apprentices were drenched with sweat within the reinforced foundry. Also in white, the Commander didn't seem to notice the howling winds, the screeching of the animals outside. Coolly, with the calligrapher's brush, he applied the fine clay to the broad back of the blade, leaving the edge exposed. Now the edge would retain its super hardness while the blade bent and curved a million times. In the hands of the right warrior, the blade could hack through armor, cut a swath through a troop of horsemen. He thrust the blade into the flames and watched closely.

The fire licked around the gleaming metal like a lascivious lover. At precisely the right moment, when the metal glowed violet-gold with flickers of viridian, the Commander withdrew it and held it over the narrow swordbath. Keeping it parallel to the plane of the bath, he prayed to the soul of the sword, asking forgiveness for any imperfections he had made. Then he plunged the sword into the bath. The metal seemed to sigh like a lover. Always it was a different sigh, perhaps a fifth of a minute long. It was the last sigh of a dog killed on a road one fine morning by indifferent, galloping hooves. It was the first bitter intake of air into the baby-pink lungs, and the last sigh of the earth when the orange fire of the sun threw spokes of finely spun gold into the horizon and faded as the evening star appeared. The Commander inspected his work and judged it good. Now he handed the sword to his ablest apprentice. He leaned his weight against the reinforced foundry door.

Some hours later when he awakened, the storm still raged; the hilt had been attached to the sword. The hilt guards were of silver damascene. The polishing had been left uncompleted.

"Yes," said the Commander, "you have done as I asked." He handed the sword to the apprentice, then grasped the latch of the door.

The apprentice was alarmed. "You cannot intend to go out on such a morning."

"I intend no less! Stand aside!"

Reluctantly, the apprentice gave way. Both apprentices braced themselves behind the door, ready to squeeze it shut as soon as the master swordmaker passed.

The Commander seized the sword from the sweaty palm. The door opened with a whoosh, the fires flared, the sparks danced crazily like stinging bees around the faces and the bodies of the apprentices. "It hurts! It hurts! Ouch!" the apprentices cried as they wrestled the door shut.

Though he had fasted for days in order to complete the sword, the Commander leaned into the wind, planted his feet like roots into the ground. His legs grew hard as tree trunks. He pushed the sword forward through the wind which veered left and right. With his arms rigid, and the point of the blade slicing the wind, the Commander strode forward.

"Now I am ready for you, Susanawo! Now we shall do battle!"

Susanawo broke the backs of the heartiest oaks, and still the Commander plodded forward. The fulminous Kami sent shafts of lightning across the dark brow of Heaven, knitting the sky with pain. As though from a tree held upside down, the Kami shook branches of lightning into the earth, killing all the fish in the electrified lake. The ground trembled under his feet, but the Commander strode forward.

At the sacred tree in the clearing he knelt with the sword. "Now, if my vision has been true," he shouted, "if I have seen truly, and understood wisely, if I am worthy—let it happen according to thy will, Great-Spirit-Beyond-Our-Final-Knowing!"

He stood straight in the ratcheting storm. He held the hilt of the sword in both his hands and lifted it above his head, exerting the last measure of energy and will to hold it straight. He bent his knees, cocked his elbows until the blade touched his back, then flung it into the sky. It skirled and turned on its axis, shearing the wind as it hurtled above the tree tops and above the clouds, polishing itself to a mirror gloss as it turned.

*

Will looked up into the clouds, wondering what he had heard. A jay flitted among the treetops, hurling invectives against all other birds in its territory. Will finished undressing, stepped out of his undergarments, unwinding the breechclout. After he soaked himself, he would rub his garments in the hotsprings.

There was no fat on him. He was wiry, agile, and his eyes were always searching. He was not starving as he had been 18 months before at the Battle of Ishibashi-yama. Now he knew how to take care of himself in the forest and along the seacoast, catching game and fish, eating berries and raw kelp. But the whole country was hungry now. Fathers sold girl babies on the country roads, and no one bothered to ask what use the hungry purchasers would make of them. The God of War languished while the God of the Winds withheld the rains, and the winds scattered the seeds from dry seedbed to dry seedbed. The fortunes of the Tairas and the Minamotos seesawed, and the people were caught in the bellows between them. For months there had been no fighting, not even the pretense of fighting. Both armies were equally crippled as farmboys returned to their villages, and allies reconsidered their options.

Will eased himself into the steaming water; the vernal sun eased itself behind purple mountains. The heat relaxed his muscles, the sulfurous fumes he inhaled cleared his head. He wondered how Ginyo and Lance were faring in the capital. Some months before, he had returned to the village, accosted Kaoru, who nearly screamed when she saw him.

"Have my scars so changed my countenance you cannot recognize your friend?"

Kaoru hurried him to a bower. "It is dangerous for you here! How can you come here? Oh, Will! It is good to see you, but I'm frightened."

"I have grown eyes at the back of my head since last we met, and ears in every pore. Don't be afraid."

"But there are spies. Even now, when the spies themselves go hungry."

Then he noticed her hands, the lacework of bones. Her skin had lost its luster; sallow, it stretched over her cheekbones. "I'm ashamed to have you look at me," she said, remembering her old pride.

He pitied her suffering. "The fire in your eyes is deeper now."

Then she wept and told him how Lady Gio had died, saving her food for the children, squirreling morsels away, denying up to the last few days what she was doing.

"Ginyo?" he asked in a shaky voice, "and Lance?"

They were the only good news. An aunt had seen them in the capital in Lord Munemori's entourage. They were safe for now, and well-fed. Will sighed relief, pressed the little money he had into her hands and left her alone in the bower, still weeping.

He leaned back in the hot springs and stretched his toes out. His stomach growled. It no longer pained him as it had before. He had learned which of the wild grasses to eat for the pain, but the growling was more difficult to abate. "Well-fed," he said aloud, recalling Kaoru's words again. He closed his eyes. He must have dozed. When he opened his eyes, a pink-nosed white monkey was seated opposite him in the spring.

The monkey tilted its head in contemplation. Will tilted his head in return, then shut his eyes and drifted back into the steam. "Do you have any *sake*?" a voice asked.

Will jerked around. There was no one.

The monkey shrugged. "I just asked if you had any *sake*."

"No," Will said evenly. "No, I don't."

The monkey sighed. "Aren't you going to introduce yourself?" the monkey asked.

And without thinking about it, out of weariness and loneliness, Will told the monkey his story: from the destitute village of his birth, to Camelot; from Yamato to Heian-kyo; all of it: his love for Ginyo and his knowledge that it was hopeless; the battles he had fought and how he had enjoyed them.

The moon rose while he talked.

"Well, that certainly was interesting," said the monkey. "And now I'm afraid I must be going."

"I feel better after speaking to you," Will said. "But . . . won't you tell me about yourself?"

The monkey withdrew from the water, bent over on its hands and feet and shook itself vigorously. "Oh, I'm nothing special, I assure you."

"But I have never heard of a talking monkey," Will protested.

"Is that so? Isn't that curious!" The monkey scratched its head. "Why I've drunk *sake* many times with humans—and you say you've never heard of it?"

Will shook his head. "I'm not sure I can believe any of this," he said. "Probably I shall awaken and laugh at myself. Probably it is just the hunger. It is just the hunger talking now. The hunger in the belly and the hunger in the heart. I'm not sure what I believe anymore."

"You creatures certainly do have a problem with that," the monkey said emphatically. "We find it is not so much a matter of what one believes as *why* one believes—and *how*." The monkey dilated its wide, pinkish nostrils and with large black eyes contemplated the figure in the spring . The steam rose into the cool air like a breath of compassion. "Well, I wish I could stay and chat," the monkey said, "but I do have some other obligations."

"Of course," Will said.

"Not at all," said the monkey. It nodded good-bye, then sauntered into the moonlit woods.

*

They thought the cheering would never end. One-hundred thousand horsemen rode down Red Bird Avenue towards the Rajomon Gate. All morning and all afternoon the pride of the Taira paraded in the finery of their garments. Even the Tang Dynasty of China could not boast a better class of men. All day the Shinto priests hustled between the various city shrines: offering prayers to the ancestors; waving branches of the sakaki tree and asking the ancestors for safe passage and a chance to bring home honor. The Buddhist monks who still served the Taira were pressed into service, chanting mantras, clacking blocks of wood together, marching with their *tabi* socks and shaven heads in columns behind the soldiers.

The cavalry were the Tairas' best and brightest. The gilded hilts of their swords shone, and the silver horns of their helmets. The silk threads that fastened the fishplate armor shone, and the silk shirts and pantaloons under the armor, and the red brocaded robes over the armor. The gold and silver-studded saddles shone, and the eyes of the horses and men.

One could forget the year-long famine. One could forget the battles and losses. Fathers and mothers waved their sons to war. Wives and children caught the festive mood. The famine had ended, winter had ended, and spring burned bright with promise. Never had the nation assembled such an army. They would make fast work of the rebels! Once again, the words of Kiyomori's brother-in-law, Tokitada, were said with conviction: "Unless a man is a Taira, he is not a human being."

But not everyone cheered in the same way. Some of the old people wept as they smiled, making a brave show. Wives smiled and cheered for the sake of their children. Children put their hands to their ears, as though muffling the future sounds of war.

"How many men have they left in the city?" Lance asked Ginyo.

"I have heard it whispered that the gates are guarded. Not much more."

Lance shook his head. "There was a general of Ch'in who had to defend a city. He had few troops, while his enemies had many. So he left the gates open, and ordered the people to go about their business. He told flute players to play sweet, happy songs on the gates of the city. When the enemy general approached, he heard and saw. Then he turned back."

"The Taira have done the opposite," Ginyo said.

"Even so . . . If all the fish are taken from the rivers, the people will eat well . . . until next year! If the forests are burned and all the beasts corralled, the people will eat well . . . until next year!"

Ten days later, Major General Koremori, now twenty-five, led the one-hundred-thousand against a fort defended by six-thousand Minamoto troops. The Taira victory was swift and total.

Lord Munemori himself entered the converted corridor where Ginyo did her work. Ginyo bowed. "To celebrate this victory I have ordered 4500 cocoons from the finest silkworm dealers in the provinces," Lord Munemori told her.

"Sir?" Ginyo queried.

"Enough for one new kimono, my dear! I want something bright this time! You understand? Something to celebrate, to throw off the mantle of these dreary days." He inspected the bin of her silken twines. He held up one for closer inspection. "Mandarin orange," he said, showing Ginyo his choice. "Something with mandarin orange."

"Yes, my Lord."

Munemori turned to go when he noticed Lance in the corner. "Biwa singer! I didn't see you!"

"Nor I you, my Lord."

Munemori indulged the blind man's quirks. He had come to appreciate the subtle mind behind the morose expression. "You should bow in my presence," he gently reminded him.

"Yes, Sir, I should," Lance said without bowing.

"Biwa, I understand your malady has made you madder than most. Nevertheless, be careful."

"Yes, my Lord."

"I do require something of you."

"Yes, my Lord." Now Lance bowed.

"Ah . . . very good . . ." Munemori smiled at the two ministers who accompanied him. "I would like a happy song. To celebrate our victory. We have had enough of dirges! Can you manage it?"

"I am eager to *see* if I may, my Lord."

"*See* that you do!"

"If I *see* aught, I shall *see* to that, my Lord."

"Yes . . . well . . . you may stop bowing now."

"Yes, my Lord." Lance continued to bow.

The new threads were delivered to Ginyo and Lance selected from Ginyo's preselected "happy" colors. Lance had finished composing his song when the news of Major General Koremori's second engagement with the Minamotos reached the capital.

The Taira had divided their army into a main force of 70,000 and a smaller force of 30,000. Yoshinaka, the Minamoto General, divided his 50,000 men into seven forces. Yoshinaka dispersed his forces and waited. Some troops were ordered to hide in the hollows of trees, and some hid behind mountain boulders. The vanguard of the Taira forces faced the vanguard of the Minamotos' across a wide valley. Will and fourteen other Minamoto bowmen shot turnip-headed arrows into the Taira camp. The Taira responded in kind. Next, the Minamotos advanced thirty horsemen. And the Taira responded in kind. The Minamotos advanced fifty horsemen. Fifty horsemen advanced the Taira. One-hundred Minamoto horsemen faced one-hundred Taira horsemen.

The Minamoto generals had been ordered to hold their warriors in check. The Taira, too, were eager for battle, but also enjoyed toying with their enemy, since they were certain they held the distinct advantage of numbers. As the Taira sent more and more of their forces into the valley, the sun faded from the sky. On the peaks behind them, one of the Minamoto forces howled their war cry as they beat their quivers. The main Minamoto force joined the cry of their confederates, and all over the mountain peaks and in the forest the white banners of the Minamotos unfurled as the howling resounded through the valley.

The Taira tried to escape through the narrow passes of the valley. The Minamotos hurled rocks and boulders and spears from above, and the Taira horses stumbled over the fresh carcasses of men and horses. The Taira drew their swords and fought each other at the passes. When it was over, blood trickled down the rocks from where the corpses had piled up, flowed into rivulets that flowed into a river into the valley. Of the Tairas' main force of 70,000, only 2,000 had escaped!

As he wandered the halls of his palace, a distraught Munemori heard the biwa singer's voice:

> In spring when the flowers bloom
> praise the God of War!
> Red are the flowers of the Fourth Month.
> Ruby red are the lips of my beloved.
>
> Even my horse must feel it—
> for he gallops headstrong now—
> victory over our enemies
> has fired up his blood.
>
> Sweet are the War God's laurels,
> sweet are the flowers of the Fifth Month.
> Victory is sweet when the soldier returns
> to find his beloved behind red curtains.

*

The noose around the capital tightened. The Minamoto forces threatened from the north and from the east. Kiyomori's sons argued about everything now. They spoke loudly, their voices trembling with emotion. "We must send the Cloistered Emperor out of the capital at once," one argued. "For his own good—as well as ours. He is our seal of authority. Without him, our edicts lack divine sanction."

"But we cannot force him," argued another. "Or he will oppose our plans."

"Our father did not hesitate to confine him in Toba Palace," said the first. "He is an old man, but he bends like the willow, and so survives."

"It's a good plan," Munemori agreed, clinching the argument. "We must send the child Emperor and his mother, as well."

But before they could execute their plan, Go-Shirakawa got wind of it. With the help of a priest he was secreted out of Toba Palace—disguised as a priest himself! He took refuge at Mt. Hiei, where 3,000 warrior monks were prepared to defend him.

The Taira brothers were like sailors caught in a storm in a leaky ship. No sooner would they caulk one leak than another would appear. They made plans for flight. They sent emissaries to their allies. They called in debts and came up empty. They dispatched troops to Kyushu to suppress rebellion in the southern island.

"We must kill these members of the Palace Guard," one brother insisted, handing Munemori a list of names.

"These men have served us faithfully these many years," Munemori objected.

"They are from the East! They cannot be trusted now."

Munemori ordered that the men be brought before him. When he looked into their eyes, he could not give the execution orders.

"The crane need not fear a grain of salt on its wings when the huntsman readies his bow. You have served us faithfully. Go to your families in the Eastern provinces. Live quietly. This is not your quarrel."

The guards kissed the ground Munemori walked on.

In the converted corridor Ginyo looked at the mandarin orange fabric of the *obi*. She knew she would never finish it. "I am frightened," she said frankly.

"I will not let harm come to you," Lance swore. "Nor will the God I serve."

"I still do not understand this God of yours, this three-in-one God."

Lance smiled. "I do not understand how the silkworms weave—yet, they weave."

"It is dangerous! I don't fear for myself. I have seen enough, but—"

"And I see too much . . ."

So they went to one of the lesser gates of the city. Spools of silk thread were all they had. "I don't care much for the finery, Ma'am," said the gatekeeper. "How 'bout a kiss?" Ginyo shuddered, and the gatekeeper relented. "I'm not such a bad fellow, ya know."

"The next one may not give in so easily," Ginyo said when they were past the gate-keeper's hearing.

"Trust your God, and I'll trust mine," Lance advised.

They reached the temple at nightfall. Two more pilgrims caught in the floodtides. The abbot took them in, gave them rest and food.

After they had refreshed themselves, the abbot joined them in their chambers. He addressed Ginyo: "Though your kimono is of a simple style," the abbot said shrewdly, "you speak with the accents of the court. Your speech is layered like a sword, tempered many times. You have survived many trials. Now tell me, child, what brings you here."

Ginyo prostrated herself before the abbot. "Pray for me, Father! Pray for me! I am too weak for the world's sorrows." She choked on her tears.

The abbot sighed. "Have you forgotten what Saint Honen taught? Merely to call upon Buddha Amida's name will lift the veils between the worlds. Walk on the fine white road, my child."

But her tears did not cease. "I have forgotten how to call the name. And I am in the black river of this world."

"Then I will pray for you." Now he turned to Lance. "Though you are quiet, you speak volumes."

"I listen, and I try to learn."

"That is a talent I can honor. Yet, I think, you have not journeyed here merely to listen."

"I have a wish, Holy Father, that these poor spools of thread may please you." Lance emptied the spools from his satchel.

"They are handsome," said the abbot. "In the morning, bring them to the offering room. Now, tell me, what may I do for you?"

So Lance told him of the vessel Lord Kiyomori's wife had donated two years before.

"I remember seeing it—but in what storeroom it may be now, I cannot say." The abbot stroked his chin. "Is it a family heirloom?"

"It has been in my part of the world for many years," Lance assured him.

The abbot considered. "The Lady Nii donated gold and silver. And fine jeweled swords, jeweled earrings from the ancient times. Sutra scrolls with crystal knobs. *Makie* boxes inlaid with mother of pearl. But neither her gifts nor our prayers could add a hair's breadth's length to Lord Kiyomori's life—nor spare his suffering . . The heart of God is infinite, yet men must answer for their crimes . . Yes, I do recall that vessel. Because it was so simple, so plain. I'll have the students look for it tomorrow."

They heard the students chant their evening prayers. "You must excuse me now," the abbot said. He lit the wick of a second candle. A moth fluttered around the sizzling tallow, scorched its powdery wings. "Shall I lead you to your chamber?" he asked Lance.

"Yes. Thank you."

"Thank you, Father," Ginyo said.

The abbot smiled, slid the door of her chamber open. When the door shut, Ginyo moaned softly. The large sleeves of her kimono muffled her weeping.

*

They woke to the gongs and the chanting of the sutras. After a breakfast of bean curd, miso soup, kelp and rice-millet porridge, the abbot joined them. "Have you dined well?" he asked.

"Very," Lance said. "And your sleep was restful?"

"As restful as one might hope in times like these."

"How can we repay your kindness, Holy Father?" Ginyo asked.

The abbot wagged his finger gently. "For many years the House of the Taira were generous friends of our temple. Now that they have fallen from the limbs to the roots, we shall not abandon them . . . There is just one thing . . . "

"Yes, Your Reverence?"

"Since the troubles started, we've had the devil of a time getting fresh fruit. We had a nice grove of persimmon trees, and one morning all the fruit was gone. When was it? In the Twelfth Month last year. It's said some Minamoto horsemen rode by and denuded our trees! Not only that, they chopped them down! If they had asked, we would have gladly shared . . . I do so like persimmon! I know it is silly to mention it in these times, but . . . "

"We will be happy to send you some fruit from the capital," Lance said.

"Well, that would be fine. That would be very fine."

A young voice asked if its bearer might enter their room. A novitiate entered, carrying the Holy Grail on a brocaded pillow. The abbot took the Grail, appraised it shrewdly, decided it was of little value, and bade the student leave.

"Hold out your hands, Biwa Singer," the abbot commanded.

Lance knew the shape at once. Had the flames not sucked the moisture from his tear ducts, he would have wept.

"It must be a very important heirloom," the abbot ventured.

"After all this time!" Lance answered.

"Have you no fear to stay here, Your Reverence?" Ginyo wondered.

"Me? Not at all. We have been friends to both clans, and have bones to pick with neither. Personally, it seems to me, Japan is big enough for two talented families to share responsibilities. Alas, it cannot be. We must put our faith in Buddha, not the vagaries of this floating world. I have lived long . . . As for you, my children, do be careful . . ."

Lance bowed respectfully. The abbot's personality had touched him. And now, after all this time, he had the Grail!

"But what will you do with it?" Ginyo wondered when they were on the road back.

"Return it to its citadel," Lance said cryptically.

"It doesn't look like anything a citadel would want," Ginyo said, teasing him.

"That depends on the citadel," Lance responded.

Four barefoot children ran up beside them, two girls and two boys from six to ten years of age. The oldest, a boy, beat a crude drum while the other boy bent over backwards, touching his hands on the road, and watching them upside down. The younger girl squatted, then lifted herself on her hands and bent her legs forward so her toes touched under her chin. The oldest girl danced while the drum beat. The oldest girl suffered from a clubfoot, a deformity she had largely overcome, her slightly wobbly or tremulous movements and intense concentration making her dance even more poignant. Ginyo was delighted. "How cute!" she cried. "Let's rest a moment," she told Lance. The young acrobats walked on their hands, somersaulted and did cartwheels while the girl with the clubfoot tried to dance like a courtesan. Ginyo sighed, remembering.

After a few moments, the drummer stopped, and the youngest child held out his hand. Ginyo extracted four coins from her purse. The child's eyes lit when he saw them in his palm, as did, in turn, the eyes of each child he showed them to.

"Won't you come to our house, Auntie?" the dancing girl beseeched Ginyo.

Ginyo looked about warily. "We have a ways to go yet," she explained.

But the child was insistent. "Please, Auntie. It's just over the hill. I have been practicing the White Suit Dance. Someone from the capital must see me! Please, Auntie!"

"The White Suit Dance? Where did you learn it?" Ginyo's senses reeled.

"I have my costume just over there," the child insisted, taking Ginyo by the hand.

"Will you wait here?" Ginyo asked Lance.

"Nay. I'll abide with you."

"Let me guide you, Sir," said the oldest boy, taking Lance's hand.

"What if the Minamotos . . ?" Ginyo wondered, too confused to finish her thought.

"Minamotos?" The older boy laughed. "I'll beat them with my drum sticks!"

"I'll kick them with my feet!" the younger boy boasted, falling backward onto his hands then springing to a standing position.

"I'll charm them with my dancing," sang the younger girl, with a poor, whirling imitation of her older sister. All the grimy-faced children laughed.

"Hurry, Auntie," the older girl said. "Just over this hill." She pulled Ginyo forward over the hill and into a valley where the river flowed fast and green.

"Just be here," the girl cried, pulling Ginyo into a clearing beneath a great tree. When they had all assembled, the children laughed again, then quickly ran into the woods.

"Have some demons of the forest deluded us?" Ginyo asked Lance.

"Tell me where we are," Lance asked, listening to every rustling sound. He felt the trunk of the massive oak, centuries old. "Can it be?" he asked.

"We had better go," Ginyo said, feeling the sudden chill as the sun vanished behind high clouds. "How cruel of those children to hoax us so!"

"You must not blame the children," a voice said from the woods. Ginyo grabbed Lance's arm. From the dappled shadows, a *rokubu* emerged. He had blended like a lizard with his surroundings. Ginyo had not seen him, though she had looked straight at him. Now it was as though he pieced himself together, stitching a little light here, a little shadow there. The cabinet of drawers harnessed to his back emerged, the bamboo staff in his hand, the basket and the bowl suspended from the cabinet, his bald head, white pants, gray *hakama*, rope sandals. It was not so much emerging as coming into focus. The *rokubu's* demeanor was mild and calm. Ginyo watched in fascination.

Even when he stood ten feet from them, the man's face was somehow indistinct. He had mastered some trick of moving with the shadows of the clouds and trees, subtly shifting his body just before one could get a fix on him.

"I paid the children to bring you here," the *rokubu* explained.

"What do you want of us?" Ginyo asked, a slight tremor in her voice. "We are just a poor blind man and his attendant niece."

The *rokubu* unharnessed his weighty cabinet of drawers. With its bamboo pedestal rising to his knees, the entire structure rose two hands' breadth above the man's head.

"We have no need of your tricks and prayers," Ginyo asserted. "My womb does not cry out for children. Take your charms and potions! You must look elsewhere for a living!" Then, with a less assertive tone, she added, "Please . . . Please leave us alone."

Lance advanced a few steps towards the *rokubu*. The fertility priest-doctor looked him over sadly. "He will not hurt us," Lance told Ginyo. Then the two men embraced.

And when they embraced, the face of the *rokubu* stopped moving, the shadows stopped their ceaseless play upon his features. He kissed Lance on the cheek, then gazed steadily at Ginyo.

"Will!" she cried. "Is it Will?"

"A thousand tricks and prayers have brought me here to hold you in my arms."

Ginyo fell into his embrace. The treetops circled around their heads. Will kissed her wet cheeks. She kissed his wet cheeks back. Lance's fingers played over Will's features. "Have the years been so unkind?" he asked.

"I saw more than I cared to," Will said. "These years have etched their sorrows on my brow."

"But why are you dressed like this?" Ginyo wondered. "Have

you reversed the usual routine? Are you a butterfly who carries his cocoon?"

Will smiled. "I may be." He untied the cord that fastened the hinged doors in the middle of the cabinet. "This cocoon contains my folded wings," he proclaimed. Now he opened the doors. In place of the religious paraphernalia there was shimmering body armor laced with amethyst silk cords. The drawers of the portable altar were actually false drawers. Will showed Ginyo the hidden hinges and opened the top and bottom compartments. His bow fit on grappled hooks in the back of the cabinet, the length of it rising bottom to top. In the bottom compartment were his helmet, armored neck fringe, a lacquered iron mask, shin and thigh guards. In the top, his breechclout, pantaloons, armor robe, metal sleeves and shoulder guards. A leather quiver with twenty-four arrows was fixed securely in the middle compartment.

"You are transformed!" Ginyo said with awe.

"I have become more of myself," Will answered.

Lance's fingers stroked the scale-like armor. "Would that we had this at Mt. Badon . . . Can such light work keep the swords' points from you?"

"All but the heaviest blows, and only those aimed with precision. What one loses in protection one gains in flexibility—and then some!"

"How did you know that we were here?" Lance asked.

"I've watched you since you left the city. These woods are thick with soldiers—and with spies. I would not let harm come to you. Nor would I hinder your journey . . . But now, there's not much time. Our forces ripen in the fields; the Taira cannot overcome their blight. The capital is doomed. I've come to take you back with me."

"Oh," Ginyo sighed. She sat down upon a boulder. She would not meet Will's eyes.

"There isn't much time," Will said again.

Lance put his hand on Will's shoulder. Even under the priestly hempen garment, he could feel the sinewy muscularity. "Will," he said, "I have the Grail."

"The Grail?" Will kneeled and crossed himself. "Little did I know its worth . . . I was a child, I spoke as a child . . . Where is it?"

Lance removed the satchel from the bamboo pole. He removed the Grail, swathed in the black silk cloth the abbot had entwined it in. Lance was about to undo the twines when Will heard a branch crack in the distance.

"Nay, Lance, not here. The forest has a thousand eyes." He bid Lance put it back.

"It's over now," Lance said when he had wrapped the satchel on the bamboo pole again. "We can go home now."

"Home?" And now it was the world that went out of focus for the *rokubu*. He seemed to stand on swaying ground. Ginyo and Lance floated away from him, floated back.

"Will, this is the place," Lance continued, "the very ground where Commander Nakatomi first revealed his plans. I cannot think you've found it for no purpose. Here they invoked the Kami of Yamato—seven hundred years ago. I was here . . ."

"Yes," Will said, looking around admiringly, "I was drawn here. I stumbled on some stones, and looked, and found my place."

"Will," Lance continued excitedly, "it is no accident that reunites us here. If ever I were sure of anything, by Jesus' wounds, I'm sure of this. We have, I think, merely to call out the names— not even that! Merely to think of what we know—to be restored as we once were—in this place, some seven-hundred years ago, back to our time, where we belong."

But Ginyo saw the sadness in Will's eyes. "Is that where we belong?" he asked. Now his eyes met hers. The ground stopped moving underneath his feet. Her face came into focus. Famine had not chiseled her features as they had his, nor had the gore of war spattered her. Yet there were changes—a deeper loss, a hurting knowledge that sent crows' wings of furrows across her brow.

"Ginyo will you come, too?" Will asked. And his voice was young again, almost like a boy's.

She looked helplessly at him, then at Lance, as though he, somehow, would know what words to say. But Lance could find no words. "I can't," she said softly. "I can't . . ."

Now Will put his hand on Lance's shoulder. Lance understood at once. "Excuse me," Lance said, and he guided himself with a staff, walking down a footpath towards the river.

Will knelt in front of Ginyo, as he had knelt years before. The years fell away. Each gazed into the other's eyes. Ginyo touched Will's cheek. "It's too late," she said softly.

He kissed her palm. "Then, you have sealed my fate," he said.

"No, Will, I beg you. Do not add to my sins by murdering yourself. Save yourself. A year ago I would have rushed into your arms." Her eyes hardened. A glaze came over them. "Yes, it's true. I would have broken all my vows. I could have held you then . . . with the purity of broken vows . . . Don't ask me to explain . . Believe me, that woman that you thought you knew, died thinking of you a year ago . . ."

Will rose. He saw Lance by the sacred oak, feeling it with his fingers, waiting to invoke the Kami of the place.

"When she died," Will told Ginyo, "she took my breath with her."

"Please, Will . . . Please understand . . ."

Will walked over to Lance. His steps were steady, deliberate. "I must stay," he said.

"You cannot save her, Will."

Will turned to look at Ginyo. Her cheeks were wet with tears. "While she lives here, here is my world." Forcefully, he expelled the air from his lungs. "I am a warrior," he said, straightening his shoulders. "I never knew . . . I never would have known in Britain, compassed by that little world of daubed huts, collopes, my step-father's hands."

"I am a warrior. There is no white road for me. Only the red river. In the thick of battle, I tasted blood. My own warm blood rose to my mouth, and the blood of my enemies splashed in my eyes and nostrils. I gorged on blood—"

"Will—"

"Nay, let me finish!" Again he expelled the air, but he could not expell the memory. "Every second was a little world, a lifetime suspended, lifetimes hanging by threads. Every sound was magnified. A rustling in the trees roared like the sea, an insect's chirping seemed the whistling stertor of a dragon's den. I held time in my hands, or saw it frozen on the faces of the men I killed . . . Men and boys . . . boys dressed up like men, in armor, with girlish-boyish faces. I killed. I gorged on killing . . . And afterwards, I felt alive . . ."

"Will—"

"How can I go back?" He looked at Ginyo again. She sat lifeless, staring at the river. "If there's one chance that I can save her, I must stay for that."

"Will, this is her world, not yours."

"Can you tell me that, good friend? Does your heart not ache for another world than this? Do your inner eyes no longer see that feline poet of the long dark hair?"

A chill wind blew over them. The sky darkened with an ominous cloud.

"I have begun to understand something," Will continued with quiet resignation. "It is hard to say it. Yet somehow I believe I have some purpose . . . Do you hear who is talking, Lance? That silly sapling you pulled from the rushes . . . I believe the Kami have some use for me, they have not had their will, yet." He smiled, thinking. "I made a pun, Lance."

"You would fit in well at Camelot."

"Would I? That is well. I would like that. Once I could have asked no more . . ."

"What are your dreams of now?"

He sighed. "To ripen as I must. To fill my moment of time with the best of me, the whole of me . . ." He watched the scudding clouds. "Ye Gods! I'm jabbering!"

"Then, I'll stay, too," Lance said with resignation. "My time has not yet come."

Warily, Will watched the clouds. "You'll be going back to the capital?"

"Yes."

"Be with her, Lance."

"You need not ask."

The two men embraced again. Will strapped the *rokubu's* harness on his back.

"Forgive me," Ginyo said as they turned to leave.

But he was already stitching himself into a mantle of shadows.

"You understand, don't you?" Ginyo asked Lance as they entered the capital's gate.

"Yes."

"If only . . ." But she did not finish the thought.

At Lord Munemori's palace, the guards let them pass without a word, as though they had been awaited. Once they entered the corridors there was a hubbub and they were sucked into it. Runners came from Munemori himself; the runners looked them over, then returned quickly to report to their Lord.

After midnight, after they had bathed and Lance had retired, Munemori entered Ginyo's chambers. "I thought you had escaped," he said softly . . .

In the forest, Will opened the doors of the *rokubu's* cabinet . . .

"I didn't," Ginyo said . . .

Will removed the panel from the back. Carefully, he withdrew the *makie* box he had secreted behind it . . .

"I don't know what I should do if you left," Lord Munemori confided . .

With trembling fingers, Will opened the box . . .

Ginyo said softly, "I know . . ."

Will held the white, silk sash in his hands . . .

Munemori rested his head against his lover's breast. She stroked his head. How helpless he was! How lost! . . .

Gently, Will stretched the silk over his fingers, held it up against the lambent moon.

The light fell through the sash, fell through the lattice of the palace. Ginyo looked up into the soft light.

Munemori knelt and embraced his lover in a pool of light. He pressed his lips against the silk that covered the down of her sex.

Ginyo shuddered. The pool of light closed in around her.

*

Munemori did not have long to enjoy the solace of his mistress. During the last week of the Seventh Month he visited his sister at Rokuhara Palace. "You must prepare to leave the capital tomorrow," he informed her.

Kiyomori's daughter, the Empress-dowager Kenreimon-In, was barely twenty-eight years old. At sixteen she had married the reigning Emperor. At twenty-three she had borne him a son. Three years later, her husband was dead; dreamily, she watched as her father had her son Antoku coronated Emperor of Japan. Now, her brother told her, her son's life was imperiled.

"Has the Lady Nii consented to this move?" she inquired.

Munemori raised his brows. "Our father's first wife—that insufferable woman!—has nothing to do with this. I am in command. I will make policy. That is final."

The Empress-dowager nodded. She was used to her brother's brusqueness. She did not have Lady Nii's talent for exerting herself against imprudent policies. She did not pretend to know about strategems and tactics. Now she cared about nothing but saving her son. If fleeing the capital for the Western provinces would do that, she would gladly go. "Have you got your umbrella?" Lady Nii asked Munemori as he checked in on their carriage the next morning.

"Mother, why must you always ask me about the blasted umbrella?" Munemori exploded. "Can't you see how busy I am?"

Lady Nii was perfectly composed. "I wouldn't want you to forget is all."

"Yes . . . Yes . . ."

The day was bright, hot, humid. Antoku, the child-Emperor, leaned out the window to watch the court children who had assembled in his honor. As the oxen were prodded forward, the children began to sing a song about the red-crested cranes of the north. *"Kuru-kuru,"* the children sang, imitating the cranes' call. Antoku laughed with delight.

"Just hearing about the cranes makes me feel cooler," the Empress-dowager remarked.

"That so?" said Lady Nii archly. "Tell me, do you think it proper that the Emperor of Japan stretch his neck out like a goose?"

"Antoku, dear," the Empress-dowager addressed her son. She patted the seat beside her in the carriage and nodded. Reluctantly, the boy closed the curtains and settled back for the long journey.

"Did anyone remember to bring the sword?" Lady Nii asked after they had passed the gate.

"The sword?" The Empress-dowager was confused.

"Where is Lord Munemori?" Lady Nii called out to the drivers. "We must go back!"

But Lord Munemori could not be summoned. He was already riding to the Uji Bridge where Taira forces commanded the road that led directly to the capital. As he rode, he noted the noisily cawing crows that circled the roof ornaments of a temple. He covered his thumbs with his fingers, as though he were passing a funeral.

"We must pray doubly hard," Lady Nii proclaimed. "In every temple and shrine on the way. Wherever we stop! Lord Buddha, how could that fool forget the sacred sword?"

"Lord Buddha, protect us now," Ginyo said as she watched the last carriage of the Emperor's retainers disappear down the dusty avenue.

In the garden at Rokuhara, Lance sat in the sun, bathed for the last time in the fragrance of the lilies.

"It is no good," Munemori told Ginyo later that evening. "The Minamotos are closing the circle. My brothers say we should stay and make a fight, but I know it is useless. We may gather strength in the West. Let the Minamotos battle each other for the ashes!"

A few days later the Minamoto generals watched the smoke rise from Rokuhara Palace. Within an hour, the Taira fortunes were reduced to rubble.

"Hurry," Munemori commanded, as the men ran about with their torches. "Let not a stick of furniture remain to comfort the usurpers!"

"It is a happy day," said the Minamoto adjutant.

"Is it?" Yoshinaka Minamoto cocked his eye in the direction of the fires. "I had sooner a thousand times have met my foe in battle." Catching a whiff of distant smoke, his horse snorted, shook its mane. Yoshinaka patted the restive neck. "The wind that blows our way today, may blow another way tomorrow."

In the smoky city, the voice of the biwa singer rose above the ashes:

> Though the flames rise high in the morning,
> the fragrance of lilies fills the evening air.
>
> The pomp of the court's unwinding—
> as though a great kimono were wound back
> on its miraculous spools.
>
> Forty-five-hundred cocoons
> in the dew-drenched evening air . . .
> Do they recall
> the feel of a girl's white shoulder,
> the *tabi* brushing the polished floors?

> The threads are shirred
> in the great Loom-maker's hands.
> Out of the flames come lilies;
> out of the lilies, flames.

*

On the fourth day of the Second Month the Shinto bonzes carried the *mikoshi* to the Kamo Shrine where they recited prayers for a bountiful harvest. In his private garden, Go-Shirakawa brushed a dusting of snow from his winter kimono. A white owl perched on a sycamore, rolled its head on its balled sockets to left, to right, nearly upside down. Alone in his garden, the Cloistered Emperor allowed himself an uncustomary chuckle.

He had reasons to feel satisfied. With Yoshinaka's support, he had insinuated another one of his sons onto the Imperial throne, displacing the impostor Antoku. From the Goddess Amaterasu to the reigning boy-Emperor, whatever the ebb and flow of political and military power, the sacred trust between the Goddess and the Imperial family must never be broken. Else the nation itself would sink into the sea.

Yoshinaka, that blustering fool, had managed to drive the Taira from the capital. Within a month he'd established a dictatorship more absolute than Kiyomori's. From his military headquarters in Kamakura, Yoritomo Minamoto ordered fresh troops to rescue the capital from his reckless cousin.

Cousins! It had always been a war of cousins and brothers, half-brothers, uncles, sisters and mothers! All claimed descent from one of the branches of the Imperial line. The Fujiwaras had honored the bloodlines and ruled in peace for 300 years. Tairas and Minamotos had sought to start new dynasties. Like gaming cocks, the little spurs on their feet must be sharpened against themselves. It could be managed!

Now the capital was once again in Yoritomo's hands. The Master of the Eastern provinces had sent his ablest general, his half-brother Yoshitsune, to destroy the Taira once and for all.

Yet they held on in spite of the odds. Go-Shirakawa had ordered their allies to expel them from their southern stronghold in Kyushu. Vastly outnumbered, the Taira had fled in small fishing boats, encamping on the island of Shikoku. Still the Taira name drew valiant men to their banners. If they could merely survive, perhaps the tide of fortune would once more turn in their favor. They fought with the desperation of the abandoned and they held their ground. They crossed the Inland Sea and fortified themselves on the opposite shore. Now they controlled the sea lanes to the capital.

Twenty-five-years-old, General Yoshitsune Minamoto marched from the capital at the head of 3,000 horsemen. He divided his forces in two, sending 2,000 men to guard the passes to the capital. He further divided the thousand that remained, sending 700 to attack the Taira frontally at Ichi-no-tani. He led the 300 best horsemen up the snowy mountain passes.

Five-thousand Taira sharpened stakes and put them in the road facing East. To their rear, the cliffs rose precipitously into misty mountains and snow-clad conifers.

"We shall never get down these mountains," Yoshitsune's generals complained.

"Unless our horses grow wings," the troop commanders countered.

All laughed. All except Yoshitsune.

He strode about on his three-inch wooden sandals. Despite his moustache and scanty beard, the young Master General with the buckteeth cut a most unimposing figure. "I have seen stags elude our hunters' arrows," Yoshitsune said. "They disappear behind a crest of mountain. When we catch up and look over the precipice, they are far below, racing into the forest. Bring me a man who knows this area!" he ordered.

An old man was led to Yoshitsune's tent. "From Harima in the spring the wild stags come to graze our province's rich grass. To Harima they return when winter comes," said the old man.

"Horses and stags are equally sure-footed," Yoshitsune declared. "Where stags go, horses can!"

But his generals were not so sure. "Stags do not have men and armor on their backs," one told another.

"That headstrong boy will get us all killed," another complained.

"While he talks tough through his buckteeth, the Taira sharpen their claws!"

"Yet, he defeated Yoshinaka," said another thoughtfully.

"Good luck and men's lives—neither are endless," said the quiet bowman with the short, thick arm.

That very day Yoshitsune ordered his horsemen to train with one hundred pound rice bags attached to their saddles. The next day the men trained with one hundred and fifty pound rice bags. The horsemen grumbled and pointed to their foreheads when they mentioned Yoshitsune.

"Going downhill everything is heavier," Yoshitsune explained to his adjutant. "We should have more days to train. But delay would be costly. We are outnumbered and they are dug in. But they think like old women. Surprise and strategy are everything here. Let us trust in Hachiman—and train without ceasing." That night he burned the incense for the God of War.

At dawn, on the 7th of the Second Month, Yoshitsune addressed his best horsemen, the cream of the crop of three-thousand. "Listen to me, men of the Eastern provinces, honorable allies and friends. For four long years the Tairas fled before us. They battened on our dissensions. Now, the viper in our nest is slain; united, let us rain terror upon our foe. Do not forget Taira Kiyomori—how he dared imprison the Cloistered Emperor, how he burned the Nara temples. The blood of those the Taira tortured cries for revenge. Be men of steel! The God of War will guide our horses' hooves. Like lightning, let us descend!"

The first thirty horsemen started down the mountain. Among

them was the strange, short-armed bowman whom nobody knew. He always seemed to show up just before the battles, or else one would see him in the thick of it, hacking with his sword like ten men, or shooting arrows from his bow, quicker than the eye could follow. All the commanders assumed that someone else could account for him, someone else could tell his name and history, recite the litany of his deeds. Everyone assumed, and everyone was wrong. The strange bowman seemed to disappear into the smoke of battle. When it cleared, he was never found, and all would assume he had been lost. And all would be wrong.

Yoshitsune himself led the horsemen down the precipice. Even he had not calculated the steepness of the cliffs. The horses straightened their legs and slid down the sandy cliffs. The men bent back in their saddles and stretched their legs straight out, trying to brake their headlong descent. Over a hundred yards they slid until the ground leveled.

The 300 above watched the 30 below. And the 30 on the level ground saw the Taira encampment below them, with their defenses pointed east. Yoshitsune paused to catch his breath. The last 50 yards were a mossy escarpment.

Then Will rode forward. "Where I come from, we ride down slopes like this to catch a grouse. Methinks this is a racecourse to try my mettle." Then he plunged down, and the 30 followed. And after them came the 300.

Many stumbled. Horses broke their legs and threw their riders. Men fell headlong over one another and cracked their heads like eggs on the boulders. The horses neighed wildly and some men screamed in terror and some screamed the war cry and it seemed to the Tairas below that the whole mountain was falling on them.

Then the Tairas bolted from their forts and rushed into the enemy forces facing them. They were slain and cut and torn, and yet they hacked through, knowing there was no retreat for them, nothing but the sea now, where the child-Emperor Antoku waited on the boats with General Munemori. One of the Taira horsemen hacked at a Minamoto footsoldier. Will came up behind the man and grappled him from his horse. The two of them fell with a grunt to the ground.

For a quarter of an hour they hacked at each other's swords and armor. The terrified footsoldier cowered behind a dead horse. Then a Taira arrow pierced Will's left underarm as he raised the two-fisted sword. The world stopped moving. When it started again, there was no sound, and the Taira swordsman turned as in a dream of dance, slowly and with exquisite deliberateness. The swordsman raised his visor as Will fell back.

As the arrow drained his life force, Will recognized his enemy. It was the Captain of the Guards of Yamato, the "Blue Man" who had pursued them into Heian-kyo, the man who had blinded Lance and severed the tendons in Will's arm. Now the Blue Man raised the hilt of his two-fisted sword to his head, the point aimed at Will's chest.

Then the skirling sound distracted them. Some sort of missile was hurling towards them, some shining thing turning over and over, fast as a silver hawk plummeting for the kill. It was Commander Nakatomi's sword, forged in the smithy of eternal time. It fell into the hands of the cowering Minamoto foot soldier.

The young foot soldier seemed dumbstruck to find himself with so magnificent a weapon. The weapon seemed to pull him into battle. It hacked at the armor of the Blue Man. It cut his sword in half and drove a deep wedge into his helmet, so the man staggered back, blood gushing over his eyes. Then the Blue Man turned and ran, joining the general rout of the Tairas.

The foot soldier cradled Will's head in his arms. Will studied the smooth face of his benefactor. "You saved my life," the footsoldier said. "And I saved yours."

"Beansprout!" Will said before he fainted.

*

A year after their defeat at the Battle of Ichi-no-tani, the Tairas remained masters of the sea. They built forts along the coasts and retrenched their forces. The hero of Ichinotani, Yoshitsune Minamoto, was distrusted by his half-brother Yoritomo. Thus, Yoritomo sent inferior generals in pursuit of the Tairas, and the stalemate could not be broken. Finally, Yoritomo overcame his doubts, and commissioned Yoshitsune to destroy the Tairas once and for all. Yoshitsune's name worked as a magnet for the wavering clans of the Western provinces. They switched support from the Tairas and supplied ships and men, munitions and supplies. Now Yoshitsune commanded 3,000 ships in the Inland Sea, while the Taira ships numbered a thousand. But the Taira ships were larger, and the Tairas had been sea warriors for a hundred years. They knew the currents. The opposing forces shaped themselves around the straits of Dan-no-ura. The Taira were in their element. They were confident at last.

"On the first page of the *Art of War*," Munemori told his assembled commanders, "Sun Tzu has written of the Five Fundamental Factors, namely: moral influence, weather, terrain, command and doctrine.

"Now, let us be as objective. In moral influence, our forces are superior. Why? The true Emperor of Japan is Antoku, Lord Taira Kiyomori's grandson, in whose name we fight. As to weather, it is a neutral factor, as likely to do good or ill for us as for them. In knowledge of terrain, we are superior. In command, we are superior on the sea, our generals are cultivated men who have read the classics and know philosophy. As for doctrine, we represent the legal government under which the country prospered for twenty years. Didn't we preserve the system of the Fujiwaras? The Minamotos are upstarts. Their "God" lives in a shrine of wood in the fishing village of Kamakura. Our God's shrine floats on the bay at Itsukushima. No shrine or temple on Mt. Hiei is more pleasing.

"Let us crush these impostors once and for all. Tomorrow, thousands of Minamoto heads will cry out for their missing bodies!" He paused to gather in their laughter. There was none. "Now," he continued, "sleep well. The Hour of the Hare comes on."

It was a little past dusk when Munemori dismissed his generals. In spite of his bravado, he walked about the deck of his ship with a sense of finality, and a sense of relief. From somewhere far ashore the fragrance of cherry blossoms drifted over the thousand vessels of the Taira fleet, tethered like horses and rocking peacefully in the calm, dark waters. He thought of the cherry trees of Yoshino and the days of his youth when he sat beneath the scattering blossoms drinking wine and composing poems for maidens.

"You sent for me, my Lord?"

Munemori recognized the voice. He sighed. He kept his eyes on the water. "I didn't hear you approach."

"I have practiced walking in a quiet manner."

"Come. Stand beside me."

Still he didn't look at her. "You see that glow far over there?"

"Yes, my Lord."

"Those are the evening fires on the Minamoto boats. Perhaps they are warming *sake*. Or cooking a late meal for strength."

"It's strange," Ginyo said.

"How so?" He looked at her now. In the pale light of the ship's torches her skin was golden: in her silver kimono—silver as the moon—she was a fully ripened, golden beauty.

"It is almost . . . lovely," she said.

Munemori smiled. "How well you understand . . . That was my thought . . ."

"May I ask you . . . ?"

"Ask . . ."

"Shall we stand together tomorrow evening and see nothing from this deck but stars and moonlight?"

Munemori looked at her for a long time. Then she lowered her eyes.

They heard the soft sounds of the biwa coming from below

the decks. Munemori was moved to confess, "I loved you from the first time I saw you, when I was a young man and you did the White Suit Dance in my father's palace."

Ginyo sighed. "It seems . . . another lifetime."

"Yes," he said softly, "so it was . . ."

*

At the Hour of the Hare the dome of the sun crept over the horizon and the first arrows were exchanged. Accustomed to shooting from horses, the Minamoto bowmen were pitched and tossed by the swelling tide and the first deluge of arrows clearly favored the Taira. The Admiral of the Taira fleet had chosen to engage in the straits where the currents were fast and treacherous. It seemed he had chosen wisely. The morning tide propelled the Tairas' heavy boats while the Minamoto sailors struggled against the waves. The first barrages of arrows all fell short of their marks, but the spent arrows of the Tairas landed on the decks of the Minamoto ships.

"Has Susanawo turned against us, too?" Yoshitsune's Admiral wondered.

Yoshitsune withered him with his look. "Row!" he screamed to the oarsmen. "Row against the tide!" Through his buck teeth he screamed, "Row! The God of the Wind is not more glorious than the God of War! Row!"

As the Taira vessels bore down on the Minamotos, Taira arrows began to strike their marks and blood ran on the Minamoto decks. "Row!" Yoshitsune screamed, spitting through his buckteeth, cursing and whipping any laggard oarsmen. "Bring our best bowman!" he commanded. "Let them see how we return their arrows."

They summoned the man with the thick, short right arm. "The courage of our captains flags," Yoshitsune explained. "Our allies from the Western provinces grow faint. Show them what we country boys can do."

Will bowed. He steadied his feet on the rolling deck, contemplated arrow, bow and target at once. He held the bow out at 60 degrees to his body and paused, steadying his breath. He extended his left arm straight, crooked his right arm and lifted the arrow above his head. He drew the bow back slow and steady until the white crane feathers passed his ear. When the base of the feathers was at his earlobe, he tilted his head slightly from the plane of the arrow and sighted along the shaft. His gloved hand released the arrow.

Two seconds later, the captain of a Taira ship fell forward onto the arrow wedged under his sternum. The Minamoto sailors roared.

But the currents favored the Taira. More Minamoto sailors fell, and their bodies were pushed overboard to lighten the load. Susanawo puffed up the sails of the Tairas and the Taira fought with the energy of their ancestors, with the skill and courage that had made their name renowned. One of their thousand vessels carried the Emperor Antoku and the Lady Nii, Kiyomori's sharp-tongued wife.

Now the lead ships threw out grappling hooks and the soldiers engaged in hand-to-hand combat. Beansprout leapt onto a Taira ship and fought as a man possessed, wielding Commander Nakatomi's two-fisted sword. As Will watched with pride, an arrow struck Beansprout from behind and lodged between his shoulder blades. He fell forward, trying to withdraw it.

From a smaller boat, Will climbed onto the Taira deck and pulled the arrow from the boy's back. Behind his own back, the Blue Man's sword found its way under Will's fringe armor; the point would have dug deeper had the swordsman not been felled by a Minamoto halberd. In the reddening sea, the Blue Man struggled to get out of his armor.

"That's twice, Beansprout," Will said softly.

Beansprout's wound wasn't serious. He held Will in his arms as the combat flared around them. Will took the *makie* box from where he had it tucked inside his body armor. He fell back exhausted.

"Open it for me," he whispered.

With trembling fingers, Beansprout opened the box. A gust of wind blew the silk sash upward, and it drifted on the currents of the air, turned above the smoke of the battle. It was the last thing Will ever saw.

"Look!" said Yoshitsune Minamoto as he watched the turning sash. "Is it not like the white banner of our clan?"

The Tairas and the Minamotos saw the white sash rising into the clouds, turning like a great butterfly. On one of the rear vessels, Ginyo ran forward on the deck, disregarding the sailors who ordered her back. She struggled with them and cried for Will, shouted his name, and fell back into Lance's arms. Lance wept without tears.

Now it was mid-day and the ships were flaming and smoking all over the sea. On shore, the newly hatched geese choked on the soot, and the downy white feathers of their parents were covered with it, and the cherry blossoms rose up in a swirl and fell back onto the sea with the ashes. The white sash settled on a Minamoto boat and Susanawo lost interest in the games of men and the currents of the straits turned as they always did. The heavy boats of the Tairas struggled against the currents. "See how Hachiman has given us a sign!" Yoshitsune cried in joy. And indeed the conclusion seemed inevitable now as the vessels of the Minamotos swarmed like killer whales against the leviathans of the Tairas.

Lady Nii swept the young Emperor into her arms. "Granny, I'm frightened," said the precious boy, whose long, dark hair glistened like a girl's. Lady Nii kissed his cheek, and turned with a sneer to the nobles gathered around her.

"Now I will speak truth to all," she said. And her children and her grandchildren were held by her flashing eyes. "Lord Munemori, who struts and primps like a peacock on the stage, is neither son of mine nor Taira Kiyomori's! My late husband, fretting for an heir, for then there was just our one son—Shigemori—exchanged our girl baby for a son but recently born to a merchant—a maker of umbrellas!" She practically spit the words out. She trained her eyes on the startled Munemori. "Here is that merchant's son!" she screamed. "Is it any wonder the Taira backbone and intelligence is nowhere to be found in him?"

Ignoring her as best he could, Munemori ordered that the vessel be scoured from prow to stern so that their enemies might find nothing unseemly about the boat that bore the Emperor.

With Antoku clinging desperately, Lady Nii ran below decks, seized the sacred sword from the temporary shrine, and appeared on deck brandishing it like a crazy woman. While the battle raged around them, an other-worldly quiet descended on the principal boat, and Lady Nii's eyes were glassy calm. "Woman though I am," she cried, "I have sworn upon my husband's bones to meet him in the lands beyond, untainted by defeat." She walked to the prow of the boat, the poor boy-Emperor like baggage at her hip.

"Where are we going, Granny?" the boy asked in a nervous, girlish voice.

She knelt beside him and spoke gently. "In a former life, you mastered the Ten Precepts. Thus blessed, in this life you ascended the Imperial throne. Now the threads of fate are cut; some evil karma drags you down." For the first time she wept, and the boy wept out of fear. "Turn East," she commanded. "Turn to the Ise Shrine . . . There your Holy Mother, Amaterasu, bid farewell."

Antoku turned and bowed.

"Now West," said his grandmother, turning him. "Say, 'Hail Amida Buddha.'" She put his hands together, while those who watched him wept—the ladies-in-waiting and the strongest soldiers.

Now she took the boy into her arms again, and rose defiantly. The Minamoto ships were racing towards them. Arrows whizzed across the deck. The Taira bowmen answered in kind. But something seemed to deflect the arrows from Lady Nii and the boy.

Lady Nii kissed the boy's wet cheeks. "No more fishing boats for a palace, dearest boy. Let those who will, follow us! Here is our capital!" Then she plunged into the waves.

The water bore them, ruffled the skirts of their kimonos, her roseate and his moon-silver, and they rode the waves like two flowers intertwined, as a hundred hands stretched out to them like oars from the boats. Dazed, Kenreimon-In, the child-Emperor's mother, wafted at the prow; strong hands constrained her, and she watched as the others watched the slow, dreamy sinking. Even the hearts of the Minamotos broke, as the rose and silver vanished beneath the water.

While Lance consoled Ginyo in his arms, an arrow severed her carotid artery. She spurted a fountain of blood, choked and died.

"Damn you, Merlin! Damn you Buddha! Damn you God!" Lance cried, ripping the *magatama* jewel from his throat, casting it into the sea. A blue hand caught it, then disappeared beneath the waves.

Lance carried Ginyo's corpse like a broken doll in his arms. "Nothing is worth this! Take me, too! Damn you! Damn you, Commander! Damn you! Damn you all!"

He was still raving when the Minamotos boarded the ship.

PART THREE

Atlanta

"O divine Master,
Grant that I may not so much seek
To be consoled as to console,
To be understood as to understand,
To be loved as to love."

—*The Beggar of Assisi*

11 | The Man in the Blue Seersucker Suit

The old DeSoto purred smoothly down I-85. The man in the blue seersucker suit beat his fingers against the steering wheel and the insistent rhythm of the blaring rap music seemed to move in synch with the indigo tail fins slicing their way through sparse traffic.

The willowy peroxide passenger, between chews on her tasteless gum, observed in a whiny voice, "Ain't it a little loud?"

The Blue Man ignored her. And the rapper rapped on:

'Got the beat on my feet
an' I can't stop now.
Got my gun on the run
an' I don't care how—
gonna take'em wit' me,
gonna make'em miss me,
gonna win, gonna win
or go out tryin',
gonna take some down
cuz soon I'm dyin'—
an' I don't care how."

The Blue Man caressed the Glock 23-.40 S&W caliber, nesting in its boned holster under his seersucker jacket, riding his thick leather belt. On a heavy gold chain around his neck, he wore the *magatama* jewel.

Follwing Atlanta's dull winter, the dogwoods had exploded in symphonies of pinkish white blossoms. Gummy sap rose in the trees and bushes, oozing luxuriant leaves. The fragrance of sex cascaded over highways and teenagers mated like lightning bugs, glowing phosphorescently for a few prurient moments.

The Blue Man turned off exit 12 and followed the signs to the Renaisance Festival. The peroxide mannequin who had stuffed cotton from a pill bottle into her ears, snapped out of her trance, turned glazed eyes to the Blue Man. She gave him a large, toothy grin when he shut off the rap.

"Dis must be da place," the Blue Man said, shutting off the motor.

"You're so funny," she said.

"Alice," said the Blue Man in his best Ralph Kramden, "you're the greatest!"

Peroxide poked him gently in the ribs. "I tole you my name is Velvet, honey." She cuddled up to him as they walked, liking the feel of her own willowiness twining his oaklike muscles.

He hurried past most of the exhibits, murmuring disdainfully, "It wasn't like that. This is bullshit!" But he lingered at the armor-making set. "This we can use," he said, and he made notes as though he expected to travel back in time.

Which, of course, he did.

He bought her some toffee candy and they watched the jousting. They were such a peculiar couple—the large, mustachioed Japanese man in the blue, seersucker suit, with his Twiggy-like moll—they got stared at a lot, and photographed a little, and even distracted the attention of the jousters who raised their visors to get a second look. Ordinarily, the Blue Man would have glared back at everyone with malice and menace. Now he let them look so that he could study their faces.

Especially the jousters he studied, and their footmen. When they fell off their horses, he studied how they fell, looking for almost undetectable tricks of knowledge, telltale signs from centuries past. But there were none. None in the way they clumsily handled their swords or struck their poses or pretended to die. His enemy would know better than all that. He would give himself away with a reflex, a nod, a twitch in a muscle half a second's beat ahead of his opponent's.

He was somewhere in Atlanta. The Blue Man knew that in his bones. The same forces that had propelled them from Yamato to Heian-kyo to the Battle of Dan-no-ura, had brought them to the capital of the New South. He'd taken care of the pesky sidekick at Dan-no-ura, but the big fish had slipped out of his hands again. He'd get him, though. He always got his fish!

How easy it would be, he thought, to remove the Glock from the holster, muzzle it, cover it with a newspaper. At the next performance when the jousters collided, he'd fire and no one would hear above the crash of metal, and no one would notice the bullet hole in the armor, or the knight falling back. He'd grab the bimbo and they'd saunter away before the shouting started, before the cops came. It would be so easy!

Now they hurried past the mud wrestlers—a covey of men drenched in mud, eating mud, only the pale whites of their eyes slitting their mud-enveloped universe. "This was a popular pastime of the peasants of the day," the unbesmirched young man explained as the mud-beings romped and rolled and slithered and flung mud-pies at one another while the gawking tourists stepped back prudently. Spots of mud splattered across the Blue Man's white-leather shoes and his blue, knife-creased cuffs. He cried out in a kind of horror, like a wounded animal, at the uncleanliness, the filth and degradation. He grabbed the bimbo's hand hard and hurried her away.

Two eyes watched through the slits of mud. The eyes tried to remember what was important. Something about the man in the blue suit should have worried the eyes, should have focused the attention. But the eyes could not remember why they should worry. They had seen much, they had forgotten even more.

Another clod of mud broke across the cobalt, blue eyes. Lance cleared his vision, grinned with muddy teeth, and broke a clod, in turn, against his worthy opponent's chin.

*

That queasy feeling was starting up again. It began as a hollow in the pit of his belly, a sense of floating—as though he'd take off like one of those characters in the Chagall pictures Lorrie hung on her wall. It would reach up through the abdomen and pull at his lungs so they didn't seem to work right—he couldn't get his full measure of breath, and so his perceptions always seemed a little skewed, a little fuzzy.

It was there now as they stood on line at the Omni, this queasy sense of displacement. From one auditorium they heard beating drums and chanting—primordial shouts!—as the white-haired poet-guru greeted his adherents—the tribe of men in search of the lost father. In another auditorium, talent scouts for a national TV show watched pre-teen girls cavort across the stage in shiny, tiny majorette costumes, whirling batons and rendering classics like "Yankee Doodle Dandy," or "It's a Grand Old Flag!" while stage-door mothers fussed over their darlings' perms and hems and haltars.

"Ain't it a riot?" Lorrie said beside him.

"Mmm," he grunted, his usual communication with her.

He couldn't quite put his finger on it, but it seemed like the culture had lost a wheel, that it would spin out in one direction then gyrate in another like one of those crazy little cars the Shriners drove. (It had come as a small shock to discover that the Shriners maintained no sacred shrines.) Half the people seemed stuck in some ritualized celebration of what they called "Family Values," and the other half seemed equally committed to debunking them. "The best of times and the worst of times." Who'd said that? He'd heard it somewhere.

The line oozed forward and he felt Lorrie's hand squeeze his. She was excited. She was always excited and this pleased him. In her excitement he'd forget the queasiness and the displacement.

She had latched onto him a week earlier when he'd first signed on at Renaissance Festival. She'd come up to him the first day, before he'd gotten himself covered with mud, stuck out her hand and said, "Hey, cowboy, I'm Lorrie."

He'd never shaken hands with a woman before. Instinctively, he kissed her hand.

She stared at her hand, then at his long, golden locks, and cobalt blue eyes. "That's neat! You just sign up or something?"

"Yesterday . . ."

"Married?" she asked.

"I don't think so."

"Uh-oh." She wet her forefinger with her tongue then stuck it up in the air. "I feel a strange wind blowing." She winked at him. "Well, I don't care. Married men are safer, right?" She winked again. "See you after the show, cowboy."

A few days before, he'd been wandering around downtown Atlanta—lost, amnesiac and hungry. His tall, good looks, the golden locks and the strange clothes he wore distinguished him from the other homeless. He'd almost gotten himself killed crossing the street in a daze. Lester had hustled him to safety.

Always scouting and scheming, Lester had stroked his goateed chin and sized him up. "Can you ride a horse?" he'd asked.

"A horse?"

Lance's confusion would have deterred a lesser man, but Lester was certain Manny would find a place for the handsome stranger. He fronted him busfare to the Village, told him to get himself cleaned up and present himself for work the next day.

The next morning Lance followed the students, show-biz hopefuls and other down-and-outers to the hiring hall. Manny had taken an instant dislike to the tall, strange man with the golden locks. "I don't care what you people do amongst yourselves," Manny announced piously, "but I don't want no funny business on company time. Understand?"

"Funny business?"

Manny shook his head in disgust. He wasn't going to show off some homo bum Lester had taken pity on. There were plenty of fresh kids with long locks and they were better able to take the bruises. Manny Saphire wasn't going to make it easy for anyone to get disability. He'd been turned down three times, and he wasn't going to pay his taxes—bust his arse and pay his taxes!—so some aging, hippy faggot could get it!

"You ain't planning on claiming disability, are you?" Manny challenged, between chomps on his cigar. (He prided himself on being direct.)

"Arthur said he'd never met a man more able," Lance announced out of his fog.

Manny spit some brown juice at the white leg of the table. "And who the hell is Arthur?"

Lance tried to cut through the fog with the butter knife of his memory. He strained the muscles in his face but it didn't help. "I don't know," he said softly.

Manny stared at him. He had one of his instant, famous intuitions that amazed his friends at parties and the girls at the Cheetah Lounge. "Can you wrestle?" he asked.

"Wrestle?"

Manny exploded. "Jesus! What are you—putting me on? Who sent you here? You think I got time for this? Is this a joke? That scumbag Lester put you up to this?"

"Scumbag?"

Manny calmed himself. Allright, he wanted to play games? He'd show him how to play games! He'd give him the worst job in the outfit and pay him nigger wages!

That evening, after he'd washed up, Lorrie glommed onto

him like a bur on a dog's tail. "I'm not interested in a committed relationship," she'd said.

"Relationship?"

"Nope." She shook her head, took his arm, ushered him to her little Saturn car. "I just want good food and great sex . . ." She met his eyes boldly. "Dinner first?"

"Mmm," he'd grunted.

And she'd been as good as her word.

The fact that there was about twenty years difference between them—he wasn't really sure how old he was, so she guessed for him—only made him more alluring to her.

"God!" she gasped, after their first round. "Where'd you learn such stuff?"

"I don't know," he said. "Did you like it?"

"Did indeed, cowboy! Did indeed!"

His amnesia also attracted her. She said she'd have to reinvent him. Then if someone came looking for him, they'd have no claim on him, since he'd be someone else. She even gave him a new name.

"I christen you, Sir David Jansen," she said, touching the plastic toy sword to his shoulders. Then she laughed.

"Is it a good name?" he wondered.

"Don't you know David Jansen? That's your generation, man. You know, he's that guy in the old TV show—'The Fugitive.' He's on the lam." Her eyes brightened. "Hey, maybe that's what it is with you, huh?" She sat up in bed and studied him intensely. "You're on the lam cause you did something horrible—only you didn't do it, right? But everyone thinks you did, and this guy is hunting you down, this detective or something, you know, and he won't give up till he finds you or you find the one-armed guy . . . We gotta find the one-armed guy and prove you're innocent!" She fell back on the bed, all sputtered out.

"On the lamb?" He scratched his head.

She kissed him joyfully. "This is like the best thing that ever happened to me. This is gonna make me a better actress, you know. This is just what I needed, you know?"

He didn't know.

He only knew he was easy with her and she made the queasiness go away when he held her. She was there when he woke up screaming in the middle of the night with the weird dreams, and she'd kiss him and rock his head back and forth against her pert and fragrant breasts. "Easy, Dave. Easy, baby." She asked nothing from him except good sex and he was happy to oblige. Adept at Taoist love-making, he'd learned to hold his semen. He could go all night without ejaculating. Finally, she'd ask him to stop.

Now she presented the tickets and they found their way into the central auditorium. Occasionally, they could still hear the music from the talent show next door, or the chanting and drumming from the men's group on the other side. Lorrie squeezed his hand as Michael Yamamoto was introduced.

"It's nice to be here in an Olympic city again," Yamamoto said. "I remember telling Socrates the last time I was in one, `This is gonna catch on!' A few people in the audience tittered nervously. Yamamoto made some more small-talk and gradually warmed the audience. As he ambled back and forth across stage, mike in hand, dressed in a Georgia Tech T-shirt, black denim jeans ripped at the knees, and top-of-the-line pump-up running shoes, he gauged his audience, measured their responses, calibrated how far to go—and how fast. His slender body moved with pantherlike grace, holding the eyes of his captives.

"I'd like to see a show of hands now," he said abruptly, turning serious. "Don't be shy, huh? We're only going to spend a few hours together, so we've got to be straight with each other and peel away the masks and get down to who we are and what we know." He seemed to look at each of the 500 members of the audience. "Now tell me, how many of you can say that you've had a past-life experience? Let me see your hands."

Fifty hands were raised tentatively, then fifty more, and fifty more. Yamamoto nodded approvingly. "We're off to a good start . . . Now here's what I want you to do . . ."

*

The unctuous voice of Michael Yamamoto washed over the fertile fields of their minds as the screen spewed forth a medley of swirling spirochetes, dancing Stonehenge monoliths, whirligig phantasms, and spiffy cartoon characters that flashed a second in some subconscious basement apartment, urged further exploration, and then were gone.

"Go deep," Yamamoto intoned, "Deep . . . deep . . . deeper," elongating the long "e" sounds until it was *e*asy and all were *e*ager as *e*agles to go "down . . . down . . . down . . ." into the darkness that enfolded like the petals of roses.

Only a few were bothered by the chanting and drumming next door, or the occasional lilting jingles from the talent search of wraithlike majorettes. Most found themselves sinking into the petals of the roses, into the soft embrace of universal love that sought nothing, that judged not, that worked—so Michael Yamamoto told them—only to teach, only to bring each struggling life-awareness to the pinnacle of spirituality.

And when they were deep in the petals of the roses—and putty in the palm of his hands—he urged them remember a room in their house—the bedroom where they slept and felt safe, say, or some other favorite, cozy room. They were to visualize that room—a chair, or a bed; and the sort of floor, the windows, the light washing in from the windows; or, light from the lamps or ceiling fixtures; just so long as they felt everything was very familiar and they were comfortable, "sooo comfortable . . ." Then he asked them to shut off the light, to shut out all the light from outdoors, to go still deeper into the warmth of love and trust.

Deep in that warmth another self waited—a self who wanted

to be found again, to share the warmth of universal love, to be reunited in knowledge and mystery—to help.

"Let the impressions come in," Michael Yamamoto urged as the music in the theater shifted from Church organ to piano tremolo and strings; and the barely audible clicking sound went down, down, down from 850 to 140 beats per minute. "Trust the impressions. See this other self who was you. See the hands of this self. Is it male? Is it female? Remember, this self wants only good for you. Where are you? Look around and feel easy where you are. You have been here before. You know who you are . . ."

And had it not been for the drums and the jingles—the muffled beating drums next door and the tinny George M. Cohan jingles—it would never have worked for Lance. Had it not been for Lorrie's nocturnal, sexual gong show, and the mud wrestling that soaked and chilled his body, that stretched his nerves and made them brittle—it would not have worked. Had there been a self to resist, Yamamoto's suggestions could not have worked his magic.

But he went down, down, down and he saw it again. It was dim, it was flickering—and then it was there. And he heard someone say in the oily voice of Michael Yamamoto:

> 'Amaterasu, Goddess of the Sun,
> shamed by the misdeeds of Susanawo . . .
> shut herself in a grotto
> and plunged the world into blackest night . . .'

The self which was this other self sat hunched against the cold while the self in the theater in Atlanta shivered. Beside him, Lorrie—or, who was it? Imbe-san?—squeezed his hand. On stage, Michael Yamamoto was blurring, transforming. "Trust this other self," he said. "This other self has come to teach you." Then the fox's voice said:

> '. . . under the seas of the world,
> from under the bellows of mountains I come . . ."

Lance squirmed in the theater in Atlanta. The queasiness was bad. It had taken the balloons of his lungs and pinched the ends of them. The queasiness crept up his spinal column like a scorpion and embedded its curled tail stinger in the back of his neck.

"Oh!" he gasped.

Lorrie/Imbe-san squeezed his sweaty hand. "Are you all right?"

"It's all right," Imbe-san said, reassuringly. And the snow began to fall in the theater as the drums beat softly.

"How shall we restore this harmony?" Lance asked aloud in the theater.

"Dave, what's wrong?" Lorrie asked, her voice alarmed.

"Don't be afraid," Michael Yamamoto said soothingly from stage, as he felt the putty slipping from his hands, rearranging itself, shaping itself.

"Hey, Mister, don't take it so personal," some good Samaritan advised Lance.

"Men must have *wa*," Lance said loudly, standing up, so everyone was now looking at his dark shadow projected against the light of the screen.

"Hey, sit down!" someone called angrily.

"You're spoiling the mood!" another complained.

"Without *wa*, death and madness are the lot of men!" Lance answered.

"Carol, turn up the lights," Michael Yamamoto called from the stage.

"How shall we restore this harmony?" Lance asked them all.

The lights went up and the whole theater gazed with awe and apprehension at the tall forty-year old with the long, golden locks, who was turning to face them all now, proud, sure, determined— a natural leader; except for the inescapable fact that he was nuts.

A woman stood up and aimed a camera at Lance. The bulbs flashed in his face, the torches of Yamato flared.

"With this," Lance declared, holding the sword aloft in his hand. "This restores *wa* to the land!"

Lance looked up with pride. He could feel the weight of the sword in his hand. Only, there was no sword. There was nothing but Lorrie's polka dot umbrella.

*

The Blue Man watched in delight as the brown Coke liquid spurted out of the central spigot, made a wide arc in the air, then filled his waiting cup to the brim.

"How they do that?" he asked Velvet.

"It's magic honey," she said between chews.

He carefully placed a wad of gum on the underside of the counter. He smoothed it out so a kid wouldn't toy with it and even a fastidious cleaning lady would just let it go. It was the twentieth time that day he had smoothed out such gum. He took a sip of the Coke and thought back over the plan.

The man-with-no-pinkies had put it all together. The Blue Man admired the symmetry of it, the perfect convergence of the technological and the demonic. He couldn't have expressed it that way, of course, but that's what it was and that's what appealed.

He had arrived in Atlanta a little before Lance. He had simply awakened in the body of someone else, a body that had been prepared for him, the body of a Yakuza lieutenant. The dark, shamanic powers that ruled his life had bested the powers of the Commander and Imbe-san. Lancelot—mortal, frail, conscionable—had lost his mind at the Battle of Dan-no-ura. He had broken the first rule of the quest: he had lost sight of his purpose.

Man is a creature who periodically goes mad and slaughters his kind. Then he resumes his normal life, buying vegetables, sending the kids to school, screwing his wife, trying to put his life in order. Until he goes mad again and the mess takes over.

In Heian-kyo Lance had read too much of the philosophers, the mystics and the poets. He had gotten drunk on their unearthly, visionary ideas. He wasn't up to the blood and the gore.

But the Blue Man saw the whole picture and he understood that Commander Nakatomi was his foremost enemy, and the Commander's fetch-boy, the one they called Lancelot, was merely a straw in the wind, a boulder on the road—to get around or through. Susanawo, the Thunder Being, the God of Dark Forces, would blow him away with a puff.

It was all coming together now. The hidden forces that moved the world, the underside of the warp and woof, and the visible flowing streams of images, people and events—all of it needed to work together, the tangible and intangible, hidden and revealed, people and Kami, in order to make the whole.

He couldn't have expressed it that way, the Blue Man, but he understood in his guts.

*

"Buy me some cotton candy," Velvet cooed, interrupting the flow of semi-thoughts and images that comprised the Blue Man's intellect.

He watched her as the pink, airy sugar disappeared between her pouty red lips. She offered him some, and he nearly gagged on the sweetness. "How can people eat this garbage?" he croaked.

Velvet shrugged and went on unwinding the sugar from the paper cone, licking her fingers lasciviously.

She was part of the bargain. He'd awakened next to her in his new body, found himself turned on immediately by her strange, thin blondness, fondled her and made her happy.

"You never were like *that* before!" she crooned that first night, trying to melt her body into his. "But you hurt me, baby. Try not to hurt me so much next time." She'd studied her face in the mirror on the night table. "My lips are puffy. You bit too hard."

"You liked it," he said, admiring the red shape of his hand where he'd slapped her buttocks.

"Yeah, a little," she admitted, "but not so hard. You don't want to hurt me, do you? You don't want to frighten me, do you?"

Then he took her again, hurting her and frightening her. He liked to hurt and he liked to frighten. Yet she stayed with him.

He moved instinctively in his new body, the large, muscled body of a Japanese gangster. When the man-with-no-pinkies had called, he had known exactly what to say and what to do, where to go and how to act. He merely followed the gut logic.

The only thing that wasn't in the plan was this Lancelot. He'd taken care of the other one, slit his back at Dan-no-ura. And he would have taken care of his friend if the Kami hadn't squired both of them away. The dark Kami and the light Kami were always at war and that was the way it was. He just knew he couldn't rest until he'd settled the score. He'd go back to his own time and his own place and he'd let them know the assassins of Emperor Buretsu were dead. He'd be the hero then. He'd rally the Emperor's forces and take on the Commander. He'd be the *new* Emperor!

Velvet wanted to stop at every stall in Underground Atlanta. She had to examine all the schlock, every T-shirt, every Olympic gewgaw. She tried on hats and jewelry, she looked at posters. Clark Gable and Vivien Leigh made eyes at each other everywhere. "Gone With the Wind" ashtrays and lamps and mirrors and brushes spilled over the bins and the tourists came with dollars, yen, franks and marks looking, buying, and buying.

Outside of Underground, the sun was going down. Velvet and the Blue Man sat beside the statue that looked like an ordinary Will Rogers' type citizen taking the breeze, enjoying the atmosphere. The Blue Man stuck the gummy plastic bomb under the statue's hind quarters. It might work there, it might not get removed.

The man-with-no-pinkies had explained it all: "It will all be ours," he had said, tapping his index finger on the city's map. It starts here in the Center for Disease Control itself so everyone will know there's no place to hide. Then—*Pandemonium!*"

No Pinkies said the word like it was a magical elixir. The Blue Man understood less than he thought. He knew just enough for a henchman. No-Pinkies knew just enough. Everyone up the line knew just enough. And behind it all was the Plan. Hammered out over the years and ripened in the darkest, most diabolical minds. The Plan had brought the Japanese Yakuza and the Middle East Dictator and the irredentist Soviet Colonel—"that's *Soviet*, not *Russian!*"—together.

"A thousand years of darkness," No Pinkies had said. "Like the West's Dark Ages, but now it's everywhere."

"A thousand points of darkness," No Pinkies had laughed. And when the dispirited citizens of the New World Order saw their manufactured dreams of glory exploding, they would take up their guns against each other, stampeded like lemmings in their fears. "New World Anarchy!" No-Pinkies declared. "And we inherit the whirlwind."

It was all so simple, all so elegant, the Blue Man kissed the stubs of No Pinkies' hands. No Pinkies blushed.

The Blue Man didn't care a hoot about the politics. He just wanted to wreak havoc. So he spread out the smooth bombs—forty bombs a day, and three more months to go.

Revenge! Destruction! Chaos!

They were simply gumming up the works!

*

Michael Yamamoto slammed down the latest issue of *Creative Loafing*. "Have you seen what they've done to me?" he asked Carol as she entered the office.

Carol leaned over his desk; her lacteal softness spilled over her bodice, brushed the fine hairs on Yamamoto's neck.

"Jesus, baby, not now!" Yamamoto whined.

Carol picked up the tabloid. *"Life Regression Regrets"* the headline read, and on the cover was Lance, holding up his polka dot umbrella.

"I've worked so hard to re-establish my credibility," Yamamoto muttered into his hands. "Now this!"

"Maybe it's not so bad," Carol sympathized.

"It's just like that time in Austin," Yamamoto muttered. "Just like Austin."

"Nothing could be that bad," Carol shuddered.

Now Yamamoto studied his office/bed mate. "Do you know how much time I spent with this reporter?"

"I remember that late evening . . ."

"I told you that was *business!*" He grabbed the paper from her hands. "Look . . . Look: 'The conclusion is,' Dr. Phillips warns, 'those who believe in past life regression are apt to be especially sensitive to these sort of auto-suggestive techniques. Once the genie is out of the bottle, there's no telling what the genie will do. The genie may not be a top-of-the-line kind of guy. Anyone with deep psychological scars—and that's most of us—had better seek professional counseling in a licensed psychiatrist's office. Remember what the Romans said: *Caveat emptor*—let the buyer beware.'"

Carol sank her buttocks into the soft leather of the Harvard University chair. She leaned back against the emblazoned emblem, *"Veritas."* She sighed. "So, what now?"

"What now? What now? The house is off, that's what. This thing is published in Charlotte and Tampa, too. No doubt they'll be canceling. Has anyone canceled yet? No? Well, they will, don't worry. The Emory gig is off, I'm sure of that. I guess it's back to Michigan for me. Jesus Christ! And winter's coming on!"

"It's only springtime, honey . . ."

"That's soon enough! Don't you get it, baby? Don't you?" Michael shook his head. "The whole thing I've been trying to do is get people to relax with this. That's all. Once they accept the idea, the possibility of life-regression . . . How's our account?"

"We don't owe a thing. And our credit's good."

"Thank God for tender mercies."

"There's always Hawaii," Carol said hopefully.

"I told you, competition's too strong . . . Who was that maniac, anyway? Did you find out anything?"

"All he could remember was his name—Lance something. He kept saying, 'Lance do lack.'"

"Lance do lack what?"

Carol shrugged. "That's what I said . . . His girlfriend called him David Jansen."

"David Who?"

"You know, *The Fugitive.*"

"Oh Jesus," Yamamoto whined. "And things were going so well."

"By the way," Carol said, fingering the pink memo. "She called this morning."

"Who?"

"The girlfriend—Lorrie something."

"She wants to turn the screws?"

"Worse . . . She wants to make an appointment. Says it's urgent."

"Tell'er to go to California. That's where she belongs. Her and her David Jansen."

Yamamoto scanned the article again. "'Licensed psychiatrists,' huh? Most of them get into it cause they're half nuts."

*

The knight in shining armor lay in a heap of metal and dust, attended to by the paramedics. The red and blue lights on the squad cars flashed in series as kids in mutant costumes sprayed each other with water machine guns full of red dye. "Poor guy," the onlookers sympathized. "Is he dead?" the kids wanted to know, pausing in their water play, their interests aroused for the first time that afternoon.

Manny Saphire ran up and down the fenced enclosure wondering how they were going to pull off the next four shows with the college kid quitting the day before and their star attraction heaped like cans of sardines on the tourney field.

"Mr. Saphire," the nubile, brown-tressed cashier called out. Manny watched her breasts jiggle as she ran up to him. "I was just wondering," she sputtered, "like, with what happened and all . . . David can ride a horse, you know. He told me he used to—"

"David?"

She smoothed a wayward tress back, "You know, the mud wrestler."

Manny heaved a weight-of-the-world sigh. He considered his options.

"Well, it was just an idea," Lorrie said, turning.

"Have you seen him ride?"

"Well, not exactly, but, you know . . ."

Manny didn't know. He looked at his watch. "Tell him to get cleaned up and see me in the trailer."

Lorrie beamed. "Yes, Sir! Thanks, Mr. Saphire." She went skipping away, wiggling her fanny.

"Tell him to hurry!" Manny called.

*

Michael Yamamoto surveyed the messages that had piled up since lunch. "Call the News Editor at *The Atlanta Journal*." "Call Features Editor at *Atlanta Magazine*." "Call Bob Edwards at the *Tampa Tribune*." "Mary Cassidy of the *Charlotte Observor* wants to interview you for the *Living Section*."

Carol breezed into the smartly-appointed office. She wore a Cheshire-cat grin and her eyes twinkled like diamonds. She gave him a big, wet kiss.

"This is great," Yamamoto gasped, indicating the memos. "What happened?"

"The best is yet to come," Carol teased, wetting her lips with the pink tip of her tongue.

"Tonight, honey. Wait for tonight."

Carol removed the folded memo from the perfumed crevice between her breasts. She unfolded it like a flower. "The *creme de la creme*," she said.

The memo gave a name and number to call at *Esquire*.

"That's national," Yamamoto gushed. "I've never been national before." He kissed her. "Have this laminated," he said about the memo.

"It's your time, honey," Carol assured him. "Your ship has come in."

The phone rang and he picked it up. "Yes . . . Yes . . . Why yes, be happy to . . . That's: Y-A-M-A-M-O-T-O," Michael obliged the caller.

*

"Sign this form," Manny said, shoving the legal release in front of Lance's visored face. Lance drew the visor back and made a large "X" at the bottom.

"What the hell is this?" Manny fumed, purpling slightly.

"It's my mark, Sir Manny. I don't know where my seal is."

Manny threw some Maalox tablets into his mouth. "Awright. Awright. God help us. You look awright, though."

"We didn't use to wear so much armor in those days," Lance said, straining to remember, to catch something definite through the fog. "The horses weren't so well-protected, either." Lance patted the neck of the crinet-protected sorrel.

"Right," Manny said, half wincing. He checked out Lorrie's well-exposed brown thighs. "Remember now, no one's supposed to get hurt."

"I understand," Lance assured him. He placed his metallic

shoe in the stirrup. With Manny pushing at his rump, he clanked onto his mount. "No one was supposed to get hurt back then, either... But many did..." He nodded to Lorrie, who saw herself reflected pridefully in his armor. Lance tugged at the reins and the horse began to trot onto the field.

"Wait!" Lorrie called. She ran up to him and gave him her handkerchief. "I seen it in a movie," she half-apologized.

He took it gratefully. Another piece of the puzzle seemed to click into place.

But the fog was still impenetrable.

"Ladies and gentlemen," the announcer blared, "your attention puh-leez. Welcome to the greatest show on earth, the tournament of kings. As our worthy knights take up their lances, behold the green knight on the white charger." The green knight saluted with a dip of his lance. Manny Saphire popped another Maalox. "Sir Gawain is his name," the announcer intoned.

Lance stared at the green-tinted glow at the end of the field. He wondered why he was fighting Sir Gawain. They had always been good friends.

"On the sorrel charger," the announcer crooned, "adorned in shining silver, our very own Sir Lancelot, the pride of Arthur's court."

Lance lifted his visor. He was looking for someone. Who? A woman with wheat-blond hair. Who was she? Where was she?

"What's he doing?" Manny asked Lorrie.

Lorrie shrugged. "Beats me."

"I didn't ask about your sex life," Manny muttered.

"Huh?"

"Look... run to the fence and tell him to stop it, will you? Tell him to get on with it."

With his helmet off, Lance rode back and forth along the fence, looking for two faces: the blond woman's and the beneficent, sagacious face of the king.

Tall and straight-backed against the loinguard, helmet off, with his long locks flowing, he was every inch the exemplar of the Table Round. "He's gorgeous," one woman said to another. "He could cross my moat any day," her companion replied.

"Looks like Lancelot's looking for someone," the announcer temporized. The green knight trotted in a circle, wondering what he was supposed to do. "Could it be Guenevere?" the announcer joked.

And just then one of the kids with the water machine gun shot a stream of red dye into Lance's face. And Lorrie said, "Dave, you okay? Mr. Saphire says to get on with it."

Lance wiped the dye from his eyes as the kid's mother hustled her brat away. "Say you're sorry to the nice horsey-man," the mother urged.

The ten-year old shot his middle finger at Lance, then at his mother. "Cute little bastard, isn't he?" the mother wondered.

Lance looked down the field at the shimmering green horseman. "Guenevere," he said softly, and fifteen hundred years of longing and love and sorrow were in the name. "Arthur," he said, and the name rang like absolution. Tears streaked down his cheek, diluting the red dye.

He put his helmet on and the crowd cheered. He rode the sorrel back to the starting position. He secured the lance under his right arm.

At the signal, the two knights rumbled towards each other. Lance lay the weapon across the charger's outstretched neck, over the dividing fence. He aimed for his challenger's breastplate, realized some twenty yards away that his opponent was unworthy, and lightly tapped him off his saddle as though he were flicking a fly.

The crowd went wild.

*

The 50-inch screen on the wall spurted a montage of images as the hand on the remote played with the channel changer. Lorrie lay against the satin pillows on the king-sized, circular bed, deftly applying lipstick to her nipples. With a towel around his middle, Lance stood a foot away from the screen, studying the dancing images. His hand reached out to comfort a starving child in the Sudan. His hand recoiled at the images of the latest outbreak of violence in Los Angeles. A fat man made a fist at his wife and said, "To the moon! To the moon, Alice!" The magic box laughed.

Lorrie studied her nipples in the dressing table mirror. She had gotten the idea from an article in *Cosmopolitan*: "Fifty Ways To Spice up the Bedroom."

She swiveled towards Lance. "Hey, honey, whaddaya think?" She arched her back. Her nipples were hard, the areola red as blood. Lance turned quickly, nodded perfunctorily without seeing anything amiss, then fixed his attention on the CNN report.

A duststorm of white flies cascaded on cotton and peanut fields near Americus, Georgia. The camera showed the view from inside the car as the wipers cleared a swath of vision through the dark clouds. The wipers made a scraping noise against the windows, which soon turned black. "It's jus' lak dah end uv dah world," said a frowsy, pink-faced matron of the region.

Lance felt Lorrie's hands encircle his chest, felt her red nipples rub against his back. She kissed the nape of his neck, ran her hands down his body, caressed what she called his "tall order".

"Now that's more like it," she said, pleased with his response. He turned, and she showed him her breasts. "You like it?" Now he saw what she had done. He sucked her nipples, tasted the lipstick, the salt of her sweat, the perfume and powder. He threw the remote on the bed, and she fell back on it, the rhythm of her buttocks gyrating the images on the screen.

"To the moon, Alice! To the moon!"

"And in Moldava, clashes continue between . . ."

"The President says he has a plan to get us out of this depression. Well, what is he waiting for?"

"Norm!"

"Jus' lak dah end uv dah—"

"—moon, Alice! Pow! Zoom!"

They heard sirens in the street below, crisscrossing the city like harpies. The sirens enmeshed their love-making, raced down Tenth Street, past Piedmont Park, took I-75 South. More sirens raced across I-20 from West and East, gathered into columns at I-75, flowed south towards Hapeville, East Point and College Park.

At the projects, three black men lay in the streets, their dark blood staining the pavement. The flashing red and blue lights cried pornographic violence into the crack-crackling bricks. Out of the chinks in the bricks, the eyes looked down, saw the white eyes in black faces, pinched above crisp, black collars, watch back. White, darting eyes questioned the witnesses—who had seen nothing, heard nothing, remembered something like distant thunder and a smell like gun-powder mingled with magnolia.

While the hands wrote and the eyes saw nothing, the Blue Man moved in the shadows, tinged the shadows with his indigo, silk cape, huddled over the corpses and drank the blood from the wounds, with a soft, delicate slurping sound as a baby makes nursing. The last body still had life in it, and the Blue Man relished the warm, sweet taste.

"Don't let him. Please," moaned the last body.

But the officers heard only the static of their radios, the accusations in the compliance of the witnesses. There was muffled gunfire somewhere not far off, running down unseen wires, searching for them, calling their names. They waited for the ambulance doors to close, then sped off into the blue-black night.

Lance and Lorrie shuddered against one another for a long orgasmic minute as Desi and Lucy made up and megaweeds destroyed the Australian wheat crop and threatened the world's graneries. Plump and shapely, her buttocks reverberated with the aftershocks of their love and the remote played a wanton symphony on the 50-inch screen on the wall:

The TB epidemic in Atlanta claimed another—

200,000 were suffering from milk poisoning in—

Norton was fleeing the fat man's wrath . . .

And in Five Points, downtown, Angel Hernandez, age 40, coughed another clump of sputum into his hands. He held it out to the moonlight, as though making an offering, as though he expected to see something other than the net of red filaments and yellowish pus.

"I never got no breaks," Angel said to the blue figure that came softly out of the shadows. He wept and lay his head back on the gutter. The cold concrete took some of the fever. The iron slats of the sewer cradled him as the Blue Man's cape brushed over his face.

"*Quien eres?*" Angel asked the shadows.

"*Tu hermano azul,*" the shadows answered. With exquisite gentleness, the Blue Man raised Angel's head, then cracked it open against the curb.

"Baby, you're the greatest," the fat man said to his wife. Lorrie flicked off the TV set. "I thought it would never end," she said breathlessly, slithering against Lance's supine body. "How do you hold out so long?"

Lance shrugged. Lorrie wiped him off with his waist towel, then put it between her legs. She sighed with deep contentment. "I'm happy," she said. "I've never been so happy."

Lance kissed her cheek. He looked around the comfortable condo. "Will your father let us live here?"

"Sure . . . Now that he's run off to Europe with Raven. Like I said, the place is ours. He just used it for a tax write-off, anyway. Hand me those ciggies, will you?"

Lorrie took a deep drag while Lance studied the Kandinski prints on the wall. He especially liked the one called "Strife." Bold, suggestive strokes depicted a rainbow, a blue mountain, two horsemen with large red hats battling each other with lances. But if he looked at the painting another way, the white horses seemed to describe the outlines of a dove. The strife was resolved into an image of peace.

"Would you like to hear some music?" Lorrie suggested,

putting on her robe. "Dad's a square. He doesn't have anything past the '60s or '70s."

Lance winced. "You mean that noisy talking stuff?"

"No, no. That's rap. You're so funny. I'm talking *old* stuff."

Lorrie searched in the cabinets for a few minutes while Lance watched the city. How strange it was! In his world, long ago, the sky had glittered with diamonds and the earth was black as pitch. Now everything was reversed. The sky was a soft, grayish glow and the earth glittered and pulsed with lights.

"I guess Dad took all the good stuff," Lorrie said softly. "Probably brought it to Raven's. She's a freak for Bob Dylan and Elvis and the Beatles and all those guys."

"What's that you're holding?"

"Oh, these guys go way back, man. Mose Art and Poo Sini"

Lance looked at the silver discs. "Let's try them."

They sat in the darkened room as sirens wailed and flashed below, as skylights played across the night sky and huge aircraft flickered like lightning bugs. A woman with the sweetest voice Lance had ever heard sang in a strange language an aria of beauty, longing and grace.

"What's wrong?" Lorrie asked.

"Nothing."

She watched him in the faint light. "Are you . . crying?" she asked softly.

When the aria was finished he turned to her again. "Who did you say this is . . . Mose Art?"

"Yes."

"I would like to meet this Mose Art."

Lorrie giggled. "Not even you can do that. He's been dead a thousand years."

"Nevertheless, I would like to meet him."

Lorrie studied the ruggedly handsome face. A chill played a piano scale up her spine. "I've never known anyone like you," she whispered. "I was thinking . . . the way you handled that horse today . . You just brushed that guy out of his saddle like he was a feather. Where'd you learn to do such stuff?"

"It's been a long time . . ."

"Oh right, Mr. Modesty. Like you just do it all the time."

"Not all the time. Only on the festival days. We didn't have the magic box then."

"You're not gonna give me that Lancelot stuff again?"

"Do you doubt my word?"

She sat up suddenly in bed. She stared at him, played with the long, blond locks. "So you're saying I've just been screwed by Sir Lancelot, right?"

"Screwed?"

"Yeah, you know, balling!" She humped her hips.

"Ah . . ."

"Hey, what if it's true!" Lorrie exclaimed. Now there were tears in her eyes. "You're really something special, Mister. I don't know who you are and I don't care. You balled me like nobody's ever balled me, and if you wanna be Sir Lancelot that's fine. If you wanna be John Kennedy or Elvis Presley, that's fine, too. What we gotta do, honey, is get you an agent. We gotta go to Hollywood and get you an agent."

"Yes . . . I would like to go to the Holy Wood."

"You're a piece of work, man. Do you know what a piece of work you are?"

But he had seized on her idea. "I would like to go to the Holy Wood," he said again. "Maybe there I can discover . . . There is something I must do . . . But I don't know what or why . . . I was someone . . . a long time back . . . Someone who saw things and understood things . . . Someone who made a difference . . . I see the blurry outlines; can hear the crowds, and faces swim into my ken. But I'm only the husk of who I was . . . There was something that I had to do . . . I can't remember what it was . . ."

"You're on a . . . whaddaya call it? A quest! Some kind of quest . . ."

"I think so . . . but . . ."

"But you can't remember. You just flew through time, right? Like you've got a mission, like those Star Trek guys. Like you gotta save the world or something. What was that guy's name? Merlin? That ring a bell?"

"Merlin?" He strained against the blankness.

Lorrie leapt from bed, raced to her pocketbook, emptied the contents on the bed. Lipstick, matches, condoms, cigarettes, candy, combs, brushes, receipts, papers, gum spilled out. She rifled through her papers. "We gotta get you back to see that guy Yamamoto. He has to see us." She opened matchbooks, looking for the number, checked receipts and chewing gum wrappers. "I know I have it somewhere. Want some gum?"

The Blue Man smoothed a gummy bomb under the little desk at the elementary school. The night watchman's flashlight moved slowly, cautiously over the room as a blue rat scurried across the radiator and disappeared in the wardrobe closet.

"Here it is!" Lorrie said. "We'll call him tomorrow and I won't take no for an answer!"

"I don't get paid to chase no rats," the watchman muttered to himself, closing the door behind him. "No, Sir. No, Siree."

12 | The Petunia Petunia Show

Dear Diary:
I'm sorry to take so long to get back to you. You know how it is when things pile up [see previous entry!] and you know how I am about letting them pile! But, I think you'll forgive me when you understand what's been going on.

The big news, of course, is David—or, I guess I should say "Lance." We've been living in sin for two weeks and I'm loving every moment!

Diary, I don't know what it is about this guy, but I can tell you this—he's *diff!* And I gotta say: *For the first time in my life, I'm really in love!* (There, I said it!) (And no, it's not just the sex, though I can tell that's what you're thinking! And I have to admit it's *fab!*) (Or at least it was . . .)

The thing about Dave—I mean Lance—is, he's got this idea that he's—are you ready for this? Maybe you better sit down! (Ha ha!) Okay, he's got this idea he's . . . *ta-ta-taaaa! Sir Lancelot!* Yeah, you know, that old-timey knight! Aside from that, he's a great guy.

The thing is—now don't laugh, okay?—he's got me half believing it. (Well, okay, I know it's pretty *weird*, but I guess it's no *weirder* than the Loch Ness monster or Big Foot or E.T.—and I believe in them, right?)

Well, two weeks ago we move into Dad's condo. (He's run off to Europe with Raven, so I guess it's our condo now.) Prob is, Lance has discovered Dad's library—all those old books he keeps around just to impress his clients. The day after we move in,

Lance asks me to call Mr. Saphire and tell him he can't go to the Festival anymore. Well, of course I did. (You shoulda heard that old guy curse!) Well, I guess you know the rest—how we've been living on the good old plastic. (I guess Dad won't mind, cause I'm keeping it in limits, like he always said, though I gotta admit he never said I should support my boyfriend! Well, I won't tell him if you don't. Ha ha!)

Anyway, supporting him is no problem. (Or maybe that *is* the problem—that it is *no* problem—if you get what I mean!) Because David (I mean Lance) just isn't very expensive. I mean, he never wants to do nothing—just stay inside and read books! I mean, from morning to night! He reads when he's eating, he reads in the bathroom, he reads when he's in the tub. If he could read in his sleep, I'm sure he would. (He's even started to listen to "Books on Tape" when he sleeps!) He reads all kinds of stuff and then he starts talking like the characters in the books. He read *The Grapes of Wrath* and he started talking just like Joad Whatsizname—"Yes, ma'am. No, ma'am"—and I *cain't* seem to convince him that people don't talk that way anymore. (Actually, it's kinda cute!)

The only time he's not reading is when he's listening to music—which is a pretty close second to his reading. He says music is holy and he listens to all the old guys—that's who he really likes—Baytoven (sp?), Bakh (sp?), Mose Art (sp?) and Pooh Sini (sp?) . . . Someone named Russ Columbo—like the detective . . . and someone named Satchmo.

Well, the thing is (and this is just between us! Okay?) the thing is, it's driving me nuts! (Okay, I said it!) And it's really cut into our sex life, if you know what I mean. I mean, he's still there when I want him—which is often!—and he still performs like any five guys I've ever known—all right, Diary, enough of your snickering! But, you know, something is missing. I mean, his mind is somewhere else. (Probably on the music, which he plays while we're doing it.) (By the way, Rimsky Korsakoff (sp?) is especially good for it!)

The thing is, Diary, I love this guy, and I don't want to lose him. He's touched something I didn't know I had. (And I don't mean my G-spot!) It's what they call the maternal instinct, I guess. I want to help him and I want to do for him. Only I don't know the best way how. (Does that make sense?)

Now I gotta tell you something strange, maybe even a little *weird*. But after I tell you, maybe you'll understand how *diff* this guy is & why I love him so.

The thing of it is, he *cries*. I mean, he cries a lot!

Not a bawling, boo-hoo, cry-baby kind of crying. But it's more like a sadness or something that comes over him and the tears start to fall.

He cries when he listens to the old time music and he says strange things like, "The spring of human suffering is as deep and limpid as time." (I wrote that one down. Don't ask me what it means! When he doesn't sound like Joad Whatsizname, he sounds like Shakespeare or something.) He cries when I turn on TV and there's one of those kids with the swelled-up bellies in Haiti or some place, and he cries when he hears about a murder on the local news. He cries whenever there's any news about Japan, about how bad it is over there with them eating their babies and all, or when there's another race riot or more civil war in Russia or trouble with Iraq and Iran, and on and on and on and on.

I never knew a man could cry so much. He says it makes him feel better. I never knew *anyone* could cry so much. When he studies the art books, he cries and says, "How beautiful!" and he cries over Marilyn Monroe's picture and John F. Kennedy and the Challenger disaster with the school teacher, and on and on and on and on.

Now this is no wimpy guy, Diary. Like I said, he's got five times the *stamina* of any guy I know. He's built like a god and he knows things about pleasing a woman—well, modesty *forfends* me giving details! (Ha ha!)

But I just don't know what's wrong. I would just like to help.

Well, I finally made contact with Yamamoto, the guy who

started all our problems. He's been tied up since that article appeared, getting interviews and giving speeches. His dumb secretary kept giving me the brushoff like I was just another airhead. (Like she should talk!) Finally I explained that I needed to see Mr. High and Mighty for Lance, not for me, and maybe, just maybe, Mr. High and Mighty owed his surge of popularity to us, since Lance's outburst at the life-regression session had started the ball rolling, so to speak. Well, within an hour I get a call back and Mr. High and Mighty himself—who really isn't such a bad guy—says he's been trying to contact *me* all this time and didn't I get the message from Manny Saphire which he left me weeks ago? (I never trusted that old *lech* anyway!)

Well, the long and short of it is, we've got a private session arranged for tomorrow. Mr. Yamamoto seems just as anxious to see Lance again as Lance is to see him. (Lance keeps saying he's missing something, and maybe Yamamoto can help.)

So, that's where it's at, Diary. I really want to help this guy. He's really *sweet*. He's really *diff!*

*

The words of the poet still rang in Lance's mind: "Time is but the stream I go a-fishing in. I drink at it, but while I drink, I detect how shallow it is. It's thin current slides away, but Eternity remains. I would drink deeper; fish in the sky whose bottom is pebbly with stars."

The lake in Piedmont Park was not as clear as Walden Pond, nor was he as great a dreamer as Thoreau. Joggers, strollers, and roller-bladers circled the lake, and the lights of the city pulsed about the fringes of the Park. He felt his spirit flying out of him like a hundred kites turning in the humid air of May. What had Eliot written? "White again, in May, with voluptuary sweetness." He pulled on the kite strings, tried to gather himself, recall the fibers of his life and lives. He knew he had failed.

None of his vast amount of reading had helped dispel the

darkness. He was a cave explorer with a dull lantern wandering through limestone caverns. The face of a woman would seem to emerge—a dark, exotic singing a Mozart aria, then shattering like china. Other faces came—a wizard with brown-gray ringlets of flowing beard and a white skyrobe of pentagrams and dragons; a man with a fox face dancing in the snow, and a boy learning to ride horses. And, somewhere, too, something ever lurking, waiting, watching—a tumorous presence, a dark, ominous blue.

"Lance!"

Lorrie's voice startled him back to the floating world. She ran breathlessly to his side. "I was worried, honey! Why didn't you tell me where you were going?" He let her crook her arm in his. "You're all right, aren't you?" she asked.

"Aye. Thou needst not fret."

"What?"

"No need to worry, Missy."

"Oh." She studied him with that bemused, quizzical expression of hers. It was her typical approach to the universe. "Did you wanna be alone?" she asked with uncustomary insight.

He had, but the mood was broken. He patted her arm gently and smiled weakly.

They started back to the condo. She stopped in mid-stride, turned to him, looked up to him. "I'm really glad to be with you," she said. "I just wanted you to know. I'm not trying to lay any fantasy island on you. If you know what I mean. I mean, the door's always open. Not that I want you to go—that's not it. You understand?"

"I think so."

"I'm just trying to say . . . I'm not making designs on you. But I'm glad we have what we have. It's something special. It's *diff*, but it's special. Am I . . . Do you know what I mean?"

He studied her, bemused by her confusions. She interlocked her fingers, scooped up air as she made a swooping arc of her arms, paused at the moon, as though she'd take it out of the sky for him. "Are you worried about tomorrow?" she asked.

"Nay . . . Should I be?"

She laughed. "Nay . . . I don't think so." He watched her struggle with the words again. It was good he had learned to look beyond her struggling. "I just wanted to say . . I hope . . whatever happens tomorrow . . . whatever you find out . . you can always count on me . . . if you need a friend . . . I wanted you to know . . . I mean . . . I *respect* you . . . That's something new for me . . . Do you know what I'm saying?"

He put his arm around her shoulders, grateful . . . grateful.

*

"You understand," Michael Yamamoto warned, "there's no guarantee."

Lance nodded. "Just let's do it."

He settled back in the couch in the mahogony-paneled office. Outside, car tires made a swishing sound against the rain-soaked streets. Yamamoto adjusted the colors on the wall monitor. "Normally, I charge a pretty steep fee for a personal regression," he said, smiling. "But this time, I almost feel I should be paying you."

"I'll send you my bill in the morning," Lance said wryly.

Yamamoto inserted the tape of images. "I guess we all pass the bill around, one way or another. We're linked in ways we don't understand. That's why it's so fascinating."

"You find links . . . to your patients?"

The young therapist positioned his chair behind Lance's head. "From time to time. Nothing definite . . it's more a kind of vague imagery that resonates with something deep inside me. You know about the Theory of the Sixth Remove?"

"No . . ."

"It's something like this . . if you can go down to the sixth level, everybody in the world knows everybody else. Say there's a starving kid in Haiti. Well, someone you know knows someone who knows someone who knows someone who knows someone who knows that kid. And that's just the way it works in this lifetime. If you add past lives, you can see what a web of entanglements human existence really is..."

"Have you regressed any famous people?"

"You mean, famous in the past? ... Well, I once had a woman who was an aspect of Byron. You know, the poet."

"An aspect?"

"I've never met anyone who was a direct descendant of someone else. Souls seem to combine like DNA, constantly begetting new patterns ... So, are we ready?"

"Go for broke."

Yamamoto activated the VCR. A soft humming filled the room, blotting out all street sounds. Behind the hum was an almost inaudible clicking sound—a soft whirring of 850 beats per minute. "I want you to relax completely," Yamamoto said, as the imagery of growing flowers appeared on the screen. "See how *slowly* the flowers grow, how *deeply* relaxed in the sureness of time, relaxed and sure in eternity?"

"Yes ..."

"Human life is like that, too ... You too can relax into the sure, patient rhythm of eternity ... You, too, are held in God's hand, in the hand of a sure, radiating power, a protective goodness that only wants the best for us ... Now, remember, any time you want to stop this, you just count up to three. `One, two, three, awake!' Try it."

"One, two, three, awake."

"Good. Very good ..." He started his tape recorder. "Just let your eyes focus softly on the screen," he said. Church organ music played in the background as the flowery imagery continued. "Send the relaxing power to your toes. Feel your toes relax .. Down your toes to your heels ... and your feet are com*plete*ly relaxed .. Up your feet to your calves ... and your calves are com*plete*ly relaxed ... sooo relaxed ... com*plete*ly relaxed ..."

Thus proceeding, Yamamoto brought the wary knight to a

state of suggestibility. Years fell away like the petals of the rose, and still he went deeper into the soft, maroon heart of the rose, feeling the warmth and the tenderness and the love of the rose, as the clicking slowed to 140 beats per minute and the contours of the office faded.

"Can you tell me who you are?" Yamamoto asked.

"The biwa singer..."

"The bee-wa singer?"

"Yes..."

"And what do you see?"

"Blackness. Only blackness..."

"Is there no light in this blackness? Not a chink of light anywhere?"

"Only blackness."

Yamamoto made a note in his journal. "This is a blackness that cannot harm you," he said. "This is a blackness that can teach you. There are many paths in this blackness. Tell me the path you are on."

Lance shifted uneasily on the couch. "I am in the black river of the world," he said.

"It cannot harm you.. The water is warm.. The water will buoy you up..."

"I listen and I try to learn," Lance said, catching a thread in his hand, a silken thread, following the thread.

"What are you learning? What are you listening to?"

"The students are chanting..."

"Yes...?"

"There are gongs and chanting..."

"What do the students chant? Can you make it out?"

"*Namu Amida Butsu.*"

"And what do you feel? Can you tell me?"

"Something cool in my hands. A cool metal..."

"Do you know what this is?"

"It is the thing I have been seeking."

"Yes... And what is this thing?"

"The Army of Salvation..."

"What? What's that?"

"I gave it to the sisters because they gave me food."

Yamamoto stroked his chin. "I see... What else? Do you want to continue on this path?"

Lance's breathing was troubled. "Beating wings in a cave..."

"Yes... Go on..."

"Oarlocks... scrape of wood against the metal..." His body began to tremble slightly. "Crying.. Ginyo crying..." The trembling increased. "Will! Will is killed!"

Yamamoto leaned forward in his seat. He wrote quickly in his own shorthand.

"Many people are crying... the Emperor... the boy..."

"The Emperor?"

"They... are... taking... him... to... the... to the... somewhere... whizzing arrows... sound of..."

"Yes..."

"Fire! All around us. Arrows of fire! The mast on fire! Flesh on fire!... Feel of silk against the flesh..."

"Yes..."

"And, they are taking the boy..."

"Yes..."

"Ginyo! No! No! No!" Now his body heaved with grief. Yamamoto waited. He'd never been taken through a battle before. He didn't know how far to go. "Lance," he said, a little louder: "Lance!"

"No! " Lance cried. "Not Will! Not Ginyo! Take me! Take me!"

"Lance!"

"Warm water on my hands... No! Blood!... An arrow in her neck... Life pouring out like a fountain... Will! Will? Are you there, boy? My friend... my brother..."

"I'm going to count to three now," Yamamoto said.

"It's not *fair*... Take me! I'm the one! Take me! Take me!"

"You'll remember everything . . . you'll be safe . . . you'll be back in this time . . ."

"Damn you Merlin!"

"One . . ."

"Damn you Buddha!"

"Two . . ."

"Damn you God!"

"*Three!*"

Lance blinked his eyes open. He was drenched in sweat. The gentle humming continued in the background and the image of maroon rose petals, seen from above, remained frozen on the screen. The cool air chilled him.

Yamamoto was also sweating. He had never had a more intense session. He sighed heavily, patted Lance on the shoulder. "You're back . . . It's all right." He retrieved a fresh towel from his office lavatory. He handed it to Lance, who stared at him, still shaken.

Yamamoto dialed the office lights to a soft glow. He turned off the VCR and the tape recorder. The humming ceased, the clicking ceased. He scrutinized his patient.

Lance sighed mightily. "I can't help them now," he said at last.

"No . . ."

"It was long ago . . . and yet . . ."

"Yes . . ." Nervously, Yamamoto flipped a pencil, caught it between thumb and forefinger, flipped it again. "Time is a prism . . . a mystery. If the past were not present now, in this moment, this moment could not exist . . . and yet, it's gone . . . or, rather, *transfigured*."

"'Time present and time past . . . both perhaps present in time future . . And time future contained in time past . . .'"

"*Burnt Norton*, isn't it?"

"Yes . . ." Lance jolted up from the couch. "I left it with the sisters!"

"What?"

"God's wounds! The Grail! It's with the sisters!"

Yamamoto checked his notes. "'The Army of Salvation.' The Salvation Army?"

"That's it! They found me wandering downtown. They fed me. I gave them all I had." A cold hand played the piano of his spine. "My God! What did I do? I've got to go!"

"I wanted to ask you about—"

But Lance was half way to the door. "I'll call you," he said.

"Lance, don't try to do too much today. You've been through a lot."

Lance nodded distractedly. He extended his hand. "Thank you. Thank you."

"Don't mention it. Do you want me to come?"

"No . . . You don't know what you've done," Lance said, pumping Yamamoto's arm.

Yamamoto felt an urge to quote something. "'If I can bring a warrior his armor . . . that will be enough.'"

"What?"

The therapist scratched his head. "What did I just say?"

Lance and Lorrie were already out the building when Lance remembered Yamamoto's last words. "Beansprout!" he said.

*

Try as they might the good soldiers of the Salvation Army had not been able to polish the chalice the big, blond man had given them. They could not know that the patina had been set in place over the millennia. Now it served its purpose as a somewhat tarnished receptacle for cellophane-wrapped perppermints.

Sister Mary Elizabeth Angelica was always trying to make things functional and useful. Had she not entered social work, she would have been one of those peculiar women who made roomsful of furniture by varnishing and stacking old newspapers. Fortunately for the thousands who flowed through her shelter, Sister Angelica had been more interested in varnishing souls.

She cast her cool, appraising eye at the couple entering the refectory. The transients, homeless and hopeless watched the couple with curiosity or downright hostility. The man with the faded blue cape hunched over a bowl of soup in the corner. Like a vulture feeding on carrion, his shoulders rose slightly as his neck curved into a question mark over the Campbell's hearty vegetable soup. Stealthily, he smoothed a piece of gum under the table.

"You'll have to wait in turn like everyone else," said Sister Angelica in her best no-nonsense tone.

Lance was undeterred. "Sister, I was here about a month ago. I left something with you—"

"Did I give you a receipt?" Sister Angelica asked warily. Her "children," as she thought of those she served, were always trying to wheedle more out of her.

"Is that it?" Lorrie asked, pointing to the cup at the end of the soup line.

Lance dropped to his knees and crossed himself. "Praise God! It's still here!"

"We save the praying for the service," Sister Angelica said sternly. She had fought off the holy rollers for decades, and she wasn't about to turn her shelter into a conversion-meat-market-for-Christ this late in the game!

Lance kissed the hem of her garment.

"Look," Sister Angelica informed him, "this isn't the place for carrying on. I run a respectable shelter. Those in need can obey the rules or shuffle on down the road!"

The shelter's patrons enjoyed the commotion. Any break in their dreary routines excited them. "Is this a movie?" an old lady with rheumy eyes asked her companion.

Coarse, bulbous fingertips ran down Lorrie's thigh. "Quit!" she cried, jumping.

"Smooth," said the old codger. A young man with a ragged beard stood up, red with indignity. "Ain't no way to treat a lady!"

"See what you've done," Sister Angelica complained to Lorrie.

"All right, Billy," she said in a softer tone, "show's over. Sit down and finish your grub."

Chastened, the boy-man sat down. Lance had risen to his full six foot six now, and the little sister confronted him boldly. "Now just what is it you were wanting?" she asked.

"I'm sorry, Sister . . . I didn't mean to cause you trouble." Lance nodded towards the Grail. "That little vessel over yonder . . ."

Sister Angelica harrumphed. She had kind of taken a liking to the vessel. "I asked you if you had a receipt," she repeated.

Lance looked pained. He hadn't expected resistance. Something about Sister Angelica reminded him of some character in *The Grapes of Wrath*. He started talking like Joad. "What's a receipt, ma'am?"

So Lorrie explained.

"Cain't say that I have, ma'am. We just kinda take folks' words where I come from."

Sister Angelica narrowed her eyes. She reckoned the stranger for a Texan. She had an abiding dislike of Texans that went back to her first no-good-skirt-chasing-booze-guzzling-gun-toting-cock-gaming-country-singing husband. First and only, she would add. "Look, Mister," she told Lance now, "I run a soup kitchen, not a flea market. Fifty people come through here a day. Times are hard and gettin' harder. The city's got money to spruce up the places where the tourists go, but me, I've got to go begging. I don't like it. But I'll keep on begging because somebody's got to feed God's children. But I don't let no one get the better of me. Now you say you donated that to one of the sisters? Well, maybe you did and maybe you didn't. But, unless you've got proof, I'm going to call the brothers from the back room and ask them to escort you out. Do I make myself clear?"

"Maybe I can help," Lorrie said, fumbling in her purse. She withdrew a plastic billfold. "I keep these for emergencies," she said, handing a hundred dollar traveler's check to the obstinate guardian of the chalice.

"Now you're talking!" said Sister Angelica, almost slapping

her knee. Then her suspicious side took over again. "You got any proof? Any identification?"

So Lorrie produced her driver's license—"That picture doesn't look like you!"—her library card— "this here's expired!"—her father's Visa card— "this is someone else's name!"—and finally her voter's registration card—never used.

"That'll do," said Sister Angelica at last. "We sure do thank you for your generous donation! . . . Please leave the mints on the table."

"God, what a witch!" Lorrie said when the door shut behind them.

Lance laughed. "I had rather any day have faced Sir Turquine and Sir Mador together." He looked back through the storefront window and saw Sister Angelica ladling soup to her children. Her expression was beatific. "Yet she was worthiest," he added. "The God-appointed one to keep the Grail."

Lorrie nodded at the chalice. "It don't look like much," she said.

"It is what it is."

"Why's it so important?"

"The wine of the Last Supper touched Christ's lips through this. His last blood sanctified this rim."

"Oh," Lorrie said, shrugging.

*

Carol fixed Yamamoto's tie for the fourth time that morning; then they caught a taxi to the downtown studio. Yamamoto had appeared on local TV before, but nothing compared with a guest spot on the networks. He would be one of two principal guests of Petunia Petunia—the hot, black, sassy, salsa-mouthed doyen of the afternoon talks. They were doing a show on New Age Nabobs. When her people had called he had jumped at the chance. He'd immediately gotten on the horn to his agent and got the book deal cranking again. The two-hundred-thousand-dollar advance would keep him in daiquiris for years to come.

"You have your choice," the make-up artist told him when he sat himself in front of the light-bulb-fringed mirror. "Heavy, extra heavy, Tammy Faye Baker heavy."

He decided on extra heavy. He was worried about the rings under his eyes. He hadn't slept well. He was concerned about the show's other principal guest.

"You look . . . different," Carol said when he emerged.

"I feel like a mummy. Pardon me if I don't crack a smile . . . How is it really?"

"Well . . . If this doesn't work, you might consider ventriloquism as a career. No one could see you move your lips."

"Very funny . . . Have you seen Lance?"

"Umh . . . He refused make-up. Said only women and Heian dandies put it on."

Yamamoto lifted his eyes to heaven.

It was Lance, of course, who concerned Yamamoto. When Petunia Petunia had asked him to bring along a patient he had successfully regressed, one who was "colorful," he had thought of Lance at once. He had tried hard to think of someone else, someone safer. He'd tried to summon from his memory someone who would reinforce his ideas—with just enough "color," but not too much; someone the matrons could relate to, feel good enough about to rush to the phones and order a copy of his soon-to-be-released book. He ransacked his files searching for names, calling former patients and patient-lovers.

Little did he know that the Kami had gotten there before him. They had raced through the fiber optical network into the receivers, jumbled his voice, garbled the message. When he tried to ooze charm, he merely sounded oozy. Inflections which had never failed to work for him before were suddenly afflicted with gravelly undertones. Men heard buoys plop to the surface and were warned off. Women heard a nasal whine that made them think of orthopedic shoes. All begged off. At last, he'd made the call to Lance; the same Kami gave his voice a buttery, authoritative quality. Lance said yes at once.

"You look *fab*," said Petunia Petunia, gushingly crushing Yamamoto's slender frame against her monumental mamaries, enveloping him in the warm, charcoal-colored, cascading flesh of her arms, smothering him against the jellyrolls of her black, sweetly-powdered belly. "Say, honey, is that a gun in your pocket, or are you just glad to see me?" Petunia Petunia slapped his shoulders and guffawed. "Now I know you're taken, honey," she said, winking at Carol, "but, tell me, who's that gorgeous stud you brought with you?"

"You've seen Lance, then?"

"Seen him? You think this here is baby fat, honey. Honey, this is radar underneath these clothes. If there's a gorgeous man around, I can home in from fifty miles. Those smart bombs got nothin' on Petunia. They don't call me "stealth" for nothin' . . . Whoo-ee! . . . You ain't nervous, are you?"

"No, ma'am," he lied.

"Well, good. I like to meet my guests before, you know. Get'em relaxed. Cuz, honey, just between you and me, there ain't nothin' tuh worry about. Cuz I'm gonna be there for you the whole nine yards." She put her little, pudgy hand up and fluttered her fingers like a child. "Bah-eye!" She winked at Carol.

Petunia Petunia cracked her knuckles. "They fall for that shit every time," she told her producer. "I'm gonna skewer that sucker!" she said, licking her chaps.

*

Michael Yamamoto squirmed under the hot lights. He loosened his tie. He had no idea it could get so hot in an air-conditioned studio. Now he peered into Petunia's jowly face; her fish-eyes cut him to the bone. They were only eighteen minutes into the show!

"You're asking us to believe," Petunia said in her trained adversarial tone, "you're asking us to believe that today's indigestion may be the result of some bad sausage we ate in another lifetime. That the child dying of hunger today was Adolf Hitler in the last life. This idea—the idea of karma—it doesn't allow for tragedy, does it? Throw out Shakespeare, throw out opera—ain't nothin' tuh worry 'bout, honey, cuz everybody's got their dues to pay an' it all comes clean in the end." Petunia turned to her audience. "Lordy, I think I'll go out and have me a *baaad* time cuz the bill ain't comin' due till the next go-round!"

Her audience guffawed. They might not follow her arguments, but they knew her style, and they loved to watch her puncture the bubbles of her fatuous guests.

"I wouldn't throw out Shakespeare yet," Yamamoto said in a squeaky voice. "Not opera, either." He felt his sweat pool under his arms.

"Not opera!" Lance told Lorrie in the front row. "Certainly not opera!"

Yamamoto took some courage from Lance's smiling countenance. "I'm not pretending we understand all the dynamics," he said, "how good and evil transfer between lifetimes. One could argue that any time we miss realizing our full potential—it's tragic."

"One could, indeed," Petunia agreed, opening the trap a little, placing her foot on the dais where her guests were seated. She had disposed of her first victim in short order, reducing the distinguished white-bearded professor-author of a scholarly book on hallucinogens into an aged hippie purveyor of failed lifestyles and degenerate morals. ("Aren't you molesting the minds of children?" she had asked at one point.) With the taste of meat in her mouth, she was now basting Yamamoto.

"Now follow me for a moment," Petunia coaxed as she moved in close for the mauling. Michael felt her hot breath on his throbbing jugular. He lowered his tie to half-mast. Petunia narrowed her eyes. Her voice was solemn, serious. "If you give up the tragic, you give up the noble and the glorious, as well. You follow me? You see, the noble and the glorious make no sense except where the tragic is an ever-present fact. Am I clear?" She cocked her left eye like a gun.

"Yes," Yamamoto moaned.

In the audience, the Blue Man turned to Velvet. "What the hell she talking about?"

Velvet shrugged. "Beats me. But she has a funny way of saying it!"

"Well, anyway," Petunia said, savoring her moment, clinching the argument and devastating Yamamoto's authorial ambitions all at once, "I believe you've brought one of your victims—I'm sorry—patients with you . . ." Yamamoto sighed as Petunia waddled towards Lance. In the therapist's mind the cash register rang up debit sign after debit sign. He wondered if he'd ever be able to practice again. Would they make him return the royalty advance?

"You're name is Lance?"

Lance had risen to his full 6-6. His flowing gold locks caught the studio lights in a sheen that made the female audience pine with envy. "Yes, Ma'am," he said in his best Joad Whatsizname.

"And you've been 'taken back' by Dr. Yamamoto? Is that right?" Petunia continued. "Don't let me put words in your mouth, sugar."

"Yes, Ma'am. Way back."

"Oh, my, and he's polite, too," Petunia oohed. "Where's your mama been keeping you, honey?" Petunia poked Lance between the ribs. Lance turned a flustered face to Lorrie as the audience snickered. Yamamoto sank lower in his chair.

"And just who was it you were in your previous incarnation?" Petunia wondered.

"Ma'am?"

"You claim to have been someone else in another life?"

"No, Ma'am. I was never anyone but myself. I just looked different."

"Ah," Petunia smiled, "and who were you called back then, if you don't mind my asking."

Lance straightened with pride. "Sir Lancelot du Lac, the son of King Ban and the good Queen Helen."

The audience leaned forward in their seats. A wave of merriment surged.

"Did you say Helen of Troy?" Petunia needled.

"No, Ma'am. Just Helen. The Good Queen Helen, the people called her... Though I don't know much about her." Lance's voice fell to a whisper.

Petunia felt the mood of the pack. Like the lead wolf, she circled her quarry. "And what is it you do now, Mr. Lancelot?... I'm sorry, I should say `Sir Lancelot,' shouldn't I?"

The audience salivated. Still in his *Grapes of Wrath* mode, Lance had no sense of irony. He couldn't understand the constant giggling. "Folks mostly call me what they please, ma'am. These days I mostly read and study," he said softly.

"You're a student?"

"Yes, Ma'am. You might say so..."

"You go to school?"

"No, Ma'am."

"Ah, an independent scholar... independently wealthy, or suffering in a garret?"

"Sir Garreth, Ma'am?"

"Never mind." Petunia shifted her enormous weight. Lance felt the carpet move under him. Petunia moved in close for the *coup de gras*. "Sir Lancelot," she said, putting her hand on his hair-fringed shoulders, "you're a handsome man!"

"Thank you, Ma'am."

"You mind if I ask you a personal question?"

"No, Ma'am."

"Just what the hell are you doing here in the 20th Century?"

The audience shuddered with laughter. Lance looked at the grinning faces. He looked at his clothes, his arms and hands, sought out his image in the monitors. Had he suddenly been transformed into the court jester?

"It's a long story, Ma'am," he explained earnestly. "It started in Yamato. Then we got caught up in the assassination—"

"We? Assassination?"

"Will and me . . . Will's my squire . . . and then we had to hightail it outa there right fast."

"High tail?"

"Yes, Ma'am . . . and we were in Heian Japan next thing I knowed. It was fine there, 'cepting the past caught up with us. The past always catches up with you. It'll bite you on the rear like a scurvy dog when a body's mind is elsewhere . . ."

"You know," Petunia said, "somehow I never imagined Sir Lancelot talking like you."

"That's a right funny thing, Ma'am," Lance agreed, scratching his head like a farmboy. "Each time I come to a place I change like one of them lizards that changes its colors." Lance turned to Lorrie. "What do you call it?"

"Camouflage."

"That's right. Camouflage . . . Chameleon, if I remember right . . . It don't last long. And sometimes I shift back and forth without I ken help it."

"And, is this your girlfriend?" Petunia asked.

"Yes, Ma'am. I guess you could say so."

Petunia gave Lorrie the withering eye. "Well, stand up. Stand up, child."

Lorrie stood, and twined her arm around Lance's.

"What's your name, child?"

"Lorrie."

"Do you believe this, Lorrie? Do you stand by your man?"

"I think . . . I think it's what he has to believe . . ." Lorrie smiled nervously into the camera.

"Well," Petunia Petunia said, "*Amor omnia vincit!* Love do conquer all! Ain't that pretty, folks? Next time someone tells you they're Napoleon, you just take them in, give'em a good, hot meal. After all, it's what they've *got* to believe. Ain't that right, child?"

With almost as dull a sense of irony as Lance's, Lorrie nodded and tried to smile.

"Especially if they look like this one!" Petunia continued. She ran her hand through Lance's golden locks.

The theme music started and Petunia did the tap-dance routine that had made her famous. She seemed to be hinged with ball bearings. Her weight flowed back and forth upon her skeleton like liquid mercury in a petri dish. "Don't go way, tomcats and kittens, we'll be back in a flash with Michael Yamamoto and his space cadets, Sir Lancelot and his squire-ette Lorrie. Got any quests? Got any dragons? Hang around to hear the pitch. If we ain't cookin', you can switch!" Petunia winked and the station broke to commercials.

Yamamoto wiped the sweat from his brow with his damp-through handkerchief. It had taken him fifteen years to build his practice. It had taken Petunia fifteen minutes to tear it apart.

Maybe he could teach English in Japan. He'd always wanted to visit his father's country. He'd always liked samurai movies. But first he was going to kill Petunia Petunia.

The Blue Man smoothed a wad of chewing gum under his seat. After the Syndicate created chaos in Atlanta, they'd get to work in other cities. No harm in starting early. As for Commander Nakatomi's golden-haired boy—there was time for him. He'd choose a place the dark Kami would approve. It had to be done in the right place and at the right time. It was not enough to kill the man's body. He must obliterate the soul. And the Kami whispered to him, "Soon . . . Soon . . ."

"Soon enough we're back," said Petunia to the camera. "We've been talking with Sir Lancelot. That's right, folks, you heard me—King Arthur's goody two-shoes. The best jouster, lover, damsel-in-distress-deliverer that ever brandished a broadsword!" She rested her hand on Lance's shoulder. "Man, I do love your hair!"

"Thank you, Ma'am."

"Lance—" she said, "May I call you Lance?"

"Yes, Ma'am."

"I was thinking during the break, Lance. You never did answer my question about what you're doing here."

"Well, Ma'am, the truth is, I wish I knew. This is where the Kami took me . . ."

"The who-what?"

"The Kami, Ma'am . . the spirit-creatures."

"Oh . . ." Petunia raised her fluffy brows.

"Well, Ma'am, you know how sometimes you do something and you're not sure why cuz it don't make no sense with anything you ever done before. And you reckon back and you think, it wasn't for me I done that, it was for someone else. You was playin' your part in someone else's movie. I reckon that's what I'm doin' now. I just happen to fit the bill."

Something in the man's demeanor moved Petunia. She searched the cobalt eyes for a hint of cynicism, a trace of mockery. But she found none. She searched her mind for a scathing addendum to his little speech, a flick-of-the-wrist-back-handed-slap-in-the-face bit of rhetorical linguine to make the speech ridiculous. But all she could think of was, "Oh."

"I'd like to sing a little song, Ma'am," Lance said, removing the guitar case from under his seat.

"How'd you get that in here?" Petunia wondered. "Past security?"

"Don't rightly know, Ma'am," Lance said, strapping on the guitar, tuning the instrument. "I'm still a little rusty . . . I used to play the biwa way back when."

Like a slow sea wave, the audience surged forward as Lance strummed the first chords. He brought them back to a better time, a Norman-Rockwell America of 5-cent Cokes and "Yes, Ma'am" and "No, Ma'am"; balloon tire bicycles and crinoline petticoats. Maybe it was a place that never was except in the imagination. But it felt good to visit.

Lance smiled his big old winsome country smile. "This here song's about changes," he said. "It's inspired by something Marcus Aurelius wrote."

"Marcus Aurelius?" Petunia said dully, holding the mike in her tingling hand.

"Yes, Ma'am," Lance smiled. "From *The Meditations*." Then he sang:

> Everything is only for a day
> coming round us in a way
> that remembers,
> in the way we are recalled.
>
> Take it from the heart
> it's the changes that have made us,
> it's the changes that'll break us
> and remake us one and all.
>
> For the universe loves nothin'
> but to make a thing that's like us
> but different from before.
> Everything that's falling
> is the seed of what is dawning
> in the heart that can't recall—"

He slowed the tempo:

> Thou wilt die soon
> and thou art but a fool,
> full of self-doubt
> when the self is but a cool
> wind blowing in the night.

He changed the tempo again:

> Just a cool, cool wind
> blowing in the night.
> Just a cool, cool wind
> blowing in the night."

The sea of the audience surged again, listening for the finale. It was the sea listening for its own voice, for he sang with the voice of all of them, and the plangent tones stirred them with remembrance, sympathy and acceptance. Petunia's hand trembled softly, adding to the tremolo in Lance's voice. He half spoke, half sang the last lines, and his voice was as sonorous as when it had stopped Lord Munemori on Red Bird Avenue:

> Nor art thou free from perturbations
> and the thing that dances holy
> is the thing that thou most fearest
> in the darkness of the night.

> Make thy heart a simple valley
> where the sunlight of all kindness
> may grow roses out of wisdom
> in the moonlight of the night;
> while the changes whirl around us,
> we fashion our beginnings
> into petals of delight;
> though the petals rearrange us
> yet we open up the door
> to find ourselves—nothing more—
> calling those we loved before
> through the petals of the night.

Yamamoto pulled up his tie. Petunia Petunia shed her first tear in thirteen years. The audience ebbed back into their seats. Forever after they would tell people they had been there. All over America, people paused and understood for a fleeting moment that it was all right, that it was all part of a bigger plan.

And the Blue Man stuck a wad of gum under the chair in front of him.

13 | The Disciple of Chi

Lance rubbed his hand gently over the rough bark of the Princess Tree in the Atlanta Botanical Garden. The large, pale green, lotus-like leaves were speckled with white pigmentation, as though snowflakes had dusted them. They reminded him of a pattern on one of Sagami's silk kimonos.

He walked past the bed of begonias that recalled the first blush of the cherry trees, *sake* cups passing under the boughs, tongues loosened into poetry. A bronze statue of a nymphlike girl with a parasol made him pause. She rose out of her rock pedestal with a vague familiarity. Had he eyes at the back of his head, he would have seen her tilt her head slightly to watch him walk away.

He followed the sidewalk to the ceramic pond with its three small, petal-fringed faces under a tiny cascade. These faces, too, were familiar, but unplaceable. He shook his head. Everything seemed so much more than itself. A world of symbols signifying...

"Nothing," Shakespeare had said. Or at least had his Macbeth say so.

Macbeth had come to nothing because he could not read—had let the witches and his wife read for him—symbols, signs, portents. At last he had denounced them as mere witches' ruses. Then the symbols rose up and chopped his head from his shoulders.

The hidden world and the mundane fed each other always. One world died into the other—the flare of extinction here was the dawn of a blossoming star over there.

He passed through the bamboo gate and followed the bamboo fence to the small sitting area in the Japanese garden. White horsetailed pampas swayed in the breeze. The stone bridge traversed a lotused pond. The sound of flowing water was cool and welcome in the humid heat of June. He splashed some water on his face, sat on the little wooden bench and a thousand images cascaded, a chorus of voices rose and fell with the breeze: Will, Ginyo, Imbe-san, the Commander . . . Fujiwara, Kiyomori . . . Guenevere . . . Arthur, Merlin . . . Sagami . . .

"So, I found you," the familiar voice said behind him.

Lance rose and extended his hand. "Hello, Michael. I'm glad you could come."

Yamamoto took a seat beside Lance on the stone bench. "It's nice to get out of the office." He placed a small stack of books between them.

"I'm getting rather tired of offices and skyscrapers," Lance said. He opened the cover of the first book. "These are for me?"

"Yes. I think you'll find them helpful. It's not really my bailiwick, you understand. People think all us New Age types are in bed with each other. But, of course, it doesn't work that way. There's rivalry and there's skepticism same as everywhere. Just because we don't accept a cut and dried, meat and potatoes universe, doesn't mean we're ready to be duped by every snake oil merchant who slithers down the pike . . ." Michael saw that Lance was getting twisted in his metaphors. He looked closely, with some concern, at the thin, pale face. "You still haven't eaten anything?"

Lance shook his head. "Not since New York."

Michael sat up straight. "That's a week, Lance."

"As you see, I'm still whinnying in this world."

"Lance, maybe you better—"

"It's all right, Michael. I'm drinking Reishi tea to keep my stomach calm. And Damiana from the country to the south. Dong Quai, Fo Ti, Gotu Kila calm my nerves and clear my mind. Ginseng for strength."

Yamamoto sighed. "I've got twenty record companies who want to sign you, and you're holed up fasting in Atlanta. Do you know what a hit you were on Petunia's show?"

Lance stood up. He listened. The Kami were trying to tell him something. He still couldn't hear. He smiled warmly at Michael. "Always keen for battle, ey Beansprout?"

"I wish you'd stop calling me that."

"Let's walk . . . I want to show you something."

They passed the beds of multicolored roses. In the distance, past Piedmont Park, skyscrapers bloomed from the ashes of Sherman's march.

Lance opened the double doors of the steel and glass-domed Fuqua Conservatory. The bonsai trees stirred as the doors shut behind them. "They say this is a lucky tree," Lance said, stroking the miniature leaves of the Juniper bonsai. He looked up, watched some movement in the distance. "I'm going to need luck, Michael. A lot of white magic."

"Those books should help," Michael reassured him. He was struck by the way Lance had changed his stripes again. The country accent was gone, the ungainly slump, the boyish awkwardness and gawking. Yet, a mystique of danger lingered in the air around him. Not that he was dangerous, but that he attracted it—and Lord help those who got in the way when danger came calling!

"Do you know how extraordinary it is for me to step into a building that's temperature-controlled?" Lance asked. "The fabled kings of Britain could not have wished for, in their wildest dreams, what your middle class folks take for granted . . . And yet I think, how poor and sad you are . . ."

Michael felt his dander rise. "You're not going to pull that `quintessence of dust' stuff on me, are you?"

Lance smiled. He motioned with his hand. "Let's visit Africa."

In the tropical rotunda, African Oscar fish swam in the spill-off of a tiny waterfall surrounded by orchids. Bat plants and begonias crowded ginger plants and banana plants grew among spindle palms. Thumb-sized lizards undulated like leaves and pinky-long green frogs hopped warily as seed-fed tropical birds flew lazily above. Lance drew deeply of the warm, moist air. "'Now more than ever seems it rich to die,'" he quoted Keats.

Michael stared into the wan and worried face. "What is it, Lance? What's wrong?"

Lance nodded in the direction of the sassafras tree. "You see those plants growing from the bark?"

"Yes . . ."

"They're not part of the tree. Those aren't sassafras flowers . . . The bark supports those plants. They take nothing from the tree. They give nothing back—nothing material. They call it an *epiphytic* relationship. The plant gets its nourishment from the atmosphere." Lance let his eyes roam the enclosed space. "From everything around it . . ."

Missing the point, Michael sighed, dabbed at his brow with a handkerchief.

Lance smiled his wry smile again. "You faced Taira arrows with less anxiety, Beansprout . . . Patience! Hear me out!"

"I only thought—"

"Your world makes much of thinking, yet it listens little. Everywhere: there's noise, a constant humming, droning, buzzing, whirring—a din. It undermines thought. Those picture boxes, the carriages you drive, what you call music. Everywhere: a pounding fear of loneliness. Yet, all of you are alone.

"I'm one of those epiphytic plants, you see. I planted my roots in the bark of my own century, in Merlin's magic, and I've drunk the air of other worlds, imbibed the atmosphere . . . Do you think they give anything to the tree, Michael?"

For the first time Yamamoto looked carefully at the tree and its plants.

"Do they add anything?" Lance coaxed.

Michael took a closer look. "Beauty . . . adornment . . ."

Lance smiled with satisfaction. "Yes . . . That's just what I was thinking . . . Beauty . . . The host could live without those things, yet how much poorer." He looked back over centuries. "We lived in hovels, drafty castles. We ate with our hands. Our hygiene was—I'll spare you details . . . Yet you look upon us with a yearning. Because we had a way to ornament our lives. We lived with the pageantry of magic . . . I want to give something back, Michael. I want you to help me."

"Of course . . ."

"Easy . . . Easy . . . Before you volunteer, turn your head very slowly, very slowly towards the orchids. Turn as a statue turns . . . You see the blue sleeve drooping amidst the birds-of-paradise? Follow the sleeve into the blue shadows . . . Do you see it?"

"I see . . . something . . ."

"That something is my death. It has been stalking me for fifteen hundred years . . . And I must meet it soon."

Alarm bells rang in the psychologist's mind. He trembled. He searched the birds-of-paradise again, saw nothing. "If somebody's bothering you . . ."

"No bother, Michael . . . No bother." Lance rested his hand on Michael's shoulder. "When I came into your world, it was so different, so strange . . . I forgot many things. I even forgot my purpose . . . Then I met you. And I began to remember. The threads were woven centuries before. And I followed them with your help. There was a reason you were saved, a reason your thread went into the loom. I'd like to think Will understood. He had come to understand more than I . . . " He sighed, then smiled. "I need your help, Beansprout. To tell my story. To help me to remember. To put it down."

Michael dabbed at the sweat on his brow and upper lip. In spite of the heroism of his supposed forebear, this "Beansprout," his soul-mate—or, soul-self—the commanding instinct in every fiber of his being now said "Run!" Run, don't walk, to the nearest exit. Get on the first plane to Hawaii, take some classes in Shiatsu, start a new business. He peered at the blue shadowy vapor amidst the orchids. Was there really something there?

He looked at Lance. What did this strange man want? If nothing else, he was certainly the most extraordinary lunatic he'd ever come across. Probably there was a book in it, a case-study book which would fatten his credentials with the academics.

Much more intriguing was the prospect of more songs. "Can we sign an agent's contract?" he asked.

"Is that how it's done?" Lance asked innocently.

Michael nodded.

"You'll help me then?"

Michael looked around again. He still saw nothing. "Of course." His voice was a little reedy.

"Tell me where to sign," Lance said.

They both laughed. They shook hands and walked out of the garden. Yamamoto turned once, thought he saw the blue vapor move from the orchids to the sassafras tree. Then a royal starling flitted above, and he reassured himself that all was well. He put a pillow over his internal alarm clock and let his sixth sense doze.

The bronze nymph statue watched them pass. "Soon," the Kami whispered to the glistening ears of the water. "Soon . . ."

*

The cool, moist skin of the python slid over Velvet's breasts, as the flat, beady-eyed head inched over her navel, over her rounded, white belly, and nestled in the brown-blond turf below. On the TV screens and mirrors surrounding her, Sylvester Stalone and Arnold Schwarzenegger were lacerating enemies with liquid lead gushing from super machine guns. The Blue Man rubbed his engorged penis between his two hands. Velvet parted her legs and the python's head eased below the pubis, nuzzled the moist, coral lips, then slid up the crack between her buttocks and glided over the dimples of her lower back. Velvet held the thick, slithering weight in her hands, felt the orgasm begin in her toes, move like a slow quake towards her center, then radiate warmth through her body. She wanted to fall back on the bed, but remained standing. When he could hold himself back no longer, the Blue Man seized the python around its thick middle and squeezed and twisted. Feeling its life endangered, the python coiled itself around Velvet's blond flesh and squeezed back. Her blue eyes shone with terror as she watched the Blue Man's hands slide further apart on the snake's body, the better to grasp the thick rubber hose of it, the better to wring and tear. She felt the coils around her body tighten, felt the blood squeezed towards head and limbs and her legs crumpled and she fell back, unsure if she were serpent or human. The Blue Man's hands worked maniacally around the snake and the thrashing, terrified creature squeezed Velvet's waist. The scales cracked and warm blood spurted from the writhing fire hose of the snake, soaked the man and woman as he entered her, rubbed her with his bloody hands. The Blue Man flung the severed snake at a mirror, its blood streaking the surface. Velvet screamed when she felt the copious semen pour heat into her womb. She seized the Blue Man's blood-drenched hair and pulled him into her blood-drenched breasts.

*

Forty minutes later the Blue Man was singing an ancient song in the shower while Velvet lay on the bloody bed smoking a cigarette. She was still trembling, fearful at what had been unleashed in her. The mangled body of the python lay in a heap at the foot of the bed. Stalone and Schwarzenegger were mincing new enemies with new devices.

Velvet calmly assayed the room. In its death throes the snake had overturned lamps, knocked over the telephone—still buzzing—scattered ash trays, water pitcher and two cans of Coke. "Things go better with Coke," Velvet said, as she rolled over and set the overturned cans upright on the floor. She set an ashtray on the night table, then crushed the bloody-finger-printed cigarette within it. She stepped into the cool, sticky Coke in the carpet.

The Blue Man was drying himself with a towel when she entered the bathroom. Suspended from a gold chain around his neck, the magatama jewel glistened like a Pleistocene tiger's saber tooth.

The sight of Velvet's lithe blond slenderness streaked with blood excited him again. "Did you come to get more?" he asked. His voice sounded eerily like Arnold Schwarzenegger's.

She entered the shower without answering, let her toes test the water gushing through the bath spigot, then pressed the dial so the shower spurted its warm, refreshing spray. She leaned her head back, ran her fingers through her hair, felt the water tap her throat and breasts gently. The red gore swirled into the drain.

When she emerged from the shower she felt totally refreshed and renewed. She imagined she still felt the warmth of the sperm inside her. She slid her feet into the gold, furry slippers she had left in the bathroom.

The Blue Man sat in his silk robe in an easy chair, smoking a Galois as he watched Stalone and Schwarzenegger flex and kill. When Velvet entered the room, she smelled the death of the snake for the first time, mingled with the stale sourness of their union. A wave of nausea and revulsion swept over her soap-sweet body.

"Did you come to get more?" the Blue Man asked in the same Schwarzenegger voice.

"If I said yes, you would worry," she said coolly.

He laughed.

The flickering TV images cast weird shadows over the darkened cyclone-ravaged room. She gestured with her hand: "What are we going to do about this?"

The Blue Man laughed again—a nasty, guttural laugh. "Call room service," he said.

He untied the sash of his robe and exposed himself to her. Blue tattoos of dragons and snakes, gorgons, phoenixes, warriors, *tengu* and she-demons covered his muscular body, appeared to change as he moved, mesmerizing with evolving, sinister patterns.

She watched, fascinated as he caressed himself, and his turgid member rose as to a snake-charmer's flute. "Come here," he said.

The wet carpet made a squishy sound beneath her gold slippers.

*

Lance gripped the carpeted seat as the motorized platform began turning slowly with a soft humming. The cyclorama of the Battle of Atlanta began to reveal its nine tons of paint and canvas. The plaster and fiberglass figures of the diorama nursed the wounded, charged on horseback, fell back bewildered in the sweltering heat of July, 1864. The eagle Old Abe, veteran of 42 battles, mascot of the Wisconsin regimen, soared above the Union field. "Merlin," Lance whispered. In ten minutes the painting had made a circuit. Five thousand men had died in a day and a turning.

At the exhibits upstairs, Lance paused in front of the costumes of Federal and Confederate generals. "They have no armor," he told Lorrie, with some surprise.

Lorrie shrugged. "I guess they figured they didn't need it. You know, it was just their fate or something."

Lance wondered how generals could go into battle without armor, without shields. (He still hadn't grasped the modern concept of war as mass slaughter.) How could the warriors display skill and courage when they couldn't get close to one another to fight man to man?

"You're missing the point," Yamamoto explained patiently. "Has your reading taken you through World War II yet? Or the Cold War?"

Lance shook his head sadly. "I'm not really past the 18th Century. The Industrial Revolution."

Michael put his hand on Lance's shoulder. "You don't really want to know what the human race has done to itself in the past two hundred years."

But Lance's piercing, sad blue eyes were, as always, eager for knowledge.

"Whole cities have been leveled, races genocided, millions of children have perished in holocausts of hunger. In our madness to control, we raped the green planet, leaving brown-yellow smoke in the ruins. We invented diseases and killed, wrapped baby Indians in smallpox-infested blankets, sold Blacks to whips and beggary, killed by dismemberment, poison, viruses, fire, hunger, cold, hanging, cutting, slashing, lead, lead and more lead. We taught our fellow citizens to hate their neighbors, then let them arm themselves against wish-fulfilling fantasies we stoked with the local news . . ."

Michael saw that Lorrie was shaking her head. Lance had a glazed expression, as though he hadn't heard much. Suddenly, with a hideous cry, Lance dropped to his knees before one of the glass cabinets.

"Look at the sword," Lance implored. Tears were coursing down his cheeks. "It's corroded!"

Other visitors turned from the displays to the strange, blond man on his knees. "What's wrong with that man, Mommy?" asked a pretty five-year old.

"Don't look, honey. The man isn't feeling well."

"Don't they know that the soul of a man is in his sword?" Lance groaned.

Michael and Lorrie helped him to his feet. "Come on, Lance. Let's get some air."

Outside, Lance seemed to revive. Michael was in favor of canceling the planned trip to the zoo, but Lorrie was convinced the animals would cheer Lance up.

The flamingoes did seem to restore his spirits. "Never have I seen such wondrous birds all flocked together!" Lance waxed poetically. "Prince Fujiwara would especially admire these. What a wonderful festival he could make with these!"

And he could have made an even greater festival with the

red-dusted elephants! "Are these the beasts that Hannibal surmounted?" Lance wondered.

"Hannibal Lecter?" Lorrie asked. "No . . . Those were lambs, not elephants." Lorrie laughed and shook her head and raised her brows to Michael. She never knew what odd thing Lance would say next. That's why she loved him so!

Lance enjoyed the "ok-to-touch-corral," where he petted the woolly backs of the llamas. A few paces beyond, the Kodiak bear astonished him. In a cool pool of water the Alaskan transplant licked its chaps and revolved its head in half arcs left to right, right to left. Lance looked around, too. "Will no boy come to bait the bear?" he asked.

Michael laughed. "I'm happy to report bear-baiting is out of fashion."

"One small step forward," Lance said, "for every fourteen back."

Somewhat hesitantly, a young woman approached Lance. Her boyfriend waited a few steps behind. "Excuse me, aren't you Sir Lancelot, the singer?"

"I am Sir Lancelot du Lac," Lance said proudly. "Son of King Ban and Queen—"

"I knew it!" the girl said, clasping her zoo map to her breasts. "Weren't you on the Petunia Petunia show about a month ago?"

"Yes," Lance said.

"I heard you sing," the girl said. "You were awesome! Would you sign my map?"

"Sign your map?"

"You know, your autograph."

"Autograph?"

The boyfriend shifted nervously. "I told you, Melody. I told you."

"Hey, I'll be happy to pay," the girl said, slightly peevish now.

"I told you," the boy repeated.

"Oh, never mind!" the girl said, grasping the map from Lance's hands.

"She wanted you to sign your name," Michael explained a little too late.

"But why?" Lance wondered, watching the retreating couple hurry away.

The girl turned back and sneered at Lance. "Snob!" she called.

"Takes one to know one," Lorrie called back.

"I told you. You gotta pay those guys," the boy's voice trailed. "They don't do nothin' for nothin'." The boy stabbed his middle finger into the air. Thinking it some sort of salute, Lance did the same. Michael and Lorrie laughed.

"Why don't we see the cats?" Michael suggested.

"You want to go back to Lorrie's condo?" Lance asked, still confused by the encounter with the autograph hounds.

"No, not those cats!" Lorrie said. "*Big* cats!"

So they watched the tigers and then the lions. And Lance thought, how strange and wonderful was the country of America that could bring the beasts of all the islands of the world to one place, put them behind glass and let them roam in habitats like their own.

And how strange and wonderful were the buildings of the land, where the houses were stacked on top on one another, and the moving cars went up and down between the floors, and the food was stored in cold boxes, and music came at the press of a button, and light at night was as bright as out of doors at noon; pictures came out of other boxes, and people walked barefooted on soft floors of fur, and there were clean, white rooms for private business, and beds of water, and mirrors everywhere—and still people were unhappy.

"How could they let the swords rust?" he asked Michael when Lorrie excused herself to "powder her nose."

"It bothers you . . . about the swords," Michael said.

It did, but he hardly knew how to say it. "If men lose respect for the things of their hand, for the things they fashion from the metals of the earth; if they use fire and bend metal with it, metal made from the ores of the earth, mined from the belly of the earth; and the wind of the bellows and the fire from the forge are joined with the mind and heart of man to bend and fashion and polish and shine so that the thing will fit the palm of a man's hand just so, and the weight will be just so—balanced to the man—and this thing will protect him and his house and his children and his wife, and it will serve him ever and anon while he measures his days, while he toils and labors and loves—how, then, will they let such a noble thing corrupt? What must it say of such men who let such things corrupt?"

Michael shrugged resignedly. "These are different times."

Something is missing, Lance thought, as he watched the cats cavorting. And they do not even know that it's missing. He would have to find a way to tell Michael during their next session with the video. He would have to try to get it on tape. Nothing seemed real to these creatures except what was refracted through a lens.

"Come here!" Merlin had said when Lance was a youngster of twenty shortly after he had first arrived at Camelot. "I want to show you something," the magician had urged. Merlin held a round piece of glass in his hand. He held it between thumb and index finger and made a round circle of light on some crumpled leaves. The light formed a point and the leaves began to smoke. Merlin blew on a spark and the leaves caught fire.

Satisfied, Merlin had nodded and smiled. Lance had stared at the burning leaves, then at the sage. Merlin never demonstrated his magic unless he wanted to make a point. Now he picked up a lady bug and held it gently in his palm. With his other hand he held the round glass close to his eye. "Now, look at it through this," Merlin advised.

Lance held the round glass and looked at the bug. He jumped back, dropping the glass.

"Careful!" Merlin cautioned, snatching the glass before it hit the ground.

"I saw a dragon!" Lance exclaimed.

"Nay, Lance, you saw the very creature I'm holding in my hand. Look again."

Lance looked, and saw that the creature was harmless, and

the scooped valleys it moved through were the ridges of Merlin's palm. "What does this teach you?" Merlin asked, letting the bug fly off.

"Things may not be what they seem."

"Go on," Merlin coaxed. "You had two lessons, did you not?"

Lance scratched his head. Queen Guenevere and her maids had entered the distant garden. He was already distracted by the Queen's beauty.

Merlin noted the lad's loss of concentration. "The fire, Lance . . . the burning . . ."

"Ah, yes . . ." He concentrated again. "That things may have a double use. What destroys in one instance may help our understanding in another."

"Go on . . ."

Lance watched the Queen and her maids play a game of shuttlecock. Their giggling came on a light breeze, seemed to cool him and make him hot at once.

"All right, Lance," Merlin said with some regret. "I see you will take a while. Though your mind is sharp, it flits like a hummingbird's. Only nectar will sustain it."

"What did you say, Merlin?"

"I said, the dragons of the mind are those most difficult to kill. They loom in the imagination like mountains on a darkling plain. What we perceive rightly, we may weigh justly. Without right perception, there is no justice. Now do you understand about God?"

"What? What did you say?"

"I asked you about Lorrie."

"Lorrie?" Merlin's face faded. Behind the protective glass, the great, maned cat bowed its head to drink, swishing its tail in its unamused mate's face.

"She's very fond of you," Michael continued. "I only brought it up because you said you wanted to talk about it."

Lance took his bearings, fought off a slight vertigo by seizing the wooden guardrail. "Are you all right?" Michael asked.

"Yes . . . I'm fine." He looked back and forth from the cats to Michael. If he could just remember all the lessons! If he could just remember the lessons and focus on the present and prepare for the coming battle! That was the nature of his quest—no more, no less! "Can you take care of her?" he asked. "I don't want her to be hurt. I'm afraid for her. I told you about Will. What happened. Sometimes it seems everyone who gets close to me—"

"That won't do," Michael said in his professional voice. "People get hurt one way or another. Nobody's hexed."

"I thought I'd tell her this weekend. She wants to take me to Lake Allatoona."

"You're still determined to go up north to the Cherokee land?"

"Everything persuades me I must go. The books you lent me about the shaman practices. The dreams I have waking and sleeping. Voices I hear. Ripples on ponds make a pattern. Leaves fluttering. I've practiced breathing like the Yogis. I've fasted, taken herbs. My nemesis approaches. I must prepare. Have you read *The Art of War*?"

"I guess that's one I missed."

"Sun Tzu says that the wise general bases his strategy on his enemy's `shape.' Observe your enemy; know him. That's what he means by `shape.' We start by thinking of the enemy as amorphous, shapeless. That shapelessness is our ignorance, our fear. Then we probe; we explore. We see where the enemy's fire-breathing head is, where the armor-plated tail; where the soft spot that a spear may enter.

"For months now, I've been shadowed by my enemy. As he observed me, I have been observing him. We might have had a confrontation anytime. That would have been very *cheng*, very direct. This happened before. I was blinded that way; my friend Will was killed . . That's how I went into battle when I served in Arthur's court. But now—all my traveling, all my travails have taught me a sliver of subtlety: *Chi* was the chink in my armor."

"*Chi?*"

Lance watched the graceful cats move on soft paws, all their joints and sockets seeming well-oiled springs. "They would know what I mean," he said, nodding towards the glass. "*Chi* is the other way of fighting—flanking, circling, distracting. There I lacked skills . . . And there I paid . . .

"Think of them as skins on the same drum—one on each side—*chi* and *cheng*. Perhaps you would say *Yin* and *Yang*, though you should not think of them as male and female; rather, two very different ways of action that may transform, at any moment, one into the other. These things I've come to understand through the work I've done with you: by looking back and seeing larger patterns . . . But, there's still too much I don't understand . . ."

Michael cleared his throat. "There's still too much *I* don't understand. But I'm in it now. I'm going to be there for you. I don't know why you had to come here, but I'll help you any way I can. I've been practicing the drumming, as you asked me to. I'll be ready."

Lance clutched Michael's upper arms. "I must tell Arthur: at the Table Round, two more seats are due. One for Will and one for you."

Michael clutched Lance in like fashion. "I can't say that I totally believe in this . . . I can't say I'm not scared."

Lance tossed his head back. "Belief comes as it comes, my friend. It can't be forced—no matter how hard one applauds!"

"The Sangreal," Michael asked, suddenly concerned. "You put it in the vault?"

"As you advised me."

"So, you guys, did you learn anything from the cats?" Lorrie asked when she returned.

"What should we have learned?" Michael wondered.

"How to treat a woman," Lorrie said, taking Lance's arm.

"You wouldn't want me to swish my tail in your face, would you?"

Lorrie appraised Lance's posterior. "I don't know. Might not be a bad idea. You've got a cute bum."

Michael laughed. Lance shook his head. "I don't understand these modern girls," Lance said.

"No one does," Michael said. "Just go with the flow."

They made faces at the orangutans and gorillas and failed to get a response. The animals had been jaded by too many tourists making faces. When they left, the animals were distracted by a blue shadow crouching in the trees, moving scentlessly among the artificial boulders. The Kodiak bear rolled its head, then bowed. The lions aimed their ears in multiple directions, then looked at each other with a warning. The indolent, always-lounging orangutans sat straight up and waited patiently.

Outside the zoo, Michael kicked the crank of the 1948 Indian and the motor roared to life.

"When you going to teach me to drive that thing?" Lance asked.

"Tomorrow. After our taping session. It's not easy. Have you ever driven a cycle?"

Lance laughed, his eyes twinkled. "Have you ever jousted on a horse?"

*

The largest exposed granite stone in the world reached long scapulae under the Piedmont plain, undergirding Terminus/Atlanta/Atlantis: the phoenix-risen city, resurrected out of the ashes of Sherman's cannonade; out of the blood of the martyrs at New Hope Church, out of the terrible dreams of the Home Guard's old men and willow-green, fat-back-raised farmboys still wet behind the ears.

"It's impossible to get around this city," Lorrie complained, nosing the Saturn carefully in front of a police night-cruiser.

They'd hardly spoken a word for an hour, since their drive back from Allatoona Lake. Uncustomarily, Lance was glad for a break in the silence. "I thought you liked it here?"

"Look at that!" she exclaimed, noticing the camera lights ahead. "Another goddamn journalist doing another goddamn story about the goddamn homeless! I'm goddamn sick of it! I really am!"

Lance looked at the poor Black with the tattered Olympic T-shirt enjoying his fifteen seconds of television fame. "I was once homeless," he said softly. "You took me in."

"Yeah," she said. She made no attempt to disguise her bitterness.

In the condo, she went into the bedroom and fell straight back on the bed. She stared at the twirling ceiling fan.

"I didn't mean to upset you," Lance said tenderly. "You've been a true friend. You once said we would always be friends. I don't know what I would have done without you."

"Yeah," she said, "a true friend."

He sat down on the bed beside her. She moved slightly away, still staring at the ceiling fan. "Lorrie, I'm not good at this," he said haltingly. "I was never any good at it."

She narrowed her eyes. "Have you done it so often?" She thrust her hands under her head, pointed her elbows at him, wouldn't look at him. "You said all you wanted to at the lake, didn't you?" Her brows rose and fell with her thoughts, her need to be held warred with her desire to lash out.

"I never meant to hurt you, Lorrie."

Now she looked at him with love and hatred. "You used me! Now you've got that movie contract, you don't need me any more."

"What movie contract?"

"You think I don't know?" She played her trump card. "Michael told me. Some movie agent wants to sign you."

Lance laughed in spite of himself. "Is that what you think? Oh, Lorrie, if it were that simple! I told Michael yesterday a movie's not in the cards."

"But you sold your song?"

"To pay you back for everything you've done."

Her features softened. "To pay me back?"

He took her hand in his. "Yes. And for the sister. Sister Angelica . . . Is that what was eating you?"

"I thought . . ." Her eyes were glistening now. "Lance, why must you go?"

He sighed heavily. "It's as I told you, baby. There's something that I have to do."

She sat up. "Let me help you. Haven't I helped you good up to now?"

"No knight was ever better served. Nor was a damsel ever more deserving of what I cannot give."

She wrapped her arms around his back and pulled him to her. She held him tightly. "I love you," she said for the first time. "Please don't go."

He stroked her hair and kissed her softly on the cheek. "I told you at the lake, I never meant to hurt you. I'd rather cut my right arm off." Gently, he unfastened her arms and looked into her eyes. "Where I'm going, you cannot go. There's danger and—"

"I told you I'm not afraid. Don't you trust me? Take me with you. I can help."

He shook his head.

She put her arms around the nape of his neck. Like a child she looked up into his eyes. "You'll come back, won't you? I'll wait for you. I don't care how long it takes."

He rose from the bed and walked to the window for one last look.

"Lance?"

He didn't turn. It was better she should remember him that way—leaving her cold.

Below, the red and blue lights of patrol cars stitched the fabric of four million lives together: laughing, singing, dancing, screwing, dying, getting born. Waiting for the grand drama to lift them up, to call forth the best and worst in them.

"Time is but the stream I go a-fishing in," he thought.

He slung his bags around his shoulders.

Outside the door, he heard the muffled sounds of one soul tearing from another.

14 | The Quilt

Sometimes she could finish a quilt in 18 hours, sometimes it took a hundred times that long. She never knew when she started how long it would take, nor what shape it would come to. Her old black fingers would just get into what she called "their dancin' shoes," and they'd start putting the colors together, and the colors would make her think of a sunset and she'd remember how she felt on some particular day at sunset and what she had been reading or listening to on the radio or overhearing that she oughtn't have. It was best when she didn't watch those 75-year old fingers, those dry, gnarly knuckles; when she just let them get into their "dancin' shoes" and pull here and push there, making the applique movements and the embroidery movements as they pleased, kind of pulling the rest of her body along for the ride; soon the ground fabric would be covered with all kinds of things she didn't understand, but somehow she'd make connections, one thing to another.

She'd been doing it more than sixty years. Sometimes she sewed men's neckties into it and they'd come out in a circle pattern like some strange kind of sun. Some 14 years before, she'd been to a festival and found a quilt about the University of Alabama. But all it had was Bear Bryant and his famous hat and a football, and she said to her daughter, "Where's the rest of it?" So she made her own quilt and she put in a panel that showed George Wallace standing in the schoolhouse doors banning her people from entrance.

She made a quilt about Martin Luther King and one about the Civil Rights Movement which showed the Edmund Pettus Bridge in Selma and the Dexter Avenue Baptist Church in Montgomery. That was when her fame started. The quilt went on tour and got put into an exhibit by some Massachusetts college. Then, four years ago, the people in D.C. gave her a Heritage Fellowship. Now, the big satellite dish outside her patchwork trailer home pulled in all the baseball she cared to see, and plenty of the rest of the world besides. She'd watch things on the Learning Channel and CNN and Discovery and "I Love Lucy" and cartoons and it would all run together in her mind and in her dreams and then her fingers would get into their "dancin' shoes" and she'd try to figure out what it meant.

But now she hadn't a clue. There were the knights and the Japanese sunrise; a golden goblet and a cross; an old—ageless, really—gray-bearded magician with youngish eyes and a Native American holy man; a woman in a silk kimono and a man riding a motorcycle; Petunia Petunia and boats in flames; cherry trees and dogwood blossoms; a king with a ruddy face; and a patch of blue in the corner that wouldn't take shape no matter how many times she applied another piece of fabric: she just kept ripping it off and starting again. Then the fingers made a tear-shaped jewel and a sword; and they sewed in a little handmirror. It was then that the news came over the satellite and into her living room. She always kept the TV on for company, and now it was telling her about the explosions. Her fingers stopped their dancing. Her daughter came in, slack-jawed, and they stood together with millions of other people around the world in front of the pictures coming in on CNN.

"Now why'd they wanna do a thing like that?" her granddaughter Sally May asked. And all over the world they were asking the same question.

The Blue Man stood in front of his set and watched the pictures as he caressed the head of the blue-gray rat . . . Velvet took a break from her cooking and came to watch.

In the cabin at Red Top Mountain, Lancelot sharpened the picture on the portable set, and in his oak-paneled office Michael stared in horror. In her father's condo, Lorrie stopped pining for Lance, dried her eyes and watched the people being carried on stretchers from movie theaters, blood-spattered bodies crumpled in telephone booths, terrified children being rushed from schools.

The Mayor was appealing for calm.

Were there enough police to handle the crisis?

Would the National Guard be called in?

"Why they gots to do that?" Eugenie's granddaughter asked again.

And a cold ran up Eugenie's spine. A cold like when she'd stood on the Edmund Pettus Bridge in Selma long, long ago. She was all in dread that it would start again, only it would be worse now, it was all so much more complicated now, so much more dense with so many different patterns to make sense out of.

She went back to her quilt and the fingers danced this way and that and she tried to go another way but the Kami said, "This way," and the fingers put in a puff of smoke, and the Kami said, "Over here," and a red flare appeared so that a cloud rose—a dark blue pall of anger and hatred that covered the patterns, the bright colors, and the hope of the world.

*

Velvet wore the netted black stockings to mid-thigh. Her panties were a rose-patterned, black lace translucense and so was her bodice. Leaning over the stove, she exposed thighs and buttocks, belly and navel, arms and upper chest. In all the glory of her blond whiteness, she worked the bubbling pots, sniffing and pouting and knitting her brows. Intermittently, the Blue Man would gaze up from the TV news and watch the muscles of her gluteus maximus tighten or relax as she bent or leaned or stood.

She was getting on his nerves. He was tired of her always prancing around like a French whore. He wanted a woman with class!

"Why you got to be cooking all that stuff?" he called from the living room. "All we ever eat is pizza and TV dinners. Why you gotta be dressed like that?"

Velvet brushed the burdock roots until they were clean. She sliced them while she sang back to the Blue Man, "I tole you, honey. I take them for my allergies." She sniffed the boiling yellow dock and turned down the heat.

"That ain't no way to dress when you're cooking," the Blue Man said. "Why don't you take pills like everybody else? What kind of allergies you got you can't take pills?"

Velvet sipped the tea of bittersweet and celandine. It was just right. "I like to dress this way cause it makes me feel *slinky*. When I feel *slinky* I cook better. Those pills the doctors give you just make you wanna sleep. I wanna watch TV later; I don't wanna sleep."

The Blue Man shook his head. "No class," he muttered.

"What's that, honey?"

Sullenly, the Blue Man flipped the remote. The little explosions were all over the city. There was a curfew. Bomb squads were looking for bombs, looking in all the wrong places; or looking right at the bombs and not seeing them, mistaking them for chewing gum.

Velvet emerged from the kitchen to watch the latest report. "Ain't it terrible?" she said, biting her lower lip. "Who'd do such a thing to kids and all?"

Without a word, the Blue Man rose from the easy chair and got his jacket from the closet.

"You goin' out, honey?" Velvet asked with surprise. "I was just gonna order some pizza."

"I don't want no goddamn pizza," the Blue Man said. "I'm going for a walk."

"You want I should come?"

"No!"

"You better be back before the curfew," she called as he slammed the door.

Outside, there were cops everywhere and the pedestrians moved leadenly and suspiciously, as though they were maneuvering through a minefield. Red and blue lights would flash as sirens blared and police cars and fire trucks rushed to the latest disaster.

"The whole damned world's coming apart!" a homeless man said, catching the Blue Man's forearm. "Don't nobody cares the trouble is." His slurry speech and boozy breath disgusted the Blue Man. "You got a quarter, man?"

The Blue Man pushed him aside. "You got no right—" the man complained. The Blue Man glowered, and the outcast hurried away.

There were crowds milling in the streets. The disasters had brought them out, as though sheer numbers might protect them, and there was an eerily festive mood, as though they were partying in a hurricane. Suddenly it seemed that things had gone to hell all at once. The civil war and famine in Russia had claimed a million lives since the spring; the Iraqi dictator was on the prowl again; England was literally sinking into the sea. Pesticides were increasingly ineffective: using 33 times more pesticides than they had in the '40s, U.S. farmers were losing 37% of the harvest to chemical-resistant bugs—about the same that had been lost in medieval Europe! Japan, the world's basket-case, had secured nuclear weapons from Khazakstan; now she was threatening nuclear war if Russia did not withdraw from her northern islands. TB was rampant everywhere. The hole in the ozone over the Arctic was now as large as the hole in the ozone over Antarctica; Australians were migrating *en masse* from the southern part of the continent and South Africans, especially the blacks, were dying *en masse* from melanoma. Somewhere in Tennessee the AIDS virus was figuring out how to spread itself through the blood of mosquitoes.

Everything was as it should be, and the Blue Man was pleased to have played his part. A warm sense of fulfillment spread in his veins and he didn't see the band of naked roller bladers until they descended screaming from the side street, elbowing and kicking at everyone in their way. "The end of the world is here, mother-fuckers!" they screamed, and one of the in-line skates found its way into the Blue Man's solar plexus.

"You hurt, Mister?"

Even as he sucked in air and pressed the bruised muscles of his abdomen, the Blue Man knew that he had never heard a sweeter voice in all his life. He felt little arms around his shoulders guiding him to a bus stop bench.

"You all right, Mister?" the voice said again. The Blue Man looked up into the young face of innocence lost. Lorrie tendered a tentative smile. "You all right?" she asked again.

He grunted. In a previous incarnation he would have chased the skaters until he caught them, then made the one who kicked him eat his in-line skate. Now he let it go. Was he getting mellow?

"Don't I know you?" Lorrie asked, carefully appraising the exotic face, the way the heavy 5 o'clock shadow seemed to tinge the face blue. She was half mesmerized by the pattern of blue tattoos that rippled above the clavicles and ran down the bulging arms.

He shook his head. Did she know him? If she had any peripheral vision at all she would have seen him dozens of times in recent months, hugging the shadows of buildings and trees, dissolving into mists and fogs and summer dew.

Lorrie kept pondering, and something might have clicked if the high-frequencey loudspeaker hadn't crackled with static just then. "This is the Atlanta Police Department's official proclamation," the loudspeaker bristled as the cruisers began their slow sweep down Piedmont. "It is now 7:30. You have half an hour to clear the streets! Anyone on the streets after 8 P.M . . ." The speaker crackled again, then ended with, "violation of the Penal Code, article . . ." The rest of the message was lost in the whir of overhead helicopter rotors. "Shit!" Lorrie cursed. "Everything's going to hell in a handbasket . . . Uh, you want some coffee or something?"

Ordinarily, she wouldn't have invited a total stranger into her condo for coffee and refreshments. She had always taken more chances than she should have, but she certainly knew where to draw the line. Besides, she had learned from her recent experience with Lance that good samaritans often got shafted. But she was lonely and scared now. Bombs were going off everywhere, in all sorts of out-of-the-way places. The utter arbitrariness of the violence was just plain scary. She was as much numbed to senseless violence as any other good American, but this was *diff*, totally *diff*. She wanted company. The way things were happening she figured she was as likely to die sitting alone in her apartment as anywhere else. A lot of the end-of-the-world party-goers in the street seemed to share her sentiment. The blue-faced guy looked like a big, friendly bear type. If things got out of hand, she had cans of mace hidden strategically throughout her condo.

A few minutes later, the Blue Man propped his foot on the ottoman and peered through the steam of his coffee. "It sure is sticky out there, huh?" Lorrie asked. "Every time I go out in the streets I feel like I'm in a sauna. You mind if I freshen up?"

He grunted.

While he was waiting, he surveyed the condo, looking for any tell-tale signs of Lance. He sniffed the air for a man's odor. Whatever had been there had long since been drowned by hair sprays, nail polish, polish remover, soaps, eau de cologne, Pine Sol and baby powder. Not to mention the immanent frangrance of woman. He lifted the toilet seat and let a stream of blue piss pour into the bowl.

"Oh, there you are," Lorrie said when he came out. She wore a fresh Japanese cotton kimono—a *yukata*—and she had freshened herself with a washcloth and powder. She sat down on the recliner opposite the sofa, and lit a cigarette. "You don't mind if I smoke, do you? I always forget to ask."

He thought it was classy that she asked at all.

"How's your stomach?"

"Much better. I think it was this herb tea."

"Isn't it great? Chamomile's my favorite."

Lorrie crossed her knees, wagged her foot nervously. "I'm not in the habit of inviting strange men into my apartment," she said, suddenly alerted by the way the man was staring at her. "I don't even know your name."

"Blue," he said, because that was what Velvet called him.

"Blue? . . . That's . . . unusual . . ." She rolled it over. "Is it Mr. Blue, or just Blue?"

"Blue," he said again.

"All right," she smiled. "It suits you, you know. I mean, your skin, if you don't mind my saying, it does have a blue tinge to it . . . And, of course, those tattoos . . ." She leaned forward to study them, felt herself pulled into the swirling patterns, and pulled herself back. "Whew! What was I saying? About your name, right? It's a nice name. Unique and all."

Blue smiled. His teeth were perfectly aligned, perfectly white except for one incisor which was a blue gemstone. Lorrie caught her breath when she saw its sparkle.

"You live alone?" Blue asked, knowing the answer already.

She felt a low decibel warning, a tremolo of fear in her blood. "Well, actually, I have a roommate . . . It's a guy . . . We're not intimate or anything. But he's like my big brother." She looked at her watch. "He should be back any moment."

Blue smiled again. There was something attractively menacing about his smile. He liked the way she lied so easily and smoothly. It took class to cultivate that kind of lying.

It made him feel good to be in the house of his enemy, talking to his enemy's woman. He knew Lance had left her a few days before. He knew where Lance was and what he was doing: waiting for *him* in the mountains, honing his skills, preparing for battle.

The sirens started their caterwaul in the streets below. A ripple of small explosions sounded like firecrackers. Somewhere, people were screaming.

"Your friend—he's missing the curfew," Blue said, the slightest sardonic grin playing at the corner of his eyes.

"I guess he'll be here soon," Lorrie said, fidgeting with her watchband.

Blue rose from the sofa and took her hand. She rose and gazed into his dark eyes. She fell into the eyes as one falls into the dark pools of time, as one gets lost in possibilities, fun-house mirrors, smoky silver trays that bear exotic fruit. Suddenly she felt cold. She shuddered as Blue's arms curled around her waist and pulled her to him.

*

Eugenie Eleanora pulled the blue thread, wound it around one of her lower teeth, then snipped it with the shears. She looked at her quilt with surprise. The patch of blue was spreading like one of the curses of Moses on the house of Pharaoh. She hadn't even been aware of it. She thought she had been doing something else, then she looked up from the close work and saw that the blue kept making inroads into the rest of the design. It wasn't the color so much as the shapelessness of it that perplexed her.

She wiped a sheen of sweat from the back of her neck. "Sally May," she called out, "bring your grandmama a glass of lemonade!"

"What's that?" the girl asked a minute later, pointing to the amorphous blue. She placed the lemonade carefully on the windowsill.

Eugenie shrugged. "How'd I know?"

Sally May considered her grandmother well. The sharp, dark eyes that considered back allayed any doubts about the old woman's faculties. "You usually woulda ripped it up by now," Sally May said, defending her suspicions.

"Not this one," Eugenie said, not knowing herself why it was special. She studied the pattern with a sense of befuddlement. "Not this one."

*

"Is this the one that injured itself against the cage?" Sachiko asked.

"Not this one," Sagami said, carefully placing her hand through the bamboo door of the lark's five-foot tall cage. She stroked the feathers on the bird's back. "This one sings in spite of its confinement. Half an hour of freedom in the morning, then it pops back to its house. It likes to know where its next meal's coming from. And is quite content to sing for seeds and insects . . The other one—she ate the proffered food, but hurt its wings against the bamboo cage. It could not live unfree."

Sachiko sighed. Her sister smiled weakly back at her, placed the little captive back in its cage. Sachiko tried to hide her thoughts, but Sagami understood.

"Don't be sad, Little Sister," Sagami said. "I am really quite content . . ."

The bonzes tapped little prayer bells with wooden rods, and the murmur of evening liturgies began.

"Will you come again next month for the festival?" Sagami asked brightly.

Sachiko laughed. "Do you think I would miss the festival in honor of our great, great grandfather? Of course! And I'll bring you *zuiki* and *saitomo*, too."

Sachiko clapped her hands. "Delicious!"

Arm in arm, they walked to Sachiko's waiting carriage. Sachiko struggled to hold back her tears. "Are you really all right? Is there nothing I can bring you?"

Sagami shook her head. "Yorifumi?" she sighed at last, as she always did before they parted.

"He's a fine young man," Sachiko said. "You would be proud. All the ladies of the court are after him. And, on top of that, he writes the most up-to-date verse!"

Sagami smiled.

The onlookers lowered their heads out of respect for Sagami. Suddenly, a chill wind blew from a distant mountain lake. Sagami's decorous nun's robes could not deflect the cold. Her old bones shook. Sachiko saw how dry and brittle the once lovely cheeks had become. The ascetic's diet had winnowed the flesh, and the spirit shone more brightly. But the flesh would not survive another winter.

"Do not cry, Little Sister," Sagami said, wiping Sachiko's tears. "We cannot choose our lives. Only our reactions to our lives . . ."

They embraced, and Sachiko entered the sedan car. The oxherders poked the ribs of the oxen, and Sachiko watched her black-robed sister get smaller and smaller in the little window of the car. She waved her plump, little hand and Sagami waved back bravely.

How many years had it been since the strangers had gone into the river and vanished? Sachiko still shuddered recalling how her sister had followed them into the river, how she had dove repeatedly to recover the body of her lover. The *hina* dolls had been torched, and in the light of the flames Sagami had dove and called out "Britain! Britain!" At last she had collapsed weeping on the shore.

With his rival out of the way, Sagami's weasel husband had no problem claiming the boy as his own. It elevated his stature in the court ever so slightly, though no one supposed such a handsome boy could come from the loins of such a ferret-faced father. Nevertheless, he raised the boy so that he enjoyed all the advantages of fine food, good company, literature, dance and music. If the boy missed his mother, he gave no sign of it.

He could never have imagined how his mother missed him. For years after she had taken the tonsure, she would dwell on the image of her baby at her breast. Alone in her cell after her prayers, her heart would rebel against acceptance, and she'd cry out in silent anguish for Britain and her baby. The Blue Man's torch had seared her soul, lit a coal that still smoldered: a fire she nursed in spite of herself, nursed like a bitter child.

Now she was dry and brittle, alone in her drafty cell. She made a cup of her palms and warmed them around the candle flame. She prepared the ink on the inkstone, dipped the brush and wrote as she always did.

Such jeweled and glittering words! Yet they eased the torments of her soul. All she had ever wished to say, all she might have said in a lifetime to her lover Britain, she poured into her verse. How much she missed him still! In spite of everything she'd learned about the transitoriness of life, she could not let the flame of his memory die out.

In the morning, she would crumple the papers, as she always did, then watch her words uncurl and flame on the brazier. She'd start to cook her miso on the humbling flame.

*

Commander Nakatomi couldn't stop shaking. He shook in rhythm to the drums and the gongs. The rattle of bones he held syncopated his movements. Imbe-san had never seen her husband shaking so. The devotees watched with awe and fear as wave after wave of memory broke over the ancient body.

Imbe-san had begged him not to journey anymore. Even with all his spirit helpers, her husband could not indefinitely overcome the rigors of old age. Now their hair was snowy white, peace reigned in Yamato, and still he ventured forth into the arcana.

"Something has been blocking me," he had told her. "In my last years, when I should see farthest, the net of magic comes back rent with holes. The world that we are knitting, the time lines, may be pulled to dross unless I fix this hole in my own heart."

"But," Imbe-san had weakly protested. "Surely others can complete this work . . ."

The Commander had held up his hand: "We know the way the time-lines travel back and forth. Our safety here and now depends on what's to come. This little, peaceful world we've made is but a nugget from a golden vein. What's to come is fluid as a dream. I must go forth and see what I have missed. Some pain that will overwhelm me has blanked my magic out. An absence beckons me. In that absence I may find myself . . ."

Now they gathered at the *saijo*, to feel closest to the Kami. Inside the circle of sacred ropes, the Commander stood in his ceremonial robes, his white hair flowing over the red foxmask.

"Where have you been, Commander?" Old Gonsai called out. "Tell us your dream."

Gathering his strength and will, Commander Nakatomi stopped shaking. His voice was steady and firm, but it seemed to come from the bottom of a chasm:

> "A lifetime I have waited, practiced, fasted,
> eaten of sacred roots, chanted, prayed, listened.
> For my people only, no hope of gain for self . . ."

As his voice trailed off and he seemed lost in reflectionss, Imbesan wondered if her husband could ever again walk in the Land of Clouds.

"This is what I saw," the Commander continued. He had stopped shaking. Through the holes in the foxmask, his eyes gazed fixedly upon past, present and the land of Future Music. His voice had a resonant pitch:

> "A village of two thousand souls
> perched along a riverbank,
> growing corn, beans, gourds, pumpkins.
> Women with wooden hoes turning the soil
> with shells fashioned from the sea
> while the men hunt deer and gather
> cane traps buried in the currents—
> jetties of stone funneling
> gar and box turtles, catfish and drum
> into the woven cane.
>
> "And the children sing.
> Under the cottonwood poplars,
> under the hickory trees

> they gather black walnuts,
> shells from the river basin.
> The two sexes play together
> until the bleeding time.
> Then the girls are taught
> the ways of women.
> Then the boys are taken
> Into the circle of the men.

Some watched the Commander with rapt interest, and some had their eyes closed, sitting serenely in the vernal sun. A soft breeze blew the first plum blossoms onto a devotee's hair. The young woman didn't seem to notice the white petal perched in her raven blackness.

> Some planted sunflowers, some tobacco,
> some worked the chirts;
> and they were always building.
> Their houses were of wattle and daub.
> Around the 2000,
> a twelve-foot high log palisade
> rose beside a ditch.
> Fifteen-lengths-a-man apart,
> watchtowers rimmed the palisades.
> Then there were the mounds..."

"What are `chirts'?" a young boy wondered.

> "A rock that chips like glass.
> The hafted points they bound to spearshafts.
> They worked in plazas, in the common grounds:
> Pottery they make with swirling patterns—
> not unlike our relics
> of the Jomon folks of long ago.
> And their eyes are much like ours...
> But I was speaking of the mounds..."

"Tell us of the mounds," Imbe-san urged gently.

"Seven earthen mounds rise
from the flat banks of the Etowah.
Four are softly molded by the rains
and breezes of five hundred years.
Three are of more recent vintage.

"Five times a man's height
to thirteen times a man
rise three flat hills.
Baskets and baskets of red clay and earth
from borrow pits and the defensive ditch:
upon their backs carrying the mud,
with ropes tied around the temples of their heads—
two hundred years to when I stood on it,
with six or seven layers underneath my toes.
And I was Chief, in the temple, on the tallest mound.
Under me the other Chiefs lay buried.
One hundred log steps to the temple's platform rose
steep and high, and on the roof, three symbols:
a great hand with an eye inside the palm,
plumed snakes, and a cross
for the four corners of the world.
In the temple, constantly alit, I kept the Sun-God's
flame."

They are like us, Imbe-san thought. Then the devotees turned to each other, looked silently, and understood. Some stalk of the main branch had blown across the sea. Susanawo, intending something else, destroying more than he had saved, had saved a little, in spite of himself. The Commander shook again, then spoke:

"Five hundred years in war and peace they dwelled,
mostly in peace, five hundred years.
Then, one day, in my forty sixth year,
we heard a sound that we had never heard—
metal against metal, swords against a cuirass,
and horses trotting, and the horses also armored.
There were thirty of them.
Along the watchtowers, our best bowmen
had their arrows half-way drawn
when one of the iron helmets called out in our language
that they came in peace—to trade.

"We let them in our gates, closely surveiled,
and they had, indeed, brought wondrous wares
of shining things, and we marvelled at their horses.
We had seen other kinds of men before,
coming from the west and south.
Obsidian from the Rocky Mountains,
red pipestone from Minnesota,
micah from Appalachia—we traded for our ochre,
graphite, greenstone, galena and quartz.
We were used to other men.

"But these men dressed in iron,
they made rudeness to our women.
They camped outside our palisades,
flashing their shining swords.
They had a different kind of eye.

"Each day their number doubled
until there were six hundred;
and with them, black men kept like dogs.
One day our boys came back from hunting—
bruised, angry as men, and told the story
how the beards had set on them,

roughed them in the woods.
Some young men counselled war.

"But we were not a people
who set out easily for war.
Our defense was good.
And we knew
the irons wanted gold more than our lives.
We did not want to squander our good life
so we bit our tongues and waited.
We knew we could out-wait them.

"Outside the palisades
they took what they wanted.
Women, boys and men
they pressed into their service.
Those who had shunned
the safety of our sharpened logs,
living beside the flowing river—
the freest souls among us—
became the most unfree.
The "Spaniards"—so they called themselves—
beat our cousins with iron fists and leather thongs.
When they left,
the very air was sick of them,
contagion dripped from the magnolias
and our people started falling.

"One after the other
had the red marks covering their skin.
Or else the act of love grew painful
and puss came from the genitals;
or the babies turned blue or yellow
and there was much vomiting
of a green, smelly fluid,

and much shitting
with blood in the stools.

"And those who survived were five hundred.
And they said, 'Here is a place of death;
let us leave it.' But others said we must not leave
the bones of our ancestors;
if we leave the bones untended
we will curse our souls forever.
So we stayed; and we said the ancient prayers;
and we waited for our gods."

The Commander paused. His sadness hurt them all. Even the youngest had been brought into the words. The drumming stopped. All watched the Commander now and they knew that he would leave them soon and there was no one to replace him.

The diseased joints buckled. Commander Nakatomi fell to his knees, supporting himself on his staff. Old Gonsai and Imbesan rushed to his side, but he waved them back. He furrowed his forehead, concentrated his vision and energy into a crease of memory between his eyes. The snake-like crease pulsed ever so slightly, and his voice rose from the cavern of his lungs:

". . . waited . . waited for our gods . . .
I, in my holy office, offered tribute, as I always had,
but with the greatest urgency.

"On my chest, a shell gorget
held a circle in a circle, fastened by a cross.
Within the inner circle, the forked-eyed serpent.
My head was orange, ochre-dyed.
With copper-headed headdress
and wooden-headed rattle
I sang to the Eagle Being:
'Come down to Your hurting children.
Take of our heart-felt offerings:

> venison, turkey and quail.
> Take what Your God's heart craves . . .'"

"Did he come?" cried the boy. "Did the Eagle Being come?"

> "Nay . . . Nay, he would not show himself.
> We knew not why he would not.
> And then . . . we understood . . ."

"What was it?" Old Gonsai asked, frightened to think that a god could abandon its children. And all of them were frightened by that thought.

"It was the one the Spaniards had left behind," the Commander sighed.

> "The one who spoke our language,
> the one who eschewed the Spaniards' ways . . .
> He had brought herbs
> which cooled the children's fever.
> He seemed to have a sixth sense
> where to fish the streams.
> The irons left him when they went
> clanging after gold.
> This one was gently dispositioned.
> Our sweetest maiden
> claimed him for her own.
> That maiden was my daughter . . ."

A lost lifetime of love surged in the Commander's breast. On his knees, supported by his staff, he wept his bitter tears.

Gently, Imbe-san placed her old, white hand on her husband's shoulder. He placed his hand on hers. "I'm all right," he said softly. "Just salt and rain in my eyes . . ."

"Perhaps we'd better . . ."

"No," he said, "I will go on . . ."

Imbe-san returned to the circle. She waited. All of them waited a long time.

> "That maiden was my daughter," he continued.
> "The best of us . . .
> At first, they seemed as happy as two fawns
> discovering the world.
> I don't know when it changed.
> I remember seeing on my daughter's back
> a bruise—about the size of a man's hand.
> When I mentioned it, she said she'd fallen in the woods.
> Then I noticed she concealed
> more and more of her skin—
> like our oldest women,
> and her step, that had been light,
> grew heavy; a kind of sullen humor
> grew about her eyes,
> and her birdlike voice grew heavy,
> and she would not meet my eyes.
> And then, one day, she died . . ."

The Commander looked around the circle. He was in two worlds now. In the world of Yamato his corporal form seemed to waver and blur. "He is becoming transparent," Imbe-san thought, and she feared they would lose him. But the voice was strong.

> "In my grief, her husband pressed me,
> importuning all secrets,
> the meaning of all ceremonies:
> what the gorgets symobolized;
> the plumed serpent, whom we had worshipped
> for a thousand years, and had forgotten why;
> the eye within the palm—
> all the hidden meanings he pried from my dreams.

> "It seemed a mist was falling,
> a blueness that enveloped me
> and soughed my secrets out.
> There was no air in my dreams.
> And I knew
> that I was killing all the gods:
> those of my mother's mother
> and those of my father's father.
> Yet I told,
> for this was the magic of the mist,
> this was the evil magic."

"Then what happened?" asked the boy, who had grown so much older.

> "The bones of our ancestors cried out,
> 'You must not leave this land!'
> We knew we would never rest in the worlds to come,
> that a growing hollowness must ever
> gnaw away our entrails,
> that we must wander like the blind
> in a land of riches
> if we left the land.
> But our children died in our arms.
> The gods refused to show themselves.
> The husband of my daughter
> spoke in all our dreams:
> 'This is a cursed place—Go!'

"We left . . . and we are homeless still."

The Commander raised a pitiful howl to heaven, then collapsed into his wife's old arms.

15 | Showdown

Yamamoto pressed the fast-forward button on the tape recorder he'd planted on the console between the seats of his Lexus. There was a whir, and then, Lance's voice: "Western society is everywhere working overtime to create the illusion of the individual while concretizing the reality of man-in-mass."

They had talked all day, pausing only to stoke the wood in the fireplace, to eat, and to piss in the woods. Yamamoto had been amazed at how Lance had changed. Months of fasting, reading and solitude had made his skin sallow and his eyes limpid. Some weeks before, he had observed Lance walking through the woods, with a book in his hand, his journal and pen in his back pocket. Now he saw how the constant peripatetic discipleship had hardened the limbs and tightened the muscles. Yoga, sit-ups, push-ups and chin-ups had honed his body just as his diet of Western and Eastern literature had honed his mind. Through the cobalt eyes, the fire of ideas burned with mesmerizing intensity.

Yamamoto pressed the fast-forward button again and stopped it arbitrarily. Lance continued expounding, "They never killed God in the East. The Christian drama, on the other hand, is inextricable with the agonized and agonizing figure of Christ on the cross."

He had not yet achieved discipline of thought. He would throw out ideas like a crazy pitchman in a Hollywood studio. He tested, prodded, provoked and preened to see what sort of reaction he might get. Yamamoto played with the buttons again.

"Because we do not know how to evaluate properly—the essence of wisdom—we quantify reality—the illusion of wisdom."

Yamamoto had managed to get words in edgewise only twice: when he had convinced Lance to let Petunia interview him again, and when he had talked about Lorrie.

"She called you?" Lance had asked, unable to conceal his wrestle with the angel of conscience. "How is she?"

"Concerned about you," Yamamoto explained.

Lance wandered over to a stack of books. "None of these have taught me how to heal a broken heart." He sighed, and gazed long at the glowing coals. "Long ago another girl was hurt for the love of me . . . Have I learned so little, Michael?"

He had assured Lance that times had changed since the Lady of Shallot. Nevertheless, Lance had made him promise to look in on Lorrie as soon as he returned to Atlanta. Now he weaved through the bottleneck around Marietta. The lights of the city drew him like a magnet, and it seemed that the cars streaming down I-75 were blood corpuscles racing towards the beating ventricles of the city, only to be pumped out again.

Everything was going to hell in the world, but his own life was coming up roses. The advance on his book had sweetened his outlook. Now that Petunia Petunia was coming down to talk to Lance again, he was sure he'd have a best seller on his hands. After all, he had the authorized biography!

So the ozone holes were getting bigger . . . He and Carol would shuffle on down to Barbados and he'd life-regress the rich and famous. Kids starving to death in Africa? He'd send some money to CARE. American cities going up in flames? He'd soon be out of it! The Hindu-Moslem War killing millions? What was it Lance had said? "The three greatest curses of man: racism, nationalism and religionism. All of them subsumed by tribalism."

A carload of skinheads cut him off at the junction with I-285. The bald, tattooed teens in the back seat gave him the bird and the Hitler salute. One of them stuck his ugly bovine face out the window, then aimed an Uzi at Michael's head. Michael fingered the holstered Beretta in the console. Laughing maniacally, the kid sprayed a round of bullets straight up into the air as the car sped away.

People were being killed for nothing now—more and more often. There were too many people and they were always juiced up on drugs or alcohol or the media or the rush of life. Lance thought he could make it right, he could turn it around, somehow, if only he could meet his final challenge. He thought it all hinged on his completing his quest. He didn't understand that it was too far gone. All the martyrs' blood of history had swollen into the ocean of time, and still the ocean washed the hungering ideals away.

He'd have to do what he could to save Lance. He didn't want to see him get hurt. Lance was his meal ticket. He'd have to keep him going and keep him talking and keep the money coming in. People needed to hope, and Lance gave people hope. People wanted to believe, and Lance was convincing as hell. He had half-convinced Michael.

He pulled into the driveway at Lorrie's condo. Sporadic gunfire and explosions lit up the night sky, syncopated the wailing sirens, screams of anguish. He announced himself to the security box. The gate opened, and he parked in the visitors section. He removed the holstered Beretta from the console, tucked it under his belt. Strange that she hadn't gotten over Lance in all these months! Most kids were more elastic.

He hadn't told Lance about the fear he had heard in her voice. No need to worry him. She'd gotten herself mixed up with some unsavory characters. Lance was well out of it. Michael would hold her hand, listen patiently, sooth her with some psychobabble and be on his way.

The front desk man barely glanced up from his copy of some tabloid rag. The headline blared: "Elvis sighted in U.F.O. Piloted by Hitler!" He rang Lorrie's apartment, but there was no answer. That wasn't unusual. The intercom hadn't worked right for years. No reason to fix it now.

"You say she's expecting you?" the bored clerk asked.

"That's right."

"Go ahead then." He stabbed back with his thumb towards the elevator.

There was soft music coming from Lorrie's apartment—Rachmaninoff... *Piano Concerto*... Michael rang several times, then knocked. He called her name and finally turned the doorknob.

The lights were turned low, romantic. *The Piano Concerto* suggested epic loveliness and grandeur.

"Lorrie?" Michael called.

He followed the stained footsteps to the bedroom. Lorrie watched him steadily from the propped up pillow, her head motionless and serene. For a moment, it seemed that her eyes were follwing his movements...

He found the rest of her body in the bedroom closet.

*

"I never know what's gonna happen," Eugenie Eleanora told the unblinking eye of the camera. "That's what makes it int'restin'."

Petunia Petunia let the camera linger on Eugenie's face, then directed the lensman towards the quilts. "Now this one here," Petunia said, indicating the new one.

"Oh, that's not finished yet," Eugenie said. She hovered protectively over her work, as though trying to shield a great-grandchild from the glare of lights.

"It sure is different," said Petunia admiringly. She walked around the improvised frame, letting the camera follow her fingers. "This person here," she said, "he seems to be some kind of knight."

"Yes'm. I don't know where he come from." Eugenie chuckled to herself, wove her shawl more tightly around her shoulders.

The lensman focused on the peculiar figure of the knight. Petunia Petunia recognized Lance's intriguing features even if no one else could.

Small wonder they couldn't! The mouth was twisted into a rictus of horror. The eyes were glazed by the unspeakable.

"It looks like Munch," Petunia said.

"Theolonius?" Eugenie wondered. "Well, I don't know . . ."

"This here," Petunia said, pointing, "it's a woman's head, kind of floating in space."

"Yes'm," Eugenie said, shifting uneasily. "I done it. But I don't know *why* I done it."

Petunia moved to a corner of the quilt. "All this blue here. It hasn't taken shape."

"No, Ma'am. That's been worrying me. I worry it back and I worry it back, but it keeps on reaching down. It's like a chill you can't get warm from."

"I want the folks to see how it moves down into the rest of the quilt."

The camera followed Petunia's eyes.

"Yes'm," Eugenie continued. "Like icy fingers—that's what it is. I keep worrying it, and it keeps on comin' . . ."

"It's not your usual grandmotherly quilt," Petunia said.

Eugenie laughed. "No, Ma'am, it sure ain't that."

Petunia caught the signal from her producer. "We're going to take a break now," she told the camera. "Then we're going to see this remarkable lady in action."

During the break the make-up people mopped Petunia's prodigious brow. Eugenie was cool and collected. Petunia shifted her operatic weight before the quilt while Eugenie settled into her working chair. "I never done this before," Eugenie said, "on camera . . ."

"Ain't nothin' to worry about," Petunia assured her.

When the producer nodded, Petunia welcomed her audience back and set the mood of expectation. Eugenie's fingers put on their "dancin' shoes" and started moving and shaking, picking fabrics and sewing, snipping and sorting, sewing and choosing while the cameras moved back and forth between her face and the quilt, her face and Petunia's. All the while Petunia prattled on and Sally May watched from a corner. A few deft movements and there were tears on the face of the knight.

They were cold tears. Tears that ran down the cheek and into the ears when midnight came on Red Top Mountain. Tears from eyes that had seen the love of folly and the folly of love.

Michael Yamamoto had seen the tears. "Come back to the city, Lance," he'd urged.

"Could I have saved her? Is there some way I might have saved her?"

Michael stared into the fire at Lance's cabin. The October wind rattled the shutters.

"Everyone who loves me is cursed," Lance said, "even as I am cursed. Because I dared betray my King. Fifteen years of penitence could not annul my treachery. Ten years of an ascetic's gazing at the moon could not bestill the serpent in my heart . . . Is there no mercy in the world, Michael? Not even Christ's blood can wash away my crimes."

"Lance, I . . ."

Lance held up his hand. "The chalice, Michael . . . Let me gaze upon it . . ."

Carefully, Michael unwrapped the black velvet from the Holy Grail. Lance held his breath. He had not seen it since the day he had entrusted it to Michael's care. Even that gesture had not saved Lorrie. Michael stood back. The Grail was dull and tarnished. Lance reached out as a blind man reaches for his lover. But his fingers trembled violently and he could not touch it. He put his face close to it and peered at the centuries-dull surface. His breath made a haze on the metal. A stain seemed to take shape. The Blue Man's face grinned with malice. Lance blinked twice, rubbed his eyes and the face vanished into the patina. As he stared, another shape emerged: ageless, wise and sad. And the goblet rang as though it had been flicked by an unseen finger. Michael felt the little hairs on the back of his neck stand up, and the goblet vibrated slightly. It caught the glow of the burning logs and diffused the light around the cabin. Then the Grail began to sing.

It sang in Merlin's voice, high-pitched, out of a yearning dream. Lance and Michael were frozen in a web of space and time.

> "'Michael and his angels fought against the dragon...'"
> "'Gird up now thy loins like a man: for I will demand of thee...'"
> "'If the blind lead the blind, both shall fall into a ditch...'"

In his mind Lance said that he was weary. Somehow Michael heard him say it. And though his lips did not move, nor his tongue utter it, he heard him say also in a plaintive, weary voice, "Show me the way back, Merlin. Show me what I must do. Show me... how to go home." And the ringing voice of Merlin answered from the Grail:

> "Weary?...
> I am weary of mornings that never come
> and nights that bring no balm;
> only the continual listlessness of loss,
> falling like rain amidst desolation."

"Take this cup from me," Lance said aloud. Then he fell to his knees before the Grail. He clasped his hands in silent prayer. The singing commenced again:

> "Fifteen hundred years I waited.
> There is a place that I have seen
> covered with mists, where cottonwoods grow:
> seven mounds rise by a winding stream.
> Go! Your death awaits you there.
> Your death's name is Etowah."

The vision faded, the chalice stopped ringing and the two men stared at one another.

"It was all true," Michael said, his whole body trembling. He could not get warm. "Everything you told me! All of it!"

"You heard him, too," Lance said, gratified.

Michael approached the tarnished goblet. He stared back and forth from Lance to the chalice. He flashed on Lorrie's headless body parts. "I just wanted to tell a story," he said, backing away. "I thought there was a book here . . . You see what I mean . . ."

"There are no jesses on you, Michael."

Woozily, Michael walked to the fire. He couldn't get warm, couldn't stop trembling. He couldn't face Lance. He saw Lorrie's head propped on the pillow. "It's not like I didn't try to help," he said. "I was there from the beginning. I always believed in you. I set up an interview for you. I was going to tell you. Petunia Petunia's in Atlanta. She's taping some quilt-maker in Alabama. I set it up for her to talk to you. You made me your agent, right? I've been looking out for you. I set it up for you. I didn't do this for myself, you know? I mean, where do you think the money comes from? I only make an honest living. Somebody's got to take care of the practical things. She's here, anyway. She will be. Two days from now. I promised I'd meet her. So, you see, I've got to get back. I'm expecting her call . . ." He started backing away from the fire, back from Lance and the Grail. "Gotta be back." He inched towards the door. "You stay in touch, okay? . . . I'll call you. Don't try to call me. I don't know where I'll be. I'll call you . . . You've got that cellular phone I gave you? Just give me a beep. I'll keep my beeper on." He knocked over a small end table and scattered some books and magazines. "I'll call," he said. "I'm sorry . . ."

"It's all right," Lance said gently. But the wind gathered at the open door and hurled the words into the swirling flames. Sparks flew into Lance's hair.

Michael turned once to see Lance brushing a swirl of sparks from his hair. He raced to his car, raced the engine, dug two trenches as his back tires backhoed the earth.

Eugenie's fingers danced a red streak across her quilt.

*

The old Indian cycle cut a swath through the stream of traffic fleeing the city for the relative safety of the north Georgia mountains. Bleary-eyed youngsters pointed, and their rifle-clutching elders scowled at the strange blond man with the flowing locks. Was he one of the end-of-the-worlders? One of the crazies who killed for the sake of it? Lance kept his eyes on the ribbon of gray winding into the flamegold of the piedmont.

In the city itself urban survivalists battened steel doors on Peachtree Street, stocked canned goods and water, polished their gun scopes. Fatalists sat back and enjoyed the show. Having predicted apocalypse for years, they relished their vindication. On Ponce de Leon the homeless gathered around no fountain of youth, but garbage infernos in rusty cylinders; eyes in the back of their heads watched their neighbors, as outstretched hands sucked up the heat. Every now and again an explosion would rattle their heat-happy hands and sly eyes would dart from neighbor to neighbor.

It was too cold to be out on Halloween, too cold to be riding a 1948 Indian cycle. Even the grinning jackolanterns were covered with frost, and it seemed their pumpkin teeth were chattering. In spite of the curfew, in spite of the warnings, die-hard celebrants of the peculiar readied their costumes and masks. Various versions of "the Mad Bomber"—hand grenades sprouting on a camouflage jacket—were the costumes *de riguer*. Rumors were rampant: an attack on the Center for Disease Control was imminent! Whatever had happened before could not prepare anyone for the madness to come. Even Petunia Petunia felt it: something manic about to combust.

"You get me this interview," she told Yamamoto, "I'll P-R your book like nothing's been P-Red since St. Paul P-Red the Sermon on the Mount."

"He's not going to like it," Michael said nervously.

Petunia motioned to one of the waiters, ordered a mocha

almond fudge sundae. "Honey," she said when the waiter was gone, "let me worry 'bout who likes what and how."

Michael folded his hands together to try to calm the shaking. "There's something I haven't told you" he said softly . . . "about the Holy Grail . . ."

"The whaaattt?" Petunia cocked a bulging eye in Michael's direction.

So he told her the story. She listened carefully, then ordered another sundae. "You don't expect me to believe this crap, do you?"

"No," Michael admitted.

"Good . . . But I do admire your gumption . . . And your creativity . . . Hey, whatever sells . . . You just get me where our boy is going," she said shrewdly. "Let me worry about the rest . . ."

Michael considered his options: betray a friend, or make a million dollars in book sales. "No cameras," he said softly.

Petunia licked the fudge from her spoon, then shook it at Michael. "Ain't no need to worry, honey." She stirred the same spoon in her coffee as—

—the brown liquid in the big pot went round and round under Velvet's nose. It smelled right to her. It had not been easy to find the liver of a wolf, but Blue had obliged her with a trip to the zoo. Seneca snake root, spignut, elecampane and balmony had not been easy to find either, but her persistence in phoning every health food store in the area had eventually paid off.

"What you want all that for anyway?" Blue had complained.

"I tole you, honey, it's for my asthma. You want I should breathe, don't you?"

Blue wasn't sure. He narrowed his eyes into slits and watched her creepy blondness. He hated her to her blond core and could not understand why he hadn't killed her. He imagined especially gruesome ways to mutilate her, but something always intervened: a good ballgame or a wrestling match on TV; a compulsion to plant a few bombs in a children's nursery; polluting a hospital's supply of healthy blood with AIDS-contaminated blood. He got his coat and hat from the closet.

"You going out again, honey?"

"Yeah . . . Don't wait up for me."

She was always waiting for him, even when he disappeared for weeks at a time. Even when he'd come back to her with blood on his hands.

He had more important things to worry about. That bastard *Hata* was almost in his clutches. He smelled his blood. He wouldn't let him get away again. That bastard had escaped once too often, thanks to his uncanny luck, his meddling magicians!

He knew how to deal with magicians. He'd outwitted them before, and he'd do it again. As long as he moved with the Kami of the dark rites, he'd win again. Then he'd come back for Velvet. Her and her goddamn herbs and stews. He'd stew her. He'd *stew* her up to her neck!

He parked the DeSoto at the Grant Park Zoo. The zoo was closed, of course. One elderly attendant kept nervous watch at the gate. "Can I help you?" the old man asked, his friendly disposition showing through, in spite of the tenor of the times.

With the flat of his palm Blue shoved the cartilage of the man's nose into his brain. The man dreamed lightning, then dreamed nothing.

The big cats felt the earth tremble through their paws, shot their pointed ears up, sniffed and waited. Howler monkeys made a weird bellowing noise, and hyenas laughed.

Blue took off his clothes. Peacocks raised their eldritch cries. Blue's broad, splayed feet walked on the sodden earth, leapt over the gate of the orangutans.

"So, you have come," said one of the orange creatures.

"I need guidance," Blue said.

"What have you brought us?" asked another orang.

Blue took the magatama jewel from around his neck. The orangs gathered around.

"It is nothing but a stone pizzle," said one of the clever ones. "We have our share of pizzles, thank you!" he said, thrusting his pelvis forward while the others snorted.

"It has magic," Blue said. "With this you may understand the language of men."

The orangs huddled for a closer look. One of them stroked it. They chatted rapidly among themselves. What they had spurned, they now revered. The leader reached for the magatama. Blue held it back. "If we understand the language of men, we will understand the designs of men," the leader said. "We will know why they build—and why they destroy what they build. Then we will walk as men and be as men, and be more than men, for we shall have our language and our traditions as well . . . Will you part with so precious a jewel?"

"It is a toy I have grown weary of," Blue confessed, but he did not tell them it had never worked well for him. "If I have victory tomorrow—"

"If God grant me victory tomorrow . . . " Lance thought as the freezing white water of Amicalola Falls splashed from his shoulders, "If the son of Mary . . . if the son of the Princess of Demetia may grant it . . . If the gods of the woods, and the spirits of the air, the genies of the water, and the unknown Kami grant it . . ."

He fell upon his knees, overcome by the cold and the force of rushing water. Wave after wave of white water pummelled him. Then, and only then—in all the millions of years the water had fallen and would fall—a particular configuration of wind and chiseled stone made a *torii* curtain of water over his head, enclosed him in a frame of parallel cataracts. Standing, he imitated the holy gestures he had watched the monks at Mt. Hiei practice centuries ago. He had forgotten that he knew them. Hands and feet flowed into the symbolic gestures, flowed out again.

Beyond the curtain of white water: dim forms of breath took shape, quavered, and were gone. Lance began to chant the words unspoken for a thousand years. Something in the pines smiled back, raised a hand of shadows to the sky, pointed its other hand to earth.

The pine trees rustled their silk garments in the wind. Amida Buddha floated down on the needles, an entourage of female deities accompanying him, welcoming the traveler. And all of them were only: pine bark, cones, needles, stone, wind, water.

The God of War came next; grimacing, turning his fiery lariat. Even when the water turned to flames, Lance did not budge. The lariat brushed his skin; it was covered with razors.

The God of Love came, a lion roaring from his hair. With bows and arrows and multiple arms, the Love God pierced the knight with memories sharper than razors. And Lance moved through the sacred gestures and through the slicing pain.

The curtain of water parted. The *torii* of water vanished.

Exhausted, Lance stretched out on the rocks at the bottom of the falls. He wondered if his strength would ever return.

If they granted victory . . . what?

He hardly knew what it meant anymore.

In the old days it was easy: send a dastardly foe to hell. Then on with the feasting.

He pulled himself from the rocks and stood naked in the cold air of dusk. When the stars appeared he watched the wheels they formed and thought of what men said of them, and all he did not understand. He pulled the cold around him like a mantle, and stood shivering under the wheeling stars.

Then the engine of the Indian growled, and the headlamps flashed across the forest.

*

He kept thinking of a story Will had told him. Will had heard it from one of the warrior-monks. A day-dreaming basket-seller had walked in front of the horse of a proud samurai, and the startled animal had reared back. The horseman also had been dreaming, but as soon as he realized what had happened he was seized by fury. Most men of his rank would have decapitated the hapless merchant on the spot, but this samurai devised an exquisite torture. He challenged the little man to a duel one week later. The poor merchant ran about like a headless chicken. What was he to do?

What did he know about swords? He wanted to flee, but he knew that the samurai would track him down and then take vengeance on his family. At last, the merchant resigned himself to his fate.

At the appointed hour, the samurai and his footmen met the lonely merchant on a barren hill. The samurai took one look at the man standing resolutely with a battered old sword. Then the samurai turned and went on his way.

"Lord, why did you not make short work of that idiot?" one of the footmen asked.

The samurai looked at the footman shrewdly. "That man is not afraid to die," he told him. "No man is stronger . . . "

Now Lance watched the helmet of the sun rise in the Eastern sky. He dabbed his index finger in the mixing bowl of ochre and water and dabbed three lines across each cheek. He was not afraid to die.

He knelt before the Grail and crossed himself. What forces had guided him across continents, across centuries? They had their purposes. One played one's part.

Blue and his ragtag army of orangs filled the trunk of the DeSoto with Benellis, Uzis, Remingtons. They tightened belts of ammo around medal-emblazoned chests. They had practiced their magic all night and they were in high spirits.

Meanwhile, Lance put the final point on the oak staff that would serve as his lance. He wrapped the Grail in its velvet cloth, placed it carefully in a leather knapsack, and fastened it around his shoulders.

Michael Yamamoto looked nervously from side to rear view mirrors. People were fleeing the cities in all kinds of conveyances, but Michael saw no sign of the Indian cycle he had abandoned to Lance. Behind his seat in the van, the camera-crew were matter-of-factly polishing their lenses.

"Relax, honey," Petunia Petunia said, patting his twitchy shoulder.

"I asked you not to bring the cameras," Michael said weakly.

"Honey, what you see is what you know. Who's gonna believe

us otherwise?" Petunia played with her favorite scarf, fashioned from one of the pennants of the '96 Olympic ceremonies.

They were the first to arrive at Etowah. The camera crew quickly gathered that they were alone, then took footage of Petunia in front of the abandoned museum.

Lance arrived while they were setting up the cameras at Mound A. He rode the old Indian around the perimeter where the moat had once provided the first line of defense. If he saw the cowering figure that was Michael, he ignored him. Petunia instructed her cameramen to film. While he rode, Lance sang his power-song:

> Everything is only for a day
> coming round us in a way
> that remembers, in the way we are recalled.
>
> Take it from the heart
> it's the changes that have made us,
> it's the changes that'll break us
> and remake us one and all.

He drove the cycle up the 105 steps of Mound A, found it occupied, scowled at Michael, Petunia and the film crew, then rode down Mound A, and up the smaller Mound B. There, oak staff-lance at hand, he waited.

"Isn't he magnificent!" Petunia Petunia enthused on camera. Yamamoto held his head in his hands.

"Do you think we can get him to show us the Grail?" one of the grips asked Petunia.

"Jesus, don't do that, please," Yamamoto whispered.

"Show us the Grail!" Petunia Petunia bellowed from Mound A.

Lance ignored her. He watched the eagle circle over the ancient grounds. He tried to remember where he had seen such an eagle before—something about the Civil War.

The Blue Man and the orangs arrived a couple of minutes later. They drove the DeSoto up to the defensive ditch, then fanned out quickly. They started shooting wildly at everything in sight. (They were not, after all, good soldiers.) A .416 bullet pierced the lens of the lead cameraman, bored a tunnel through his eye and brain and exploded the back of his skull.

"Oh my God!" Petunia Petunia cried. "What are they doing? What are they doing?"

Yamamoto didn't hear her. He was digging himself into the soft earth of Mound A. The three remaining crew members dropped their equipment and scrambled down the mound. They were cut in half by Uzis fired at close range by two berserk orangs. Petunia Petunia soiled her size-80 pants.

Then they heard the rattle on Mound C. The two orangs who had torn up the film crew stopped jumping up and down on their spongy corpses. The three orangs sheltering amid the poplars along the river stopped sneaking towards Lance. Lance had still not shifted his position on Mound B. From the borrow pit, the Blue Man studied the mounds through his binoculars. I know this place, he thought. He went searching his meager memory banks and came up empty. Then they heard the drums.

And they saw Commander Nakatomi dancing. To the four corners of the world he lifted his arms and shook his rattle of sacred bones. Yamamoto raised his head a whisper's breadth to behold the Holy Man of Etowah, returned to rectify an ancient wrong. Dyed with ochre, his hair was bright orange. Around his waist, kneecaps and ankles, small bells rang to the beat of the drums; around his chest, gorgets. Resurrected with him, the drummers of Etowah now beat the ancient rhythms. The Commander sang to the eye in the middle of the palm, to the plumed serpent, to the Eagle Being. The air vibrated, and the banks of the Etowah were peopled as they had been long before. The great plaza was swept and the women fashioned cane baskets and the men went out to fish. The orangs scratched their heads. They had not prepared for counter magic.

From the borrow pit the Blue Man ran to the base of Mound A. He ran through the spectral crowds in the plaza as though they weren't there. Something out of the nebula came back: the Commander, the Shaman. Hadn't they played their parts in another world? Had he himself been there? Had someone like him been there? Then what was he? What were they all?

It was all the introspection he could muster. It made him dizzy. Now he crouched, aimed and fired at Lance, still perched on the Indian cycle.

Velvet caught the bullet between her teeth. She was swathed in black velvet and her skin was white as bone. Then, as quickly as she had appeared, she was gone.

She ran faster than a swooping hawk. She kicked the orangs in their buttocks—a terrible insult to them. Smarting and humiliated, their leader approached the Blue Man.

"He has invoked an unfamiliar magic," the orang lamented. "Perhaps we'd better rethink our options."

The Blue Man grabbed the beast by its chest hairs. He pulled it forward until their faces were an inch apart. "I've tracked this bastard 1500 years!" he shouted. "Haven't you heard the news? He dies today! The only question is, Who dies with him?"

The orang returned to the cluster of other orangs. He shook his head resignedly.

Petunia Petunia crept to the cameras. She clutched the handle of the smallest, the hand-held one. Crawling to the best vantage point, she propped herself on her elbows and began to pan the scene. In spite of the cool weather, she was sweating like a pig. She wiped her brow with her Olympics scarf—five linked rings on a field of white.

Below in the village, spectral people were eating persimmons, shaping antler and flint arrow points, cooking acorn meal with hot stones in a basket. They were the souls of the Commander's dream, invoked as he remembered them: loveliest of all—a reed of a girl, his daughter.

When the Blue Man saw the girl, his heart raced and he understood. Magic vied with magic. He called upon the dark Kami.

Down from the north the Wind God, Susanawo, blew the tannic waters of Pumpkinvine Creek, swept across the plaza, overturned the cooking pots, whipped the children into their clay and daub homes, broke the will of the adults to struggle back to life.

Petunia's scarf whooshed into the air, and still she filmed. To keep himself from blowing away, Micahel grabbed her ankle. Her great bulk held them both in place. He saw the scarf turn above them, then shut his eyes again. He remembered another battle, another scarf. A sound like "Dan-no-ura" fluttered in his ears. Someone had saved his life and died in his arms, shattering the mirror of his soul. When the soul came back together, the fragments coalesced like pieces of stained glass, stained with the horror of war.

Susanawo whirled the dust of the village to the four corners of the world. For dear life, the orangs clung to the trunks of the bending poplars. When they opened their eyes, the village and plaza were gone.

The Commander was gone, blown back through time by the Blue Man's magic.

Only Lance remained, astride the Indian cycle, on top of Mound B, the oak staff in his hands.

On Mound A, a black hillock struggled to come back to life. The black hillock of Petunia Petunia propped herself on her elbows and started filming again. Still fastened to her knees, Yamamoto lifted his head and looked towards Lance.

He had not moved in an hour. Now he kicked the cycle's crank and roared down the mound towards the river. The orangs were still blinking the dust from their eyes when Lance skewered the first one. With a mighty effort, he hoisted his lance and the beast slid down towards the hilt guard. Lance turned on a dime, then skewered the second beast.

The second one did not die easily. He howled and beat at the impaling wood. Lance paused behind a poplar and used his boots to free his blood-soaked staff.

The remaining orangs ran helter-skelter in a panic.

Using the bedlam, the Blue Man made it to Mound B and he

aimed the Benelli at the nape of Lance's neck. If one of the orangs hadn't backed into him at the last second, he would have pulped the medulla oblongata. The bullet hit the Holy Grail instead.

Blue wrestled the terrified orang to the ground and beat it to death with the stock of his rifle. The last three orangs watched with morbid curiosity.

"Idiots!" Blue screamed. "We are four and he is one!" At this news the orangs grew cocky again. They threw their grenades at Mound B where Lance had perched. They threw their grenades at Mound C where the Commander had stood. Mound C was the burial mound. Unwittingly, they had opened the graves of 350 Etowah Indians.

Like centuries-long sleep-walkers, the spirits emerged from the graves. But there was no one to guide them. They moved in circles around the mound.

Blue decided to get to the top of Mound A, the best vantage point. But what if Lance was already there? He sent two orangs to the other side, then ordered a charge up the mound. They found Petunia and Michael shaking on top. With one maternal hand, Petunia pressed Michael to her breasts; with the other, she kept the camera rolling.

"What the hell you doing here?" Blue yelled.

"Getting it on tape," Petunia said. "For posterity."

"Posterity?" Blue liked the idea. He smiled for the camera. Then he noticed Yamamoto. "You stay," he told Petunia, "he dies."

He was about to make mincemeat of Michael when Velvet jumped on his back like a mountain lion and bit off the lobe of his right ear.

Blue spun around, but she was gone. "Now I'm mad!" he said. "I'm *really* mad!"

"Who are you?" Lance asked Velvet when she crouched beside his cycle. "You look like—"

"Listen to me," she said, "while there is time." She looked at the scudding clouds. "The wind that sent the shaman back through time gathers now for a reprise. You cannot fail. If you miss this moment, you must forever wander in a maze, torturing yourself."

"I have the Grail," Lance said. "Get me back to Merlin."

"I'm not the one to take you," Velvet said. She pulled a silver flask from her belt. "Drink this," she said, "so pain may render vision."

"I have no pain," he said, but he drank. The taste was of the earth and barks of trees, carapaces of dead insects, horned toads' urine, monarchs' wings. He gagged, spit, handed her the flask. She pulled his hair back tightly, held the flask to his lips, buzzed in his ear. "Drink again . . . for redemption's sake."

He drank, and she was gone.

But the world was clearer now. His eyes were like a hawk's with telescopic powers. Every blade of grass, every grain of sand was keenly marked. On the top of Mound A, he saw Blue looking in his direction. Around his neck, like a talisman, Blue wore the magatama jewel.

"Where's that bitch?" Blue ranted. "I'll kill that bitch! I'll flay her alive!"

The orangs were ecstatic. They loved the idea. They began to dance in a circle, holding each other's hands, singing "Flay her! Flay her!" Then they heard the roar of the Indian cycle racing up the mound. They started shooting wildly, and one was killed by the others while Lance rode between their bullets. The tip of his lance caught the gold chain around Blue's throat. Lance ripped the *magatama* free of its golden clasp. He caught it in his left hand as he roared down the mound.

Blue raged. He turned violaceous-blue. He hungered for the kill. He wanted to stomp the black mountain of flesh who kept the camera pointed at his face. He wanted to stomp the little quivering yellow man who clung to her feet.

He raced back to the DeSoto with the surviving orangs. They crashed through the wooden gate in back of the museum, sped around the ditch until he found where it was most shallow. He looked to the sky. Susanawo huffed his cheeks full of the air of north Georgia and blew. The grenade-softened earth of mounds B and C filled the ditch. The DeSoto varoomed over the ditch and down the central plaza of the forsaken village. In high spirits, the orangs smashed the windshield out.

Suddenly, Lance came flying over the top of Mound A. Agape, the Blue Man and the orangs watched as the Indian cycle appeared to pause in mid-air. In slow motion, they saw Lance shift the oaken staff. The sun broke through the clouds that instant, then cycle and rider blotted out the sun and gravity called its flying hero home. The point of the staff thundered into the soft spot under Blue's sternum. On the other end of the staff, Lance dangled. Lance and Blue were like two bugs at opposite ends of a pin. The Indian cycle fell in slow motion, then crashed onto the DeSoto and the car spun around like a dying dragon.

Blue seeped cyanic blood. He began to melt into his own blood. The oak staff cracked and Lance fell onto the DeSoto's hood, then crashed to earth.

One of the orangs turned the steering wheel slightly so the car rolled over Lance's legs. The orangs stopped the car, retrieved the razors from the trunk. "Flay him alive!" they sang, "flay him alive!"

With the stunning clarity that Velvet's drink had given him, Lance watched as they skinned him alive.

"Oh my God!" Petunia cried. She dropped the camera. "What are they doing?"

Michael tried to get himself to go down the mound to help his friend. He tried to crawl to the weapons of the dead orangs. But he couldn't move.

The orangs took their time. Strip by strip they peeled, hour after hour. Lance saw Petunia's Olympic pennant-scarf turning in the dusk. He couldn't move. He watched with a detached disdain.

He died as they were scraping bone.

*

After the orangs had done, Velvet kneeled beside the mutilated corpse. "You have done your usual sloppy but essential work," she told the grinning, blood-smeared apes. "Now, get the hell out of here!"

Emotionally wounded by her words, tails between their legs, the beasts skulked into the forest.

Velvet gathered the bones and washed them in sacred water from the river. Stupidly, as usual, the orangs had neglected to look for any talismans. In the heat of the battle they had forgotten all about the magatama. Velvet found it where it had fallen from Lance's pocket as he had dangled on the cycle above the blue DeSoto. Dented by bullets, the Holy Grail was still in the small knapsack on Lance's back.

Muffled, as though from a long way off, the sound of drumming came from the grenade-cratered mound. Velvet, Petunia and Michael saw Commander Nakatomi emerge from the shadows, still dancing to the rattle and the drums. His magic had brought him back. But with no sense of urgency now. Rather, with a somber tranquility.

With a similar resignation, Velvet brought the bones to the mound. The spirits of the chiefs and holy men gathered round as Velvet wrapped the fingers around the magatama. She cradled the skull on the Holy Grail. The Commander rubbed the thigh bones together and a spark leapt onto the dry straw offered by an assistant. Commander Nakatomi blew, and the straw crackled and lit. The kindling was placed on a bed of straw in a stone basin. Twigs and wood were carefully stacked on top until the old temple fire lit the evening sky.

"So let it be restored in this valley," said the Commander, and he placed a thigh bone on the flames.

"So let it be restored in all the valleys of this land," Velvet said, and she put the other thigh bone on top of the first, so that they made a white cross in the flames, pointing to the four directions.

"That which was without place has found its place," the Commander said. "Let it be restored."

> "Let it be restored," the spirit-chiefs chanted.
> "If a thing has no place, it is no thing.
> If a man has no place, he is one of the forlorn.
> If a people have no place, they are despised by all:
> their art has no flowering; their magic
> is cast to the four directions
> like a faint breeze that cannot
> carry a song."

The Olympic banner flickered in one of the poplars, caught a current of warm air from the fire, lifted itself high above the mounds. The eagle that had hovered over the battle swooped and caught it in its beak. Petunia and Michael had gotten it all on film. When the sun had vanished, the fire still burned. Velvet, the Commander and the chiefs were gone.

Petunia washed her clothes and body in the Etowah. Her fat protected her from the cold. She felt wonderfully new.

On the riverbank, she found some dried persimmons, blown up by Susanawo from the village of four hundred years before. She washed them in the water.

Silently, she huddled with Michael around the sacred flame. Her clothes were drying on some propped up branches.

They ate the time-blessed food. She was certain she had never eaten persimmons before. But the taste was vaguely familiar, and as she ate she thought she heard the sound of a temple bell and felt that a promise had been kept.

*

It seemed that Lance had walked for years. One moment he was on the plain at Etowah watching himself being flayed. The next moment he was a skeleton walking across a desert. In bony fingers he clasped the magatama. Fastened around his neck, the Holy Grail clattered against his bones. Devoid of flesh, mouth, eyes, ears and nose—nevertheless, he perceived as a man. He had failed! The entire quest had been in vain. He was nothing but bones now: bones and memories. Every memory was a chasm of regret.

Years he walked before he arrived at the Mountain of Death. This mountain was a flatiron of darkness; cold, and smooth as steel. Only his memory of blindness enabled him to find his way around it. On the other side, he came to the river of three ways. The small-time sinners crossed at the shallows; those who had done good deeds passed over a bridge of chalcedony; the thoroughly perverse had to battle ogres and goblins, *tengus* and rotting corpses: the putrid corpses of those one once had loved. Lance crossed at the shallows, was sent back over the bridge by an old crone. Before she sent him back, the crone molded a thin layer of clay on his bones, so that he might feel again. Then she whipped him with the nettles of desire.

Lance struggled against the ogres and the demons. Guenevere embraced him and her flesh was worms in his hands. Her hair turned to straw, her breath reeked of offal, her lips were purplish and cirrhotic. Still she clung to him. He beat her and she turned into a slime that covered his body. It took years to wash her off of him. He could not wash her off without washing away the clay that covered his bones.

Sagami came and her breasts were large and pendulous, covered with maggots. Lorrie came, holding her head in her hands. Will came. "Why did you kill me?" Will asked. "Why did you kill us?" Lorrie's head asked.

He beat his way through them all. Arthur stood before him, in the panoply of kingship, weeping tears of blood. "Betrayal," Arthur said, pointing with his sceptre. The marrow froze in Lance's bones.

Then two guards seized him under the rib cage: one with a horse's head, one with an ox's. They carried him to Emma, the King of the Dead. Under his steel biretta, Emma creased his fiery brow. "Who is this bag of bones?" the red-faced God thundered. Two scribes consulted their records. Emma looked in a smokey mirror, and the mirror played the images of Lance's life. The warlord-deity scratched his scarlet beard. He raised his staff. Two faces on the top of the staff looked down on Lance. One face was nothing but an eye and a mouth; the other, nothing but a nose and a mouth. The eye blinked and stared. The nose sniffed.

"He went questing for the Holy Grail," said one of the scribes.

"He seems to have it there," said the other, seizing the Grail.

Lance closed his bony fingers over the Grail. He pulled it to him. The scribe pulled back.

"Let him go!" said the Seeing Eye of the staff.

"Keep him!" said the Nose.

Emma came down from his molten throne. The scribes gasped. They could not remember when Emma had descended from his throne.

Emma stared into the cavities of Lance's skull. "Who sent him here?" Emma asked, without turning from Lance.

"Vivian, that troublesome she-devil," said the more fastidious scribe.

"Hah! I might have known." Emma stroked his chin. "What sort of mischief is she scheming now?"

"Keep him," said the face with the Nose. A fountain of gaseous flames shot through the gules of smoke.

Emma seized the magatama tied around Lance's rib cage where his heart should have been.

"Do you know the purpose of this?" Emma asked. His voice bellowed and ricocheted among the caverns, and his hot breath melted the stalactites of the underworld.

"It is—to see into the hearts of men," Lance said.

"And have you seen, traveler?"

"It is a net with no bottom, my Lord. A maze of mirrors that confounds the possessor. A serpent and a golden throne."

Lava spurted from the gullies of the Lower World. Emma stroked his chin. "Can you, pilgrim, see into Emma's heart?"

"No, Lord Death . . . I have no such magic."

"That is because, pilgrim, Death has no heart. Only judgment and will . . ."

The cavities of Lance's eyes met Emma's onyx eyes. "And what is Your will, Lord Death?"

"To judge well, pilgrim." Emma turned on his fulminous heels. "Go," he said softly.

PART FOUR

The Return

"The Tao of heaven
Is like the stretching of a bow!
It brings down what is high;
It lifts up what is low.
It depletes what is abundant;
It augments what is deficient."

—*The Tao Te Ching*

16 | The Ocean of Time

Merlin awoke in a hawthorn bower. A soft mist caressed his beard and brow. A soft hand gathered the mist and soft eyes smiled upon him. The moonbeams fell through a tracery of branches, made an auburn nimbus of a young girl's hair.

He looked around. Where were his books? Where were his flasks and scales, homunculi and reptile skeletons, chronometers and maps, scrolls, cats, globes, baubles, talismans and measuring devices? Where was his bed of stone, the turret window that shut out light, the tower winding out the mortal world?

"The tower!"

Vivian smiled back at him. He sat up with a start. He felt his face and hands, smelled hawthorn, roses, mist and bark and earth. He stood up and the girl stood with him. He touched her cheeks and hair and lips and smelled the mist on her and the youth of her. He laughed and she laughed with him.

He ran to the circle of trees that enclosed the bower. Haltingly, he stretched his hand towards the invisible circumference. Nothing stopped him. No border hemmed him in. He poked the air. "Ha!" he laughed. He poked the air again. "Ha! Ha!"

He slipped his head through the invisible circumference. A white owl considered him, turned its head like a dial, clockwise, counterclockwise. He mimicked the owl's movement.

He stepped beyond the copse of trees into a moonlit clearing.

"Vivian!" he called, dancing in a circle, with his arms out like a child.

She glided towards him, took his hands, joined him in his dance.

"I'm a man again, with all the feelings of a man!" he laughed. And now he saw how beautiful she was, the woman she'd become.

His head spun. A spider's web caught dewdrops and moonlight up above. He stopped revolving. "Was it all a dream?" he wondered. "Nothing but a web of dreams?"

She removed the shawl from her shoulders. She held it out to him: the five linked circles seemed like little moons in a white sky.

"Lancelot!" he said. "Where?"

Vivian put her forefinger to her lips. She led him out beyond the clearing.

The knight had made the rooted tentacles of a great oak his bed and slept in the moss between them. His pillow was the Grail. A canopy of leaves sheltered him, and hawthorn flowers made a coverlet. Around his neck, the magatama glistened.

"The sword and mirror?" Merlin wondered.

"All will be divulged," she said wisely, mysteriously. She led him back to the bower.

"Then, it's over?" he asked.

She smiled. Who had she become? What was she now?

The spider spun a strand of moonlight, slid down towards earth; inspected the world of men and women, judged its own world better, climbed back up.

"It has hardly begun," she answered.

*

For a long time Yamamoto tried to forget what had happened, he tried to put it from his mind. He was "in denial"; he knew it, he was doing what he told his patients never to do, doing what his practice was based upon *not* doing.

But how do you deal with a friend being flayed alive before your eyes?

And how do you deal with your own cowardice?

Petunia Petunia would call him once a week. They had an unshakable bond now. She wanted him to come on her show again and talk about what had happened. He'd always put her off, fabricate some meeting, some conference, the work on the book—whatever.

She had signed some deal with Hollywood to make a major motion picture. She wanted Michael's input on the screenplay. Or was it a documentary with PBS, needing him to give credibility? Or was it both? She had so many deals going this way and that no one could keep up with her. And with it all, she'd lost 100 pounds!

His agent kept calling about his book. He had kept him on hold for six months now. He didn't know how to end it. He couldn't end the book withouth knowing who he was.

Carol had gone back to Michigan, lured back by her high school sweetheart, after 15 years of putting him off while waiting for Michael to make up his mind.

"Which mind?" he'd asked her.

She'd kissed his forehead and wished him well.

He tried to remember what it had been like before Etowah, before Lance had restored the balance. Only he and Petunia remembered how it had been; only they had been there to witness the changes.

Everyone else went to sleep one day and woke up with different memories the next. And what was human life but the sum of its memories?

How could he tell them that a spiritual chiropractor had come from the heroic age, made a couple of adjustments on the *Zeitgeist's* spinal column and altered all perceptions?

Everything was far from rosy, but the despair was gone. Something Lance had accomplished at Etowah had reached back and changed the shape of things after the Second World War.

Michael didn't understand it. It was like playing four-dimensional chess!

The Secretary General of the U.N. was a continual inspiration to women all over the world.

How could he tell them that she had been an Indian princess in a mound village called Etowah? That Sir Lancelot had come out of the West to save her soul?

Only Petunia knew what he was talking about. "Go with the flow, honey," she'd advise during a weekly telephone call.

"He asked me to tell his story," he said.

"Come on my show. I'll give you a forum."

"You got it on tape, but people think it's a movie."

"It's all in the packaging, honey. Don't you know that? The truth has got to sneak up on folks. You can't hit'em on the head with it. You give them popcorn and make them comfortable, and then you tell them the truth—maybe."

Then he asked her what he'd been afraid to think. "Could it change back?"

"What you mean?"

"It changed once . . . It could change again."

He thought he could hear Petunia drumming her fingers on some table on the other end of the line. "Now you got me, honey. I don't know . . Maybe that's why we seen it. Maybe we're the ones who have got to keep it moving. Maybe it clicks out again without us, and it all goes helter-skelter like it was." She sighed. "God knows, it sure was *baaaddd!* And I don't mean good!"

"You remember," he said gratefully. "You haven't forgotten anything?"

"Shoot no, an' I never want to. But we gotta go on now, honey. Ain't no use livin' it over and over."

"Where'd it go?" he asked. "That world? That life?"

"Shoot, honey, you looked up at the sky recently? You ever try counting all them stars? What did Carl Sagan used to say, `*bil*lions and *bil*lions!' And that's just in this time here. Maybe once you imagine somethin', it never goes away. Maybe that's what all those stars are for . . . so we can fill them up with imaginin' . . Hell, I don't know . . .

"There's someone on the other line. Can you hold?"

*

"Can you hold this?" Eugenie Eleanora asked, passing the mirror to Sally May.

Sally May craned her neck towards the nearly-finished quilt. "What is it, Granma? It don't look like nothin' I ever seed before."

"That's *seen*, baby. Don't look like *anything* I ever *seen* either!" Eugenie contemplated her masterpiece. "I don't rightly know what it is," she confessed. "But I think I'll call it 'The Ocean of Time'."

"Is time a ocean, Granma? I heard it called a river once, but never a ocean."

"River flow one way, baby. River overflow its banks, river cut through the mountains and makes the valleys. River get small and go dry . . .

"Ocean, though, ocean got every whichway to go. Ocean go forward, ocean go backward, ebb and flow, ebb and flow. Ocean get mean and angry, ocean get calm as glass. Ocean got leviathan inside . . . and sea anemones . . and itsy bitsy finger fish with tiny eyes; and them itsy bitsy fish swimmin' this way and that way an' makin' their own way in this world. Ocean got a mean streak, an' ocean sweet like your granma's pumpkin pie."

Sally May laughed. "Granma, you always jokin' me."

"Sure, baby. How you know I love you otherwise?"

She tickled her granddaughter's belly. Sally May doubled over.

"Careful, baby, don't drop that." Eugenie took the mirror from the small, black hands. Now where was she going to put a mirror? What did it signify?

"Didn't there *ust* to be a whole lotta blue in this?" Sally May asked.

"Did there, baby? I don't recall that."

Sally May considered her grandmother well. The old gray eyes looked back and smiled. They were cat's eyes that could see what other folks couldn't. They could see in the dark, they could see what wasn't and what was. They could see into the soul of things and take out what was needed. They knew how to cut what was not needed. They were cat's eyes, with diamond swords in the centers.

"Maybe there was a little more blue," Eugenie said softly.

*

Arthur opened the umbril of his helmet. He held his mailed hand up and the six and fifty armored knights behind him pulled their reins and their horses snorted to a halt. Arthur watched the lone horseman approach.

"It's our philosopher!" said Sir Bors when Lance was within hearing. The other knights snickered.

Arthur turned, narrowed his eyes, and Bors and all were still.

Lance steadied his mount. The horses' breath was foggy in the morning air. They had ridden hard, and more hard riding lay ahead before they joined the main contingent. The animals were as impatient as the men to join the battle. They smelled the blood to come, the horror and the glory.

Lance bowed his head to his King. The knights and horsemen watched with contempt. Arthur nodded, and his eyes were kindly. Yet he could not hide his disappointment. Lance wore a leather hunting shirt adorned with nothing but the curved magatama jewel at his neck.

"Greetings, compatriot," Arthur said.

Lance dismounted. He kissed his liege's hand. "Nay, Lance, we'll none of that," Arthur said.

"Methinks he comes to claw his way through Mordred's heart with that jewel thingamajig around his throat," Sir Bors said to Sir Griflet. The men in their proximity laughed and their armor clattered.

"I had sooner see you otherwise attired, Lance . . . but I am glad to see you, nonetheless," Arthur said. "Take my blessing . . . and let us on to war."

Lance removed the goblet and the wine flask from his satchel. "Before you face that rude boy, that bastard sting of mordant humors, drink this spiced wine, my King."

Arthur turned the goblet in his hand. "It has a pleasing shape. Have you brought it from your travels?"

"Aye."

Arthur considered the wine in the chalice. Within the liquid, he saw the silver of his helmet gleam. He remembered Guenevere's last tears. "Would that this wine were Thetis"s spring where she cast her boy, Achilles, holding him by his heels. I'd let her let me go awhile and come up swimming, protected fully and new-baptized."

"'And every inch a King,'" Lance said.

Arthur drank to the lees, then handed Lance the Grail. "Have you enchanted me?"

He held the bear-man's eyes. "I would that I could, my Liege."

Arthur smiled sadly, pulled the reins, then rode off to his destiny.

Lance watched the six and fifty clatter by, the rude wooden crosses borne aloft, the pennants, and druid talismans dangling from saddles. Romance would batten them with glory, cure their gouts and clear their pustules, ambition them with noble causes.

And Arthur would survive. Thanks to the wine he'd drunk from the Grail, Mordred's lance would wound him but not kill, no more than the lance of Longinus could kill the spirit of the King of Calvary.

Lance watched the dust rise after them as the sun broke through the morning fog. And the leaves turned on the giant oaks and the Kami whispered "Soon . . ."

*

"Eighty percent of the people in the state of Georgia are stupid," the radio's talking eminence proclaimed. "No, in fact, let me modify that for all you right-wing ditto heads out there—eighty percent are *extremely* stupid and always have been . . . I know I'm not stupid, and you know it, and all the smart people out there who listen to my show know it—which isn't very many in a state like Georgia . . . "

Yamamoto turned off the radio. He called Petunia Petunia on the phone, but couldn't get through. He badly wanted to talk to her, needed to talk to someone about how things were souring again. People were wrapping themselves in symbols and others were attacking the symbols and leaving them naked. People were dying and killing and wounding for symbols and it all had to do with other things, things barely understood or perceived—boundaries being blurred, and identity and mom and apple pie and the romance of the lost cause.

They had gained a year, the *Zeitgeist* had shifted, but the same strains played in the human heart, the same medley of mistrust, arrogance and ignorance. Lance would have said it that way. He had learned so much from Lance, and he missed him now.

Michael played one of the tapes he had made of Lance's regressions. The voice had a soothing, easy quality: "'To unite resolution with resilience is the business of war,' one of Sun Tzu's commentators has written. But as I look about this modern world, I see resolution *without* resilience. Everywhere, men and women are petrifying their positions, so there are merely temporary victories: a crushing of the enemy under the weight of mass brutality. After a while, the internal contradictions in our petrified position cause it to crack from within. Then the enemy comes and crushes us." Lance's voice was filled with the sadness of history: "Only when we can learn from our enemy, will there be peace in this world. Only when we can love our enemy's children as our own."

Michael had interrupted him there. "Wait a minute, Lance. I'm not sure I understand. Or maybe you don't understand how deep the enmities go . . How does a Jew learn from a Nazi, or a black learn from a KuKluxKlanner? You see what I'm saying. There are irreconcilable differences."

"To learn from my enemy is not to respect his ignorance. It is to find the causes that explain his ignorance, and then to dispell it. I have to make a conscious effort to learn those causes. Unless I'm willing to make the effort, I can never gain from the encounter . . . And I *must* encounter my enemy. That is the human condition."

Michael demurred. "I don't know, Lance. You're asking a lot from us simians, no matter how much evolved. Most of us just don't have the energy to do what you're asking. Life is short. We just want to have a little fun."

"Yet we have the energy to go on petrifying ourselves. Sure, life *is* struggle: a constant struggle to learn, to edify and enlighten. Cast out ignorance from one soul on this planet, and you alter the course of the wheel of stars."

Michael stopped the tape. He clearly remembered the rest of their dialogue. "Where's the pay-off, Lance?" he'd asked. "Even your Sun Tzu talks about the general rewarding his troops."

Lance had sighed. "Peace, understanding, moving a few rungs up the evolutionary ladder. Not good enough? You want something tangible, something to make the senses sing?"

"We're sensory beings. Even Freud—"

"Can we make this final leap, Michael? To do right for the sake of doing right without reward? Or maybe the reward is knowing we're building something adamantine, a monument to *homo habilis*—the tool maker. And here's a secret, Michael: if you do it right, you can have fun, too!" He'd paused, and the weight of imminent battle seemed to fall upon him. His voice had softened. "I don't know, Michael. I'm a poor vessel. I'm surely no one to be preaching . . . And yet . . . what choice do we have? Resilience or petrification?"

Now, a soft rain began to fall. Michael opened his window. Magnolia blossoms eddied to the street below, their poignant scent filling his office. He unlocked his desk drawer. The silk bag was exactly as he had lain it months ago, its contents undisturbed. "When you are ready, look at this," Lance had said when he'd presented it.

"What is it?"

"A gift . . . `to make yourself whatever form you please.' The greatest gift of all—the gift of transformation."

Incredulous, Michael had asked if he could see it then. He had opened the bag. It contained a mirror, with tintinnabula on the back, Jomon flame designs, druidic symbols, Etowah mounds. With some trepidation, he'd looked at the polished glass. A familiar face peered back. "I only see myself," he'd said.

"Put it away," Lance had told him. "Look again when you're ready."

Now he looked. And he saw his face changing before his eyes. He saw it aging, as with stop-motion photography. It grew old and withered like a dried-out peach, and then it died. He saw the mask of flesh grow hard then and crack from within, little fault lines criss-crossing the intelligent brow, the high cheek bones, the proud mouth. The flesh tumefied, sagged and fell away until only the skull remained. In the eyes of the skull, images appeared: faces he would love; wives and children; teachers; parents; friends—and the faces called him back and forward. Was it himself they called, or someone like him? Weren't they all him, really, putting on new bodies as one put on clothes, changing the moods and colors and the background music, keeping the leitmotif the same generation after generation?

He saw himself at Dan-no-ura, a frightened child, traumatized by war; and he saw himself at Etowah, all the trauma come back, paralyzing him with fear.

What had Lance said? We *must* encounter our enemy. That is the human condition. We must learn from the encounter.

Fear was the enemy they shared. All of them. All the legendary knights whose names still stirred the blood. All the great warriors and teachers.

Lance had gone around the world, through fifteen hundred years, to meet the death he feared from sin—to conquer fear.

Michael put the mirror back in its silken purse. He turned the screen of the computer's monitor on, then listened as the computer whirred to attention.

He could tell the story now. It was all of their story: the one who railed on the radio, and those he railed against. The black and the white, the male and the female, the Jew and the Muslim, the gay and the straight: carnivores, herbivores, omnivores.

He would tell them about the struggle and about their fear.

Maybe they wouldn't want to hear? a dim voice said. They would laugh at him, mock him, take it all away. All he had worked so hard for, all he had . . .

"Nay," he said, and began.

*

"Nay," I will not take it, Ansell told the Queen's messenger. The seneschal stood in the shadow of the portcullis, the late June sun casting menacing shadows through the grill-like bars. Ansell folded his hands across his chest, and seemed weirdly sectionalized by the sun and just as impassable as the gate he guarded.

The poor young messenger knew better than to test the will of Lancelot's infamous seneschal. During the year of his Lord's absence, Ansell had assumed more and more responsibility for Lancelot's estate, dictating to the other servants, and increasing the wealth of his absent Lord, even though the country endured blight, revolution and war.

But the young messenger was almost equally reluctant to suffer the displeasure of the Queen. She would not sting him with harsh words like the proud seneschal, nor have him cuffed or kicked in the shins. But he dreaded her downcast eyes; eyes that seemed always to hunger for morsels of hope these days;

eyes that fed always on a secret anguish, and were never nourished.

"Won't you reconsider, Sir?" the youth implored one last time.

"Do you controvert me, villain?" The seneschal's face reddened with indignity. The lad turned to go.

"What's all the racket?" Lancelot asked, emerging from the doorway of Joyous Gard. He appraised the situation from several yards away. "Well?"

"I just happened to be going out," Ansell explained, "when this varlet accosted me with some importuning missive. I knew my Lord would not wish to be disturbed—"

Lance held his hand up to staunch the flow of words. He took the message from the Queen's factotum, and scanned it quickly. "You do your job too well," Lance told his seneschal. "I think we need to have a talk."

"I live to serve, my Lord," Ansell said, bowing. His face reddened with indignity.

"Tell your mistress I will meet her, as she asks," Lance told the youth.

When the boy had mounted his horse, Lance put his arm around his seneschal's shoulder—a very unlordly thing to do. "Ansell, old sport," he said, "let me tell you about something called `anal retentive behavior.'"

*

In his laboratory, Merlin adjusted the flames under the alembics, checked his alchemical scales, consulted the sacred formulae once more, then stroked his long, brown-gray beard. Amongst his bubbling chemicals, his homunculi and astronomical charts, he was perfectly content.

From a shelf above, Jasper the fat cat jumped onto Merlin's shoulder. "You're pretty pleased with yourself, aren't you?" Jasper teased, ever one to make mischief.

"And why shouldn't I be?" Merlin retorted. "I'm back

amongst the things I love, doing what I love. I can walk freely in the world and feel the sun on my shoulders. I am a man again and beloved of a woman whom I love."

Jasper arched its back and stretched its claws ever so slightly into Merlin's flesh. "Yet, if I'm not deceived," the cat said with a yawn, "the philosopher's stone eludes you."

Merlin adjusted the flame under the alembic. He watched the vapors distill into the glass tube. "Your meaning, Jasper? I've no time for riddles now."

"If I'm not deceived," the cat repeated, "you cannot turn base things to gold."

"Aye, Jasper, that trick yet eludes me." Merlin looked into the cat's green eyes. "So?"

"So . . Be careful of that woman. She fooled you once—"

"Ouch!" Merlin pulled his hand back quickly. It had drifted too near the draft-fanned flame. He sucked the injured forefinger.

"Once burned, twice shy," Jasper purred.

*

Guenevere's lady-in-waiting led Lance through the maze as far as the pergola and then departed. Beyond the trellised gate, the Queen sat on a stone bench waiting for him. She would not gaze in his direction. Her posture, though, was demure and resigned. She nodded when Lance stood in front of her, and bid him sit on the opposite bench.

"How well you look," she said. "And changed . . ."

"And you . . ."

Thrushes flitted amidst the periwinkles, looking for colorful insects. Lance felt the humidity oppressing him. He remembered a day in the Fuqua Conservatory, the bliss of air-conditioning.

There was so much he wanted to tell her . . . and so little he could say. He'd like to describe the cities: Heian-kyo and Atlanta; the sights he had seen, and the people; the dreams, and the fragments of dreams.

"This is more difficult than I imagined," she said softly. With a white handkerchief, she wiped a tear from her eye. She gazed at her laced shoes, the shining brass eyelets. She folded her hands in her lap. "I wanted to see you . . . and now . . ."

"I should have called on you before . . ."

"Yes . . ." She struggled with how much to tell. "I had hoped . . . I waited for you . . . A year . . . and a day . . ." She met his eyes now. "Why are quests always a year and a day? It is a strange thing. The year goes quickly, but the day trudges on forever . . . And now you have been back—how long? Never mind—it's forty seven days! Why did you not tell me you would go?"

He said softly, "I didn't know . . ."

She searched his eyes. "After that night . . . our last night . . . you will think me very foolish now . . . I was torn in two with wanting . . . and self-loathing . . . I had a thought—God forgive me—to take this gift of life and give it back to God."

He had had the same thought—to dash his skull on the rocks below the promontory!

How much he wanted to tell her! How little he could say! "Let me sit beside you, Guen. Let me hold your hand."

"Nay, Lance. I cannot trust myself. Even now." She turned her eyes away, and steeled her will. "I wanted to see you one more time . . . to ask you . . . for forgiveness."

"I? . . . I forgive you?"

"I . . . I met a Sister from Amesbury . . . we talked . . . when you were gone . . . Poor Arthur . . . all of you were off at once . . . I think he thought you'd stay. No one thought Sir Lancelot would go chasing after grails! . . Arthur strode about the drafty castle sighing, "Where's Lance? Where's Percival? Where's Gawaine?" When he sighed your name, I broke. I could not bring him solace then . . . So, I asked you to come today. So that . . . So that . . ."

She smoothed imaginary wrinkles on her dress, gazed at her hands in her lap. After a while, she continued, with resolution.

"I ask you to forgive me, Lance . . . you left on my account . . . Not the first time . . . Let it be the last . . ."

"I'll not forgive you, Guen . . . In the first chapter of the Book of Love, let all forever after find the holy name of Guenevere."

"But Arthur—"

"Is gone to meet his glory . . . Nay, Guen, we cannot weigh our lives. Only Godlike eyes can see the scales."

She smiled then, for the first time. "Are you *Lance*? What has become of Lance?"

He stood, then sat beside her. He took her small, white hand. They were perfectly at ease.

"I met a Sister from Amesbury," she said again. "We talked when you were gone . . . She had such . . . *satisfaction* in her . . . I need that sort of peace, Lance . . . I never knew . . . such *satisfaction* . . ."

He looked at her thick, auburn hair, imagined it all shorn. She forced a smile. It was time to go.

He stood and watched her white hand fall slowly as a blossom. He paused at the pergola and looked back. She dabbed at her eyes with her white kerchief. She would not meet his gaze.

He wandered for an hour in the labyrinth before he found his way.

*

"I cannot find my way back," Lance lamented, "I was hoping you could help me."

Merlin lay Lance's voluminous notes aside. They had not nicknamed him "Merlin the Crab" for nothing. He disliked attacking anything head-on. He especially disliked having to say no. He didn't know how he could help Lance, but he didn't want to tell him so. He feared the task was beyond his powers. After all, it was not *he* who'd sent him questing in the first place. But as long as he didn't say no, there was always a chance something would turn up. Rattle the cosmic clock a few times, shake enough springs loose, and, who knew? If he kept nudging the problem maybe he'd find the solution.

"All these things you've written of—are they all true? Is it possible?"

"Every word is cobbled with the truth," Lance said. He studied the mage's eyes. The sadness Merlin tried to hide revealed he could not help.

They sat in the garden of the Castle of Broceliande, where Merlin and Vivian had made their home. Crystal towers rose behind them, humming like soft chimes in the summer breeze, catching like prisms the colors of a summer sunset.

A silver shaft of light appeared on the horizon. Bearing a silver salver of fruit, wearing a linen frock adorned with occult symbols, and a samite tunic out of Alexandria, Vivian came wafting on a breeze.

"How fare my solemn gentlemen?" she asked, stepping into the arbor. She set the salver on the little table.

"Overwhelmed by your grand entrance," Merlin said, kissing her cheek.

Lance kissed her hand and kneeled.

"Lance has been telling me such wondrous tales," Merlin enthused, his face turning ruddy. "He's given me his notes to read. You wouldn't believe what he's been through."

Vivian smiled knowingly. "You forget, love, I was there."

"Of course, of course." Somewhat embarrassed, Merlin shot quick eyes to Lance.

"Won't you have some grapes?" Vivian offered. "They come from the Isle of Sicily where the climate's sweeter."

They sat in silence a long time. The centuries he had lived through seemed to weigh on Lance. He grew weary, wearier than he had ever been. Merlin and Vivian were chatting about something but their words seemed to come underwater. He turned his head underwater to watch them and he gestured underwater and he laughed underwater when they laughed. Was this Vivian? Was this Velvet? How had she played her part in the drama? He still didn't understand.

He watched the bubbles rise from their mouths and from his own. Their words were strange and garbled. At last, with enormous effort, with the ocean of time on his shoulders, he rose, and made some excuses about needing to get home, and he felt himself trudge underwater to his faithful steed.

"He wants to get back," Merlin sighed.

"I know..."

"I don't know how...."

"It's not for us.. That task is not for us." She took his hand. "The people of Yamato have a saying, `When the student is ready, the teacher will come.'"

"He has suffered as much as a man may suffer. What more can they want of him?"

"It's not for us... That judgment is not for us."

"Nay..."

They watched the sun cast amethyst-pink silk about the sky. Venus lit the candle in her bedchamber, Mars fired up his forge.

Ages ago, Merlin would have hastened to his lab. Hypatia's ancient scrolls would have beckoned, the vast storehouse of Alexandria, the 36,000 volumes of Thoth, hieroglyphics and cuneiform to be deciphered and memorized, the lost songs of silent syllables. Now he was content to watch the sky put on its mantle of evening, while he contemplated the moonlit face of love.

He held her hand—warm and mortal, like his own. Though they might live ten thousand years, yet their days were spun on the loom of time—precious and precarious.

"That chant with which you locked me in my thoughts—" Merlin said at last, after many days of thinking about it.

"I was wondering when you would ask."

"`The five moon's night—'"

"Not `night,' but `knight.'"

"Ah ha, of course! Foiled by a homonymn. And Holy Wood?"

"Foiled by imperfect hearing. Not Holy Wood, but Hollywood. A magic kingdom in the Future Music."

"And that one that you told me of—"

"Our daughter ..."

"Yes."

"For her sake, everything I did, I did."

She turned her doe-like eyes to his: "A thousand years I held her in my womb. I watched the race of men brutalize their kind. The female of the species most of all—hunted, raped, murdered; harnessed like beasts of burden; kept from light; burned alive for country wisdom—which herbs would cure an infant's cholic, what remedy for an old man's gout. For speekwell and marigolds, sage and spearmints, spignuts, purslane, sweet flag, cinnamons and cloves old women and young girls were boiled in oil or cast into the river, hands and feet bound. Or, they were threaded through the spokes of wheels, every bone in their bodies broken. For looking with the eyes the Goddess gave them, eyes were plucked out; for singing sweetly, tongues were ripped out; because they had the means to make within their bodies new life—they were feared, despised, tortured, killed. For worshipping the Goddess of the woods and hills and valleys, for gathering beneath the moon in summer rain, for joying in the feel of snow or sunlight, for every liberty they took for being born and loving life—spurned, despised, and killed. Hypatia they killed, who kept the ancient scrolls. Eve they cursed and blamed for all their sins. I could not bring our daughter into such a world. I held her in my womb a thousand years . . .

"You slept and dreamed. Dear Merlin, how you slept and dreamed! I'd go out from the tower that you dreamed and I'd look about the world and hold our daughter wound as a coil in my womb."

"I didn't know," Merlin said softly.

"Nay, husband, nay . . ."

"Why didn't you . . . ?"

"Soft . . . soft you now . . . What would you say? Break the spell? Bring my Merlin back into the world? It was not mine to do . . . After your enchantment, I read your books; I moved beyond the spells and runes of Power without End. The path I walked showed me the end of power." She took a long, hard look down the corridors of time. "When the Sky Gods came, we women were dethroned. We had to bring our gifts back to the world. To find a Way that would not lose our gifts along its Way."

"And you have found it now?"

"Aye, Merlin, where it has ever been—within the very symbol of the Grail—our female selves, waiting to receive, to transform and to give forth. Open to the world of the divine, transforming in ourselves divine laws into worldly facts. Our magic struggled to bring forth that sense of holy life again—the shared Divinity from which we'd fallen: male and female fallen . . . We had to give to human kind the contrasymbol for the Holy Lance. Under the Lance the empires were born. Under the Grail, the compassion of the Goddess."

"And while I slept, you set all history aright?"

She touched his lips. "Nay, love, not history, but world story. History is but a chink of what we know. And what we know is but a chink of what has been . . . "

"Was there no part for this old magic man to play? . . . " Merlin wondered. "If you had told me . . . If you had let me know—"

"You would have done more than your share—or wanted to. Merlin, this struggle was our forge, our female forge, a fire that we had to walk through, to make us strong, the way that women can be strong. The Grail that nourished, and the Grail that caught the holy blood is what we offer now in reconciliation."

Merlin's eyes twinkled. He understood. He was filled with peace and understanding. Then a dark fear entered. "What of our girl? This coil of love?"

"I could not hold her. She unwound . . . slowly . . . surely . . . In my roaming, I found a place: secluded, lost in time; a gentle people with a magic of their own worshipped gods with other names than ours, but much like ours. I left our child there with one of their holy men. A good man, much like you. But . . . " She lowered her head. "I think you know the rest . . ."

Merlin lowered his head, too.

"Nay, love, do not weep; no silent tears bedew my Merlin's cheeks! Would you hear more?"

"Nay . . . Aye . . ."

"Then let me tell . . . And let us speak of it no more when that moon rising now is set . . .

"A thousand years I carried our child, child of our magic, sweet may of our human love, no human child—yet human. Then I gave her to that holy man to coddle and direct. He loved her as his own. She was his, too: his spirit-child; you know how these things work.

"But an evil wind came, Merlin, a blue wind that killed our child . . . And that wind hollowed me, so I was nothing but an emptiness that walked this earth . . . Two things I became. Two things that made me live. A hope to murder what had murdered her . . . And self-disgust . . . Yes . . . self-disgust; a loathing of this female thing I am: this mothering, febrile fertility; this humid den of life and yearning spewing forth ever into a world that takes and spoils and kills. I . . . hated . . . this—breasts, buttocks, musky dampness that spews forth life . . .

"When I found that thing that killed our daughter, I prostrated myself. Do you understand? It was my way of conquering—what? Myself! Him! What?

"Revenge was warring with my self-disgust. It was a way to conquer self-disgust. To make that supernoval monument to male stupidity and rage, rage with his own lust. You understand? He killed the very thing that might have saved him—the serpent-spirit of his own virility—and he too dumb to know! He did not even know that I was Nemesis come from out of time to blast him back. He did not know me . . ."

She sighed. "That is what I had to tell you . . . You waited . . . You were always good at waiting . . ."

"Thank you," Merlin said after a long while.

And they watched the moon together, and the purling shooting stars.

*

"Can you hold this?" the hoary Commander asked his aged wife.

Imbe-san received the sacred sword. She watched her husband's horse trot forward, through the gate of the tumulus. Her husband turned, and bid her advance. Gently, she heeled her palfrey.

They trotted over the bridge of the outer moat, then the bridge of the second moat. They came to a huge lake with a keyhole mound island in the center. The mound covered an area the size of a village. It rose a hundred feet. It was shaped like an inverted goblet, without a stem, something like a grail.

"Do you know this place?" the Commander asked.

"It is Emperor Nintoku's tomb. Why have you given me this honor? Why have you brought me here—a woman—to this place?"

"Let us dismount. Walk with me a while."

Ever dutiful, Imbe-san followed her husband around the bell-shaped lake. After a few moments, the Commander took the sword. "Kneel," he told his wife.

With trepidation, she knelt. She watched him raise the sword above his head. She shut her eyes and shuddered. She felt the blade touch gently on her shoulder.

"Too long I traveled in the unknown lands," her husband said, as he raised the sword again. "Companionless, half of what I was. Not knowing what I was. Now I have seen as far as I may see alone. I see—my other half was you."

The sword touched Imbe-san's other shoulder. She opened her eyes.

Her husband took her hand and gently bid her rise.

"What has happened to us?" she asked, looking at her hands, touching her husband's face, feeling her face and breasts. "We are younger . . ."

The Commander smiled. "How long has it been since Lance departed?"

"Eleven years . . . eleven years of peace we've known . . ."

"Eleven years of peace . . . And yet, within my heart, no peace. A block of granite lodged within my heart . . . Something had happened to me—or something was going to happen, something so terrible it would destroy me, destroy my work and power forever, change everything forever. I felt this, yet I could not see.

"So I traveled in the Future Music, trying to understand. I saw us growing old—your hair turned white, and mine white and thin, and my bones were thin as paper. And I did not understand the sadness."

"I have seen that sadness often," Imbe-san admitted. It creeps upon you when you sleep. You hide it from me when you wake, but I have seen it crease your brow . . . But not now. That weight is lifted—from your heart and mine. And both of us are younger."

"The weight of sadness makes us age . . . I did not understand that sadness. So I traveled—up to my ultimate farewell. And then I saw what I'd been missing. I took a final journey and I saw what I could not bear to see . . . All this happened years from now."

Imbe-san shook her head. "It happened . . . yet, you're here. You talk of the future as though it were the past. How can I understand such things? Will the things that happened then, not happen now? And will a future *you* take back eleven years from now and undermine this moment too? I cannot see through this smoke."

"There is much to learn, and much I cannot tell, except as you learn it." He held the sacred sword aloft. "This sword that separates the worlds will help. Hold this sword. It will guide you in your travels."

With trembling fingers, Imbe-san took the sword. As soon as her hand touched the hilt, the trembling stopped, she felt in control.

"I'll tell you this," Commander Nakatomi continued, "we think of time as a straight line from past, to now, to future. I have learned:

there are no straight lines in the vast expanse of sky. We thought sky and earth were separate, but now we have seen the earth within the sky and know that time and space are derived from a single egg, curving around all objects. Time-lines knit the world into a whole. We travel time-lines and think they are our lives. But in the Master Mind of the Sky World, there is neither ending nor beginning . . . only infinte possibilities."

*

Lance awoke with the strains of *Tosca* lingering from his dream. Mario Cavaradossi bid a fond farewell to the impassioned diva of his adoration:

> The stars were shining then
> and the earth was fragrant.
> I heard the creaking of the garden gate . .
> and then she was there.
> She fell into my arms.
>
> O sweet kisses, languid caresses!
> I trembled as I loosened her veils,
> revealing her beauty.
>
> . . . never have I loved life more.

As soon as he realized where he was, Lance sent an urgent summons to his seneschal. His manservants attended to his attire and heated the water for his bath.

Sweating profusely from wearing too much clothes and hurrying to his Lord's bidding, Ansell was escorted to his dour master, seated in the steaming water. Ansell made eyebrows at the other servants who hurried out of the "bathroom."

Starting his day with a hot bath was just one of many peculiarities their Lord had adopted since his return. While the other nobility might boast of bathing once a month "whether they needed it or not," the Lord of Joyous Gard opined that bathing brought him closer to the gods.

Ansell bowed with a sweeping gesture. Lance bid him sit.

With a slight grimace, Ansell settled on the moist woodblock. If he had been uncomfortable before, he was tenfold more so now. His sweat formed little puddles at his ankles, and plashed droplets from his underarms. The Lord was babbling about some dream he'd had, how unhappy he was, how he had come to some decision. Ansell steadied himself on the stool, yet swayed back and forth in spite of himself. He seemed to lose consciousness for a moment. The next thing he knew, Lance was rising into the steam, wrapping a towel around himself.

Then Ansell was trying to find his way through the steam. His Lord's face was in front of his. He felt his face being slapped.

"Ansell! Ansell!"

"Good, my Lord?"

"Are you well, man?"

"Good, my Lord?"

"Did you hear what I was telling you? Come, get up! Let's get some air."

Outside the castle, Ansell immediately revived. The humidity of morning had dried with the rising sun. Ansell felt his clothes and body cool and dry.

"Did you hear anything I said inside?" the Lord wanted to know.

"A little, Sir. About some dream."

"And what about the will?"

"The will, Sir?"

"The will that you will write for me. You know the way these things are phrased."

"The *will*, Sir?"

"'Zounds, man, must I say it thrice?" Lance ticked off the particulars: "Take an account of all my properties. Add to it an account of all who work for me: the length of service of each man and maid; how many little ones they feed. The more productive ones—acquit just rewards. But see no one is left out. All must be taken care. And I want you to be sure there's money left to found a school."

"A *school?*"

"Yes, yes. For the little ones. And anyone else, of course." He thought a moment. "And, yes, of course, I almost forgot, a hospital."

"A hospital?"

"That's right . . ." Lance looked to the sky. "Yet I'm afeared of our day's quackery . . . No bleeding, mind you."

"No bleeding?"

"Nay . . . nay . . . I am too much ahead of myself, good man." Lance pinched his nostrils, said in a high nasal, "By the way, man, you might try bathing a bit more often!"

Ansell flushed. "Aye, Sir, I shall try it."

"About the hospital . . . I'll leave some notes about the circulation. No need to wait for da Vinci, huh?"

"Da Vinci, Sir?"

"And Harvey . . . What was I saying? The key thing is, they must study—the doctors that you bring here. Diet's necessary, too. They'll have to dissect corpses—"

"Corpses?"

"Yes. Fresh ones." Lance looked around. Beyond the pretty estate, he saw his fields, and the serfs and villains in the fields, already laboring, hostages to his prodigality; and the children were laboring beside their parents, stunted already in mind and body. He remembered Ansell. "Man, what are you waiting for? Shake a leg! Up to it! Fifty four forty or fight! Rah, rah, rah! Remember the Alamo! Go, team, go!"

Lance watched his seneschal run from him as from a madman. He laughed until his stomach hurt and he fell to his knees.

*

Now he rode over the green Cotswolds and over the Mendip Hills. The strange dwellers of the fens watched him as they gathered their fish and fowl. He rode over the Fosse Way where the Romans had ridden before. A hundred years before, the wealthy had gathered their wares, fearing the Saxon hoardes. Silver and gold on their backs, mules laden with jewels, they took to the network of roads, and buried the wealth on their backs. The hooves of his horse clinked on a plate in a bog at the end of a road, where no one had passed for decades. Under the encrusted dirt he saw the dull gleaming. Washing it in a stream, he saw two circles emerge from the silver: in the rondure, the God Oceanus, surrounded by nymphs of the sea, surrounded, in turn, by the Bacchae, Satyrs, Maenads and Pan. Silenus offered a wine cup, while Hercules readied to fall.

He buried it where he had found it, grateful for his eyes that beheld it, grateful for having been blind. Grateful, grateful, grateful!

He had given his will to the clerics and carefully seen to the copying. He had placed the various manuscripts with the priests and abbots of the region. Merlin, apprised of his scheme, had brought him a skeleton used for his own investigations. Then Merlin had embraced him and bid him adieu. He himself had smuggled the skeleton into the scullery like a sack of onions. He had brought it himself to his chambers, laid it down in his goose-down bed. "We don't come to much," he thought, arranging the sallow bones.

Then he ignited the straw and the coverlets. Racing from Joyous Gard, he had sounded the alarms before passing through the tunnels. He'd paused once on a hill to look back. Flames leapt at the sky and the dark smoke billowed from the chambers. The fire would be contained—and only his "bones" would be mourned. He rode like the wind, like a lover to an assignation, like a condemned man tasting the air of his freedom.

At Glastonbury, he roused the good abbot from sleep.

"Say, man, do you know the hour?" the abbot complained,

glowering at the prelates who had failed to intervene for him. The abbot approached the wayfarer, drawn like the prelates by the man's insistent air. He peered into the cobalt eyes.

"Who are you, Sir? In spite of your country jerkin, you are not cut of flaxen cloth."

"I come from the Islands of Langerhans."

The abbot looked suspiciously from the wayfarer to the prelates. The prelates shrugged. "I have never heard of this place," the abbot admitted. "Is it far?"

"Far in time, Your Excellence. Near in place as your liver."

The abbot remembered his weariness. "Look, Sir. It is late. Come back tomorrow. *Late* tomorrow." He glowered again at his prelates.

"I beg your pardon, Your Excellence," the wayfarer said, and his voice was easy, and redolent of aromatic herbs, silk and romance, and other times and places. Seduced by the voice, the abbot turned, and smiled.

"I have a gift for the abbey," the wayfarer said, setting his satchel on a pew, removing a tarnished goblet.

The abbot inspected the gift with a critical eye. "Yes, well, it's very nice of you, but—"

"I do not ask you to keep it in a special place, Your Excellence. It is only a simple goblet. Place it in a storeroom with a hundred of its kind. Yet keep it, pray. Remember that our Lord was but a simple carpenter who changed the world." Lance pressed a bag of gold coins into the abbot's hand.

The abbot looked to the prelates. Each shrugged in turn, and finally the abbot shrugged. "Very well, Sir. We are pleased to honor your request. Is that all?"

Lance thought of the land of Yamato. He thought of Commander Nakatomi, swirling in the snow in a foxmask. He thought of the boy with the rusty sword, grinning for his approval. The bonzes of Mt. Hiei chanted the Lotus Sutra and the crystal elephants of Prince Fujiwara's festivals glimmered in the sultry air . . . Sultry nights with Sagami, the layered colors of her silk kimonos, the sound of her throaty laughter . . . He thought of blindness and hunger and the good sisters and the crackling ships of fire and the death of the boy with the sword . . . Atlanta and Lorrie and the miracles of science, the icy waterfall at Amicalola and the ice of the future cities, and desolation in the heart. He thought of Petunia and Beansprout, judgment at Etowah and the Kingdom of the Horse-faced God . . .

"Yes," he said softly. "That's all."

*

That's all, he thought. Hadn't he done all that he was meant to do?

The hot, greenish mineral water of the hot springs of Bath soothed his muscles after the hard riding. Thanks to the inclement weather, the usual gaggle of tourists were blessedly absent, and he luxuriated in watery solitude, while a single elderly female attendant puttered about at a distance. Above the gray stone ledges, the Roman Goddess Minerva looked down from her pediment. Respectful of the local gods, the Romans had surrounded Minerva with the stony likenesses of Celtic deities, druids and bards.

"'Time present and time past,'" Lance said aloud, liking the way his voice echoed, "are both perhaps present in time future . . . time future contained in time past.'"

The elderly attendant, used to eccentrics, gazed in his direction to see if he desired a massage or a drink of cool water.

What was the rest of it? He had memorized it once, at Lorrie's condo:

> If all time is eternally present
> All time is unredeemable.
> What might have been is an abstraction
> Remaining a perpetual possibility
> Only in a world of speculation.
> What might have been and what has been
> Point to one end, which is always present . . .

The great bard had got it nearly right. Time was not what men imagined, which only mirrored the way they thought, organized with a beginning, middle and end; moving always, inexorably, from beginning to end, with the present ungraspable, a sigh that expired the second it was heard.

Men connected the dots with their minds and they mistook their connections for the thing that was always there, waiting for them to make patterns. It was what sustained them, what they came out of and would pass into only to be transformed again.

Had it not been for the victory at Mt. Badon, how could he sit in the Roman bath? The Saxons would have overrun the country and slain him long ago. So the past *was* present, the present bound with it like a sheaf of wheat was bound, like a sword that was layered and still sang and stung with the resilence and strength of the layering. The past was not a thing that was *done* and finished, but a thing that was *happening*: stretching into time present and time future and as malleable as either, understood and refracted by all the prisms of perception, changed by and changing all things connected to it. The nails were driving through Christ's hands and feet, even as Arthur rode back in victory from Mt. Badon; even as Antoku ascended the Sun-God's throne. All of it happening at once.

Time wasn't "unredeemable," fixed in stone. Ouroboros devoured its own tail and nourished itself to grow its tail again which it continued to devour. The "perpetual possibility" of time was exactly the thing men had failed to grasp, the one thing that could reconcile their marriage to the gods.

"Will you be wanting anything, Sir?" the attendant asked from a distance. Her voice called him back to the familiar world. The water steamed about his head, seeped into his bones. Over his head, water splashed out of the mouth of a copper turtle.

"No . . . I'm fine . . ."

"If you'll be needing anything . . " She let her words and

meaning trail, the way they did it in the East. Something about her seemed comforting and familiar.

The East . . . Sagami's world . . . Five hundred years away from him—the world to come—and present now. But he didn't know how to get there . . . Even Merlin could not help.

He hadn't let himself think of her. He'd been torn from that world, ripped from that womb of time, bloodied, compelled by some purpose he had barely understood. If he had thought of her as he had wanted, he never could have continued.

Now he knew what had compelled him. All the trials had shaped his soul into another thing, and given him a shaman's song. What was the hexagram he'd read so long ago? "Teh-Khieu: Great Accumulation and Major Restraint . . . The Gentleman stores in his mind the grains of history . . . Thus he knows rightness . . ." And the *Book of Judgments* had advised: "Stay the course . . . Restraint together with accumulation . . . The Gentleman serves the public, the King smiles upon him, he undertakes enterprises of great height."

He had been "gathering virtue," shedding the unnecessary, annealing vision and immaculate grace. "Polishing the mirror," they said in the East.

He leaned his head back and watched the water spout from the turtle's mouth, tried to remember where he had seen the green of that patina.

If time were fluid, it was possible to capture a moment again, and change the outcome of all that would transpire. Yet the infinite possibilities contained within the seed of time would also transpire. Spirit mechanics could move in and out of the time flow, tightening pipes here, fixing levers there. All artists rearranged the elements of their media, but the Great Artist rearranged time itself and made the pattern of eternity.

"Time is but the stream I go a-fishing in," that other bard had written. "I drink at it, but while I drink, I detect how shallow it is. Its thin current slides away, but Eternity remains. I would drink deeper . . ."

He wished he were not so tired . . He might yet accomplish something if he were not so tired. Even Merlin had a partner to assist him now . . .

He felt himself sinking into the green water. Some had drowned in it from time to time, drawn into the heat and the green, fluid opacity.

The towel-folding attendant watched the head slip under. She watched the water pour out of the mouth of the patina-green turtle. Lance's black hair floated like a sea anemone's. "Go with God," Imbe-san said softly.

*

Sally May turned the TV off and came into the room where her grandma was putting the finishing touches on her quilt. "Them Olympics over?" Eugenie asked, knowing the answer.

"Nah . . . I just don't like to see that ballet swimming. It's weird when they come out of the water pointing with their toes. They look like some kind of strange fish."

Eugenie put her arm around her grandchild's waist. "It's just out of the ordinary is all, honey. You keep looking at it, it don't look so strange."

Now Sally May pondered the quilt. "You put a turtle in it! Is it finished now?"

"No one ever finished a work of art, child. You just give up on it. You can't learn anything more from it, so you give up and get on with the next one."

Sally May tilted her head this way and that. Colors lanced across one another, bled into one another. Knights emerged out of the pattern, damsels in distress, dragons and demons, athletes and warriors; a sword, a mirror, a spear, a palm with an eye in it, a serpent eating its tale, an old, blue DeSoto.

"The Ocean of Time," Sally May said softly, liking it better than all the others her Grandma had ever made. "The Ocean of

Time . . ." She looked in her grandmother's gray, cats' eyes. "Will you teach me how to do this, Granma? Will you? Will you?"

*

Lance looked at her again. It seemed a fog was clearing from his eyes . . . Never had he heard a woman speak as she did . . . "They tell me this is a symbol of long life," he heard himself saying, handing her the jade turtle he had been awarded for the contest of scents. "Take it, and live long. And put away these thoughts."

Sagami urged the turtle back. Lance closed her hand gently upon it. "Tell me soft your name."

"Sagami . . ."

Months later, they joined Will, Sachiko and Old Nurse at the riverbank of the Kamo. The torchman was about to light the last boat of dolls. The oarsmen were already pulling the other boats. Only the chain to the last boat lay slack. The torch went down and the straw lit. The oarsmen pulled and all six boats were flames on the water. The first boat had already disintegrated. But its steel keel held the links to the lead boat and the others.

The torchman held the torch above his head in an awkward gesture. Lance turned to look at him, and thought he recognized him. The man smiled wryly.

Reflexively, Lance grasped the hand that held the torch. In an instant, Will seized the man around his throat and wrestled him to the ground.

The other festival-goers applauded. It was such good entertainment! So thoroughly up-to-date. Prince Fujiwara thought of everything! Long live the shining prince! Long live Heian-kyo!

The Blue Man struggled out of Will's arms and ran into the river. Will pursued him. The Blue Man dove, and vanished under the waves. Will threw the torch at him. It sizzled and went out.

"Who was he?" Sagami asked, rushing to Lance's side. "Are you hurt?"

Her concern had pumped the blood through her body. She shone with loveliness and the grace of the moment.

"I am unscarred while yet you bide with me," he said.

"That I shall do," she vowed. "Forever and a day."

Lance smiled ironically, "The day," he remembered, "is the hard part."

Will came back from the water's edge. He was young, and strong, and laughing, drenched and shining in the sun. "He's gone, Lance. That's the end of him."

Lance wondered how it would turn out this time. He knew he was seeing the underside of the tapestry. The Minamotos would have to win their battles without Will at Ishi-bashi-yama, without Will scaring up the ducks at the Wisteria River. Perhaps they would not win? The Taira would just manage to survive while the Minamotos destroyed themselves from within. And what would happen then? What would happen if Beansprout failed to light an evening fire on a hill and Will failed to tell a beetle a white lie?

He closed his hand over Sagami's. Whispering tongues loosened about him. It didn't matter now. He would have a child to raise in the knowledge. His and Sagami's child.

Will would have to earn his medals some other way. Or would he languish, uncertain always of his course, hearing the strains of unplayed music, ruining his life with *sake* and women, deprived of the grand sacrifice his soul would ever crave?

"That's the end of him," Will said again, almost with regret.

"Is it, Will? . . . Is it?" A soft breeze rippled the river, rustled the watery willows.

And the Kami whispered . . . *"Soon . . ."*